WHEN DARKNESS DESCENDS

The Relevation Trilogy: Book I

G. W. LÜCKE

With Distinction Publishing

Published in Australia by With Distinction Consultants
PO Box 97, St Marys, Tasmania 7215
https://withdistinctionconsultants.wordpress.com/
First published in Australia in 2020

Book website: https://relevationtrilogy.com
Author Facebook page: https://www.facebook.com/GWLucke/
Maps produced under commercial licence by G. W. Lücke using
Inkarnate software https://inkarnate.com/
Cover design, typesetting: WorkingType Studio

National Library of Australia Cataloguing-in-Publication Entry:
Creator: Lücke, G. W., author

A catalogue record for this work is available from the National Library of Australia

Title: When Darkness Descends. The Relevation Trilogy: Book I.
ISBN: 978-0-6488207-0-3 (Paperback)
ISBN: 978-0-6488207-1-0 (ePub)
BISAC Codes: FIC009020 FICTION/Fantasy/Epic;
FIC009100 FICTION/Fantasy/Action and Adventure

For Frances, Jack and other lost souls

Ostamp
N
Nordargen Sea
Occidian Sea
Elephai Bay
Germalia
Ephesus
Afonwee
Mons Harena
Disputed Territory
Slyencia Bay
Portum
Pordillo Territory
Ghadang

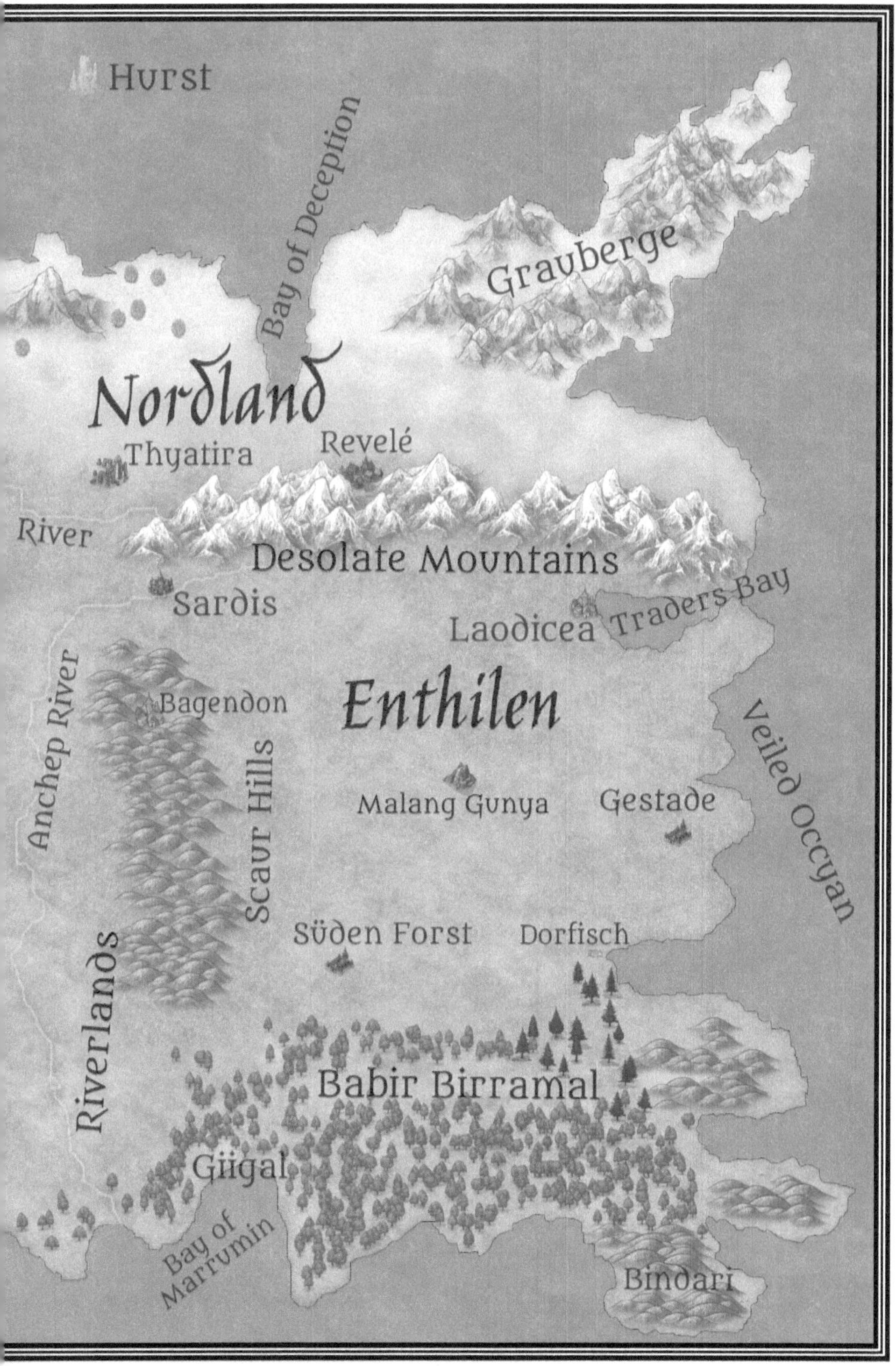

Hurst
Bay of Deception
Grauberge
Nordland
Thyatira
Revelé
River
Desolate Mountains
Sardis
Laodicea
Traders Bay
Anchep River
Bagendon
Enthilen
Scaur Hills
Malang Gunya
Gestade
Veiled Occyan
Riverlands
Süden Forst
Dorfisch
Babir Birramal
Giigal
Bay of Marrumin
Bindari

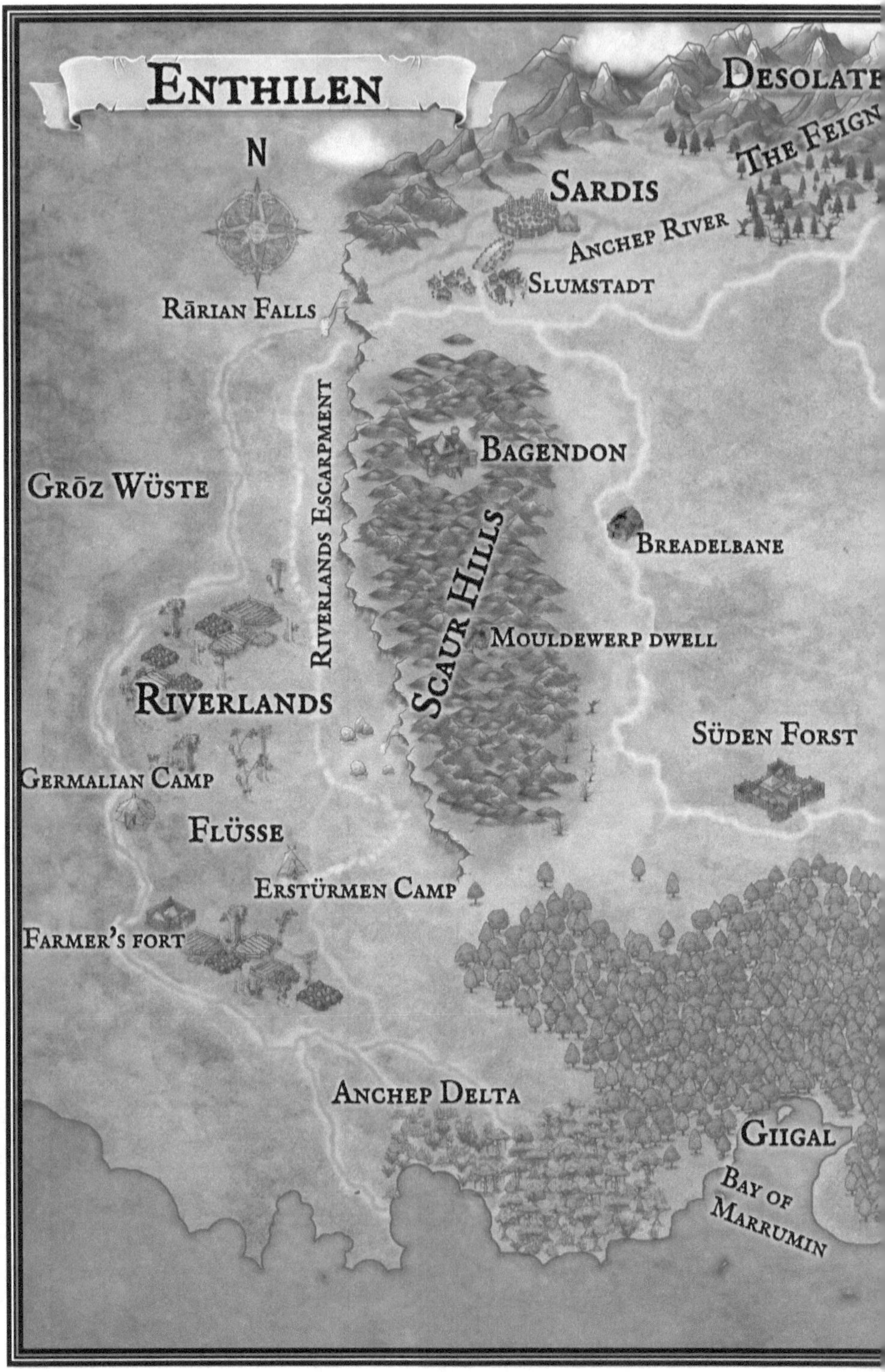

ENTHILEN
N
DESOLATE
THE FEIGN
SARDIS
ANCHEP RIVER
SLUMSTADT
RĀRIAN FALLS
GRŌZ WÜSTE
BAGENDON
RIVERLANDS ESCARPMENT
BREADELBANE
SCAUR HILLS
MOULDEWERP DWELL
RIVERLANDS
SÜDEN FORST
GERMALIAN CAMP
FLÜSSE
ERSTÜRMEN CAMP
FARMER'S FORT
ANCHEP DELTA
GIIGAL
BAY OF MARRUMIN

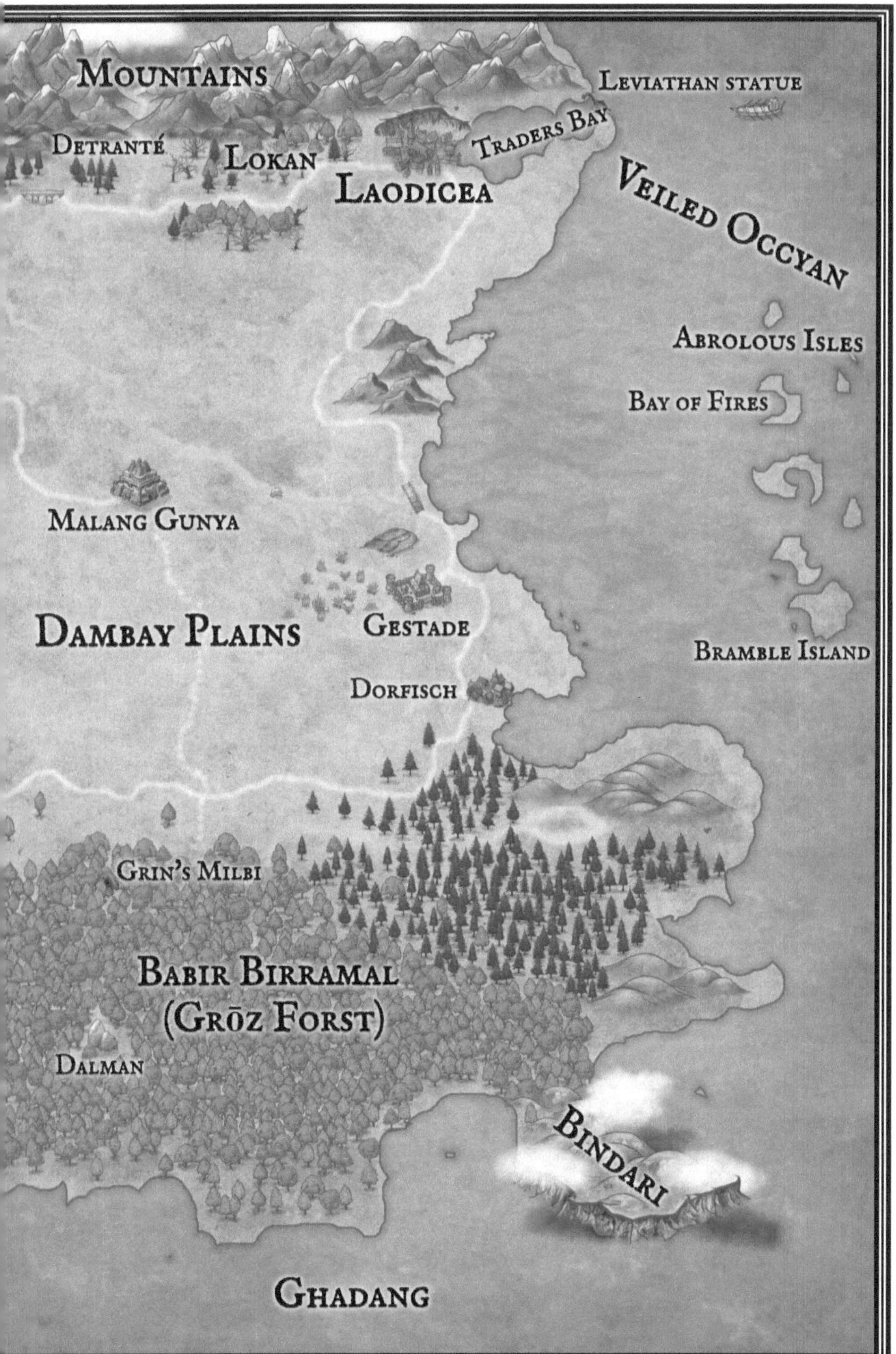

MOUNTAINS
LEVIATHAN STATUE
DETRANTÉ
LOKAN
TRADERS BAY
LAODICEA
VEILED OCCYAN
ABROLOUS ISLES
BAY OF FIRES
MALANG GUNYA
DAMBAY PLAINS
GESTADE
BRAMBLE ISLAND
DORFISCH
GRIN'S MILBI
BABIR BIRRAMAL
(GRŌZ FORST)
DALMAN
BINDARI
GHADANG

Rel`e*va”tion *n.* [L. *relevatio,* fr. *relevare.*]
A raising or lifting up.

These things saith the Son of God,
who hath his eyes unto a flame of fire…
(Revelation 2: 18).

Prince Oldaric galloped his courser through the crowd of giant, lumbering stone-grells, hacking at the half-naked bodies of the heathens with his sword. Blood splattered across his face, droplets tasting of metallic salt dribbling into his mouth as he screamed a battle cry. He urged his battalion of Erstürmen cavalry onwards, leading them through the sandstone streets of the grell city of Malang Gunya. The hooves of two hundred and forty horses clattering across the flagstone pavers behind him sounded like an avalanche of boulders tumbling down the side of the steepest mountain.

Oldaric smiled as the grells shrank in the wake of the Erstürmen attack, the terrified faces of the vanquished retreating into the false comfort of stone houses. Battering rams will smash those mortared walls, he thought. Victory will be done before the moons rise.

Amid the chaos unfolding ahead of the invading cavalry, two dozen stone-grells gathered at a roofless, circular temple with white marble columns surrounding painted floors. The giants clutched stone-tipped spears, pointing them out towards the oncoming enemy. Oldaric knew that the grells would do everything to protect the most sacred place in Malang Gunya: the calendar of life. It depicted the entire known history of grell culture. They cherished the calendar above all else; the grell slaves that served him back in the royal city of Sardis talked about it endlessly.

He rounded the base of the stepped pyramid that towered over the calendar of life, leading his cavalry towards the grell defenders. From the corner of his eye, he caught a glimpse of the jagged rock too late. It cannoned into his spangenhelm, knocking him from his saddle and sending his sword clattering across the stones. Instinct saved Oldaric's life. He rolled out of the path of the cavalry's crushing hooves, pressing his body against the bottom step of the pyramid. A punishing whine filled his ears. He blinked again and again, trying to clear the opacity that clouded his mind.

As the savage whoops of Erstürmen soldiers slaughtering grell defenders echoed through the calendar of life, a shadow blocked the sun from Oldaric's face. He scuttled backwards on his feet and elbows, retreating from a male stone-grell that hovered over him. The grell's lilac eyes grew wide with fear and panic, and at the end of a raised arm, a trembling hand fought to grip another rock.

Oldaric lifted a gauntleted hand in surrender and softened the scowl on his lips. He fixed his gaze on the bald, pale-skinned giant, tracing his eyes across the black ink of the facial tattoo that adorned the faces of all adult grells. The arm muscles of the grell relaxed for a brief moment.

He's wavering, thought Oldaric. He kept his left hand raised and used his right to push himself off the pavers. Standing, Oldaric was still head and shoulders shorter than his ambusher. Never taking his eyes from the grell, he moved his right hand slowly towards the grip of his sheathed long knife, simultaneously flashing a distracting smile and speaking like this was an expected and welcome encounter. "What is your name?"

The grell shifted on unsteady feet. I am Brennian stone-grell, first son of Binnian and Orenan. Protector of Malang Gunya."

"Do you want to survive this day, Brennian? Live peacefully among these beautiful streets and grand halls once again? I can secure a place for you, serving a glorious Erstürmen Kingdom."

"I have no master other than the land itself. The land from which all life comes."

"I understand. Yet, you're surrounded by soldiers with no way out. The land is not going to spare your life. But I could." Oldaric's fingers wrapped around the handle of his knife.

Brennian tensed his arm, drawing his hand back, as if preparing to throw.

Oldaric unsheathed the knife. Brennian thrust his arm forward the same moment an arrow whooshed past Oldaric's ear. A rock thudded into his greaves right before a limp Brennian toppled onto the blood-stained pavers, the red and black fletching of an Erstürmen arrow jutting from the grell's neck.

The midday attack on Malang Gunya ended before the sun set, as Oldaric had predicted. The Erstürmen soldiers had routed the grells, killing hundreds and taking hundreds more for slaves. A handful of grells escaped, fleeing south, likely into the vast tracts of forest they called Babir Birramal.

Oldaric limped towards a private room in one of the grandest halls in Malang Gunya, the leather lining of his greave rubbing against the violet bruise spreading across his shin. He knocked on the polished timber of the door and pressed his ear to the wood.

A muffled command seeped through the grain. "Enter."

Oldaric opened the door and stepped inside. A healer knelt beside a cot made from deer skins stretched over a wooden frame, applying a poultice to the wounds of King Alaric.

Alaric brushed the healer away. "Enough fussing. Leave us."

The healer stood and placed his right fist against his heart. "Hail, King Alaric." He turned and scurried from the room.

Oldaric stepped forward. "Father. Are your wounds deep?"

"Mere scratches. I'm not going to let a pagan grell be the death of me."

"Thank Volerdie's mercy. We've taken the city. Our people will rejoice at your victory."

"We let the grells linger here for too long. Your grandfather, Faramund, should have cleansed this place a generation ago. I've redeemed our family for his weakness. Come, sit next to your father. There are things we must discuss."

Oldaric dragged a small, wooden stool across the floor and sat next to the diminutive king, tucking his boots in underneath the seat.

Alaric groaned as he lifted himself upright and rested his back against the wall. "When did you last attend chapel?" he asked.

"In Sardis, the day before we marched for Malang Gunya."

"Supplication to Volerdie's mercy only when the fear of death compels you is the action of a weak man. A coward. Your absence from chapel at other times hasn't gone unnoticed. Even that snivelling fool of a curate had mind to speak to me directly about your lack of piety."

"I'll recommit to my duty, Father, when we return to Sardis."

"See that you do. If you'd paid closer attention to the teachings of the scripture verses, you may have gleaned such knowledge that now enlightens my thoughts."

Oldaric narrowed his eyes. He'd seen the smugness of his father's expression before. King Alaric revelled in knowledge he believed few shared. He also took sadistic pleasure in demonstrating the intellectual weaknesses of others, even his first-born son.

Alaric lowered his voice to a whisper, as if Volerdie himself may overhear his revelation. "The curate allowed me access to the scripture verses."

"That is forbidden. How did you..."

"I'm the king. My desires are never forbidden. I studied the scripture. Day and night. Season after season. My dutiful inspection revealed something the curates should have realised long ago."

Oldaric crouched forward on his stool, inhaling the stale odour of his father's battle-soiled body.

Alaric continued, "Somewhere in this cursed, endless plain is the lost city of Pergamos. Somewhere among the swaying grass is hidden Volerdie's ancient seat of power."

"The Dambay Plains are flat and featureless. How could we miss seeing an entire city amid such banality?"

King Alaric reached out and clenched the neck of Oldaric's tunic in his fist and sneered. "Are you saying I'm wrong? Do you think your father a fool? The scripture verses didn't divulge its exact location, but I'm convinced it's hidden in these plains. I'll wager those faithless grells have cast a spell over the land, masking Pergamos from our view. Now that we've expelled them once and for all, the spell will be broken."

Oldaric pulled away from his father, stood and paced the room to the rhythm of his marching thoughts. "If we find Volerdie's seat of power, then..."

"We?" spat Alaric. "If I find Pergamos, I will be the greatest Erstürmen king to ever live. The greatest ruler since the ascension of Volerdie, our Divine Creator. What treasures might the halls of Pergamos hold? The scripture verses spoke of a throne fashioned from the corpses of unbelievers. This must be Volerdie's throne. The throne of the dead. All his power is connected to it. Secrets that could entrench my rule for an eternity. When I rise from this infantile excuse for a bed, my search must begin."

"You should rest, Father. Renew your strength before undertaking this quest."

"The healer assured me I'd make a full recovery within days." King Alaric slunk into the bed, pulling a woollen blanket up under his chin.

Oldaric turned his back, blocking his father's view, and reached for a burgundy cushion resting atop a bedside table. He clutched the cushion to his chest, trying to smother the beat of his thumping heart.

"Leave me, now," ordered Alaric. "I need to sleep."

A cold, distant voice responded. Oldaric convinced himself that it was Volerdie's voice that spoke this evening. That spoke through him. "Of course. A long rest before the pursuit of an eternal reign."

Oldaric spun around and faced his father. He sprang forward before the older man could sit up, thrusting the cushion over the king's face. He's weak from the battle wounds, Oldaric thought. But still Alaric thrashed, snapping bony fingers around Oldaric's wrist and digging broken nails under his skin. Oldaric grimaced, then clenched his jaw in determination, pressing harder down on the cushion. Alaric gasped for air, trying to twist his body out from under the smother, but Oldaric held firm and smiled as he sensed aged muscles falter.

* * * *

The dying breaths of King Alaric startled a rat resting under the cot. It scurried to the corner of the room, disappearing into a hole in the wall. Down a dark, dank tunnel it ran, skipping over generations of dust and mould. Through walls and under floors, deep beneath the city of Malang Gunya. Under the grey soil of the Dambay Plains, it squeezed through a crevice in the bedrock and raced down into a place that had not seen light for an eternity.

The rat scuttled through a crack in the thick, oak doors of a grand hall. It stopped and tilted its head up, sniffing the sour air. Its entire body shuddered, as if an atmosphere of dread had filled its nostrils. It didn't linger, scampering across the tiled floor towards another hole.

Through the veiled black, the rat passed a chair perched high on a marble platform. A throne made from petrified human bodies and crowned by the head of a horned beast. And next to the platform, partially buried under dirt and rubble, as if remorseful hands had tried to hide their shame, lay two glass eyes like obsidian marbles, their flaming pupils the only flicker of light fighting against the consuming darkness.

"Nanna?" The whisper stumbled from Tommy's trembling lips as he hid under his bed, curled up like an unborn baby. Framed by the untucked sheet and worn timber floor, a bad man straddled Nanna's recumbent body and slashed at her flailing arms with a knife. Tommy recoiled from the assault, slinking further beneath the bed springs, his fear tracked by his grandmother's tears glistening under the bedside lamp.

The bad man dropped the knife and pulled something from his coat pocket that clinked together as he wrapped his hand around them. He pushed a clenched fist onto Nanna's chest, but her body arched and bucked, throwing him aside. The man thudded to the floor and, for a brief moment, locked eyes with Tommy cowering under the bed.

Nanna raised herself onto one elbow. "Please…Tommy, get help…"

The bad man flung himself back on top of her.

Tommy heard something crack and Nanna's arm stuck out at a strange angle. She collapsed under the weight of the bad man as he jammed his fist against her chest again, dropping his body onto the shuddering hand to fix it in place. Her arms and legs thrashed, but this time the man held fast, like a starved wolf clinging to the rump of a weakening deer.

Tommy's grandmother gasped for air through a foaming mouth. With frothy spit dribbling down her chin, the convulsions ended and Nanna's body went limp, her cheek pressed against the floorboards, glazed eyes casting a frozen glare towards her grandson quivering in the dark.

Tommy's throat constricted as mournful sobs fought against anxious breaths. "Nanna?"

The drifts of dust under Tommy's bed tickled his nose with every breath until a sneeze threatened. Teeth clenched; he forced the intrusion back down into his body.

Keep still, he thought. *Still and quiet.*

A pool of Nanna's blood seeped across the floor towards him, collecting dirt as it oozed under the bed. He pulled his knees in tight, retreating from the advance.

The bad man stood, his heavy breaths echoing amid the fearful silence. The edge of the bedsheet brushed the top of black boots, rusted buckles holding leather straps across the foot and above the ankle. The man trod on a book laying on the floor. Tommy's new favourite book — *The Lorax.* Too young to read the book himself, he'd pleaded with Nanna to read it to him tonight. For the third time. She did her best to explain what the story meant. Tommy liked the ending.

"I care," Tommy whispered. For a second, frustrated anger replaced his fear. *Get off my book. Leave Nanna alone.*

Tommy reached for the book. The bad man's feet moved. Fear swamped the anger and Tommy jerked his hand back into the safety of the darkness. He closed his eyes and tried to escape to the land of the Lorax, hoping the bad man wouldn't follow. But he did, sucking air from the room, as if his horrid deed began to smother him.

"Nanna...leaving, Tommy. Leaving. Not coming...back."

The man's faltering voice made the back of Tommy's neck tingle. A hair lodged in his nose and he sneezed, then burst into tears.

The bad man offered no consolation for Tommy's sorrow. "Nanna left...a present. A special present...in your secret hiding place. She wants you...to keep it secret and safe. Don't tell...anyone. Not anyone. Ever."

Tommy calmed his sobbing. *Secret hiding place.* Only he and Nanna knew about it. Sometimes they hid things together and promised they'd never tell anybody else. Their special secret to keep between the two of them.

The bad man crouched next to the bed and the bottom of his coat splayed open, exposing a hem of metal rings locked together. They glinted in the lamplight, catching Tommy's eye. He'd seen the stitched metal before, in storybooks about knights and princesses.

Chainmail.

The bad man whispered into the dark under the bed. "S-sorry it happened like this." He stood and walked to the doorway, his heavy boots clicking on the floorboards. He paused in the hallway, a final snivel floating through the still autumn night down to the dusty floor under Tommy's bed. "Forgive me."

Tommy shivered. The bad man disappeared.

*   *   *   *

11 years later

Hand on heart, Tom Anderson counted the beats shuddering through his fingers. Perched on the front porch of his home, anxiety threatened to overwhelm him. An old woman, faint and frail, stood at the bottom of the driveway next to a towering redgum tree. An old woman that looked like his grandmother.

Tom clenched his jaw, jumped to his feet and strode towards the tree. As he reached the halfway point of the long driveway, the woman stepped behind the trunk of the eucalypt, vanishing from Tom's view.

He sprinted to the tree's base, but caught only his breath. Nanna had disappeared. Again.

Tom slumped against the tree trunk and dug his elbows into his thighs, resting pimpled cheeks on white knuckles. A dying cicada rolled around in the grey dirt, its vibrating wings kicking up tiny puffs of dust as they stuttered towards a final silence. Tom scuffed his sneakers in the dirt, disrupting a convoy of black ants scaling the eucalypt, likely on their way to harvest honey dew from accommodating lerps. Closing his eyes, he rubbed his shoulder blades against the rough bark. For the last eleven years, he'd tried to forget that night in his bedroom when he hid under the bed while a stranger murdered his grandmother.

Murdered? Maybe.

Nanna's death remained a mystery, even though five-year-old Tommy saw it happen. When the bad man left the bedroom, and Tommy found a fragment of courage buried in the lint and dust under his bed, he ran to the neighbour's house. He took Mrs Duffield by the hand and dragged her to his room. Nanna had disappeared. Mrs Duffield rang the restaurant and spoke to Tommy's mum and dad. They came home straight away and saw the blood and a knife on the floor. They rang the police.

The police put the knife in a plastic bag. One of them sat on the couch with Tommy and asked him the same questions, over and over. Tommy's mum cried, a lot.

The police couldn't explain what happened. They listed Nanna as a missing person. She hasn't been found yet. Except, in the last month, Tom had seen her six times counting today. Her or her ghost. Always from a distance.

He'd tried to explain it to his mum. She told him it was probably delayed onset trauma. Ghosts aren't real.

Then why did he keep seeing her? wondered Tom. The bad man said Nanna wouldn't come back. He lied.

Tom opened his eyes, dug his heels into the dirt and twisted around to face a hole at the base of the redgum tree. The secret hiding place where he would keep treasures as a child and tell no-one except Nanna. This is where he'd found Nanna's present eleven years ago, buried inside an old wooden box. A mysterious book that had dominated his short life. Tom called it the 'blue book' owing to the dark blue, patchwork-leather cover that enveloped the pages like bruised skin.

Attached to the book was a photograph of his grandmother with a handwritten note on the back.

> *My Dearest Tommy*
> *This is your special present. Keep it secret and safe. One day you'll be able to read all the words in this book. Cherish the words, like I cherish our time together.*
> *With Love*
> *Nanna*

At five years old, Tommy couldn't read his grandmother's note in its entirety, but he understood 'secret' and 'safe'. Over the years, guilt fuelled his desire to follow his grandmother's instructions to the letter. He'd never told anyone about the blue book, but he always wondered why Nanna had told the bad man about their hiding place.

Maybe the book could explain Nanna's reappearance? Tom checked for prying eyes. A quiet, dirt road ran past the front of his family's five-acre property. Across the road, sheep grazed under a sparse canopy of pink gums. Dense revegetation flanked the outer perimeter of Tom's home, masking the views of neighbours. With his parents out for the day, nobody would see him retrieve his prized possession from its new hiding place.

Tom interlocked leafless, fallen branches around the base of the redgum, building a makeshift ladder tall enough to reach the first fork in the trunk where the aging tree split into three stems. He scrambled up the ladder with deft familiarity a nd p ulled h imself i nto a b owl shaped by centuries of growth. Choosing the stem growing diagonal to the ground, he shinned his way along its smooth bark, pressing into the branch with his elbows and knees, until he reached a hollow. Balanced far above the ground, Tom thrust his left hand into the hole and almost slipped from the branch as panicked squawks rang out.

"Bloody birds," he grumbled to himself. "They've built another nest on my book." He regained his balance and gripped the branch tighter with his right arm and legs, sending his left hand to explore the hollow again.

"One…two…three nestlings…getting noisier. I hope they don't attract any attention." They did. A brown treecreeper landed on the branch and let out a cacophony of alarm calls. Tom didn't want to disturb the birds, but he needed to retrieve his treasure. He dug around the outer edges of the nest, searching through layers of loose bark until his hand brushed against the leather-bound prize. Grasping the book between his thumb and index finger, he pulled it out from under the nest, careful not to dislodge the nestlings, and climbed back down the tree.

Tom grabbed a mustard-yellow backpack from his bedroom, threw the blue book inside, locked the back door and marched down the driveway. He walked for an hour until reaching a remnant patch of eucalypt woodland left over from the clearing of one of the farms on the outskirts of his rural hometown; Littlehampton, South Australia.

After jumping the rusted barbed-wire fence surrounding the woodland, Tom navigated his way around thorny shrubs and fallen timber, dead leaves and twigs crunching under his sneakers. Kangaroos thrived in the woodland, particularly on its fringes nearest the wheat crops. Tracks marking their crepuscular commutes from sheltering to feeding areas weaved through acacia and casuarina trees like macropod highways.

He followed a track to the top of a steep, rocky ridge dotted with

granite boulders. Underneath the lip of one of the boulders, he'd exca-
vated a shelter where he could escape the pressing awkwardness of
teenage life and calm his anxiety; a weeping sore first infected on the
night he watched Nanna being murdered. From the shelter, Tom could
see the entire woodland spread out before him, stretching from the
ridgeline to the sharp edge abutting cleared paddocks. He loved being
surrounded by nature. It helped him to heal. To put aside his worries
and anxiety. At home, he'd spend hours with his nose buried in books
about plants and animals from all over the world.

Tom relaxed into the shelter, unfastened his pack and wrapped
his hand around the heavy, blue book. Flicking hair from his face, he
opened the book's cover, worn through fervent possession, and ran his
finger along the frayed, yellowed edge of the first page.

He'd studied the blue book for almost his entire childhood, counting
and numbering its five hundred and sixteen pages. He often counted
things, trying to control his anxiety by distracting his mind with the
mundane. Sitting among the boulders of the rocky scrub, he traced his
finger over the unusual design that adorned the first page of the blue
book; a golden sun positioned between two orbiting spheres painted as
eyes with black irises and flaming red pupils. Elongated rays of sunlight
connected the three celestial bodies. Underneath the design was an
instruction written in English.

*Learn the language here presented and read the stories of
conquest and heroism.*

Tom didn't recognise the neat, flowing handwriting, which graced every
page and told stories in a strange, unfamiliar language that he'd christened
'Bookish.' The first half of the blue book translated English to Bookish, and
the writer had taken particular care to spell Bookish words phonetically to

facilitate correct pronunciation. Tom knew no other language like Bookish, and he decided that the writer of the blue book had made it up. Nevertheless, he wanted to learn the language, for Nanna's sake.

Tom revelled in the second half of the book, which contained stories of the heroic deeds of princes and kings that ruled over a people called the Erstürmen. One recounted the settling of refugees of war in the city of Laodicea in a land called Enthilen. Another story, one of Tom's favourites, told of a young King Thiemo who discovered the secret to eternal life, but, after becoming immortal, sacrificed himself to enable the return of Volerdie, the Divine Creator. The Erstürmen welcomed the sacrifice with fanfare and admiration, blessing King Thiemo's last days with all his heart's desires. They believed that such a sacrifice would lead them all to an everlasting paradise.

Tom had become so engaged with the Erstürmen that he wrote his own stories about them, banged out on his cherished, turquoise-blue typewriter. His mother always encouraged his fertile imagination, although he knew that she worried about it feeding his anxiety. She'd warned him that a creative mind can be a double-edged sword, locked in an endless battle between despair and brilliance. Lately, despair had taken the upper hand, Tom often retreating into his mind to imagine alternative pasts or futures; an encyclopedia of *what ifs*?

The blue book contained two more peculiarities that perplexed Tom. A statement embossed on the front cover: *The eternal reign begins with you*, and a scrawl in the margin of page four hundred and sixty-two, written in a different handwriting to the remainder of the book: a lemniscate next to the word *Revelé*.

* * * *

Tom sat in his bedroom, listening to his parents in the kitchen of their small stone house engaging in another pointless argument about some-one's age. It made him think of Nanna. In two days, she would have been sixty-five; born February 19th, 1918. Her birthday was exactly one month after his.

Guilt started to gnaw at him again. Guilt that the bad man got away. Guilt that Tom didn't do more to protect his beloved grandmother. Guilt that justice had never been served. He longed for justice, hoping it would end the torture of his anxious mind.

"Tom! Dinner's ready."

Tom sat up at the sound of his mum's voice. His bed springs creaked as he stood and opened the bedroom door. He wandered into the aging kitchen with its peeling laminate benchtops and checker-patterned linoleum floor and sat opposite his father, Bert. They didn't acknowl-edge each other. Tom fixed his eyes on the dining table in front of him and waited in silence.

"What'd you do today, Tom?"

"Nothin', Mum. What's for dinner?"

"Corned beef."

Tom screwed up his nose. He hated corned beef.

Bert took a sip of beer and turned to his wife. "I'm thinkin' of fellin' the old redgum at the bottom of the driveway."

Anger burned Tom's cheeks. "No."

"Why'd you care? It's dyin'. Dead branches droppin' everywhere, making a mess. Only good for firewood now."

A fist tightened around Tom's chest. He counted the petals on the yellow flowers that covered the placemat between his knife and fork.

"Why don't you leave it?"

"It's too old, Elaine. Gonna fall over and land on the road one of these days. End up killin' someone."

Fifty-eight, fifty-nine, sixty petals. It's not helping. The field of yellow flowers disappeared under a plate of soggy cabbage, mashed potato and corned beef drowning in white sauce. Tom twirled a piece of cabbage on the prongs of his fork. "I saw Nanna again today."

"Oh, Tom. We talked about this. They're only hallucinations."

"Maybe she's tryin' to tell him somethin'?"

"Please, Bert. Leave it."

Tom raised his head to meet his father's stare. "Like what?"

"Grow up. Face your fears like a man."

Fuck you. Tom knew his father blamed him for Nanna's death. For doing nothing to raise the alarm. He suspected that his father didn't believe there was a bad man in the first place. That, somehow, Tom had killed Nanna or was responsible for her disappearance.

"You were only a little boy, Tom. There was nothing you could have done. We've been through this so many times." Elaine glared at her husband.

Tom dropped his head and pushed mashed potato around his plate.

"We could talk to someone about these hallucinations," said Elaine.

"Who?" asked Tom.

Bert interjected, "I'm not payin' for a quack."

Elaine placed her hand on Tom's forearm. "We could think about it. Are you looking forward to school? Year Twelve this year."

"Sooner it ends, sooner he can get a job."

Tom's mind simmered in silent frustration until the end of the meal. After dinner, he walked to the bottom of the driveway and sat under the redgum tree, rubbing his hand over the bark. The tree *was* dying. Naked, grey branches now the lifeless gems of a failing crown. Yet, Tom had known this tree his whole life, sharing secrets with its aging heartwood. He'd played chasey around the tree with his Nanna. Showed her his secret hiding place and the treasures he kept there. When Nanna disappeared, Tom stopped hiding things under the tree except the blue book. When he could climb the tree, he moved the book to the tree hollow. Now, his father threatened to destroy both hiding places.

Tom pinched the skin on his thigh and started to count, glancing back towards the house. His father stood on the front porch, arms crossed, leaning against a rotting timber post, glaring at him.

*   *   *   *

Two days later, Tom woke to a chainsaw screaming outside. He threw back the blanket covering his bed and jumped onto the timber floorboards. Pulling on a pair of shorts, he raced outside already knowing what he'd find. His father had felled all of the lower branches, attacking the old redgum with the squealing chain of death while standing in the bucket of a front-end loader, Mr Duffield at the controls — the accomplice in the murder of Tom's childhood memories.

"Fuck this." Tom stormed back into his bedroom, pulled on his sneakers and favourite *The Jam* t-shirt, and grabbed his backpack. He tossed in a half-full water bottle, two mix tapes recorded from the radio, his Walkman, and the latest issue of *Starburst Magazine*. He pulled his dresser away from the wall, the sticker-covered mirror perched on top rocking with the shunt, and thrust his hand into the dark, lint-filled space behind the drawers, wrapping his fingers around the blue book that he'd rescued before the slaughter of the tree began.

As Tom went to shove the book into his backpack, it slipped from his grasp and fell onto the floor. He bent down to pick it up and something caught the sunlight streaming in through a hole in the curtains. Something jammed between a gap in the floorboards.

Tom took a pocketknife from his bedside table and prised the object free, holding it up to the light; a small, silver coin. Inscribed on one side

18

were three words written in Bookish: *King's Quarter Treasury.* On the other side was the profile of a man with a strange crown and the name *King Alaric* engraved underneath.

How the hell? Where did this come from? Too flustered to think more about it, Tom slipped the coin into his pocket, picked up the blue book and tossed it into his pack. He slung the pack over his shoulder and stormed into the kitchen. Grabbing a slice of cold toast and a banana from the breakfast table, he headed for the front door, brushing past his mum.

"Where you going?"

"For a walk."

"The tree's dying, Tommy."

Tom stopped at the kitchen door. "He doesn't care, Mum. He's never cared."

"You know we love you. Your father's worried the tree might fall on the road."

"He doesn't have to cut down the whole thing."

"Where are you walking?"

"I dunno. I might go to Ritchie's place."

"It'll be good for you to spend some time with your friends. You've spent too much time alone this summer. Your anxiety…"

"Yeah, I know." Tom's anxiety festered in undistracted solitude.

"Do you have a clean hanky?"

"What? Don't be stupid."

Elaine fetched a white handkerchief embroidered with Tom's initials from the clothes-drying rack and shoved it in his pocket. "My mother always said that whenever you go out make sure you have on clean underwear and a clean hanky."

"So, if someone pulls my pants down or I have a sneezing fit, everything will still be OK?"

Elaine smiled at Tom and kissed his hair. "Mum also used to say success in life is a confidence trick. Maybe, this year, you'll gain some self-confidence. It'll help you get a job."

Life after school terrified Tom, but he knew his mum wanted the best for him. He gave her a hug and walked to the front door.

She called after him, "Phone me from Ritchie's if you're going to be late."

The warmth of Elaine's embrace turned cold as Tom stepped onto the porch in time to see his father and Mr Duffield set a fire at the base of the old tree. The flames raced up the trunk, fuelled by a pile of dead branches and the combustible oil of eucalypt leaves. Tom trudged down the driveway and out the front gate, eyes swelling with anger and heartache.

Ritchie wasn't home and Tom found himself wandering through the rocky scrub again, head bowed, kicking rocks along kangaroo highways. He sulked his way among the boulders near the top of the wooded ridge, dreaming of escaping his latest torment.

Tom picked up a stone and flung it as far as he could down the hill. It crashed through the tree canopy, thudding into a log. The hollow clunk echoed amid a strange quiet that had settled over the bush. He strained his ears, searching for a familiar sound. No birdsong. No wind whistling through eucalypt leaves. Only his heavy breaths after labouring up the steep slope. He leaned against a boulder, squinting at the morning sun piercing the woodland canopy.

Among the silence, anxiety crept in, exposing Tom's vulnerability, as if someone with malicious intent had pulled back a veil to reveal his location. He glanced over his shoulder. "Nobody's there. Don't be stupid."

Tom climbed towards his shelter, hoping to shut the world out for a while. He squeezed between two large boulders and stopped dead. Up ahead, an old woman in tattered clothes stepped out from behind a rock, blocking his path.

"Nanna?" Tom peered into the distance and took two steps forward. For the first time, the ghostly shape didn't try to evade him. His nerves tingled. His breaths grew shallow. Sweat stung his eyes and he blinked to clear his focus. The old woman didn't look like Nanna. Bent over by age or pain, her spindly frame wavered in front of him, leathery skin stretched thin over brittle bones.

"Sorry, I thought you were…" Tom tried to turn away, but heavy legs foiled his retreat.

Defying her antiquity, the old woman sprang towards him and as quick as lightning, an ossified hand latched onto Tom's left wrist and squeezed like a vice tightening around young wood. He recoiled from the ice-cold touch, adrenaline coursing through his body. Tom tried to yank his arm free, but couldn't escape. The woman glared at him with hollow, dark eyes; portholes to a deep maw. A menacing smile revealed a trio of rotten teeth, encircled by pale lips.

Tom gaped at the transparent skin stretched taut across the woman's knuckles. Her grip tightened and his attention returned to her face, framed by wisps of long, grey hair.

She hissed, "*Varmist.*"

"Who are you?"

"*Varmist.*"

Despite the thin, frail voice, Tom recognised the word from the blue book. It meant 'lost'. *Is she lost? How does she know Bookish?* He replied in English, not wanting to reveal anything to his accoster. "Let go, please."

"*Jun schell varmist.*"

OK, that is Bookish. I'm sure of it. 'Boy is lost.' I don't know why she thinks I'm lost. This is getting weirder. "I'm OK thanks." He fought to break the woman's grip.

"Laodicea."

Tom swallowed hard. *What does she know about Laodicea?* "What did you say? Who are you?"

"Laodicea. Enthilen."

"I have to go now. My parents will be wondering where I am."

The hoary gaze of the old woman set as hard as steel. From her mouth came English words, clear and demanding, as if she wanted to make sure that nothing was lost in translation. "No future here. Leave home. Paradise awaits."

With her free hand, the woman fumbled inside a pouch tied to a makeshift belt of frayed twine. Tom went limp as the energy drained from his body, sucked out by the lecherous fingers clamped to his wrist. The old lady prised open Tom's left hand and placed in his palm something hard and smooth, like a pebble rounded by a fast-flowing stream. She closed the hand to form a fist and the left side of Tom's body went numb. The woman relaxed her grip and reached for his right hand, thrusting another stone into his palm. This time she didn't close his fist, instead stepping back from him.

In Tom's half-open right hand, sat something black and opaque with a flash of fiery red deep within. It looked like one of the eyes from the front page of the blue book. An obsidian glass eye with a flaming pupil. The smell of burning flesh wafted into the air as the two gifts from the old woman seared Tom's skin. He grimaced, but couldn't release the eyes.

The woman motioned for Tom to close his right fist in the same manner as his left. She began a rhythmic chant in perfect English, as if she'd learned the phrases by endless rote. "No future here. Leave home. Close your hand. Paradise awaits. No future here. Leave home. Close your hand. Paradise awaits. No future..."

Entranced by the flickering red drowning in the misty black sea that he held in his right hand, Tom swayed back and forth. A bewildered mind filled with the incessant chanting of the old woman dismissed the love of his mother, the kindness of his friends, the good of this world. Right now, he wanted to be alone. With meek resignation he gave in to the hypnotic authority of the glass eyes and closed his fist.

A moment before Tom fell backwards into a swirling light, his Nanna appeared from behind the chanting old woman, her arms reaching towards him.

At the edge of a forest, Grin rested his back against a panalope tree while his mind wandered. Waning sunlight, filtered through broad, trident-shaped leaves, warmed his face as he cast his eyes skyward. Birdsong fluttered on the breeze. In the distance, wild pigs snuffled, likely burying their snouts in sticky mud. Recent rain accentuated forest aromas. Mendeal herbs in their last throes, the aged, papery flowers of yurali bushes, and the sickly-sweet smell of panalope leaves.

Grin bathed in the final days of gawimarra, the harvest season, before guma, the storm season took hold. He felt at one with the forest of Babir Birramal; his only home since birth. The ancestral home of the stone-grells, Malang Gunya, was far away and now deserted. But soon, he would visit the stone city for the first time. March with his father and the other grells to honour those who fell during the Erstürmen invasion.

Palms warming damp ground, Grin caressed blades of grass through long, thick fingers and inhaled the forest scents that gave purpose to his existence. Next to his bare feet, a field mouse darted across the emerald tops of moss-covered rocks. Insects buzzed around the yurali flowers searching for the last store of nectar, and wind whistled through the needle foliage of the bilawi tree, wailing like the ghosts of lost ancestors.

Grin's body relaxed, drifting away with the murmur of the forest. His shoulders rubbed against the bark of the panalope tree and he sank backwards, meeting the resistance of an ancient creature with roots strong and spreading. The tree and the grell became one until only the forest remained.

Like sap flowing t hrough t he x ylem, G rin's m ind e xplored e ach branch, twig and leaf. Floating among the canopy, the rays of the sun fuelled pullulating thoughts. A psychological photosynthesis. Renewing, replenishing, empowering. Fulfilled, h is m ind d rifted hi gher. Bl issful, unguarded. It rested at the peak and absorbed the pleasure of the tree-tops; a blanket of green promising safety and comfort.

A gust of wind trembled the outer limbs of the tree. Grin teetered, then fell, his mind tumbling through the entanglement of twigs and branches, down through the heartwood, down past the topsoil, down into the darkest, deepest burrowing roots. A blackness closed around him. His thoughts wavered. His energy drained.

A vision emerged through the darkness. Another grell, stooped and pale. She leaned on a sparth, its shining blade setting a glimmer in ruin-ous eyes, and offered a tainted hand to Grin. The smothering claustro-phobia of the underworld lay siege to his sanctuary.

Did the pale grell promise an escape? He took her hand, his mind recoiling at a flash of iridescent white, ears ringing with screams of distress.

Grin jolted awake; his dream disrupted by splashing and panicked cries. He leapt to his feet and bolted to a nearby stream. Standing on the bank, rapids flashed past his keen eyes. Churning whitewater smashed against boulders strewn across the streambed. Among the tumult, a desperate hand clung to a slippery rock. Grin tensed his muscles and raced into the water. At waist deep he stopped, paralysed with fear as the current jerked his legs sideways. Like most grells, he couldn't swim.

The outstretched hand lost i ts g rip. A s tranded b ody fl ailed in th e water. A boy bobbing about in the rapids like driftwood. A boy dressed in strange clothes.

Grin steeled his nerves and leapt onto the nearest boulder. Belying his heavy frame, he navigated into the middle of the stream, jumping from boulder to boulder with the surety of a mountain goat scaling a cliff. He positioned himself downstream of the boy. In one fluid motion, Grin knelt forward and thrust his hand under the water, grabbing a fistful of shirt and wrenching the floundering stranger from certain death. He hoisted the thin, limp body above his head and rushed back to the embankment.

Grin laid the boy down, searching his face. The stranger's closed mouth drew no breaths. Grin slapped the boy's chest, hard. No response. He tried again. Water spewed from the boy's mouth as he gasped for air.

Grin waited until the stranger's breathing calmed, picked him up, threw him face down over his shoulder and raced into the forest.

*   *   *   *

Many days walk north of the forest stream, in a damp cave buried under the Desolate Mountains, the empty eye sockets of a horned beast carved into the backrest of a throne of tortured souls glowed with crimson menace.

"Worshipful Master. The throne of the dead. Look, the beast glows. The beast glows, master."

"Yes, you're right, Mother. He's here. Send word to Eroberung. Take the boy alive."

~ Chapter 3 ~

Tom lay sunk into thick fur stretched over a timber frame that suspended his body above the floor. Through bleary eyes he stared at a wall past the end of his nose. The cold water of the stream still chilled his tongue and thinned mucus ran from his nostrils. He sniffed and opened his eyes wider. The smooth, polished wall reminded him of the granite boulders that dotted the bush remnant near his home. Tom blinked hard, focussing on faint patterns decorating the grey stone. He traced one of the patterns with his finger; a spiral within a spiral. Then another. The lines interconnected, all part of a much larger design. He pushed himself back from the wall to absorb the intricate pattern. Spirals became veins on a leaf, leaves on a twig, twigs on a branch. Tom counted the leaves.

"You are awake."

Tom froze. Behind him, someone spoke Bookish. Not the thin, hissing whine of the old woman that had ambushed him in the scrub. This person had a deeper, almost guttural voice.

"You are awake and you can hear me. There is no use pretending."

Tom rolled over to face the stranger and a lump caught in his throat. Before him stood a giant with broad shoulders and a bare, barrel chest. *It must be nearly eight-foot tall. Is it...human?* A tattoo dominated the giant's pale face; black ink spread across both cheeks and joined at the chin, like the wings of an eagle.

"Are you afraid?" asked the giant.

Tom pressed his back against the wall, the stranger's stern lilac eyes fixing him in place.

"My wurrumany, my son, Grinnian, saved you from the stream. I would have stopped him had I been there and saw what you carried with you. I would have let you drown. My son is too trusting. He sees all the beauty of this land, and none of its dangers."

Bewildered, Tom scanned the single, circular room for a door. He muttered in English, *"Have to get out of here."*

The giant cocked his head to the side, narrowing slanted eyes. "That language is strange to me. The common tongue is all we know. And Grellian, but that is forbidden. Do you speak the common tongue?"

Tom nodded. Here, it seemed Bookish was the common tongue.

"I can see that you are afraid. I should introduce myself." The creature stepped towards Tom; a leather skirt sewn together with twine brushing the top of its thighs. Sweat glinted on its bald crown as it held its large hands out to the front.

Tom flinched, expecting to be struck.

The giant halted. "It seems you are not ready for a formal greeting. Maybe soon. I am Frennan stone-grell. Third born of Brennian and Feyan. Protector of Babir Birramal."

Tom tried to focus his mind. *Get your stuff and get out of here.* His backpack sat in the middle of the room; its water-logged contents arranged neatly on a stone table. His eyes lingered on the blackened banana he'd taken from the breakfast table back home. It wouldn't satiate his growing hunger. His wet clothes hung from a rope stretched across one of the walls. Tom grabbed at an animal skin at the foot of the bed and covered his naked body.

For the first time, a soft smile broke Frennan's intense stare.

Tom's eyes settled on the blue book, resting by itself on a small table at the foot of the bed. *"What's missing?"* he whispered to himself in English. *"Where's my hanky?" There.* The damp square of white cotton, T.A. embroidered into the corner, hung next to his t-shirt. *"Get your clothes and find the...where's the door?"*

"You persist with that strange language," said Frennan in Bookish. "If you indeed speak the common tongue, now is the time to use it."

Tom reached for the blue book and opened the cover. The wet pages stuck together with smeared, black ink. *Damn it.* "I w-w-want to go home," he stammered in Bookish.

"Ah, so you do speak Erstürmen."

"What?"

"Erstürmen. The language of the invaders. It is the common tongue now. Grells are forbidden to speak their own language."

Not Bookish, Erstürmen. "I want to go...to go home."

"Where is your home?"

"Littlehampton. Adelaide Hills."

"What is a *Littlehampton*?"

"A town, in South Australia. You must've heard of it. Where am I?"

"Somewhere safe, for now. But you cannot stay."

Tom traced the welt in the middle of each of his palms, brushing his finger over the rough, burnt skin. Did the glass eyes bring him here? The ones the crone thrust into his hands. *Where are the they now?* He gasped when another giant grell entered the room, walking, it seemed, right through the wall. Dressed in a long, animal-skin tunic with fur lining showing through the gaps between the sewn patches, he looked much younger than Frennan.

The new arrival glanced at Tom, reached into a bag hanging from a belt around his waist and pulled out Tom's Walkman. "Is this yours? I found it on the riverbank."

"Yes," said Tom.

"What is it for?" The young grell tipped the Walkman upside down and water ran from the cassette holder.

"It doesn't matter."

The grell shrugged and placed the Walkman next to Tom's other possessions.

"You are forgetting your manners, Grin."

"Sorry, Father." Grin faced Tom and walked towards him, hands out front as the older grell had done. Tom recoiled again, mesmerised by the tattoo of a spider on the grell's face.

"I do not think he is ready for that yet," said Frennan.

The young grell withdrew and announced, "I am Grinnian stone-grell. First born of Frennan and Mirrian. Protector of Babir Birramal. I like to be called Grin."

"So," said Frennan, "you know our names, we do not know yours."

"Tom. Tom Anderson."

"Tomtom Anderson," repeated Grin, smiling.

"No. Just Tom."

"Tom Anderson of a Littlehampton," Frennan formally announced.

With the introductions over, Grin turned away from Tom and searched the dome-shaped shelter, as if looking for something in particular. With singular purpose, he strode towards a tall shelf embedded in the smooth stone wall. Reaching above his bald head, he was about to take something from the shelf when Frennan bellowed, "Wanhamarradanha!"

The older grell sprang in front of his son, thrust a hand into his chest and pushed him up against the wall.

Tom jumped as Grin's back thudded into the stone.

Grin averted his eyes from his father and whispered, "Baladhu ngaabunganha."

Frennan scowled. "Barriy. They are not for grells."

From the shelf, the glass eyes watched Tom. They'd survived the stream. With a flush of scolding panic, his anxiety swamped his thoughts. *I need to get out of here.* The etchings on the stone walls swirled around him like a rushing stream, the patterns of leaves and branches blurring together in a calamitous, botanical mayhem.

Frennan stepped away from Grin and sneered at Tom. "*Birraman.* You must take the dark eyes and leave us. They are not welcome here."

Shaken by the sudden burst of anger from the older grell, Tom stuttered, "W-w-what did you call me?"

"Birraman. Traveller. This is what you are. I believe the dark eyes have carried you here. Should we touch them, they will steal us away."

Tom returned his attention to the glass eyes sitting exposed on the shelf. He flashed back to the rocky ridge where the old woman had confronted him. *No future here. Leave home...*Tom visualized that moment, the eyes clenched in his fists, the feeling of nausea as the scrub disappeared and the world flashed white, Nanna reaching for him, his head spinning, his body travelling...travelling...

If the eyes brought me here, they must be able to take me home again. There's a stone table under the shelf. If I climb onto that table, I can reach the eyes.

Frennan grasped Grin's wrist and yanked him away from the dark eyes.

Among the anxious haze, Tom stumbled upon a shard of bravery. He jumped from the bed and sprang onto the table. Grabbing the eyes from the shelf, he grasped one in each hand, pressing his fingers into his palms until his fingernails drew blood. He ignored the pain, shut his eyes and waited for the spinning and nausea to take him back to the rocky scrub.

"Take me home, dammit!"

Tom squeezed his eyes and hands tighter, trying to will something familiar into existence. But nothing happened. He opened his eyes. Both grells stared at him. He stood on the table, dumbfounded and naked, the glass eyes fixed in his palms, wondering why he hadn't found his way back to the rocky scrub. Overwhelmed by his dilemma, Tom blurted out in fluent Bookish, "I don't want to stay here. I want to go home. This woman trapped me. Said horrible things. Forced me to hold these eyes. I went numb. My head was spinning…easier to do what she said. I closed my hands and felt sick. That book…" he pointed with disdain at his once treasured possession, "…that book…this language…stories…I don't know what it all means. It's all a mistake. I never wanted to leave home. I want to go back."

~ Chapter 4 ~

Prince Hadufuns slouched in a rickety chair, the cloth of his ragged tunic clinging to his shoulders like a sheet hung over thin wire. He picked at the tattered goat-skin covering the armrests with dirty, broken fingernails, plucking a tuft of hair and rolling it around in his fingers. It slipped from his grasp and landed among the dregs of dried gruel that knitted together forming lumps in his beard. Opposite him, behind a broad table, sat Theodoar, the Field Commander of Süden Forst, the southern-most outpost of the Erstürmen Kingdom. Hadufuns sneered at the Field Commander, perched on a throne of engraved bronze and copper, sculptures of boulder lions at the base and an eagle, wings spread, hovering above his head. The ornate cathedra doesn't mask this buffoon's incompetent leadership, he thought.

"This outpost is a sty," said Hadufuns.

Theodoar leaned forward and glared across the table. "You can talk. You're King Ewald's eldest brother. Second in line to the throne. You look like a peasant." He sat back, strained breaths labouring under heavy armour, worn for show rather than impending battle. Each rivet and surface, fastidiously polished by grell slaves most likely, reflected light around the commander's neat office as morning sun filtered through a barred window.

It's a pity Theodoar's attention to personal presentation doesn't trickle down to those under his command, thought Hadufuns. On the occasions that he'd witnessed the morning inspection of the guard, no more than a dishevelled rabble of reluctant defenders of the realm presented themselves for examination. "These outposts are the eyes, hands and shield of the king. The men should have pride in their kingdom and respect for their charge."

"I have pride in myself," said Theodoar. "Perhaps you should follow my lead. Our kingdom's crumbling. Ewald hides in his court, trembling like a mouse in a hole with a falcon waiting to pounce. The seven walls of Sardis can't protect him against the fear devouring his heart. The time has come for each to consider their own destiny."

Hadufuns sat up straight; a lame attempt at a warning. "Treasonous words."

"Why should you care? You wander aimlessly through Enthilen, lost in the labyrinth of your saddened mind. My soldiers see you scrounging for food in the forest, digging roots out of the mud. You don't tell anyone who you are, content with life as a beggar in rags, filling a pond of pitiful sorrow in hope to drown yourself more quickly. You abandoned your king long ago. Why shouldn't I and my men do the same?"

"The people of Süden Forst look to you for guidance. If the king *is* failing, new leaders must emerge, ones that offer hope."

"What hope might Hadufuns the Wandering Prince offer the Erstürmen people? You were commander of Süden Forst once. Then Umbo of the King's Shield. I was in Sardis under your command. I looked up to you before...before the *accident* ruined your mind."

"The death of my wife has nothing to do with..."

"It has everything to do with it. You've never accepted the loss. Never found the courage to move on. You're in no position to lecture me about leadership."

"Your men lack discipline, Theodoar. Some hunt wild grells for sport and leave headless bodies to the quarrel of vultures. Patrols are random and ineffective."

"Not true. We caught two rebels last eve. They're shackled in the dungeon. A few more beatings will see them sing like the fairest siren. Soon, we'll know more about the strongholds of the Dobunni resistance."

"What about the future of Süden Forst and its people?"

"Future? I care only about the present. I make no plans for the future. It's too uncertain."

"Uncertainty is the very reason to have a plan."

Theodoar bellowed, "Then I plan to eat more food, drink more meduz, sleep with more women, kill more grells and capture more rebels!" He sat back in his chair and belched, as if he'd achieved the first two objectives of his plan at that moment. Patting his portly frame through the glinting, silver armour, Theodoar flashed a wry smile at his companion in arguments.

Hadufuns sighed, lifted his aching bones from the flimsy chair and shuffled out the door. Stepping into glaring sunlight, he squinted, almost tumbling from the front porch to the dirt below. He braced himself against a timber post, letting his eyes adjust to the scene before him.

Disorder and apathy littered the grounds of Süden Forst, assaulting the fragment of pride Hadufuns still had for his kingdom. Guards teetering on primitive wooden stools sat at the front gate watching soldiers, slaves, traders and peasants mingle without consequence across the threshold meant to protect the outpost from any threat. Seemingly bored or indifferent, the guards left their weapons leaning against the outer wall of the fort, ripe spoils for any peasant keen on an uprising or simply wanting a better outcome from the next hunt. Next to the main entrance, broken crates spilled scraps of food across the dirt where dogs and children battled for meagre pickings.

A handful of grell slaves worked on the timber battlements, replacing beams rotting from long neglect with stripped trees from the nearby forest of Grōz Forst. The overseer ignored his serfs, too busy wooing a young peasant girl with stories of heroic deeds in battles he likely never fought.

Why did the slave-master bother with the pretence of courtship? wondered Hadufuns. If he wanted the girl, he could take her. Maybe he found greater joy in the willing acquiescence of affection rather than non-consensual conquest?

Hadufuns shuffled over to a corner of the outpost and planted his backside on an empty crate, legs outstretched and arms folded, leaning against the outer wall. He bowed his head and closed his eyes, losing himself in familiar tortured thoughts. While still loyal to the kingdom, he had no interest in politics. He didn't want to serve the king in Sardis, or in Laodicea where his younger brother Widald was Master of the King's Quarter, and he had no ambition to secure power for himself.

Though more than willing to offer advice to the likes of Theodoar, Hadufuns shunned responsibility. He also had no desire for a quiet, settled family life, unable to recover from the loss of his wife. With fatalistic resignation, he had accepted the mantle of the Wandering Prince, destined to maunder through Enthilen until death offered welcome release from a listless existence.

Hadufuns' wallow became his bed and he slumped into a deep sleep among the crates.

*   *   *   *

Sitting among fetid, manure-riddled hay scattered atop stained flagstones, the chill obscurity of the dungeon in Süden Forst encaged Athalee. She tugged at the chain connecting her to the wall like a rusty, rattling umbilical cord that would never be cut. A sliver of metal snapped from the shackles binding her wrists and lodged under her skin. She grimaced and kicked her heel into the floor.

"Suppress your frustration, Thaly."

Jacob, Athalee's companion and trainer, lay opposite her. He'd barely moved since their capture by the Erstürmen patrol.

He's conserving his energy in the hope of an escape, she thought. Try to follow his lead, this time. "Can you see a way out of this, Jacob?"

"We'll bide our time until an opportunity comes. We'll know when it arrives."

"I'm sorry. About our capture. I should've listened to you."

"Don't blame yourself. We were outnumbered. The sight of the enemy boils my blood, too. Sometimes it's hard to contain your anger."

Thaly lay down in the straw, fresh manure squelching under her back. She gagged at the stench, fighting h ard t o c ontrol a d ry r etch. Since pledging allegiance to the Dobunni rebels, Thaly h ad o bsessed over proving her worth, to reinforce in her own mind that she belonged. And she desperately needed to belong somewhere. Separated from her parents as a baby, she had no kin in the rebel community. But showing she wasn't afraid of anything had been her downfall more than once. Her immature brashness led to her and Jacob being captured by the patrol from Süden Forst. She should've stayed hidden, as Jacob ordered, rather than attempt to bring down the Erstürmen soldiers single-hand-edly. Having seen eighteen harvest seasons, the time had come for her to grow up. But the journey to maturity continued to be a tortured one, littered with confusion and missteps, and a bubbling frustration at not being able to find her place.

Jacob's deep, slow breaths soothed Thaly's mind. In the dull light of the dungeon, his dark skin made him almost invisible. But his greying hair stood out like a beacon.

"Try to rest," said Jacob. "Think of something more pleasant."

"Such as?"

"What about that girl you like? What's her name?"

"Ebba. I'm not sure she's interested in me. I've seen the way she stares at the male soldiers."

"Still got da energy to talk? About time for a bit more fun." The Erstürmen gaoler dragged the tip of his wooden leg over the flagstones as he limped across the room. He hovered above Jacob and tipped a cup of pigswill over his face. "Whose turn is it for da torture chamber?"

Jacob spluttered, turning his head to the side. Thaly gritted her teeth and imagined thrusting a blade into the gaoler's bloated stomach.

A soldier peered over the gaoler's shoulder. "How about the girl? She looks like a squealer."

Cowards, thought Thaly. She'd dispatch both of them soon enough.

The gaoler buried his boot into Jacob's shin. "What y'say, rebel? Yur pretty little friend gonna squeal?"

Jacob met the gaoler's gaze. "Take me instead. She doesn't know anything worth knowing."

"I need to get somethin' for da commander. Otherwise it'll be me on da rack."

The soldier poked the point of a halberd into Thaly's stomach. "Torture her and make him watch. That'll make him talk."

"Ya might have somethin' dere. Let's get 'em unlocked from dese chains. I reckon me rats are gettin' hungry."

Our opportunity will come, thought Thaly. We'll see it long before these fools know it's arrived.

*　*　*　*

Woken by the screams of a girl and the lecherous laugh of an impatient overseer, Hadufuns jerked upright and fell off the crate. He lay in the mud of the outpost grounds for a moment, getting his bearings. Past the end of his nose, a parchment rested on top of the mire, too clean to have been there for long. He leaned forward and brushed away the dirt, exposing the king's seal that bound the paper together. Hadufuns sat up and scanned the grounds of Süden Forst in hopes of spotting the messenger. A huge white horse carrying a towering, cloaked rider sauntered out of the main gate and into the Dambay Plains, but Hadufuns paid them no mind. He plucked the parchment from its undignified pedestal and prised it open.

My Dearest Son

Though lost to me, you are never forgotten. For many seasons, I've searched for a way to reunite us. Like you, I have wandered alone, discontent with my place in Enthilen. Fate brings me to you now at the time of our kingdom's greatest need. No doubt you've heard the rumours. King Ewald faces grave danger. Assassins creep closer to the inner circle with every passing moon. Rebel sympathisers have infiltrated Sardis. If Ewald falls, our dear Prince Adalwolf must take the throne. That young, innocent boy. A lonely child, completely unprepared to lead the kingdom. I fear your brothers will seize this moment and supplant Adalwolf with their own lust for power. Only you, next in line to the throne after Adalwolf, can bring stability to our kingdom. Should Ewald fall, only you can protect the young prince, your allegiance acting as a beacon for all to rally. The fate of our kingdom rests with you, Hadufuns. Your counsel is gravely and urgently needed. I'll be waiting in the Master's Hall in the King's Quarter of Laodicea on the night before Bargan next rises full.

Fondest and deepest regards

Father

Though bound by the king's seal, the letter wasn't from the king. It was from Ewald and Hadufuns' father, Oldaric, who held the throne before Ewald took power. Hadufuns hadn't seen his father since Ewald banished the old king from Sardis after Oldaric refused to cede the throne. The ancient Erstürmen custom is for the reigning king to hand power to his eldest son once the incumbent has reached the age of succession: fifty yarles. However, Oldaric wouldn't relinquish power and those loyal to the old king engaged in a vicious battle with Ewald's supporters in the inner circle of Sardis. A victorious King Ewald cast the bloodied and bruised Oldaric from the city and excised the usurpers from the kingdom like a malignant growth.

There'd been no sign of Oldaric for almost twenty yarles, and Hadufuns thought him long dead. This letter suggested otherwise. Only the king has access to the royal seal, and Hadufuns' father must have secreted one away before his banishment. The old king's talent for forward planning and to foresee events was legendary. Hadufuns believed the letter genuine, although he didn't trust the motivations of his father. Nor did he trust his brothers, Widald and Gerulf — especially Gerulf. They may well be plotting to seize power.

Hadufuns' loyalty to the ideals and traditions of the Erstürmen Kingdom urged him to take the letter seriously. Internal ructions at this time, when the king's power waned, would leave the door ajar for a rebel uprising. He folded the letter and tucked it into a worn pocket inside his tunic. He had an important decision to make. One that could affect the future of all of Enthilen.

~Chapter 5~

Too worried to be embarrassed, Tom sat naked on the edge of Grin's bed, overawed by the myriad of thoughts consuming his mind. He took a sharp piece of flintstone and prised the glass eyes from his wounded hands, fluid seeping from his palms and trickling to the tips of his fingers, then placed the eyes on the bench next to him.

The dark eyes, Frennan had called them. If they transported him here, why couldn't he use them to go home? "Where am I?" Tom asked for a second time.

"In our milbi. A shelter where we eat and sleep," said Grin.

"Yes, but where exactly is your shelter? What country am I in?"

The grells' brows furrowed.

Tom sought something familiar for reassurance. "Does the land have a name?"

"I think I understand," said Frennan. "The invaders call this land Enthilen. We call it nguram-bang, our home. The Erstürmen think they own this land, but no-one can own the soil and everything that grows in and above it. We are stewards only, entrusted with the care of the land before passing it to those yet born."

The blue book rested at the end of the bed where Tom had slept, poking out from the fur stretched over the timber. *Enthilen... Erstürmen.*

The book had many stories about this place and those people. How could anyone possibly know that one day he'd be here?

"The Erstürmen are the invaders?" Tom tried to reconcile what he'd read in the blue book with Frennan's account. He thought of the Erstürmen as heroes. Bold and brave warriors fighting savages. It appeared these grells considered them somewhat less than this.

"We were all invaders once," said Grin. "Even the grells came from another place. The Erstürmen are only the most recent. They consider themselves righteous conquerors. We prefer to call them mirrimirri, wicked thieves, for all that they have stolen from us and this land."

Tom pointed at the glass eyes. "What do you know about these things?"

"The dark eyes. The eyes of lost souls," said Frennan. "I believe that is what they are. If I am right, grells must never touch them. They are evil."

A light shone in Grin's lilac eyes. "I touched them. When I pulled Tom from the stream. I saw them fixed to his hands and worked them loose, placing them in my pocket."

"You are fortunate they did not spirit you away. When I was a child, my father told a story passed to him by his father and his father before of an evil temptation. He called them the eyes of lost souls. Transparent black with a flickering red menace deep within. They draw you to them like a beautiful, but poisonous flower. If you touch them, you will disappear from this land, never to return. And sometimes, they trap your very soul. Keep it locked inside a dark prison for eternity. I do not know how you escaped these fates, Grin. But one day, your foolishness will be your undoing."

Tom clenched both fists. "I think you have to hold them a certain way." He fought back tears. "Is *my* soul trapped in those eyes?"

"There are some in this land who linger well beyond the time when they should have returned to the soil. Age descends on them with unnatural speed and clings to their body for generations, like a bindu mussel to a rock. The Erstürmen believe the souls of these creatures have been wrenched from their bodies. Kept prisoner by cruel magic. My father told me the dark eyes have this power. The Erstürmen call the soulless, draughouls. But you are not a draughoul, Tom Anderson. You are a birraman. And you are not the first."

* * * *

As Tom slept, Grin stepped outside the milbi to enjoy the damp night air of the forest of Babir Birramal. He breathed in the sounds that floated among the trees. A bearded nightjar screeching in the distance, likely hunting moths in the pale moonlight. The booming *dollop dollop* of the spotted tree frog calling for mates among the canopy of panalope trees. The sounds gave him comfort. Content in the knowledge that life would continue long after he had passed.

Born inside the milbi, Grin had never ventured far from the forest. It anchored him to the land. Defined his existence in this world. He loved its creatures as a mother loves a child. Yet, open plains were the grell's true country. A place where they could roam widely and see far horizons. Grin had never experienced such freedom. The Erstürmen had stolen that opportunity from him.

Frennan appeared out of the forest, a limp cave python draped over his shoulders. "We can cure the meat of this yaba. It should last a few meals." Frennan tossed the dead snake at Grin's feet. "Gawimarra is about to end. Guma approaches."

Grin looked to the night sky, wondering if a storm would descend on him at any moment. "I will gather more stores in the morning, Father."

"I need to talk to you about the birraman. He cannot stay."

"He's inside, sleeping."

"When he wakes, we will return his possessions and ask him to leave."

"Where will he go? He seems to know nothing about this land."

"I do not care. He carries the dark eyes. They will draw others here. Our enemies."

"How will they know…"

Grin's muscles tightened as Frennan squeezed his shoulders. The older grell's breath gusted across Grin's face as he spoke, "They will come. They came once before. Have you forgotten? Your brother died defending our home."

Grin bowed his head, remembering the last time the Erstürmen invaded Babir Birramal. "If Tom Anderson is in danger, we should protect him."

"You are a fool. We have no hope of protecting him."

Grin raised his head and met his father's stare. "I refuse to cast him out into the wilderness alone."

Anger burned in Frennan's eyes. "You have no right to defy me. You are still uninitiated, Grinnian stone-grell."

"That will change at the coming of the long dark. Why do you refuse the birraman a hope he deserves?"

"Because his path will lead to tragedy. If you follow it with him, you will follow it to your end. I could not save your brother. I can still save you."

*   *   *   *

Tom endured a restless sleep pockmarked with troubled dreams. His father and mother found the blue book under the redgum tree, his secret treasure now exposed. They were angry with him for keeping it from them. His father tore out the pages one by one and threw them onto a fire that consumed the old tree. His mother danced around the flames laughing and singing: *eternal reign, nothing to gain, eternal reign, nothing to gain*. In the distance, Nanna stood with her hands above her head, the dark eyes embedded in her palms. A blinding light shot towards Tom and he fell into the fire.

Tom woke, alone inside the grell's shelter, sweat pouring from his brow. He wiped a scarred hand across his face and sat up. A smell like fried onions wafted into his nose. Near the foot of a bed on the opposite side of the room, lay a flat stone stained with spilt food. Frennan had called the stone guyang walang, the firestone. Wooden cooking utensils dangled from the wall above the stone, and dried plants and bulbs sat in neat, organised rows on recessed shelves. Tom walked over and sniffed the plants, recognising faint smells of lemon and rosemary. Stone-tipped spears and tools leaned against the wall, and above them, pouches and basic clothing made from animal furs hung on a timber rack.

Tom pulled his dry clothes from the line and put on his shorts and t-shirt. Instinctively, he clutched at the front pocket of his shorts and felt the coin inside, the one he had prised from the floorboards of his bedroom. He pulled it out and rested it on his palm, staring at the Erstürmen inscription. *King's Quarter Treasury*. The coin must have come from Enthilen, but how did it get into his bedroom? Did the bad man...drop it? Tom inhaled deeply and placed the coin back inside his pocket. He would ask Grin about it later. He liked the young grell, almost as much as he feared the older one.

Tom waved his hand over the firestone. Heat radiated from its surface, although there wasn't a fire or another explanation for the warmth. A single, round stone sat at the edge of the room emanating light. Tom searched for power points or any other evidence of modern appliances or electricity. He found nothing. Not even a phone so he could ring his mum.

Stories about the Erstürmen from the blue book recounted battles with swords and spears, not guns or bombs. They never mentioned cars or planes, or TV. Tom assumed they were either stories from long ago about a people he'd yet to encounter in the history books, or that all of it came from someone's imagination. It seemed, however, that Enthilen was real, and that the past was not so distant in this new land.

Next to the firestone, arranged on a pedestal, sat a cluster of eight polished, marble columns, each about the size of a taper candle. Swirls of white danced across their milky green surface. Tom picked one up and examined the surface, covered in an inscription of tiny words that must have taken many days of painstaking etching.

"They are precious."

Tom jumped and nearly dropped the column. He put it back on the pedestal and shrank away from Frennan. "What...what are they?"

"Remembrance totems of kin now passed."

"Oh...sorry."

"Through the totems we share the joy of a life once lived. Each is a celebration of one of our ancestors." Frennan picked up one of the totems and cradled it in his giant palm. "This is the remembrance totem of my mother, Feyan, who inherited her name from her grandmother. She was a strong grell who raised six children on her own when my father was killed defending the city of Malang Gunya from the Erstürmen invaders. I am entrusted with telling her story and am the holder of the totems for our family. When I am gone, Grin will care for them next and, fate willing, he will pass them to one of his children. They are our heritage and history, a legacy from the past lest we forget."

Tom stepped to the opposite side of the room and sat on the edge of his bed. Grin's bed. "What is a *grell*?"

"That is difficult to answer."

"I mean –" Tom paused, hoping the next question wouldn't cause offence, "I mean, are you human?"

"If you are asking whether we are like the Erstürmen or the Dobunni, the answer is no, we are not hu-man. We are ancient inhabitants of this land. The stories of our ancestors recall many generations of existence, back to the time when we travelled across Gadhang to arrive on these shores. I do not know, however, from where we came. There are others who have been here even longer than the grells. They are the ones who call us…invaders."

Frennan walked across to the bed and picked up the blue book, running his calloused fingers over the faded leather cover. It looked like a small notebook in his giant hand. He read aloud the statement embossed on the front of the book. "The eternal reign begins with you. Do you know what that means?"

Unexpected anger simmered in Tom's mind. He snatched the book from the grell. "No, I don't. The book's meant to be a secret."

"How did you come about this book?"

"It was given to me long ago, when I was a child. A present from my grandmother. At least…that's what I'm supposed to believe." Tom didn't want to recount the story of his grandmother's murder. Not yet. Despite being long ago, the memory of that night still haunted him. And if Frennan read the book, he'd see that it was about the Erstürmen. The people Grin had called 'wicked thieves.' Tom tried to placate Frennan's curiosity. "The book translates my language, *English*, into the language we're speaking now."

"Erstürmen."

"I was given the book to learn that language. To prepare me for this journey…" Tom trailed off.

"It would seem that your presence here is no accident."

"No. No accident."

Grin appeared through the wall of the milbi with a basket strapped to his back. Tom tried to process the grell's seeming materialisation through a solid stone wall.

"I have lots of food. The mopoke bushes are full of fruit, and I dug up yirany and caught a wadha-gung." Grin emptied the contents of the basket onto a table, spilling out handfuls of violet berries, yellow tubers covered in dirt and what looked to Tom like a rabbit or hare.

Tom returned his attention to Frennan. "You mentioned the Do... Do...barney?"

"Doe-bun-ee."

"Are they your friends?"

"Grells have lived peacefully with the Dobunni for generations. When the Erstürmen came they killed many grells. Took others for slaves, destroyed our homes. The Erstürmen have gravely tested our faith in the beauty of life."

Tom covered the blue book with an animal fur, as if that might make it disappear. "How do you know I'm not Erstürmen? I speak their language."

"Would you risk drowning in a stream to trick us into believing you are someone you are not? You wear strange clothes and carry the dark eyes. I have no doubt that you are a birraman. You have come here from a different place. A place unlike this land. A place far away."

"You said before that there have been others. Other travellers."

"This is what I believe. Many generations ago, before the Erstürmen and Dobunni came, before the battle of the tribes that split apart the stone-grells and the weald-grells, and before the building of the settlements of Malang Gunya and Giigal, a birraman lived with the first ancestors. She was small with dark skin. At that time, grells had only a basic language. The birraman taught our ancestors new words. Words that are forbidden now, though we still use them when invader ears are not listening. She showed us how to make tools for gathering food and ceremony to respect elders. The culture of the grells and her culture merged to become what we are today. The birraman lived with the first ancestors for many seasons, adopted as one of us.

"One day, a young, inquisitive grell found something strange near the birraman's shelter. As he held the treasure in his hand, he was swallowed by the darkness, captured by the flickering red. He did not know it, but the grell had found the dark eyes. The birraman had kept them secret for many seasons. Proud of his discovery, the grell paraded through the tribe displaying his prize to everyone. The dark woman wailed when she saw him and tried to take the eyes back. The young grell gripped them tightly and all of a sudden, he disappeared. The first ancestors blamed the dark-skinned woman for his disappearance and banished her from the tribe."

"Have you met a traveller before?"

"No. You are the first birraman we have met, Tom Anderson."

*   *   *   *

Stomach full, Tom pushed the empty wooden plate towards the middle of the table. Grin had lavished piles of fresh food onto the plate and Tom had devoured it. Berries, yams and seasoned meat cooked on the firestone. Throughout the meal, Grin regaled Tom with stories of his adventures in the forest, the infectious enthusiasm of the younger grell proving a perfect foil for Tom's anxiety, even under these most trying of circumstances.

Frennan spoke little during the meal, regularly casting stern glances towards Tom and Grin. Tom sensed his welcome had worn thin with the older grell and worried his presence would cause further confrontation between Frennan and Grin. He needed to prepare for his journey home. Though he had little idea where that journey might begin.

Before eating, Grin had guided Tom through a ceremony to thank the forest for providing for them, and to reinforce ongoing respect for the land. With the meal finished, any leftovers would be returned to the forest to continue the cycle of renewal.

"Everything that grows will one day return to the soil from where it came," said Grin. "I must return these remains to the forest."

Tom saw his opportunity to enjoy fresh air for the first time since arriving in Enthilen, and to speak to Grin alone. "Can I come? I haven't been outside since I arrived here."

"You may leave anytime you wish. You are not a prisoner here," replied Frennan.

"We could explore the forest." Grin stood, grabbed Tom's hand and lifted h im f rom h is c hair. Th e gr ell re leased hi s gr ip, to ok on e st ep towards the wall of the milbi and simply passed through it. Tom tried to follow and walked straight into solid rock.

Frennan failed to mask a smile. "The door is not there. You will only see it when your mind is clear and focussed on what is immediately before you. At the moment, it is clouded by the worry of what has gone before and the fear of what lies ahead. The s hroud w ill l ift wh en you focus on what you want to do right now. Then you will see the door."

Tom moved away from the wall and held his hand out towards the space that Grin had disappeared into. He expected his hand to do the same, but his fingers hit cold stone. Patterns flowed across the rock's surface. To Tom they looked like the chaotic brushstrokes of a drunken painter. He worried about how he would ever get home if he couldn't leave the shelter. As his anxiety grew, the patterns on the wall became more disordered. He thought about Frennan's words, *focus on what you want to do right now.*

Tom breathed deeply, trying to empty his mind of every thought other than walking outside. He shut his eyes and floated in the darkness, putting aside his worries one after the other; each folded like a piece of paper and slotted into numbered boxes, Tom counting as he went. *One. I want to walk outside. Two. I want to walk outside. Three. I want to walk outside.*

With the papers dispensed, Tom opened his eyes. The chaotic pattern began to rearrange itself. Forest creatures shifted before his gaze, intertwining in a dependent embrace. Birds of every size and shape flew in the forest canopy. Larger animals, deer and lion, walked across fields of herbs and grass full of snakes and lizards. And insects, thousands of insects, crawled over every surface. In the centre of the design, twisting vines climbed towering trees whose trunks and branches formed the shape of a door.

"I see something," said Tom.

"Walk towards it. Slowly. Keep your thoughts focussed on the present."

Tom followed Frennan's instructions and walked up to the doorway. He placed his hand on the wall and it disappeared right through it. The rest of Tom followed as he stepped outside.

Grin welcomed him with a huge smile. "Look at the sky! The colour is the brightest blue I have ever seen." The grell lifted his face to meet the warm sun. A cathedral of tall trees surrounded him, standing firm on a carpet of moss and lichen. A strong breeze navigated the maze of plants.

Tom had missed the outdoors. The forest didn't look like any he'd seen before, being much lusher than the battered scrub where he would hide from the world. In the treetops, birds sang; the first familiar sound in this foreign place.

"We must return the remains of our harvest to the soil." Grin pulled a stick from the belt cinching his knee-length tunic, knelt and dug a hole near the base of a large tree. He placed the food in the hole and covered it with rich, black dirt. "There. It is done."

"What's the name of this forest again?"

"Babir Birramal. Walk north, and you will reach our true home, Malang Gunya."

"I haven't heard of these places."

"And I have not heard of your homeland either. What is it like there?"

"I'm not sure I even know where to start. We have plants and animals, forests and streams like here. That animal you cooked..."

"A wadha-gung."

"It tasted like rabbit. We have those back home. But we have cars, televisions, phones..."

"I have never heard of any of those things. Can you eat them?"

Tom laughed. "No."

"Then what are they for?"

"Mostly to impress others with."

"How strange." Grin stood, towering over Tom. "My father says you must leave. Take the dark eyes and go."

"I have nowhere *to* go. I want to go home, but I don't know how to get there. I'm sorry about your father."

"Since my brother died, he has become quick to anger. Fearful of losing another child. I have convinced him to let you stay for a while longer. But, the longer you stay, the closer danger will come. For all of us."

"Do *you* want me to leave?"

"I wish we could live here in peace forever, but soon, we must make other plans."

~Chapter 6~

"Where's the stable-keeper?" asked Hadufuns.

The stable-hand pointed to the entrance hall of the kirika. "In da dungeon with da gaoler. De're plottin' some new torture."

Hadufuns entered the underground kirika of Süden Forst, a bleak, shadowed chapel used to indoctrinate the feebleminded. He would have preferred to avoid such a place, but he couldn't reach the dungeon except through the chapel. As he descended the stair, he passed an altar adorned with tattered entrails. On the blood-stained floor, peasants crawled among the rent flesh, gathering remnants of recent victims. Hadufuns shivered at the stench of ritual death and hurried further underground along a torch-lit corridor towards the dungeon entrance. Once the Field Commander of Süden Forst, he knew the path well.

Hadufuns stopped at the guardhouse and peered inside. Empty, apart from a few pieces of stale bread on the table. At least they locked the armoury, he thought.

He passed cell after cell that looked like they hadn't seen prisoners for many seasons, before coming to a cold, dim room, its stone walls decorated with rusted chains and shackles. Slumped against the wall were the room's only occupants, the two rebel prisoners that Theodoar had boasted about. They had their eyes closed, seemingly unaware of his presence.

Hadufuns studied the weary faces. Even in the dull torchlight, the scar on the older man's face, running diagonally from his forehead to left jaw line, stood out, as if the wound had been inflicted yesterday. Yet, the dark skin had long healed over. The scar likely marked a tale of battle worth the ear of any soldier. No doubt more than a few Erstürmen had succumbed to the rebel's blade.

But the girl looks young, thought Hadufuns. Inexperienced. No scars mark her clear olive skin. He knew the Dobunni rebels preferred to pair naïve fighters with more experienced ones. Their *trainers*. It appeared to be a useful strategy. The rebels continued to resist despite more than three generations of Erstürmen rule of Enthilen. Yet, Hadufuns had always been uncomfortable with female soldiers. Women had their roles in Erstürmen culture; wives, mothers, servants. Never warriors or leaders. Such ideals were distinctly foreign. Hadufuns wondered if he could ever stick a blade into a female opponent.

"Are you thirsty?" Hadufuns hovered over the prisoners, wincing at the bloodied flesh on their wrists and ankles, rubbed raw from the shackles that kept them fixed to the dungeon wall. They opened their eyes as one and looked up at him in silence. He fetched a cup of water from a bucket in the corner of the room and gave it to the young woman who emptied the cup in a single gulp.

Hadufuns filled the cup again for the man. "Food? Have you been given any food?"

"No," the man responded.

Hadufuns searched the guardhouse and returned with the stale bread. "This is all I could find."

The prisoners forced a few scraps of crumbling bread into their mouths. Through laboured chewing the man spoke, "Our captors don't usually show such kindness."

"Not all of us agree with the methods that some of us use. What are your names?"

"What is *your* name?"

"Hadufuns."

The prisoner returned to silent chewing. Hadufuns assumed the rebel was assessing his trustworthiness.

The man finally relented. "I'm Jacob and this is Athalee."

"Have you been tortured?"

"A few beatings. They're taking their time. Trying to weaken our spirit."

"I'm not weakened," spat Athalee. "I'll kill the next Erstürmen that comes near me."

"Your resolve is strong," said Hadufuns. "And yet, I stand right next to you and still live."

Athalee held her hands towards Hadufuns and with a glint in her eye, snarled, "Take off these shackles, then I'll show you what strength really is. I can better any Erstürmen soldier you care to name."

Hadufuns smiled. "I'm not sure you're in a state to better anyone."

"Then why not release us?"

"I may be kinder than your captors, but I'm no traitor."

The wizened man with the grey hair tilted his head, trying to lock eyes with Hadufuns. "No, you're not a traitor. You're the brother of the king. The one they call the Wandering Prince."

"It seems even Dobunni rebels are aware of my reputation. I'll speak with the gaoler. Try to convince him to treat you with more civility."

"Can you ask him to stop beating us?" asked Athalee.

"The beatings would be less if you provided information about rebel plans." Hadufuns turned from the prisoners and continued his search for the stable-keeper.

                        *   *   *   *

"Ho Bron! Time for yur patrol." The stable-keeper, Jenrik, marched towards two soldiers lolling about near the stables, with Hadufuns in tow.

"Yar, yar, we goin'. We want da 'dreds."

"Undreds?" asked Hadufuns.

"Yar. I dun know what dese buffoons want with 'em." Jenrik nodded to two of the stable-hands who disappeared into the overcrowded stalls. They returned dragging behind them two huge, menacingly stubborn beasts.

Hadufuns stepped aside as the undreds lumbered past, wary of the unpredictable creatures. Though of a similar build, undreds did not have the same temperament as horses. Much taller and more thick set than an average horse, and almost always jet black in colour, their blood-shot eyes advertised a manic nature that struck terror in the bravest of men. Hadufuns made sure he kept clear of the thick, spiralled horn, curved upwards at the tip, that jutted from the middle of the undreds' foreheads. The horn could easily impale a grell, and the stains and abrasions on the horns of these beasts suggested that they'd encountered many victims.

The undreds reared as they were led across the courtyard, almost lifting the stable-hands from the ground. The young men yanked on the reins, fighting to control the beasts.

"Be careful with 'em," admonished Jenrik. He turned to the soldiers. "Why not take horses?"

"Dis time, we catch grell." Bron and his companion whooped as they leapt onto a wooden step and sprang onto the backs of the saddled undreds who tossed their heads in protest.

Jenrik whispered to Hadufuns, "Why dey need 'dreds I dun know.

Dose beasts can't be tamed. Dey let y'ride if it suits 'em. But if you annoy 'em, you'll meet their horn."

The soldiers managed to get the undreds under control and headed for the main gate.

"Where are they going?" Hadufuns asked.

"De're patrollin' along da edge of Grōz Forst. Only place you'll find wild grells now-a-days." Jenrik ducked into the stables and returned leading a chestnut filly. He handed the reins to Hadufuns and flashed a cheeky grin. "Here she is. Fit for a king, but too good for you! She's young, and strong enough to carry ya to Nordland and back."

*   *   *   *

In the shadows of the last remaining grove of trees close to the main gate of Süden Forst, Eroberung stood, clutching the reins of his enormous white horse, and smiled as Prince Hadufuns Heine galloped northwards into the heart of the Dambay Plains.

He rides to Laodicea, thought Eroberung. As the Worshipful Master hoped.

Eroberung grasped the mane of his horse, the creature a descendant of seasons of purposeful cross-breeding with undreds by the Worshipful Master, and straddled it's back. A harsh ray of sunlight penetrated the tree canopy and reflected from the stark white of Eroberung's skin such that he had to squint from the glare. He knew that the few that had met him and lived to tell the tale called him the white grell.

Although Eroberung had lost all memory of happiness, something akin to pleasure entered his thoughts as he recalled the terror in people's eyes when they first saw his mutilated face, scarred from the removal of his facial tattoo. The ceremonial severing of the crest, a decoration symbolising submission to nature, was a rite of passage for all of the four tainted grells who had devoted their life to the service of the Worshipful Master.

"Eroberung."

He turned his horse and it reared, panicked, as a ghostly figure stepped out from behind a tree. A twisted old man with jagged bones poking through thin rags. A draughoul.

"Keep your distance," said Eroberung. "My horse is not fond of your kind."

"I bring another message from our master. Tom Anderson has arrived in Enthilen. The boy with the naevus. You must deliver him to the master unharmed."

"How will I find the boy?"

The draughoul reached inside a pouch hanging around his neck and pulled out a golden pentagram and a small vial full of blood. "This will aid you. Do you know how to use it?"

Eroberung scowled. "I am no fool. I understand the magic of the blood compass."

"Our master also sought word of Prince Hadufuns."

"Tell the Worshipful Master that the Wandering Prince rides to Laodicea."

~Chapter 7~

The sun set and Grin disappeared into the forest searching for food while Tom waited for him on the path back to the milbi. He'd been with the grells for at least three days, though it could be longer; he wasn't sure. There were no clocks or calendars in the grell's shelter. They measured time by the position of the sun in the sky and subtle changes in the seasons. Tom had stormed from the family home on Saturday morning, February 19th, 1983 — the date of his grandmother's birthday.

As time passed, he had little doubt that Frennan's patience had worn thin, the older grell nearing the point where he would refuse shelter for the birraman and his tainted treasure. Only Grin's intervention had saved Tom from being expelled already, but tension was mounting between Grin and his father, Tom often caught in the middle of the disputes. Though he had avoided it for as long as possible, Tom would have to soon leave the relative safety of the milbi. To somehow find a way home.

This evening was the first time Tom had been in the forest past sunset. The dusk light still lingered among the trees. Grin fossicked, unseen, near the edge of the path while birds flittered among the shrubs searching for a final meal before roosting. Not a breath of air disturbed the leaves.

Tom meandered along the path, settling easily with the waning activities of the diurnal forest creatures. He began to draw comfort from the nature of this new land, like the comfort he felt from the bush back home. He began to relax.

Night crept in. Shapes in the forest became harder to discern. Tom drifted further away from Grin until something crossed the path in front of him. He stopped dead, his heart thumping in his chest.

"Grin?"

No response.

Far away, a whining cry pierced the falling darkness. Much nearer, a rapid series of yips appeared to answer the call. Leaves rustled behind Tom. He spun around. A dog blocked the path, except it wasn't a dog, its head almost too large for its sleek body. It yawned at Tom, exposing a massive gape that could grip his head in a single bite. The creature loped along the path towards him, its head raised, as if searching for his scent. It turned side on and Tom's mouth dropped open. Even in the fading light, he could still see them; black stripes running from the middle of the creature's back to its rump, contrasted against short, light-brown fur, ending in a thin, stiff tail.

A low, soft snuffling came from the other side of dense shrubs lining the path. The creature stopped, looked at Tom one last time and then loped off into the forest towards the snuffles.

"*Shit.* Grin...Grin!"

"I am here." The young grell burst out from the forest. "What troubles you?"

"Did you see that? Did you see it?"

"See what?"

"That was a...that was a...a *Thylacine*. A *Tassie Tiger*. I don't believe it. They're extinct. Well, they are where I come from. Where the hell am I?" Tom didn't expect an answer from his new friend. He hadn't been able to gain any more clarity about his location from the grells. They didn't understand the concept of countries or planets.

Grin lifted his tattooed face to the sky. "The darkness could be playing tricks on your eyes. Seena and Bargan are both absent tonight. It happens only once in a cycle. The darkest night."

"Seena and who?"

"The two moons; Seena and Bargan."

"Of course. There are two moons."

"Is that unusual?"

"We have only one where I come from."

"It seems you have travelled a long way, birraman."

Yeah, thought Tom, *I've travelled a bloody long way.*

*   *   *   *

The next day, with the sun directly overhead, Tom sat with Grin beside the stream where Grin had rescued him. He pushed his feet into the spongy groundcover, moss and lichen stitched together in a carpet of endless hues of green and yellow. In the shrubs, butterflies of orange, white and brown skipped across whorls of taffy-pink petals searching for sweet reward. On a rock near the streambank, a lizard basked in the sun, red stripes down it's back radiant in the midday light.

"You have a beautiful home," said Tom.

"Our forest home *is* beautiful, but it is only temporary. One day, the stone-grells will again settle Malang Gunya, the ancient city in the middle of the Dambay Plains. When the Erstürmen came, they drove us from our home and ransacked the city. Many grells were killed or enslaved. The survivors fled to the forest. We have lived here ever since. Where the forest meets the ocean of Gadhang, the weald-grells had built a new settlement, but they would only provide refuge for stone-grell females and children. That is where my mother and sister live. Male stone-grells decided to settle along the northern edge of Babir Birramal to watch for Erstürmen incursions.

"During the season of the long dark, the first flowers of the panalope tree will bloom. It is then that all initiated male grells gather at the ngulubul to prepare for the march to Malang Gunya. We have done this for a generation. A pilgrimage to our ancestral home to pay homage to the fallen. Those who lost their lives when the conquerors came. I am now ready to be initiated and join the march. Soon, I will see my real home for the first time."

"How come only the males march?"

"It is dangerous. Erstürmen watch the road and hunt us down. They take young grells for slaves and kill others. Females are a particular prize."

"Aren't you scared?"

"No. I want to see my home."

"It seems we have something in common. Both of us are far from home." Tom fidgeted with an animal-skin tunic that Grin had made to help him blend into his new surrounds, trying to find a fit that relieved his itching. Although Grin and Frennan didn't wear shoes, Grin had also made Tom a pair of fur-lined moccasins to replace his sneakers. The burns on the palms of Tom's hands had healed over, though the raised scars seemed like they would last a lifetime. Every time he looked at them, he thought of home, so he tried not to look too much.

The fast-flowing water of the stream bubbled along; a stone's throw away from Tom's outstretched feet. "You saved my life, Grin."

"Of course. Would you not save mine?"

"I'm not sure I could carry you."

Grin smiled before his face turned serious. "We must leave. Tomorrow. My father has finally lost all patience. It is no longer safe for you here."

"We?"

"I cannot let you go alone, but my father must not find out. He would never let me leave the milbi."

"Where will we go?"

"I was hoping you would tell me."

Tom thought for a moment. He reached inside a pocket of his tunic, withdrew the silver coin and handed it to Grin. "I found this in my bedroom. Lodged between the floorboards."

"*King Alaric.*" Grin turned the coin over. "*King's Quarter Treasury.* King Alaric died long before I was born. He led the attack on Malang Gunya. But the King's Quarter still exists. It is in Laodicea, a city in the north, next to the ocean and at the foot of Balgagang Baldya, the Desolate Mountains." Grin handed the coin back to Tom.

Tom sighed. The time had come to tell Grin the thoughts that had been swirling around in his mind. "When I was a child, a man broke into our house and killed my grandmother, right before my eyes. He told me about a special present she'd left for me. The blue book. I think...I think she knew about the present, but it wasn't from her. The bad man left it. Her killer. But he left something else as well. Something he didn't mean to. This coin. A clue to his identity. I think the bad man was from Enthilen. Maybe he travelled to my world using the dark eyes?"

"Did you see this...bad man?" Grin asked.

"Only for a moment. He wore chainmail under his coat. And his face is seared in my memory, like the scars on my..." Tom stopped mid-sentence.

"What is wrong?"

"The bad man would have scars. If he travelled using the dark eyes then he would have scars on his hands exactly the same as mine, wouldn't he? That's how I can find him. Look for the scars. I've lived with the guilt of my Nanna's death for most of my life. Now I have a chance at redemption."

"You were only a child, Tom. You should not punish yourself so."

"That's what my mother always says. It doesn't matter. I keep wishing I did more to help my grandmother. It's too late now, but I want justice, Grin. I want to bring Nanna's killer to justice. Ever since I arrived here, all I've thought about is going home. But now...now I realise there's a reason for me being in Enthilen. I'm here to find her killer."

"Careful, Tom. It is clear that whoever left you the blue book did so to prepare you for this journey. They also have a reason for you being here."

Tom buried his face in his hands. "I feel like I can't trust my own instincts. I don't know what to trust...who to trust."

"It is a noble cause to seek justice."

Tom lifted his face. "Then I have to travel to Laodicea. Is it far?"

"It is many days walk, even for a grell. And the path across the Dambay Plains is dangerous. We must consider a different road."

"What's Laodicea like?"

"My father says it is riddled with poverty, shame and greed. It was built by the Dobunni who settled this land after the grells, long before the Erstürmen came. The Dobunni named the city Bethesda."

"I'm sorry to burden you with all this."

"It is no burden at all. You are a guest in our land. It would be my honour to help you find justice. But I ask one favour in return."

"What's that?"

"Teach me some of your language."

"*English?* I doubt you'd have any use for it here."

"Maybe, but I like to learn new things. What do you call that?" Grin pointed to the stream.

"*Creek, river, stream, brook, rapids...*"

"So many names for one thing. Is that not confusing?"

Tom laughed. "My language is very confusing. Be prepared for a lot of frustration. I'd be happy to teach you some words though." He turned to his new friend. "Grin, when I first arrived, both you and Frennan held your hands out towards my face. What were you trying to do?"

"It is the formal grell greeting. Would you like me to show you?"

"Sure."

Grin sat facing Tom, positioned one hand either side of Tom's chin and cupped his cheeks between the ends of his huge fingers. The warm touch calmed Tom's nerves.

"Now. You do the same. Place the tips of your fingers on my cheeks."

Tom followed Grin's lead and the new friends cradled each other's face, locking eyes in a deep embrace. Tom drowned in Grin's facial tattoo; muwin, the ground spider. The black lines of the inked spider swirled in Tom's mind and transported him to a place of serenity.

*   *   *   *

During his time with the grells, Tom had obsequiously dried each of the five hundred and sixteen pages of the blue book and poured over the text, looking for any clues that might explain his arrival in Enthilen, how to return home, or the identity of Nanna's killer. He had asked Grin about the stories and the strange scrawl on page four hundred and sixty-two, now a smudged blur thanks to the dunk in the stream. His new friend couldn't tell him anything that explained why someone would leave him this book. Tom thought the drawing on the front page of two eyes connected by the rays of a sun had something to do with the dark eyes, but the blue book never mentioned their use.

Although Tom tried to suppress the thought, he knew he may never return home. He wondered if that was such a bad outcome. Home life was less than ideal. He knew his mother loved him, but what about his father? And what would he do when school ended?

In Enthilen, Tom had a purpose. A chance to resolve the one thing that had plagued his mind for eleven years. A chance, maybe, to quell his enervating anxiety. Find Nanna's killer and bring the bastard to justice. Somehow.

In the early morning, on the day Tom and Grin had agreed to leave the milbi, Tom sat on the bed reading the blue book, gathering his courage for the journey ahead. Grin warmed himself by the firestone while Frennan still slept, his snores bouncing around the smooth stone walls.

"Sometimes the truth can be dangerous," said Grin.

Tom looked up from his book. "What do you mean?"

"It is best others do not discover that you are a birraman. We cannot be certain how they will react."

"I will keep it secret." *Secret and safe.*

"Curious minds need nourishment. We should devise an acceptable explanation of your origin. I have been thinking on it. You should be the son of a goat herder. I met a herder once, grazing her flock on the Dambay Plains to prepare them for sale. She came from the foothills of the Desolate Mountains. A place called The Feign. She told me that the mountains are barren and sparsely populated there. Many seasons can pass before a herder encounters another soul. They have no allegiance to Erstürmen or Dobunni, being simple peasants not interested in war or rebellion. I was the first grell she had ever seen. Later today, I will tell you everything she told me."

Frennan snorted and rolled on his side. Tom stared at the wrinkles enriching the old giant's hairless face, a web of many tales, each strand marking another day of adventure. He counted the lines at the corners of Frennan's eyes and the furrows on his brow, and traced in his mind every edge of the old grell's facial tattoo; the wings of a walga, a sparrowhawk.

Tom had learned that soon after a grell is born, during their naming ceremony, they are assigned a plant or animal that they're responsible for protecting until their death. When they were old enough, they would receive a facial tattoo, their *crest*, which depicted the creature they were sworn to conserve. Grells born into slavery didn't have crests because their overseers forbid naming ceremonies or the use of grell names.

Frennan yawned and opened his eyes, frowning at Tom.

"We are going hunting today, Father," said Grin.

"Where?"

"On the edge of the forest, where it meets the Dambay Plains."

"It is dangerous there. Patrols from Süden Forst pass by."

"It is the best place for hunting. Although, it is a long walk. We will be gone all day."

A knot twisted in Tom's chest. At any moment he expected Frennan to see through the ruse. To jump from his bed, demand Tom leave immediately and forbid Grin from going with the birraman, knowing that his son planned not to return.

But the old grell simply sat up and yawned again. "You will need supplies."

Grin nodded, glanced at Tom, then began shoving waterskins and food into two backpacks.

Tom held the blue book tight in his hand. The secret gift. His companion since childhood. He knew the stories in the book back to front. He could communicate with Frennan and Grin in Erstürmen, as if he had lived in Enthilen his entire life. But now, he wondered what the blue book had to offer him. Nothing within its pages could help him reach Laodicea or find Nanna's killer. The book had outlived its usefulness. He didn't need it weighing him down during the long journey ahead.

But he would take the coin from the King's Quarter, and the dark eyes. A nagging thought at the back of his mind convinced him that the eyes were important. Too important to relinquish without consequence. They might not get him home, but they could have other powers. Maybe he could use them to steal someone's soul?

Tom retrieved the dark eyes from the shelf, the first time he'd held them since the failed attempt to return home, and cradled one eye in each hand, nestled in the scarred tissue of his palms. He drowned in the opaque blackness for a brief moment, hypnotised by the flaming red pupil, then furtively placed the eyes inside one of the four pockets that adorned his tunic.

He needed one more thing for his journey; a clean hanky. Snatching his white handkerchief from the drying line, he ran his finger over the embroidered initials: T.A., then smiled to himself as he shoved the hanky in a pocket and thought about his mum. *I hope she's not too worried.* He knew she would be.

Tom and the grells stepped outside to meet the sunrise.

"Watch out for Erstürmen soldiers," said Frennan.

"We will keep to the forest for cover, and I can outrun any soldier," said Grin. "We will return by nightfall."

Grin and Frennan cupped each other's cheeks the way Grin had shown Tom. When they released, Frennan ignored Tom and disappeared back into the milbi without another word.

The two new companions turned and strode into the forest, Tom feeling almost invincible walking next to the huge, strong grell. "Do you think your father suspects anything?" he asked.

"By the time he does, we will be far away. He knows we have become close. Maybe he already realises that forcing you to leave means I leave also. Likely, that is why he has let you stay for so long. Do not concern yourself with this any longer. Our path leads to Laodicea. But we will need to hunt and gather more supplies first. We do not have enough for a long journey. Deer and yams are plentiful at the edge of the forest."

"Do you miss your mother and sister?"

Grin paused for a moment. "I miss the warm embrace of my mother and the ardent strength of my sister. She is younger than I, but growing stronger with every passing moon. I know they are safe in Giigal. The weald-grells will protect them."

"Why did the stone- and weald-grells split?"

"Once, all grells called themselves stone-grells. Yet, not all stone-grells are the same. Two tribes settled Malang Gunya. The grells from one tribe were smaller than the others, with turquoise eyes. My father said they always felt downtrodden. Given the most menial of tasks while the larger grells, all with lilac eyes, held most positions of power. Eventually, the tensions came to a head and there was a bloody war between the tribes, long ago. The larger grells won, but still offered the vanquished harbour in Malang Gunya. The smaller grells refused, wanting to forge their own culture. They adopted the name weald-grells and walked south to settle in Babir Birramal. The word *weald* came from the Dobunni. Not long after the war of the tribes, Malang Gunya fell to the Erstürmen."

"Is the fighting over now?"

"There has been a truce between the tribes for nearly half a generation. Now it is not uncommon for stone- and weald-grells to mate. To try to increase our numbers. Their offspring always have one lilac and one turquoise eye. Late in the storm season, stone- and weald-grells gather at the garrabari, a celebration of dancing and singing, telling stories and sacred ceremony. It happens when both Seena and Bargan, the two moons, are full. I am excited about the next garrabari. My mother and sister should be there to witness my initiation. Do you miss your family?"

"I don't have any brothers or sisters. I miss my mum...my mother. I bet she's worried about me. Frantic probably, wondering where I

am. The...authorities had no idea about my Nanna. They're going to
be pretty confused about my disappearance. I miss my close friends,
and my music, going to the *movies*..." Tom caught himself, realising that
Grin wouldn't understand what he was talking about. "I don't miss my
father and I'm sure he doesn't miss me. He doesn't care about me."

"Maybe he cares and does not know how to show it?"

"Maybe. I don't think I'll see any of them again. I'm unsure about the
future, Grin."

"Then live only for the present."

*   *   *   *

Grin directed Tom in silence using hand gestures. They stalked a fawn-
coloured doe resting in the shade from the afternoon heat. She raised her
head, ears twitching in nervous suspicion. The white spots on her hind
quarters caught the sun as it pierced the forest canopy. Insects buzzed
and chirped among the afternoon haze that shimmered through open
spaces as the forest ceded to grassy plains. The doe's muscles tensed. It
seemed she would flee at any moment.

Grin crouched as he moved towards the quarry, tensing thighs as
thick as tree trunks and keeping his broad shoulders below the height of
the understorey shrubs. He sent Tom to the other side of the clearing,
directly opposite. As Tom snuck past a row of trees, the deer flinched
and sprang to her feet. He froze and waited for Grin's command. The
grell indicated for Tom to creep closer. Soon he'd be in a position to
spring out at the deer and send it hurtling towards Grin who'd be waiting with a spear.

As Tom focussed on Grin, he noticed again how well the grell blended into the surrounding forest. His pale skin seemed to change hue in
response to the environs, and the patchwork tunic of many-coloured

animal skins proved a perfect camouflage against the mosaic brown-black tree trunks.

Tom closed in on the deer. Grin raised his hand, the signal for Tom to stand still. Tom waited, every muscle tense, eyes darting between the grell and the doe. Grin dropped his hand and Tom sprang from behind a bush waving his arms and hollering. The deer bolted. It bounded towards Grin then veered right. Grin adjusted his aim as the doe jumped past him. He threw his spear. It missed, grazing off the flank of the panicked beast and clattering against a tree, breaking the shaft. The doe escaped into the forest.

Tom raced over to where Grin stood with hands on hips and a big smile on his face. "Did you see her jump? She bounded like a wambuwuny."

"Did I rush her too soon?"

"No. Just right. It was a good hunt, but it was her day today. She is a magnificent animal. We must thank the forest for allowing us to get so close."

*   *   *   *

"By Voler-die's mercy, dis is a slow pace. Why do we need dis grell alive? Why not kill her now?"

Bron turned in his saddle to face his lanky companion, Hul. "She'll fetch a good price at da slave auctions."

"What about da baby? Kill da baby, she can walk faster."

"Even grell babies bring coin. We'll split da reward. Long as we keep da stable-keeper out of our business."

Bron and Hul sat high atop their demonic mounts, walking them along the dirt track they used to patrol the edge of Grōz Forst. Dented spangenhelms rocked on their heads, scabbards clanging against the cuisses covering their thighs as the undreds jerked forward. A female grell with a newborn resting in a sling secured across her chest stumbled behind the soldiers, tied to the saddles of the undreds. After patrolling for three days and seeing nothing, Bron and Hul had celebrated her capture. Finally, their efforts had paid off. Female grells were rarely seen anywhere near the Dambay Plains. Likely this one had come to show the baby to her husband.

Bron had bound a rope around the grell's left wrist and tied the loose end to the saddle of his undred. He did the same with her right wrist, tying the rope to Hul's saddle. Having a prisoner tied with separate ropes to both beasts should discourage any rescue. If the undreds became spooked, the grell would be torn asunder if they bolted in different directions.

"Woah. Did ya hear somethin'?" Bron tugged on the reins of his undred, the creature's power pulsing through his worn leather gauntlets and yanking his short body forward.

Hul screwed up his face. "Hear what?"

"Sounded like someone yellin'. Over in da forest."

"Yur dreamin'."

"I'm sure dere is somethin' over dere. Let's get a bit closer to da forest. Might be another grell." Bron steered his undred towards the forest and Hul had to follow lest the tension on the ropes dislocate the prisoner's shoulder.

*　*　*　*

Grin pointed towards the Dambay Plains and whispered in Tom's ear, "Over there, do you see?"

Tom saw nothing but empty grassland.

"Past those trees. Erstürmen soldiers. Let us get a closer look."

"Shouldn't we leave?"

"We will stay well hidden. Just like the hunt."

Grin's smile didn't calm Tom's jangling nerves, as the two companions crept closer to the forest edge. They crouched behind a dense thicket of yurali bushes and watched the soldiers ride their mounts along the ecotone where the forest met the plain.

Tom's eyes widened. "Those black beasts look like giant, evil unicorns."

"What is a *unicorn*?"

"One of my cousins loved them. White horses with a horn in the middle of their forehead. Her friends for life she'd tell me."

"Those creatures are not friendly. They are undreds. Their horn is used to kill."

As the soldiers passed, Tom noticed the grell trailing behind the mounts.

Grin's face set hard. "They have caught a female grell, and she is carrying a baby. They will take her to Süden Forst where she will be sold as a slave...or worse. We must help her."

"What can we do? She's tied to the back of the hor...undreds."

"That is their way, to thwart our rescue. But we can foil their plans. I will cut the ropes while you distract them."

Tom scraped his swollen tongue around a dry mouth and pinched at his tunic, counting the number of pinches in his head. He'd never seen soldiers before. At least, not like these, clothed in chainmail and armour. "Maybe we can follow them and try to rescue her from the outpost?"

"It is much too dangerous for a wild grell to wander the grounds of Süden Forst. Now is our only chance. There is a pass through the forest up ahead where the trees are closer together. You can wait near the road behind a tree and then step into their path. Be careful not to scare the undreds. Pretend you have lost your way. While they are listening to your story, I will sneak up from behind and cut the ropes."

Tom swallowed, hard. *One hundred and twenty-seven pinches.* "Then what?"

"Then we run. Even with a newborn, a grell can travel swiftly. In the forest we can lose them. I know places to hide they will not find."

For the first time since meeting the old woman in the rocky scrub back home, utter dread overcame Tom. A single, terrifying idea threatened to quash the romanticised view of Enthilen he'd formed amid the beauty and safety of Babir Birramal. He wanted to return there now. "I'm scared, Grin. I've never done anything like this before."

"I know you are scared. Once the soldiers see me, they will no longer be interested in you. They do not know we are together. When I cut the ropes, run towards the river as fast as you can. It flows parallel to the edge of the forest. Run directly away from the plains and you will find it. Remember where the giant boulders make a crossing? I will meet you there. As soon as I cut the ropes you must run." Grin put his hand on Tom's shoulder and their eyes met. "I must try and save her. Understand, I have no other choice. The Erstürmen will never stop hunting us. Not until the last wild grell is dead or enslaved. I know I am asking you to risk your life. Maybe that is too much. If you say no, I will not look on you any differently. If you cannot help me, I will try alone."

The distress in Grin's lilac eyes pierced Tom's conscience. The grell had risked his life to save a stranger from another world, and adopted him as a friend. The debt should be repaid. Tom's lips trembled. "I'll help you."

Grin pointed Tom towards a grove of panalope trees jutting out from the main forest. A dirt path dissected the grove; a perfect place for an ambush. Tom tried to block out the anxious thoughts invading his mind. *Focus on the now.* He jogged ahead of the soldiers, his mustard-yellow backpack bouncing on his shoulder blades, being careful to stay hidden among the shadows of the trees. Glancing over his shoulder, he saw

Grin move in behind the undreds, well camouflaged against the forest backdrop.

Tom hid behind the trunk of a giant tree, adjacent to the dirt path, and waited for the soldiers to arrive. The voice of one of the soldiers floated on the breeze.

"I told ya dere was nothin' in the forest. You were hearin' things."

Tom pinched at his tunic; three hundred and eighty-six pinches and counting. Beads of sweat formed on his palms and forehead. He strained his ears. The hooves of the monstrous undreds clomped in the soft dirt. They were close, a few pinches of his tunic away. *Focus on the now.*

Tom overpowered his anxiety and stepped out into the path of the soldiers. "Excuse me."

The undreds reared, throwing their heads back with a shriek. The soldiers fought hard to keep their balance. "Whoa! Ya shouldn't startle 'dreds like dat boy. De're liable to skewer ya," said the shorter soldier.

The black beasts towered over Tom; their bloodshot eyes fixed on his presence. He could feel them sizing him up, waiting for another false move that would result in his impaling. "S-s-sorry. I'm lost. Will this road take me to Süden Forst?"

"Yur a half-day's walk from dere. Whadda ya want at da outpost?" asked the taller soldier.

Thoughts flashed through Tom's head. He and Grin hadn't been through his story in detail. He tried to remember what his friend had told him about goat herding. "My father's at Süden Forst selling some of our goats."

The short one leaned forward and sneered. "Sounds like a tall tale. Whadda ya think, Hul? D'ya think this flakin' twig is a rebel spy?"

"Ya might be right, Bron. Likely he's got more Dobunni mates hidin' behind these trees."

"No. No. I hate the Dobunni," said Tom. "I was tending the rest of our flock...on the plains... when, when rebels raided the herd and scattered them. I followed one of our goats into the forest...tried to catch it. It got away. I need to find my father to tell him what happened."

Behind the undreds, Grin crept towards the prisoner. Tom returned his eyes to the soldiers and tried to keep them talking.

"Well, dat explains da yellin'." Hul smiled at Tom. "Seems like y'ull be in for a whippin' when yur father hears about dis."

Grin stood next to the female grell, holding a finger to his lips. He drew a stone knife from his tunic and hacked at one of the ropes around her wrist.

Tom jerked his head away. His stilted movement must have caught Bron's attention and the soldier glanced over his shoulder.

"Another grell. Dammit!" Bron wheeled his undred around, his rope now free from the prisoner. Hul did the same, yanking the female grell to the ground, Grin not having enough time to cut the second rope. The baby screamed. Tom stood frozen with fear. Hul urged his mount towards Grin, dragging the prisoner along behind. The female grell rolled on her back, as if trying to protect her baby.

Grin slashed at the taut rope. "Run!"

The desperation in Grin's voice shocked Tom into action. He bolted into the forest, leaping over fallen trees and rocks, fleeing from the danger. A broken branch caught his foot and he crashed to the ground, knocking the wind from his lungs. Gasping for air, Tom sat up to see Grin trapped in between the soldiers, confronting the brutish undreds with his knife raised.

Bron urged his steed forward. The huge beast lowered its forehead aiming the curved horn at Grin's torso. Grin sprang out of the way of the horn and regained his balance. Hul wheeled his beast around, the female grell struggling to keep her feet as the rope connecting her to Hul's saddle tightened. Bron charged again as Grin tried to reach the captive.

Tom gasped as Grin weaved out of harm's way, the undred's horn grazing the grell's shoulder.

Bron yelled and urged his undred towards Tom's friend with determined ferocity. Grin evaded the charging beast, diving beneath the lowered head, but thumping, cloven hooves trampled his legs. Tom winced at the shriek of Grin's screams. At the same moment, Hul spun his mount around full circle, swinging the female grell in a chaotic arc. Bron appeared to grimace as the horn of his undred shattered the back of the prisoner, bursting through her chest and impaling her and the baby in one grislymotion.

Grin tried to regain his feet, but his legs appeared to fail. Hul moved up next to him, yanked a net from his saddlebag and tossed it over the grell, entangling the injured rescuer.

Bron tugged the reins of his undred and the beast shook its bloodied head, releasing the corpses from the end of its horn. They landed with a thud next to Grin.

Crouching behind a bush, Tom gaped in horror at the plight of his friend. His mind raced. *Keep running? Go back and help? Try to hide?* He couldn't find the courage to save Grin. Not right now. Fear won. He threw off his backpack and squeezed his quivering body into a hollow log, covering himself with chunks of damp, rotting timber, as if the ligneous armour would protect him from the threat of the world outside. Laying there still and silent, he listened to the soldiers argue over their new prisoner.

"Let's skewer 'im."

"No. We just lost da female and da baby. I need some coin from dis trip. I have a family to feed."

"What about da boy?"

"I didn't see where he went. No point tryin' to catch 'im and risk losin' another grell. He could be leadin' us into a rebel trap. Let 'im go. Help me lash dis net between da 'dreds. Get dis hulkin' grell cockroach back to da outpost."

The damp of the rotting timber caught in Tom's nostrils. A sneeze threatened and he clenched his teeth. He closed his eyes, his mind transported back to the dusty retreat under his bed. A five-year-old boy again. The bad man straddled Nanna, slashing her arms with a knife. Her face pleaded for help. Tommy pulled his knees in closer to his chest.

Bert's voice pierced the dampness. *Face your fears like a man.*

Tom brushed the rotting timber from his tunic. Grin had saved his life. That must count for something. And Tom couldn't face this strange new world alone. He squeezed each of his pockets, reassured that the dark eyes were safe. *Stop delaying. Do something. Fucking coward.*

With the milbi half-a-days walk away, Tom didn't have time to fetch Frennan, and he didn't know the way. He had only one choice. Save Grin.

Tom crawled out of the log and ran back to the edge of the forest. The soldiers had gone. He found the dirt path and sprinted through the forest pass. On the other side, in the far distance, two undreds with a net tied between them lumbered towards the horizon. Keeping to the cover of the forest, Tom began his pursuit.

*   *   *   *

Tom latched onto the back of a wagon full of wooden crates, following behind the six oxen that shouldered the load, careful to stay out of view of the soldiers that had captured Grin. It led him into a bustling settlement full of people dressed in tattered clothes and living in ramshackle hovels thrown together with deadwood and dirty fabric. The hovels clustered around the main gate of a fort with tall timber walls and guards leaning with their backs to the parapets.

It looks nothing like the glorious Erstürmen Kingdoms described in the blue book, thought Tom. Nevertheless, he knew the outpost must be Süden Forst. Walking behind the wagon, his eyes darted across the faces of the peasants, expecting at any moment that someone would burst from the crowd and expose him as an imposter in this world. But nobody took any notice of him. A stranger from a strange land easily vanished among the ebb and flow of impoverished humanity; one more desperate soul looking for rectitude.

Tom ducked into the crowd as a man looking at saddles in one of the trading stalls held up Bron and Hul.

"Where you lads think yur goin' with dat grell?"

"Please, Jenrik. Don't take it from us," pleaded Bron. "We need da coin."

"Da Field Commander wants all new prisoners interrogated, even grells. Rebels been seen sneakin' round da forest. We caught two a few moons back. Dis grell might know somethin' about dat." Jenrik kicked Grin in the ribs. "Take him to da dungeon."

"We want it back after ya finished, and don't kill it. We don't get no coin for dead grell."

Bron and Hul dug the heels of their black boots into the flanks of the undreds and sauntered through the main gate. Tom steeled himself and tracked them to the dungeon. *Focus on the now.*

The soldiers halted their undreds at a stone archway supporting a thick, wooden door opening into a small room.

Too small for a dungeon, thought Tom. *It must be underground.*

Bron and Hul cut the netting from the saddles, but left Grin entangled. They dragged their prisoner into the room.

Tom hid behind a stack of crates as Grin disappeared from view. He felt for his pack and only then realised that he'd left it in the forest. He had no food or water. Night approached, and he tried to find his courage in the disappearing sunlight.

~Chapter 8~

The rusty chain rattled a chatter of death as it swayed with the lurch of three prisoners shuffling in single file through a narrow stone corridor that led to the inner most circle of the Erstürmen city of Sardis. Soldiers from the King's Shield, King Ewald's elite guard, guided the condemned through the corridor christened 'the needle'; the only place in Sardis where the outside world pierced the isolation of the king's court. A soldier poked his head out from the guardhouse, halfway along the needle, and smiled as the prisoners trudged past, each one shackled and padlocked to the length of chain that led them towards their execution.

At the point of the needle, the prisoners entered a shadowed, circular courtyard, the sun blocked by high, thick walls that extended to five levels and encircled the cobbled stones of the inner court. Flags and tapestries of all colours adorned the covered balconies of the four upper levels, advertising the lineage and allegiance of the elite Erstürmen residents who called the inner circle home. Built within the walls, directly opposite each other, the Sunrise Keep and the Sunset Keep towered over the courtyard and Sardis.

In between the keeps, at the third level, a balcony jutted out into the circled courtyard like a peninsula into the sea. Stone columns carved with the faces of past Erstürmen kings supported the structure, designed to reflect the majesty of the people ordained to occupy the space above. Perched behind the polished marble balustrade that marked the edge of the balcony, like a committee of vultures, the royal family and king's court presided over events. Fluttering banners and silk tapestries forming fabric walls surrounded the nobles. Each banner of obsidian black had the same distinct sigil; a crimson serpent with a head at both ends of its body, curled into an incomplete circle with forked tongues almost touching. Most in Sardis and beyond had long forgotten the meaning of the ancient design.

*   *   *   *

Dressed in full armour, General Jurelle Stansfield stood on the balcony overlooking the inner circle of Sardis, shifting his weight from one foot to the other. He'd endured too many of these theatrical executions, designed to both entertain and terrify King Ewald's subjects. Yet, endure he must, for now, his loyalty to the king fortified by love and fear. Love for his family and fear for their future should his loyalty ever be found wanting.

Jurelle was the only member of the king's entourage not born inside the inner courtyard. Once the revered leader of the Dobunni rebels, sworn enemies of the Erstürmen, he'd fallen in love with an Erstürmen woman, Princess Genevea, Ewald's sister. The king had used this to his advantage, turning Jurelle against his people and demanding allegiance to the Erstürmen Kingdom. The Dobunni rebels now called Jurelle the Traitor General.

Jurelle drilled his eyes into the back of the king's throne; an elaborate chair of dark wood inlaid with ivory and bone. Atop a burgundy cushion sat King Ewald Heine, a bear of a man with scruffy brown hair and a full beard down to his chest. He wore robes of royal blue and black, and on his head sat the ancestral crown of the Heine Empire, a bone-white skeleton of a coiled serpent, its head facing front, mouth open and fangs bared.

Either side of Ewald sat his wife, Queen Romilda, and his only son, Prince Adalwolf. Jurelle wondered what sort of king Adalwolf would make. Ewald would reach the age of succession in two yarles when Erstürmen custom dictated that he must cede the throne to Adalwolf. As if answering Jurelle's question, Adalwolf yawned and pushed the toes of his polished black boots up against the inside of the balustrade, scuffing the black leather until it split and tore. His mother glared at him, a scowl flashing across her face. Adalwolf rolled his eyes like a petulant child and tucked his feet under the chair.

Next to Jurelle stood other members of the king's court, entrusted with Ewald's protection or the provision of sage advice. Most ignored the proceedings in the courtyard, preferring to engage in inner-circle gossip with those closest to hand.

The guards pushed the prisoners into the middle of the courtyard to face their king. From the shadows stepped a herald holding a parchment. She stood with her back to the prisoners and addressed the king. "Your majesty. Before you today are three prisoners who have committed heinous crimes against the kingdom. The prisoner whose name is…"

King Ewald held up his hand, stopping the herald in mid-sentence, and waved her away. "Bring the man forward."

The keyholder unlocked a padlock and seized a middle-aged peasant with greying hair and a gaunt face.

"What is your crime?" asked Ewald.

"Ain't committed no crime, Sire."

"Of course you've committed a crime. You wouldn't be standing here if you hadn't."

"I'm innocent, Sire."

King Ewald motioned to Hunfrid, the Master of Executions, who brought forward a woman and a small girl from the shadows of the balconies.

Jurelle stiffened. The king's executions were becoming less about justice and more about breeding fear. Innocents were being punished for no reason other than to inflame the torment. The inclusion of a child in this macabre pantomime filled him with rage. She couldn't be more than six harvest seasons old.

Ewald continued, "Your wife and child are here to witness your punishment."

The prisoner's eyes pleaded innocence. "I ain't committed no crime. 'Ave mercy, your majesty. Mercy please."

The king nodded to the herald who unrolled her parchment again. "Standing before you, Majesty, is Darius Roebolt, his wife, Ella, and their daughter, Tilly. He's charged with interfering with the actions of the King's Shield who were attempting to punish a thief. A peasant boy who had stolen fruit from the market. His wife is charged with harbouring a criminal."

"Most serious charges."

"The boy was starvin', Sire. He only took one apfel," said Darius.

"Silence! Bring the little girl forward."

Hunfrid grabbed Tilly's upper arm and threw the sobbing child into the centre of the courtyard. Ella fought in vain against the guard restraining her.

Jurelle squeezed the pommel of his sword and clenched his jaw. A single swipe of his blade would lop the king's head clean off. Jurelle imagined it bouncing on top of the balustrade and tumbling down onto the courtyard cobblestones, Ewald's gawking face staring up to the sky. The vision was soon replaced by that of his wife, son and daughter, hanging from the wall outside the main gate of Sardis. The certain punishment for any misstep.

Darius dropped to his knees. "I'm guilty, Sire. I'm guilty. Only me. Not my family. Please. Punish me, Sire."

"Guilty! Guilty!" came shouts from the shadows of the balconies. Citizens of the king's inner circle crowded around the balustrades, always ready to deliver an enthusiastic, scripted damnation of the accused lest the dagger of accusation be pointed at them.

"I'm a judicious king, am I not? In these matters, I long only for justice to be served. You are charged with interfering with the punishment of a peasant boy. To appreciate the error of your actions, I believe a fair sentence would be for you to acquiesce in the punishment of another child. Say, a young girl?"

"No...please...sire..."

King Ewald sat up straight and puffed out his chest. "Alright, I'll offer you a choice. The child is punished, and you and your wife go free, or the parents take the daughter's place."

Ella's body went limp in the hands of the guard who struggled to hold her upright.

"You won't be offered a fairer trade. I promise no harm will come to the little girl if you take her place."

"Let my daughter go," whimpered Darius.

"Agreed!" bellowed Ewald. "Let the punishment begin."

"Torture and death!" came a shout from the crowd, met with a rousing cheer from the balconies.

Bile rose at the back of Jurelle's throat as he watched the execution unfold, ashamed of his complicity. Hunfrid signalled to the guards who dragged Ella towards a saltire.

Ella. Her name's Ella. Remember that, Jurelle. Ella and Tilly.

Guards on either side of the cross lifted Ella off the ground and bound her wrists and ankles to the diagonal timber with leather straps so her face and chest pressed hard against the splintered surface.

Ewald held up an empty silver goblet. A servant sprang to his side and filled the vessel with intoxicating meduz.

There's nothing worse than an animal drunk on madness, thought Jurelle.

A soldier unlocked Darius' shackles and handed him a whip. Twelve long pieces of hardened leather brushed the cobblestones, bound to a handle of smooth bone balanced atop Darius' open hand. Rusted metal studs, sharpened to a point, pierced the outer ends of the leather straps. Darius swayed as the murmur of the privileged nobles bubbled to a crescendo.

Jurelle thought the prisoner had become paralysed with fear. Not yet.

Darius screamed. He dropped the whip and lunged for the short sword hanging from the soldier's belt. The soldier sidestepped Darius' outstretched hand and the prisoner toppled forward almost losing his balance. He spun around and grabbed at the soldier again. Two guards latched onto Darius' arms and regained control of him.

King Ewald nodded to Hunfrid who seized Tilly by the forehead and placed a knife at her throat.

"Time for this to be over. We have other prisoners to attend to," said Ewald.

A soldier forced the whip on Darius once more.
"Beat her!" came a yell from the shadows. "Beat the traitor. She harboured a criminal."

Darius raised the whip. He pushed his arm forward, the studs on the leather straps brushing his wife's back.

"Harder!" bayed the crowd.

The bloodlust of the herd will see the end of Ella's life, thought Jurelle. How can one man fight against such odds?

Hunfrid shifted his weight, positioning himself for Tilly's execution, a warning to the prisoner. Darius swung harder, ripping the fabric of Ella's dress.

"Again!"

Again, he swung, droplets of blood forming on his wife's skin.

"Again! Again! Again!"

Darius' arm flailed like the spasms of a dying beast. Exhausted, he collapsed to the ground, the whip clattering onto the cobblestones.

King Ewald raised his hand. "Have the girl end it."

Jurelle feared a new madness was about to be revealed. He grimaced at the raw and bloodied flesh clinging to the stuttering flicker of life left in Ella's splayed body. Hurry up and end it, Ewald. Show us a skerrick of mercy still resides in that crippled heart of yours.

Hunfrid took the knife from Tilly's throat. She pulled free of the executioner's grip and rushed to her father. "Dada. Dada. Mama's hurt. You hurt Mama."

Jurelle strained his ears for Darius' response, but he heard nothing. A guard yanked Tilly from her father and took her to a taut rope at the side of the cross. Ella must have sensed her daughter's fear and, marshalling what remaining strength she had, turned her head towards the little girl.

"Do you want to free your Mama, Tilly?" asked Hunfrid. "Do you want your Mama to come home with you?"

"Yes."

"Good girl. All you have to do is cut this rope. Here, take my knife and cut your mother free."

Tilly took the knife from Hunfrid's crooked hands and sawed at the strained rope.

"Hold it tighter, Tilly."

Tilly squeezed her tiny hand around the leather-bound handle of the knife and slashed deeper into the rope. With each cut, another fibrous strand untwisted.

As the rope broke, Jurelle yanked his eyes away from the spectacle. A loud crack and swoosh echoed around the courtyard and something whistled past the balcony, thudding like a blunt axe against a dead tree into the saltire. Jurelle returned his gaze to see a spear impaling Ella's body. Darius curled up onto the cobblestones, like a whimpering dog resigned to the punishment of the hard cold.

Tilly stood frozen in shock. Hunfrid pushed her into the shadows to the waiting arms of a soldier.

The crowd yelled, "Hail Ewald! Hail the king!"

King Ewald acknowledged his subjects and turned his attention to the remaining prisoners. "Bring the boy forward. What is your crime?"

A trembling young boy, no more than ten harvest seasons old, thought Jurelle, faced the king. "I s-s-s-stole some b-b-b-bread from a stall. Our f-f-f-f-family is s-s-starvin' your majesty and..."

"Enough. You look strong. Could you better this man in combat?" Ewald pointed to Darius.

"Death by combat!" shouted the crowd.

"Give the boy a sword," said Ewald.

A guard handed a sword to the stuttering young prisoner.

"He is unarmed, S-s-s-sire," said the boy.

"He's older than you. He can use his wits for defence. Strike at him."

The boy swung the sword at the motionless body on the ground. The dull blade smashed into Darius' forearm and the crunch of breaking bones echoed around the courtyard.

"Again!" bellowed the king.

The crowd chanted, "Strike, strike, strike!" The boy swung the sword again.

Gerulf, Ewald's brother and the Umbo of the King's Shield, sidled up next to Jurelle, the top of his thinning scalp in line with the top of the General's pauldron. Dressed in flowing satin robes of shamrock green, hemmed at the waist by a band of spun gold, Gerulf's bloodline assured his status within the kingdom. He looked up at Jurelle. "There's nothing more honourable than delivering the king's justice."

Jurelle raised an eyebrow. "Are you jealous of the Master of Executions?"

"Not at all. I'm satisfied with whatever duty King Ewald bestows on me." Gerulf smirked. "How goes the Riverlands War, General? My advisors tell me that our men are being slaughtered."

"We'll have victory before the storm season begins."

"You sound confident. I heard that the peasants are surprisingly resilient."

"We're fighting more than peasants. Well trained soldiers, mercenaries most likely, have bolstered the peasant forces."

"*Hmm.* Do you have any idea who they might be?"

"Though I've not encountered these soldiers before, I have my suspicions. My sergeants tell me they're skilled in battle and can manoeuvre with lightning speed."

"It sounds like reinforcements are needed, General. Maybe even the astounding Jurelle should enter the fray?"

"I'll do whatever my king demands."

"Yes, of course."

A messenger interrupted Gerulf and handed him a rolled parchment with a wax seal. After dismissing the envoy, the king's brother tucked the unread letter inside his robes.

The letter's content piqued Jurelle's curiosity. He trusted few in the inner circle. He trusted Gerulf the least.

Jurelle smiled to himself as Gerulf attempted to redirect the General's attention. "Rumours abound of a Dobunni plot to assassinate the king."

"Nothing more than rumours."

"Yet, some rumours have a habit of...materialising."

"The inner circle is well protected. Assassins could never breach its walls."

"I'm sure you're right. And I know the loyal subjects of Sardis would rally around their king should his rule ever falter." Gerulf straightened his robes and both men returned their gaze to the executions.

The young boy tottered on stumbling feet, swaying hypnotically above a dying father. Blood dripped from the sword dangling in his right hand with morose regularity, as if counting down the last moments of life.

King Ewald yawned. It seemed he'd grown bored of the spectacle. He motioned to the guards. "Bring the old woman forward. What is your crime?"

The woman remained silent and bowed her head. The herald stepped out from the shadows and pronounced, "Standing before you, majesty, is Essiah. No surname. She's charged with conspiring with Dobunni rebels to overthrow the kingdom."

The crowd gasped. "Traitor!"

"Treachery and treason," said the king. "The worst spite on the authority of this kingdom."

Essiah raised her head, her clear, strong voice reverberating around the walls. "I do not recognise the authority of this kingdom or its pitiful king."

"Silence!" King Ewald's face flushed with anger or embarrassment.

Jurelle smiled at Essiah's grim defiance as she refused to relent. "Never have I known such a coward. Too scared to walk among your own people. Too scared to leave the walls of your inner circle. Imprisoned by imagined fear. In every dark corner of your mind stalks an assassin, every breath you draw is poisoned, every shadow hides a monster...."

An enraged Ewald sprung from his throne. "Silence! Silence!"

"Your kingdom is crumbling, little Ewald. The resistance is here. Inside this courtyard. We are here. Death is upon you."

"Kill her!"

On the command of the king, an archer standing at the corner of the balcony loosed an arrow and the old woman fell. Ewald stormed from his throne followed by his wife and son. Gerulf pushed past Jurelle, leaned over the balustrade and thumped his chest with a closed right fist. "Hail King Ewald! Hail the king!" The crowd copied the action and responded in kind.

* * * *

At the top of the Sunrise Keep, Princess Caeli peered out of a barred window to escape into the hustle and bustle of Sardis below. She avoided watching the executions in the courtyard, though she could hear the screams, distracting herself by observing the daily life of the residents of the seven concentric circles that comprised the royal city, each delineated by a high stone wall. The outer-most circle housed traders and servants. Standard soldiers occupied the sixth circle, craftsmen the fifth, merchants the fourth, and administrators and masters the third. The second circle accommodated the King's Shield, soldiers that had sworn to protect the king with their life.

In the inner circle lived the king and his court, and citizens and their servants who had, by the grace of the king or his predecessors, been deemed worthy enough to occupy its festooned balconies. Many within the inner circle had been born there, inbreeding being a defining trait of the small, anointed population. If she ever gave birth, Caeli thought, she'd only exacerbate this characteristic.

Once accepted as a member of the inner circle, most citizens could never leave, even the dead being buried in the catacombs below the cobblestones of the inner court. Only the king, his family, and the King's Shield could move freely between all the walled circles of Sardis.

Beyond the outer-most wall that protected the seventh circle, wisps of smoke from the chimneys of the peasant hovels that lay outside the main gate of Sardis floated over the parapets. The dilapidated township of Slumstadt surrounded the royal city, although Caeli hadn't visited the town for more than twenty yarles. She'd been locked in the room atop the Sunrise Keep at the coming of her thirteenth harvest season, and here she had stayed, a prisoner with a duty to fulfil Ewald's needs.

Caeli turned from the window, flipped hair from her face, and rubbed her fingers over a necklace made from a chain of interlocking lemniscates; a gift from her father. She stared into the full-length mirror that rested against a curved stone wall, pressing down on her dress, as if to brush away the bulges that threatened to burst a seam. Although she liked the way the sun caught the highlights in her auburn hair, she hated the army of freckles that marched across her puffy face.

Caeli shrugged her shoulders, dismissed the unflattering reflection and peeped through the small viewing hole in the reinforced timber door that kept her imprisoned at the top of the keep. Her mood lightened at the sight of her favourite guard.

"Jürgen."

"Yes, princess."

Caeli giggled. "Silly. You know you can call me Caeli."

"I think it's safer to call you princess."

"You're probably right. Do you want to sit on my bed?"

Jürgen, the son of General Jurelle, peered down the spiral staircase, the only access to the top of the keep.

"The changing of the guard isn't until sunset," said Caeli. "We have time."

Jürgen wavered.

Caeli persisted. "We've known each other for the entire harvest season and you've never been into my room."

"My sergeant-at-arms has reminded me many times that it's forbidden."

"Who's going to know? I have no-one to tell."

"Alright, but only for a moment."

Caeli clapped her hands. A key turned in the lock and a metal bolt slid with a clunk out from the stone archway that supported the prison door. In strode a tall, muscular young man with handsome features accentuated by the polished silver breastplate covering his torso. Caeli sat on the large, four-posted bed that dominated the small, circular room. "Come. Sit next to me. What's happening in the world outside?"

Jürgen remained standing. "Food stores throughout the kingdom are critically low and the war in the Riverlands goes poorly. My father says the peasants are defending their fertile soil like a mother protects her first born. Slumstadt is bulging at the seams, so I've been told. Farmers across Enthilen are abandoning their land and looking for salvation in the shanty town. Crops fail season after season. The vast agricultural fields to the east of Sardis wither and die."

"And what about the inner circle?"

"The king grows more distrustful with each passing moon. He's convinced there's a plot to assassinate him and Prince Adalwolf. It seems he trusts no-one, not even his closest advisors. His fear is brutal."

"His recent visits to me have been more cruel than usual." Caeli winced as she rubbed her hand over bruised ribs.

"I'm not sure where it will end. There are whispers that he may even flee Sardis."

"Ewald has not left the inner circle for many yarles. Where would he go?"

"I don't know."

"What of your father?"

"He keeps his counsel close. I'm sure he's trying to protect me. The less I know, the safer I'll be."

"That's probably for the best." Caeli sighed. "Jürgen, I tire of being locked in this room. Maybe if the king abandons Sardis they'll release me?"

"Won't Ewald want to keep you close? You're his cousin…"

"…and my duty is to bear him a son. I'm well aware of my responsibility to the kingdom. King Ewald has only one heir. They say Queen Romilda is now barren. I doubt, though, the problem lies there. He's visited me many times and yet I'm without child. Maybe it's the king who's desolate."

"Don't say that aloud."

"Please sit with me."

Jürgen leaned his halberd against the door and sat on the bed, his armoured body sinking low into the feather mattress.

Caeli rested her hand on his thigh in a gap between the cuisse and tasset. "When the time comes, will you help me?"

"Escape?"

"I'm not sure I'll ever escape. Although, I *am* sure one day I'll need help. And when I ask, will you answer?"

"Of course."

"Shall I read you a story?" Caeli sprang from the bed and raced over to her vast book collection that covered shelves spanning almost the entire wall space of the keep prison. A handful of books were written in different languages, but she could read them all, one of the few people in the inner circle who spoke a language other than Erstürmen. She pulled a book out, threw herself back on the bed and rolled onto her stomach.

Jürgen tried to stand. "I must return to my duty."

Caeli pulled him back onto the bed. "Wait. *Pleassssse.* It's only a short story. This one's about a brave young soldier who must choose between serving his kingdom or protecting those he loves."

"How does it end, Caeli?"

"I don't know. Yet."

*　*　*　*

"Name?"

"Rosalie Barron."

"Reason for leaving the fifth circle."

"I want to go to the market in Slumstadt to buy some scrap metal for my father. He's the metalsmith, Yonna Barron."

"Who's your surety?"

"My brother, Petas."

The guard at the crossing between the fifth and sixth circles of Sardis pulled up Rosalie's sleeve to check her forearm for the branding scar that identified her as a resident of the fifth circle: a sword crossed with a hammer. Apparently satisfied with its authenticity, he stamped her arm with the symbol of a lamb, a temporary tattoo that signified those residents permitted to leave and return to the fifth circle on this particular day.

"Be back before sunset, otherwise your brother will be executed."

Rosalie nodded and turned to her younger brother. "I'll return soon. Sit tight and don't make any trouble."

"I won't."

A guard took Petas' arm and dragged him to the holding cells built into the thick stone wall that separated the fifth and sixth circles.

The tattoo on Rosalie's arm permitted her to travel through the sixth and seventh circles and out the main gate of Sardis, into the peasant town of Slumstadt. She kept a brisk pace, the guard's threat about her brother's fate urging her on.

Hampered by the empty wicker basket strapped to her back, Rosalie pushed her way through the bustling crowd squeezed into Slumstadt's noisy markets. Timber-framed stalls covered in animal hides or tattered fabrics leaned with the prevailing easterly wind, seemingly only a stiff breeze away from toppling over. She passed bare trestle-tables, many traders with little stock to sell, especially food merchants. Yet, despite the lack of produce, the markets were always busy. Full of the desperate and the hopeful.

Rosalie dodged past a line of beggars and headed straight for the scrap-metal merchant; a man called Wesley Snape. He sold an assortment of metal, rusty gold he called it, that Rosalie's father fashioned into weapons, tools and rustic jewellery. However, Rosalie had an ulterior motive for always volunteering to buy metal for her father. She was infatuated with Wesley's son, Harris, who often worked at the stall. Despite his youth, Harris had seen more of Enthilen than Rosalie ever would and she couldn't resist his enlightened aura. Perceived sophistication combined with Harris' wicked charm had captured her heart.

"Hello, beautiful young lady. What wares can I interest you in this fine morn?"

Rosalie blushed at Harris' beaming smile. "Good morning respected rust merchant. I'm after some scrap metal for *Paparrr.*"

Harris laughed at Rosalie's exaggerated refinement. "Well, we can't let *Paparrr* down, can we? Today we have the finest rusty scrap you'll ever see in Enthilen. How about this old wagon-wheel rim? I'll even throw in the nails for free."

"How much?"

Harris leaned over the counter and whispered into Rosalie's ear, "A special price for you, but I need a favour." Harris grabbed Rosalie by the forearm and led her around the back of the stall, leaving his father to serve the customers alone. The fabric wall offered a modicum of privacy, away from the market crowds.

Harris unstrapped Rosalie's wicker basket, pulled her close and kissed her full on the lips. "I'm glad I came to work today."

"So am I. Can we spend some time together? On the riverbank?"

"I can't leave my father. He's not well."

Rosalie pouted and Harris kissed her again. She pulled away. "What's this favour?"

Harris checked for prying eyes, then took something from his pocket. He pressed it into Rosalie's palm. She caressed his hand. "What is it?"

"A clay mould. Of a key."

"What do you want me to do with it?"

"Make three copies of the key. You've worked the metal with your father. I know you long to be his apprentice. Consider this one of your projects."

"What does the key open?"

Harris simpered. "It's better you don't know."

"Is it dangerous?" Rosalie asked, worried and titillated in equal measure.

"Keep it secret. Don't let your father find out. Return the copies to me. Only me."

"When will you be here again?"

"In three days."

Rosalie ran her fingers through her hair, wondering if three days would be enough time to make the keys. This wasn't something she should get involved in, but she wanted to make Harris want her more. "And how much for the scrap metal?"

"Another kiss."

* * * *

"Do you trust Aldebrand?"

"Yes, Sire. He's served you and your father loyally for a generation." Gerulf sat in a small, uncomfortable chair in a corner of the king's private quarters, staring at Ewald's back as the king surveyed the inner courtyard from the window. Twirling his moustache between his thumb and index finger, Gerulf's thoughts sparkled with confidence and smugness, certain he could see a future hidden from his brother's view.

Gerulf's stature and confidence contrasted sharply with that of his king. Paranoia seemed to feed the rolls of fat that girdled Ewald's waist, and the creases on his forehead advertised a perpetual state of concern. Gerulf knew that some in the inner circle found it hard to accept that they were brothers.

The king turned from the window. "It's his service to my father than worries me. He stood by Oldaric when the old king refused to abdicate the throne. I should never have allowed him to live."

"He has the wisdom of ages that you need to rule, Sire. I see no hint of his disloyalty."

Someone knocked on the door.

"Enter," said Ewald.

A servant shuffled into the room, head bowed, carrying a tray of food.

Ewald waved his hand at a table in the middle of the room. "Put it there."

Gerulf's mouth salivated at the rich aroma of roasted meat.

The servant placed the tray on the table and stood to the side.

"Well," said Ewald. "What are you waiting for?"

The servant took a small knife, cut a sliver of meat and popped it in his mouth.

Ewald waited. "The vegetables too. And the mushrooms. Taste it all. Any of it could be poisoned."

The servant followed the king's command.

Ewald made sure he swallowed every piece of food. "Wait here for a moment. The poison might be slow to act."

The servant, the king and the Umbo waited in silence.

Impatience finally trumped Ewald's fear. "Alright. That's long enough. Leave us."

The king hacked off a chunk of roast deer and began chewing. "What about Hunfrid, do you trust him?"

"He's the Master of Executions. He's been your loyal servant since coronation. I trust him implicitly." Gerulf paused for a moment. "But I do not trust Jurelle."

Ewald walked to the corner of the room and towered over his brother. "Go on."

"He's Dobunni. I know you brought him into the inner circle because he's a skilled warrior. There's no doubting that. Better he leads our soldiers than those rebel dogs. It was a brilliant ploy on your part, Majesty. And he'd never risk the lives of his family with treachery. Yet, his Dobunni ancestry runs deep. Our spies tell us the rebels are planning an assault on Sardis. When they come, will General Jurelle still remain loyal to the kingdom?"

"If you have doubts, then we should execute him."

"That's a good plan, majesty. Although…maybe we could first use him to our advantage. The Riverlands War goes poorly. You've recently ordered the dispatch of reinforcements. Why not let the General lead them into battle? If he succeeds, we win the war. If he fails, we're rid of a potential threat. And his absence from Sardis means he'll be unable to assist any rebel plot. I can arrange for men to dispense with the General should the need arise, and to keep a close watch on his family."

"I'll consider what you say. I value your advice, brother. Kin provide clarity in times of greatest doubt. Now leave me with my thoughts."

Gerulf closed the door behind himself and stepped into the hall serving the royal quarters. He adjusted his robe and put his hand on the parchment that had been delivered during the executions. Finding a dark corner of the hall, he pulled out the message, breaking the king's seal that secured the parchment.

The time to strike is soon. Meet me in Laodicea to plan our final action. I'll be waiting in the Master's Hall in the King's Quarter on the night before Bargan next rises full. Come under the cover of darkness.

Gerulf stashed the unsigned letter back into his robes and strode to his residence.

~Chapter 9~

The bell tolled with measured frequency. A hypnotic, monotonous clang that filtered across the grounds of Süden Forst in an ominous dawn chorus. Hidden behind a stack of crates, Tom gazed with sleepless eyes at the heavy wooden door of the building where Grin had been taken. Bron and Hul had returned outside without his friend, and Tom had watched the doorway all night, trying to find the courage to search for Grin. No-one challenged his presence in the outpost, other than a stray dog with a mangy coat who had slept at Tom's feet.

As the sun rose above the battlements of Süden Forst, the door opened and out stepped a hooded man dressed in sangria robes that trailed in the brown dirt. He stood, head bowed, to the side of the open door. Across the grounds, walking meditatively in time with the beckoning toll, came a line of old men with craggy faces and grey hair. Dressed in white, their heads crowned with a circlet of golden twigs, each clutched a book at their waist and moaned laments to the breaking dawn.

Tom counted the men as they passed. *One, two, three...twenty-four. Twenty-four old men.*

A boy and girl, naked under diaphanous garments, followed the men. Their fine clothes flapped in the stiff breeze gusting across the outpost grounds, like a flag twisted around a pole.

The bell continued to toll and the sombre procession ambled into the small stone building followed by the hooded man. Throughout Süden Forst, residents stopped what they were doing and languorously plodded towards the open door. The guards at the front gate talked among themselves, ignoring the crowd milling around the entrance.

Tom thought there must be a passage behind the door, possibly leading underground to the dungeon. But he didn't know where all the people were going, and why. If he wanted to help Grin…to rescue Grin…he needed to find the dungeon. He fought against rising anxiety. *Focus on the now*. He counted in his head, estimating the number of steps to the door. *Come on, Tom. Move!*

He snuck out from behind the crates and, trying to appear calm and incurious, walked towards the crowd lining up to enter the doorway. Stepping into the cue unchallenged, he shuffled inside with the other servants of the bell; another peasant among the throng.

Soon after walking through the door, Tom descended a narrow staircase. Torches attached to walls of green-black stone lit the way, ghoulish shadows dancing on the faces of the entranced congregation. They filed into a room carved out from the bedrock. It reminded Tom of the nave of a church. More and more people came, the room filling with the stench of impoverishment; a warm, damp, putrid concoction of bodily odours wafting from the creases of the unwashed. The putrescence stung Tom's nostrils. It smelled like a carcass ripped open by scavengers and left to bake in the hot sun for days.

At one end of the torch-lit room, stood an altar on an elevated stage. The men in white robes and golden crowns sat behind the altar next to the boy and girl and the hooded man in sangria robes. *Sangria man*, Tom christened him. Seven lampstands with seven burning candles adorned the stage, surrounded by figures and symbols engraved into the stone walls; an open mouth with a tongue like a double-edged sword, a lamb with seven horns and seven eyes, a beast with a serpent crown sitting on a throne, and many five-pointed stars. Fires burned in alcoves on either side of the stage, the smoke escaping up chimneys decorated with ashen gargoyles.

The crowd stood on polished, pentagonal tiles, facing the altar. Tom stumbled forward as more people pressed into the back of the room. Sweat trickled beneath his itchy, animal-skin clothes, the air of the nave heavy and stifling. He stretched up on tiptoes trying to suck in fresh oxygen, his clarity of thought suffocating under the weight of the transfixed crowd. He couldn't see Grin or anything that looked like a dungeon, but a doorway at the side of the nave appeared to lead further underground. If Tom could escape the grip of the crowd, he could search there.

The bell stopped and the room went silent. Sangria man stepped up to a pulpit, pulled the cowl from his head and yelled, "Let darkness descend!"

The crowd responded in unison, "And engulf us all."

Sangria man continued, "Brothers and sisters, you are here to bear witness to his provenance. The power of our Divine Creator be upon you."

"And also, upon you," replied the crowd.

The man raised his arms to the ceiling. "We offer our lives to you, Creator. You who act as judge and executioner. Ruler over all kingdoms. Master of the darkness, holder of the key that unlocks the door to paradise. We petition for your return. Subjugate our bodies to your desire. Offer sacrifice to your will." Sangria man turned towards the boy and girl behind him, then faced the crowd again. "Today is no ordinary day. This is no ordinary ceremony. For today, two lambs offer themselves willingly to satiate the hunger of the wolf. To tempt our Divine Creator to return to his loyal subjects."

Tom swayed uneasy among the rippling crowd. He assumed sangria man was a priest, though he'd never been to a church like this one.

Beads of sweat congregated on his forehead and threatened to drip into his eyes. He tried to push his way towards the side door, but the crush of the crowd blocked his path.

Two men in white garments led the boy and girl to the front of the stage. Sangria man spoke to the young pair, "To appease the Divine Creator and hasten his return we willingly give our lives. Your time has come. Do you submit to our Creator?"

Deadpan and vacant, the boy and girl muttered t ogether, "I g ive myself freely and gratefully to our Creator to hasten his return."

One of the old men in white shuffled the girl to the altar and laid her there on her back, legs overhanging the stone dais. Sangria man stood beside the boy and began to chant, his words blending together in a cacophonous, righteous howl. Those at the front of the crowd followed suit and the discordance spread throughout the congregation. The peasants standing next to Tom rocked back and forth.

Sangria man raised his voice, "O Volerdie, Divine Creator, Enthilen is lost. Without you, our lives have no meaning. Your strength will fulfil us. When darkness descends amid the daylight, your wisdom will guide us to an everlasting paradise. Paradise awaits in the darkness."

Paradise awaits. Tom had heard those words before. In the scrub on the rocky ridge when the old woman urged him to hold the dark eyes.

The chanting grew louder. The crowd pulsed with delirium, swaying in synchronized waves of frenzied worship. Sangria man yelled above the din of the crowd, "Divine Creator, we submit before you, innocence and love, and we tear it asunder to bring forth the darkness."

The crowd in front of Tom parted, providing a clear view of the altar. Sangria man stood behind the boy and tore his thin gown, exposing the boy's naked body. He gave the boy a knife and pushed him towards the altar. "Take her body, and her soul. Offer it to Volerdie. L et d ark-ness descend!"

Vomit exploded into Tom's mouth. As the crowd surged forward, he struggled to keep his feet. The girl on the altar screamed, momentarily disrupting the chants from the men in white. Sweat flooded Tom's face. He wiped his brow and stared at his fingers; perspiration mixed with blood. Another warm splatter landed on his cheek. Around him, blood rained down on the crowd. He had to escape.

Don't look at the altar. Don't look at the altar.

Amid the chaos, someone standing right behind Tom pushed huge, strong hands into his back. He tried to turn around, but a flash of white caught his eye as a thick arm smacked into his face. Stunned and helpless, Tom couldn't escape the hands that continued to grab at him. His mind screamed. *Move, move, move!*

Tom pushed back on the crowd, forcing a path against the overwhelming crush. Claustrophobia and panic engulfed him as he gasped for precious breaths. With strength drawn forth by unbridled fear, he inched his way towards the side door. He glanced behind and spotted his assailant. Jammed tight among the crowd, standing head and shoulders above the congregation, a stark white face glared from under a crumpled hood. For a brief moment, Tom became trapped by black eyes opening to dark wells of torment. The pursuer flashed a smile that made Tom's skin crawl. He broke free of the evil gaze, and with one last push through the crowd finally reached the side door, shouldering it open and racing along a narrow corridor away from the danger.

Tom came upon a guardhouse near open, barred gates. He peered around the door at two guards; one asleep on his chair, the other with his back to the door, scoffing down bread and cheese. Tom snuck past and raced further along the corridor, passing empty cells that reeked of death and despair. He didn't know where he was going, but he knew he couldn't go back. He needed to find a place to hide. He ran into a dark room and tripped over something. Someone.

"Ow. Watch where you're going," came a woman's voice.

Tom stopped in his tracks. His eyes adjusted to the dim torchlight, revealing the outline of two people chained to the wall. *Prisoners?*

An older man with grey hair and dark skin looked up at Tom. "How'd you get down here? You're not a guard."

"I doubt he's come to save us," said the young woman.

"Please help me. I'm being chased." Tom peered back along the corridor.

The woman held up her shackled wrists. "We're hardly in a position to help you, boy."

The man interrupted, "Chased by who?"

"I don't know. A giant. A white monster. He's coming."

The older man seemed to be sizing Tom up. "Sure. We can help. Then you have to help us."

"Yes, alright." Tom wasn't in a position to bargain; the monster could arrive at any moment.

"We can hide you under the straw and lay over the top of you."

"You're only small," said the woman.

The prisoners pushed straw into a pile with their feet and Tom got on his hands and knees to help. A loud commotion clattered down the corridor. They quickened their pace.

Tom lay still under the pile of straw, surrounded by the stench of horse manure. His father's voice stabbed at his mind. *Hiding again, Tommy?*

Fuck off. Leave me alone. Tom tensed as voices echoed from the guardhouse.

"Who goes dere? Ya can't be in here. Oh, please...Volerdie's mercy. I didn't realise it was you."

A fierce, guttural voice accosted the guard, "Fool. Did a boy come this way? Dressed in animal skins."

"I-I-I ain't seen no boy."

Tom jumped as a thud and clatter of metal cannoned down the corridor.

"Keep still," said the woman lying on top of him.

Tom focussed on his breathing, trying to keep it as quiet as possible. Footsteps came towards him, growing louder with each breath. They sounded like a sledgehammer smashing rock. Then they stopped, replaced by a deathly silence. Tom could sense someone standing right next to him. The white monster.

The woman flinched and groaned, as if she'd been struck.

A heavy weight pressed on the straw above Tom, followed by persistent, methodical sniffing; deep, searching inhalations. The weight pressing on the straw lessened. Maybe the monster had given up? Tom bit his tongue as something sharp jammed into his calf and a fire spread up the back of his leg. *Shit! He's found me.*

As Tom prepared to burst from the straw and run faster than he'd ever run before, a scream bellowed from somewhere in the dungeon. The weight disappeared and sledgehammer footsteps lumbered off into the distance. A hand reached into the straw, grabbed a fistful of Tom's hair and pulled him up.

The man scowled at Tom. "Our lives are not playthings. You better tell us what the blazes is going on."

"I told you, I don't know."

"That white monster of yours was Eroberung. A tainted grell. Why are you being pursued by a tainted grell?"

Tom shook his head. "I've never seen him before. Please believe me."

The man's eyes narrowed. "I can tell by your accent that you're not from around here."

"I'm a goat-herder. From The Feign."

"If that's true, you're a long way from home. Would a goat-herder be willing to help Dobunni rebels?"

Tom nodded.

"Good. Then it's time for you to repay us for risking our lives. Help us escape. Go and get the keys."

"What?"

"The keys, stupid," said the woman. "The keys from the guard."

The man continued, "Go back to the guardhouse. It sounded like the guards' encounter with the white grell left them worse for wear. See if you can find the keys for our shackles. They'll probably be attached to the guard's belt."

"What if that thing comes back?" said Tom.

"We have a little time. He's probably gone to the torture chamber to find the source of those screams. Soldiers dragged another grell down there last night, wrapped in a net."

"Grin?"

"You know that grell too? What are you boy, some sort of grell whisperer?"

"Just get the keys," implored the woman.

Tom brushed the straw from his tunic and limped towards the guardhouse, hampered by the ache in his calf. Halfway there he stopped, patting the pockets of his tunic with jittery hands. He couldn't find the dark eyes. They must have fallen out in the straw. Tom turned to go back, then caught himself. The rebels would never let him retrieve the eyes unless they were freed. He had to push on.

When he reached the guardhouse, one guard lay unconscious outside the door. Inside, the other guard snored, seemingly in blissful ignorance of the events transpiring around him. Tom spotted the keys on the prostrate guard and crouched down to pull them free, but they were looped through the guard's belt. With all his strength, Tom rolled the guard onto his back and loosened the belt so he could extract the bunch of keys. He raced back to the rebels.

Tom tried to catch his breath. "Which...which one...is it?"

"Give 'em here." The woman grabbed the keys and then thrust them back into Tom's hand. "This one."

Tom unlocked the woman's wrist and ankle bands. She took the keys and freed her companion. The rebels stumbled to their feet while Tom crawled on his hands and knees searching through the straw.

"What are you looking for?" asked the man.

"Something important. I need to find them."

"And we need to go," said the woman.

"Then go without me."

The man grabbed Tom's arm and pulled him to his feet. "We can't leave you here to the devices of Eroberung. That's a fate worse than a thousand seasons in this vile dungeon."

Tom ached as he abandoned the pile of straw, but he knew he'd be caught if he kept looking. His determination wilting, he allowed the rebels to drag him towards freedom.

*　*　*　*

Eroberung loomed like a rolling thunder cloud over a wild grell that had been spread-eagled and lashed to a torture rack. Two snivelling peasants cowered in the corner, as if their deference would garner his pity. The burn marks on the prisoner's body beared witness to the captors' eagerness to inflict pain. But now the oppressors had become the fearful.

How quickly those holding a fleeting moment of power shrivel before a higher authority, thought Eroberung. "Which one of you is the gaoler?" he asked.

The stout man with the wooden leg replied, "I am, V-V-Vater Eroberung."

"Has the prisoner said anything?"

"No, Vater."

Eroberung spat on the floor. "This wild grell reeks of simplicity. Where did you find him?"

"Caught on da edge of da forest by two of our men," said the other man.

"Was there a boy with him?"

"Don't know, Vater. Didn't hear about any boy."

"If you see a boy dressed in animal skins like these stinking wild grells wear, then I must know. He must come to me alive."

"Yes, Vater. What about dis grell?" asked the gaoler.

"Finish him."

Eroberung left the torture chamber and walked back towards the guardhouse. He hissed when he found the prisoners missing and quickened his pace. Stepping over the unconscious guard, he peered into the guardhouse at the still sleeping sentinel. The white grell thought about killing the fool right there, but with time of the essence, he chose mercy over delay and lumbered out of the dungeon and into the thinning crowd of parishioners leaving the nave.

*　　*　　*　　*

Tom squeezed out from behind the small, wooden door to the armoury nestled in the corner of the guardhouse of Süden Forst's dungeon, followed by the two Dobunni rebels. Jacob and Athalee had introduced themselves in the dark of the armoury, right before handing Tom a sword; a cutlass. He held the cutlass up to his chest, pointing the blade outwards. He'd never seen a real sword before and he certainly didn't know how to use one.

Athalee crept up to the snoring guard and went to slit his throat.

"Leave him," whispered Jacob. "We need to get out of here before Eroberung returns."

"What about my friend?" Tom knew he had to abandon the search for the dark eyes, but he wouldn't abandon Grin.

"The grell?"

"He saved my life. I have to help him."

"He's probably dead by now," said Athalee. "These guards could wake up at any moment. Let's go."

Tom collected every skerrick of courage he could find. "I won't leave Grin behind. Please help me."

Athalee started to leave the room. Jacob grabbed her arm. "We should help him. He freed us."

"We don't know who he is. If we can trust him."

"He could have escaped without us. Run right past the guardhouse. But he didn't. He came back with the keys. This is the opportunity we were waiting for. A grell on our side might come in handy."

Tom's heart thumped as he listened to the rebels argue, as if he wasn't there.

Athalee rolled her eyes at Tom. "You're going to get all of us killed, boy."

"I'm not a boy," whispered Tom.

The rebels led Tom to the torture chamber. They burst in as a man with a wooden leg seared a hot branding iron into Grin's chest. A burning rage boiled Tom's skin. He slashed his cutlass at the man, but it sliced thin air and smacked into a chain hanging from the ceiling.

Jacob stepped forward and cut the tormenter down where he stood. Athalee lunged at the other man before he could reach a weapon, plunging her sword into his stomach.

Tom rushed to Grin's side and turned his ear to the grell's mouth. "He's alive. We have to get him out of here."

Tom and Jacob each took one of Grin's arms and draped it over their shoulder. They pulled him off the table and supported his weight between them. Though his eyes remained closed, Grin's giant body stirred. Tom saw his friend's calf and thigh muscles flex to take some of the strain. The escapees began the slow walk to freedom, dragging the injured grell along the dungeon floor. All three hauled Grin up the narrow staircase, past the now empty chapel and into the entrance hall.

"Wait." Athalee scouted the grounds surrounding the hall. "No sign of the white grell or any soldiers. And there's a covered wagon nearby. The driver looks like she's getting ready to leave. We can hide in there."

The escapees sneaked, as best they could, the short distance across the grounds to the wagon. They lifted Grin into the wagon tray and jumped in after him. After a short while, the driver gave a yell and cracked her whip. Six oxen lurched towards the outpost gate. Tom placed his cutlass on the filthy wooden tray and rested his head on Grin's mutilated chest, listening to his friend's frail heartbeats.

~Chapter 10~

Sitting on a gilded chair in his private quarters, Prince Adalwolf squirmed as the ample backside of his mother, Queen Romilda, waddled around him, her fingers pecking at his clothes and hair like a mother duck preening her duckling. Adalwolf longed for an excuse to escape the unwanted devotion. "*Motherrr.* I look fine."

"You *need* to look like a king. The seasons will pass quickly enough before you inherit the throne from your father. He's getting old. Soon he'll reach the age of succession. Then my son, *my* son will be the ruler of Enthilen and her peoples."

Adalwolf brushed his mother's hand away from fondling the curls of his hair, and tugged at embroidered robes of magenta inlaid with gold and silver, adjusting them back to where they were before Mother Duck had plucked them into uncomfortableness. He sat upright, his eyes burning with determination like a stubborn young goat perched atop the highest vantage point, refusing to relinquish it to any usurpers. "I don't want to be king."

"What? Nonsense. Anyway, you have no choice. It's the will of our people. It's always been this way. When King Ewald reaches fifty yarles, you will take the throne. We should start thinking about a wife."

"A wife!"

"Yes, a wife. Your father will want her to come from the inner circle.

He doesn't trust anyone outside. In fact, he hardly trusts anyone anymore. But you need to think about strategic alliances. Sardis is under our control, despite the posturing of our worrisome king. But Laodicea is not. That city needs a stronger hand. Poor Uncle Widald does his best as Master of the King's Quarter, but he's failing to manage the other quartermasters. Rebels and their sympathisers, and all manner of undesirables walk unchallenged through the Docklands and Southern Vale. We need to unite the city under Erstürmen rule." Romilda leaned into Adalwolf's ear. "Now, don't you think it would be an excellent idea to marry someone from Laodicea to bring that city and its people back into our fold? Someone who the people love. Someone who would help us build an alliance and take the steam out of this pending rebel uprising your father keeps talking about."

Adalwolf slumped in his chair. He didn't want to think about such things. He didn't want to think about the business of being king at all. Overseeing all those horrid executions. Marrying someone he never met. Adalwolf let his eyes drift out of focus, blurring the room around him, as if that would make the responsibility disappear.

His mother continued her incessant badgering, "What about Lady Queltra? The niece of the Master of the Southern Vale, Lady Lily LáDown. She's loved by her people. She's..."

"Lady Queltra? She's Dobunni. I wouldn't be surprised if she's involved in the plot to assassinate me."

Romilda tugged at the braids contorting her wavy black hair into four circlets threaded through two cauls of gold netting. "There, there, petal. No need for tantrums. She *is* Dobunni. That's the entire point. The rebels hold sway in the Southern Vale of Laodicea, but if we marry her, the rebel allegiance is torn. Her family is well respected among our enemies and the common people adore her. You know she won favour from the pool of reflection last harvest season. She must be gorgeous.

You can be her master, and through her we'll finally rule the Dobunni. *And* your sons will be Erstürmen and Dobunni. A blood mix that could rule for generations." The Queen paused her fussing and crouched in front of Adalwolf. "Bring your enemies close, my son."

"I don't want this, Mother. It's all too much. I don't know how to be king. I don't want to rule anyone." He buried his head in her generous bosom and broke down.

"Do not fear, my prince. It will all work out."

The door to Adalwolf's quarters burst open. Adalwolf raised his head and shrank in the wake of an inebriated King Ewald.

Ewald staggered into the middle of the room. "What's this?"

Romilda pulled away and retreated to a corner, leaving Adalwolf to face his drunken father alone.

"Are you crying, boy?" said Ewald.

Adalwolf bowed his head in silence.

"Answer me!"

"I'm not crying, your majesty."

"Pathetic little weasel."

Adalwolf failed to avoid the king's swinging arm. A loud smack echoed through the chambers as Ewald's open hand slapped Adalwolf's cheek, knocking him from the chair.

"Get up," said the king. "What a wretched sight you are. Get up."

Adalwolf cowered on the floor for a moment, then staggered to his feet.

Ewald glowered, his laboured breaths reeking of meduz, threads of spittle dangling from his stained, decaying teeth. "You're a pitiful boy. You've always been pitiful. You'll make a pitiful king. I should keep the throne. You're not...you're not ready to rule."

"That's against the law of our people," said Romilda.

"Law? Law? I make the law in this kingdom. I *am* the law. I deliver judgement and execution." The king towered over Adalwolf and raised his arm to strike him again, then withdrew. "Enough time wasting. I've arranged for Gerulf to begin your training. We'll see if your uncle can make a king out of you. Meet him in the gallery, immediately. Maybe you'll learn to fight back."

Ewald sneered at his son and stormed from the room. Adalwolf returned to his mother for comfort.

*   *   *   *

Jurelle sat on his daughter Saskia's bed inside their small apartment in Sardis' inner circle. He ran his weathered fingers through her honey-coloured hair and hummed softly; a tune he'd learned from the minstrels wandering the streets of the Dobunni town of Bagendon.

Tucked in tight under a quilt filled with pheasant down, her head resting on a cushion of layered animal fur, Saskia wriggled and kicked her small legs towards the edge of the bed.

Jurelle stopped his humming. "Not tired, Poppy?"

"Not yet. Why can't I stay up a bit longer?"

"You have lessons tomorrow. You don't want to fall asleep in class."

Saskia pulled herself up, resting her back against the wall. "Dada?"

"Yes, my little loved one."

"Why do you have to go fight the bad men?"

"The king has asked me to."

"We must be loyal to the king, mustn't we, Dada?"

"Yes, Poppy."

"What did the bad men do wrong?"

Jurelle peered out of the doorway of the sleeping quarters, into the koken where his wife Genevea and son Jürgen prepared dinner. Muffled laughter and the clatter of plates and spoons filled his ears. He smiled at his daughter. "Sometimes, certain people have something that other people want, but won't share it. If the other people get desperate, they fight to take what they want."

"The farmers of the Riverlands have food and we want it."

"Yes."

"Isn't that stealing?"

"In a way."

"Wouldn't that make *you* the bad man?"

Saskia's words hit Jurelle's chest like a stone. He forced another smile and kissed her on the forehead. "When you're older, I hope the world will be a fairer place. Go to sleep now."

Jurelle closed the door to the sleeping quarters and walked into the koken to the aroma of vegetable soup. "Ah, that smells good." He hugged Genevea from behind and kissed her neck.

"Not another sister," Jürgen teased.

Genevea laughed. "I think your father's too old to present you with another sister, Jürgen."

"Am I just?" Jurelle tickled the soft flesh around his wife's waist and she squealed. He dipped his finger into the soup and thrust it in his mouth. "Why aren't the servants cooking?"

"You know I like to cook," said Genevea. "It keeps me occupied and I want to make sure my men are properly fed."

"And I'm hungry now."

"You're always hungry, Jürgen. How goes the guard duty?" asked Jurelle.

"Good. I enjoy spending time with Princess Caeli."

"I knew her father. He was a decent man, led astray."

"We're becoming close friends."

"Careful, Jürgen. Your job is to guard the princess, not befriend her. That will end in trouble for both of you."

"We're careful."

"Even the most careful make mistakes. Suppress your pity for Princess Caeli and concentrate on your duty."

"Do you think she'll ever be released?"

"It's possible. When King Ewald hands the throne to Adalwolf, he'll no longer have use for her. She's not given birth to an alternate heir. I think the king will have to be satisfied with Adalwolf and hope nothing sinister befalls the prince."

"What if Ewald executes Princess Caeli?"

"Let's not think of that."

"I'm nervous about what's going on in court." Genevea placed the pot of soup on an aged wooden table in the middle of the koken. "The executions are more brutal than usual and whispers abound about a plot to unseat the king."

Jurelle pulled out a chair and sat next to Jürgen. "The king's court is nervous, though I haven't seen any signs of a threat beyond the normal. Much is driven by the king's state of mind, which is failing."

"Can I come to the Riverlands with you, Father? I want to test myself in battle."

"Battle will find you soon enough, Jürgen. One day you'll wish for it no more." Jurelle put his arm around his son's shoulder and lowered his voice, "Loyalty to the king is important, but loyalty to those you love is more so." Jurelle turned from his son and rubbed a damp cloth across his skin, washing the dirt from the pores. He flicked back his hair, frowning at the strands of grey that clung to the back of his hand.

As he went to dish out a ladle of soup, his wife clutched his wrist. "Something's on your mind. I can see your thoughts marching back and forth across your face."

Jurelle shot a glance towards Jürgen, then lowered his eyes to the table. "Am I that transparent?"

"You are to me," said Genevea.

Jurelle had been in love with Genevea for twenty yarles. Almost eighteen as husband and wife. He couldn't hide anything from her. He was a fool to try. "The time will come soon when we must leave the inner circle. Leave Sardis."

Jürgen's head jerked up; his eyes bright with a defiant glare. Jurelle's heart sank, knowing his son wouldn't be easily swayed.

Genevea whispered, as if the ears of the enemy were pressed against the front door, "Ewald's Shield watch me ever more closely. They follow me around court all day. I haven't been beyond Sardis' outer wall for ten yarles. Saskia has never been outside the inner circle. I fear they may never let her."

"We're loyal to the Erstürmen," said Jürgen. "You're about to go and fight a war for them. Why would we want to leave Sardis? Already half of Enthilen call you the Traitor General. Do you want the other half to do the same?"

Genevea hissed, "Jürgen. Please. That's enough."

Jurelle met his son's glare. "This decision doesn't come easy. The kingdom of Ewald is stuttering to an end. Desperation grows in hearts and minds with each passing moon. Maybe even, we are living through the last days of Erstürmen rule. I can't foresee what is yet to come, but my instinct says that the longer we stay in Sardis the greater the risk. You, your mother, Saskia. You're all that matter to me. If I can't protect you, then what point is there to my life?"

"How will we ever leave the inner circle together?" asked Genevea.

"I can pass through the seven gates whenever I wish. Soon, Jürgen will be able to do the same, when he's completed his final training for the King's Shield. That leaves you and Saskia. I don't know how yet, but I will get you out."

Jürgen jumped up from his seat. "I won't be part of this treason." He stormed outside.

Jurelle tried to follow him, but Genevea grabbed his arm. "Let him be. He'll come around. The Erstürmen culture is all Jürgen knows. Everything else is foreign to him. He hasn't been outside the outer wall since he was a child. Training for the King's Shield demands loyalty to the king, above all else. You know that."

Jurelle sat and faced his wife. "Do *you* want to leave?"

"Ewald is my brother in name only. The same for Gerulf. Neither acknowledge my existence. I have no family ties here. Ewald lets me live so you'll continue to soldier for him."

"I'll be too old for that soon. The battle for the Riverlands will be my last. Then Ewald will have no further use for me."

"All the more reason for us to escape."

"When I return from the Riverlands. That's when we must leave."

*   *   *   *

"Rosalie. Are you coming to chapel?"

Rosalie frowned at the bark of her father's voice. She got up from her bed and strolled into the koken, part of a small living area in her family's apartment in the fifth circle of Sardis. The Barron's apartment was large by average standards for residents of the fifth circle. Three bedrooms housed two family members each. Rosalie had to share her bedroom with her young sister, Nettie. Her brothers Petas and Allum shared the other bedroom, and her father and mother the third.

The apartment also had a wash area, rare in the fifth circle, with household and personal waste collected every day. The relative opulence of the living quarters reflected Yonna Barron's status as a well-respected metalsmith and jeweller.

As Yonna and Heady Barron's eldest child, Rosalie had celebrated her eighteenth harvest season this yarle. Every Erstürmen marked their birthday on the first day of the harvest season regardless of when they were born. At eighteen, Rosalie would now be expected to take on more responsibility with family duties.

Rosalie warmed herself by the open fire blazing at one end of the koken while the rest of her family ate their morning meal.

"I don't like chapel." Nettie twirled a dirty spoon around in her fingers.

Heady patted her daughter's blonde hair. "What don't you like?"

"There's a lot of shouting and Papa makes funny noises."

"Chapel is where we are closest to our Creator," said Yonna. "It's where we thank Volerdie for his creation and pray for his return."

"Did he create *everything*, Papa?" asked Allum, Nettie's twin brother.

"Of course. Everything."

"The rocks, the grass, the dirt, the birds, the pigs..."

"Yes, everything, Allum."

"He didn't make this." Nettie held up the metal spoon fashioned by her father.

"So, he didn't make everything," announced Petas, with the authority of an older brother.

Nettie licked the last remnants of porridge from her spoon. "Why do we want him to return?"

"When darkness descends amid the daylight, Volerdie will return and lead the devoted into paradise through the darkness."

"How will he see it, Papa?"

Heady interrupted, seemingly tired of her daughter's questions. "The Divine Creator sees everything."

"I hope it doesn't take long to get there," said Allum.

"What happens to the undevoted?"

"They wither in the darkness, Petas."

Nettie screwed up her face.

"That's why we all must remain devoted believers in the Creator." Yonna glared at Rosalie. "Are you coming to chapel?"

She slumped her shoulders and dropped her bottom lip. "I don't feel well. I can't bear chapel today."

"What's wrong?" Heady stood and placed the back of her hand on Rosalie's forehead.

"I feel giddy."

"Giddy with love." Petas smirked. The younger children giggled.

"I'm feeling sick. I can't eat anything."

"Poor thing," said Heady. "Best you go back to bed."

"I'll keep notes from today's sermon. We can go over them this evening."

"Thank you, Papa." Rosalie stared out the koken window as a bell chimed in the distance.

"We must go. I don't want to miss the beginning." Yonna urged everyone out the front door.

Rosalie turned from the window, bade farewell to her family and trotted back to the bedroom she shared with Nettie. From a hole in her straw mattress she pulled out the clay mould that Harris had given her yesterday. She cupped it in her hands and kissed her thumbs, pretending they were Harris' full lips.

Rosalie raced into the smithy that was attached to the Barron's apartment. Under meek protest from her father, she'd spent much of her spare time watching and helping him craft metal objects that they sold in markets from the fifth circle to Slumstadt. A huge stone fireplace dominated the smithy. Yonna kept the fire burning day and night, always ready to forge metal.

Rosalie moved around the smithy with brisk familiarity. Her family would be gone most of the morning. She'd have time to make one key, maybe two. She tried not to think about what it might open and hoped Harris wasn't getting himself into too much trouble.

Rosalie melted wax to pour into the mould so she had a template for the bit of the key. She then stoked the charcoal fire and pumped the bellows until sweat poured from her brow. Taking a small piece of wrought iron, she heated it in the fire and worked it on the anvil until she had the basic shape of the key. Not the best for making keys, the rusty metal would have to do.

"No choice for a peasant," she mused.

Through a combination of punching and filing, Rosalie worked the soft metal to fashion the bit and stem until it resembled the wax template. Despite honing her skills under the tutelage of the most gifted metalsmith in Sardis, she wasn't confident that the key would work. But she knew Harris would appreciate her efforts.

Will this be the key to his heart? she wondered.

*   *   *   *

"You'll have a bruise tomorrow." Gerulf turned Adalwolf's head to the side, surveying the cheek reddened by Ewald's strike. He stood with the boy alone in the gallery, a private quadrangle adjacent to the inner court-yard. Gerulf had convinced the king to allow him to begin Adalwolf's preparations for rule despite Ewald's growing resistance to his inevitable abdication. The preparations, however, would not take the usual course.

"Will we begin sparring today, Uncle?"

"A sword is not the most powerful weapon in Sardis."

"What is?"

"A prescient mind."

Gerulf guided Prince Adalwolf to a secluded corner of the gallery. They sat together on a stone bench under a carefully tended syphus tree that had sprouted long before the arrival of the Erstürmen in Enthilen. Its spreading branches provided shade from the midday sun.

"Swordsmanship is important, Adalwolf, but more so is the ability to foresee the future and the courage to expediate its arrival."

"What do you mean, Uncle?"

"Do you remember the story of Thiemo?"

"He was the youngest Erstürmen king. Crowned long ago in Thyatira when the Erstürmen still ruled Nordland."

"You will be twice Thiemo's age when you take the throne. Do you remember his greatest gift to his subjects?"

Adalwolf's face twisted in searching contortions. Gerulf could tell that the naïve prince couldn't retrieve the details of the story. His patience expired, he pulled Adalwolf closer and softened his voice. "He sacrificed his life to guide his people into paradise."

"That's right!"

Gerulf glared and raised a finger to his lips.

Adalwolf whispered, "I remember now. He was an immortal. But he forsakes eternal life to...to..."

"To hasten the return of the Divine Creator."

"The Creator didn't return though, did he?"

"Thiemo's intentions were honourable, but his knowledge was incomplete. Certain events must transpire if darkness is to descend and paradise found."

"I don't understand what you're talking about. What's this got to do with me? I'm not immortal. Eternal life is a fantasy. The story about Thiemo isn't real, is it?"

"I promise you, Adalwolf, the story is very real. Immortality is closer than you think."

The colour drained from Adalwolf's face. "I'm not ready for this. To be king. To be burdened with other...responsibilities."

Gerulf checked the bristling frustration that threatened to bubble to the surface. "Thiemo was a child, yet he displayed unmatched bravery for the sake of his subjects. If ever given the same opportunity, you should feel honoured. You're a man, Adalwolf, not a boy. Cowardice is for weak children."

Adalwolf dropped his chin to his chest and squeezed his cheeks between his thumb and forefinger.

Gerulf placed a comforting hand in the middle of the prince's back. "The Heine Empire is an unbroken line of kings from our family stretching back to King Giltbert. You will be the latest, glorious king to honour that dynasty. There's nothing to fear. We'll be here to guide you through every moment. The eternal reign begins with you."

*　*　*　*

The mirror in Princess Caeli's room rattled. She sprang from the bed and peeked out through the hole in the door. Jürgen wasn't on guard duty. Another anonymous soldier the king had sent to watch over her stared down the narrow spiral staircase leading to her room, seemingly engrossed in his charge.

Caeli skipped back to the full-length mirror that adorned the north wall of her room, out of sight of the guard. She released the hidden latches on the side of the mirror then, using her full bodyweight, pushed on its edge until it slid quietly across the floor revealing a secret entrance to her room through a hole in the wall. Although the hole was no bigger than a large dog, a full-grown person could crawl through it on their hands and knees. Barely visible in the darkness stood a tiny figure draped in shadow.

The creature took a protracted sniff of the air. "*Ahhh*, there you are, Princess," it whispered.

"You're here. I've been waiting for *ages*." Caeli knelt and thrust her arms into the darkness, giving the little visitor a hug. "Do you have any news from my father?"

"Yes, yes, yes. A letter came the other day. I have it somewhere here." Short arms fished around in various pouches that hung from a twine belt cinched around the visitor's waist. "Where is it, where is it?" The creature sniffed again. "Ah, yes, here it is. Mixed up with the mendeal herbs I picked the other day. That's why I couldn't find it."

A clawed hand held out the letter. As Caeli went to take it, the creature tightened its grip and pulled her closer. "This is an important letter. A *very* important letter. Read it, then destroy it. Those were my instructions."

~Chapter 11~

The squeaky wheel of the slow-moving wagon set a sharp pain deep in Tom's ear. He had endured the high-pitched squeal for the entire day, hidden with the other escapees underneath the stained tarp covering the wagon. Grin lay naked and motionless on the filthy wooden tray, the cuts and burns that riddled his body testament to the torture he'd suffered in Süden Forst. The grell's chest rose and fell in unison with the lurching motion of the oxen-pulled transport.

Tom placed his hand on Grin's brow, feeling for a fever. What could he do anyway? He didn't have any medicine. He didn't even know if medicine existed in this new world.

As if the grell sensed Tom's worry, Grin opened his eyes. He turned his head towards Tom, a smile splitting the blackness of his facial tattoo. "See, Tom Anderson, you did save my life."

Tom grabbed Grin's huge hand and squeezed.

Jacob slumped with his back resting against the side of the wagon, snoring. Despite the brutal scar running from his forehead to chin, he had a kindly face, one that gave Tom comfort. Yet, Jacob also had piercing turquoise eyes that shimmered against his dark skin. Eyes that were unlikely to be fooled by clumsy sleights of hand.

Unmasked by the daylight, Tom had been surprised at how young Athalee looked. *Not much older than me,* he thought. The ordeal of the dungeon had stained her olive skin with dried blood and grime, and Tom sensed a deeper pain residing behind doleful brown eyes.

"What are you staring at?" snapped Athalee.

Tom averted his gaze. "Nothing."

She kicked Jacob's leg and he jolted awake with a snort. Athalee tied her long, black hair in a ponytail using a piece of cloth torn from her prison rags and peered out from under the wagon cover. "We're nearing the Scaur Hills. We should get out here."

Before Tom could protest, Athalee loosed the tailgate on the back of the wagon and eased it open. At the same time, the wagon driver sneezed. Tom froze, ready to be discovered at any moment. But the oxen trudged on without missing a hoof beat.

"We'll need to roll the grell out first," Jacob whispered.

"He's badly hurt."

"I am alright, Tom. As well as can be expected. I think I can find my feet if you move me over to the edge and give me a little push."

Jacob, Athalee and Tom helped Grin sit upright, then dragged him along the timber planks until his legs dangled over the back end of the wagon. With all their strength, they pushed the grell off the wagon tray. Grin landed flat on his buttocks with a thump.

Athalee frowned. "*Hmm.* Well. Seems he couldn't find his feet after all."

The other escapees jumped from the wagon and raced over to Grin still lying on the ground, wincing in pain. "I did not expect that to hurt so much," he said.

"We have a campsite not far from here with provisions. In the hills, about half a day's walk. I found a piece of old cloth in the wagon." Jacob handed the rag to Grin. "Wrap it around your waist to...well, you know. I'm sorry we don't have anything to treat your injuries."

"Find me a tree branch to support my weight. I will not slow you down."

Tom found a branch that Grin could use as a crutch, and walked on the opposite side of his friend in case he lost his balance.

Athalee and Jacob led the way through the lightly wooded fringe at the foot of the Scaur Hills, a landscape that looked much drier than Babir Birramal. Tall brown grass grew in clumps between sparse, gnarled trees with smooth trunks defaced by monstrous galls. Under Tom's feet, a cracking microphytic crust covered the dry red soil, longing for rain. As the new companions climbed higher, the trees disappeared, replaced by short, stout bushes, densely packed in moister gullies. A maze of sandstone boulders streaked red, orange and yellow, dotted ridgelines running north-south. To Tom, the Scaur Hills seemed a perfect place to hide, or to get lost.

"Nightfall is coming. We'll need to rest before making for our camp. The hills are dangerous at night." Jacob led the way to a small depression surrounded by boulders and out of sight of the road that ran along the base of the hills.

"Where does that road lead?" Tom asked.

"Along the western edge of the Dambay Plains," said Jacob. "It connects Sardis to Süden Forst."

Sardis. That's the royal city of Enthilen, thought Tom. He remembered it from the blue book. Tom sat with his back against the rocks and breathed in the sunset as the dusk air chilled his bones.

"There is no need to help us further," said Grin. "We can make our own way from here."

"You're not in a fit state to travel," said Jacob. "The roads leading to Süden Forst will be crawling with soldiers after our escape. Better to stay hidden for a while. But if we're going to share your company, we'd appreciate a more formal introduction."

Grin moved towards Jacob, hands out front in preparation for the formal grell greeting that Tom had learned, but his legs failed and he collapsed. Jacob helped Grin to his knees and crouched in front of him. They cupped each other's cheeks. "I am Grinnian stone-grell. First born of Frennan and Mirrian, protector of Babir Birramal. I like to be called Grin."

"And I'm Jacob Seamaster. Son of Wilfred and Florence, the best cloth merchants in the Bethesda Docklands." Jacob released Grin's cheeks and turned towards Tom.

"T-T-Tom Anderson, son of Bert and Elaine Anderson. I'm a goat herder from The Feign."

After a moment's silence, Grin faced Athalee. "And...Athalee?"

"I prefer Thaly, that's all you need to know." She drew a circle around her face. "What does that all mean?"

"My crest? It is muwin, the ground spider. They burrow deep into the soft soil of Babir Birramal."

"A goat herder and a wild grell," said Jacob. "That's an unusual combination. We don't see many wild grells anymore. A few are our allies, fighting with the Dobunni for the sake of old Enthilen." Jacob fixed his gaze on Tom. "What were you doing in Süden Forst?"

Tom wilted under Jacob's pressing glare. *This rebel's not going to fall for any hastily concocted fable,* he thought, *but other than the truth, that's all I've got.* "I was tending goats on the edge of the Dambay Plains, near the forest, preparing them for trade at the outpost when I saw two Erstürmen soldiers on undreds leading a grell prisoner. All of a sudden, Grin burst from the forest and tried to cut her free. But he was caught. I couldn't leave him. I followed the soldiers to the outpost."

Jacob squinted. "So, you left your goat herd to fend for themselves to follow a grell you never met thinking you could save him?"

"We had met before. Tom had been grazing the goats near the forest for a few moons...and it was not his first trip. We have known each other for some time. I consider him a friend."

Tom relaxed at Grin's intervention.

"Where are the goats now?" asked Jacob.

Thaly smirked. "Most likely in Commander Theodoar's cooking pot. I want to know why the white grell was chasing you."

"Er-ober-ung." Jacob's intonation made Tom shiver, as if the malevolence of the white demon had momentarily inhabited the rebel's body. Jacob continued to press. "He's one of the tainted grells who now rain terror over these lands. Why was he at Süden Forst? What does he want with a goat-herder from the Desolate Mountains?"

Tom avoided Jacob's gaze and counted the rocks around the depression. He squeezed each of his pockets in case he'd missed the eyes of lost souls. *Still empty.* He dropped his head, his thoughts trapped again in the suffocating stench of depravity that polluted the chapel at Süden Forst. Giant hands grabbed at his clothes. *Did Eroberung take the eyes?* The chant of the entranced worshippers chilled Tom's veins, warm blood splattered on his face, sangria man drank from a cup...

Tom jumped up, leaned over a rock and vomited. He wiped his mouth with his white hanky. Grin came to his aid.

"I'm alright, Grin. I'm alright."

Grin slumped to the ground and re-directed the conversation. "The Docklands are in Laodicea. Is that your home?"

Jacob nodded. "I prefer the name Bethesda. It's what the original settlers called the city. No matter the name, the curse of indifference now lies over that place. Ripe for conquest by those with unsavoury ambitions. Nevertheless, I hope to return one day, when the Dobunni rule the city again."

Grin shifted his weight and grimaced.

"I'll try to find herbs to relieve the pain." Thaly disappeared into the dusk as the sun set and the moons rose.

"I'll keep watch. You two rest." Jacob walked to the edge of the secluded depression and stared out into the growing darkness.

Tom sought Grin's reassurance. The grell beamed a smile, as if he didn't have a care in the world.

*   *   *   *

Clouds gathered in the morning sky and Grin sniffed the air. "The season is changing. The storm season begins early this cycle."

"We should make it to our camp before the sun is high." Thaly led the other three among the maze of boulders and loose stone paths atop the Scaur Hills. The herbs she gave Grin appeared to improve the grell's strength, although his legs still hobbled under his weight. Soon, he and Tom trailed a long way behind the rebels.

The new friends walked in silence for a while until Tom found the courage to make an admission. "Grin. I've lost the dark eyes."

Grin stopped and leaned on his crutch. "Nothing good will come from those evil trinkets. It is better that they are gone."

"They might be my only chance of getting home. After...after we find my grandmother's killer."

Grin smiled. "Accept my apology. I was inconsiderate. Do you know where you lost them?"

"I thought I lost them in the straw when Jacob and Thaly hid me, but they were tucked deep inside one of my pockets. Then I realised the pocket itself was torn. I'm sure the white grell took them when I was trapped in that awful room. I couldn't move, Grin. They sacrificed children." Tom took a deep breath. "I can't get the vision out of my head. All the time, that monster grabbed at me. Searching... I'm sure it happened there. It must have."

"What would a grell do with the eyes of lost souls?"

"Who are these tainted grells? Why does one of them hunt me?"

"I know little about them. My father says they have been corrupted by a terrible malice. It is best to keep as far from them as possible."

"For most of my life, I've been haunted by that night in my bedroom when the stranger killed my grandmother then disappeared. He had... something in his hand, clenched in his fist. He thrust it into Nanna's chest and her body shuddered and twisted. Then he told me about that stupid book. Keep it secret and safe. It's all linked, Grin. My grandmother's murder, the book, the eyes, that coin..." Tom clutched at his pocket to feel the silver coin through the rough fabric, "...my being here...it's all connected. I just don't know why or what for. I feel guilty every day for not doing more to protect my grandmother. Maybe that would have stopped all this?"

"The past cannot be changed. Think only of the life you will lead today."

Tom glanced on ahead. "Can we trust these rebels?"

"At the moment, we have no choice. They seem true of heart. And Jacob is right, we will be too exposed walking on the plain. We will reach Laodicea, but the path may be longer than I had planned."

Tom and Grin pressed on, trying not to fall too far behind the rebels. The huge boulders surrounded by sickly looking trees and scraggly bushes reminded Tom of the battered scrub near his home. The familiarity gave him comfort. Here was a nature not unlike that of his own world. And he loved nature. It healed his mind. Though the occupants of Enthilen gave him pause, maybe he could find solace in its natural environment?

By late-morning, the four companions reached another secluded depression among the maze of ridgelines and valleys. "It's here." Thaly rushed up to a large boulder and dug around its base, uncovering bound packages. She ripped open one of the packages. Food and water skins bursting at the seams dropped to the ground. "I'm starving."

Thaly tossed something to Tom that resembled a strip of cured meat. He sniffed it, shrugged his shoulders and began chewing. It tasted like salted leather. The travellers sat in silence eating dried meat and gulping down stale water with a bitter aftertaste.

After finishing her meal, Thaly confronted Grin. "Why don't more grells join us? Together we could defeat the Erstürmen and drive them from our land."

"*Our* land? Grells were here long before the Dobunni."

"And others were here before the grells," interjected Jacob.

"We are peaceful. We do not want war."

Thaly picked a piece of gristle from between her teeth. "You're already at war. Except you refuse to fight. Do you prefer slaughter and slavery?"

"We survive. One day the tide will turn and all grells will be free again. The wall protecting the Erstürmen Kingdom is starting to crack. When the crack widens, we will prise a stone into the fissure and force it open further. Then the wall will break and we will push it over."

"That time is coming, my friend. But I fear that Ewald's reign may be replaced by something even more menacing. A zealot stirs in the east, directing these tainted grells. I've heard stories from Bethesda. Some of the Erstürmen are aligning themselves with a new ruler."

As Jacob spoke, thunder rolled across the blackened sky and rain started to fall. The companions huddled together and sheltered under the lip of the boulder. Tom counted each silence between the thunder and lightning. The storm sailed closer and the safety of Babir Birramal was far away.

~Chapter 12~

Jurelle shaded his eyes from the sunlight that glinted from his polished armour as he reviewed a cohort of troops assembled in the inner circle for presentation to the king. The red and yellow plumes fitted to the top of his barbute fluttered in the breeze, tapping against his spangenhelm, as if their purpose was to keep his marching feet in time. Standing to one side, a soldier held a flag pole adorned by a banner with the sigil of the Stansfield family, a creature with the head and wings of an eagle and the back legs and tail of a lion — the now mythical griffin. One hadn't been seen in Enthilen for generations.

Jurelle's sergeant-at-arms, Segie, marched beside him. He valued Segie's opinion more than his lieutenants, and considered him a trusted companion even though the Erstürmen sergeant had a deep mistrust of the Dobunni. Yet, he knew that Segie's loyalty to his kingdom and his commanders overrode his feelings about Jurelle's ancestry.

"How are the men, Segie?"

"I'd like to say they're bristling with confidence, General, but we're not winning the Riverlands War and a few have heard stories about banshees on strange beasts."

"I don't think we'll be fighting spirits, sergeant. Only peasants and well-trained soldiers. What do they think about being led by a Dobunni traitor?"

"The Dobunni are our enemy, General, you can't change that. A few of the men are grumbling. Most are loyal to the kingdom, though."

Jurelle raised an eyebrow. "Most?"

Segie changed the subject. "You're a General in the King's Shield. They've sworn an oath to follow you and protect the king. And your skill in battle is legendary."

Jurelle continued to stroll along the front line of his troops. They stood motionless to attention, their halberds pointing towards the sky, as if to punch holes in the scattered, dark clouds. Black, triangular shields rested against the grieves of the soldiers, each shield adorned with the red sigil of the two-headed serpent. He paused at one of the younger soldiers who had a face that had likely seen no more than fifteen harvest seasons. "What's your name, soldier?"

"Balack, General." Balack balanced his halberd against his shoulder and thumped his breastplate with his right fist.

"How many battles have you fought, Balack?"

"None, General. This is my first."

"Are you frightened?"

"No, General!"

"You may be the only soldier I've ever met who isn't frightened of battle. Don't suppress your fear, son, use it to focus your strength. That's the key to being a good soldier."

Jurelle turned from his men as Ewald strode across the inner courtyard, the king's robes of blue and black trailing along the cobblestones. The assembled soldiers thumped their breastplates with their right fists and shouted in unison, "Hail King Ewald! Hail the king!"

Jurelle followed suit with less enthusiasm.

Ewald faced Jurelle, turning his back on the soldiers. "With the invincible Jurelle leading the charge, victory is sure to be ours."

"Yes, Majesty."

"The men look strong and ready for battle."

"The bulk of our forces are amassing outside the city walls preparing for the order to march. We have a battalion of men-at-arms, regular cavalry and a unit of undred riders. Would you like to review *all* the troops, Majesty?"

Ewald flinched at Jurelle's goad, and Jurelle fought hard against a smile. He knew that the king feared leaving the inner circle.

"I have complete confidence in your military skill, General. I'm sure you've gathered a formidable force that will crush the enemy and secure the Riverlands for our kingdom once and for all." Ewald placed a hand on Jurelle's shoulder, led him away from the men and whispered into his ear, "I know you'll do your duty, Jurelle. There's no need to fret for your family." The king glanced across to Genevea who stood in the shadow of the balconies, clutching Saskia's hand. "I will personally see to their safety in your absence. Genevea is my sister, after all. I would hate for her to suffer a nasty accident."

Jurelle bristled at the flimsily veiled threat, as Ewald's stale breath oozed across his face.

The king lingered for a moment, then turned to address the men. "Soldiers of the King's Shield. You are the pinnacle of the Erstürmen race. Protectors of the Heine Empire. Your charge is to crush the peasant revolt and wrench their fields from their filthy, ungrateful hands. The Riverlands will be ours!"

"Hail the king!" yelled the soldiers.

Ewald lowered his voice, "I know you'll succeed in your charge and bring glory to our kingdom. Anything less would be a blight on you and your families. The Divine Creator will be watching over you. Your victory will hasten his return."

As Jurelle strained his ears to hear the king, Ewald bellowed, "Let darkness descend!"

All the assembled, except Jurelle, replied, "And engulf us all."

Ewald continued with apparent surety, "Paradise awaits in the darkness." The king stood in front of the soldiers in silence, holding his protruding stomach, as if about to give birth, then marched into the shadows of the balconies as they hailed him a final time.

"Segie, prepare the men for departure." Jurelle turned from his sergeant and walked over to Genevea. He traced a gauntleted finger across the fine fabric of the linen wimple covering her dark hair.

"Promise me you'll keep safe," said Genevea.

"It's war. I can't make any promises. If I don't return…"

Genevea placed her finger on Jurelle's lips. "You will. You will because you must."

"Why do you have to go, Dada?" asked Saskia.
"To protect our kingdom, Poppy, and to protect you and Mama and Jürgen. Where is Jürgen?"

"He's guarding the princess." Genevea searched in a pocket of her flowing white gown, the traditional attire when sending loved ones to war. "He wanted me to give you this." She handed over a small, silver griffin attached to a neck chain.

"This is his amulet. I can't take this."

Genevea pushed the jewel into Jurelle's hand. "He wanted you to have it. To protect you in battle."

Jurelle cradled the family treasure in his palm and closed his fist. He battled with a terrible thought. A thought of betrayal. "Jürgen won't…I mean, he wouldn't…"

"He's our son and he loves you. I've never doubted his loyalty."

Jurelle hugged his wife close and whispered in her ear, "Look after Saskia. Keep your eyes open and your senses keen."

He didn't need to say more. Every resident knew of the treachery that festered in the inner circle. Alliances could change on a whim. As the wife of a Dobunni, Genevea was especially vulnerable. Jurelle ached at the threat his ancestry posed to his family.

Saskia latched onto his leg and pressed her freckled face against the cuisse covering his thigh. "I love you, Dada."

Jurelle smiled at his daughter. "I love you, Poppy. Look after your Mama and big brother for me."

"I will. I've been practicing." Saskia pulled away and demonstrated her developing swordsmanship, feigning lunges and parries to her father's delight.

"Careful now! You'll skewer me before the battle even begins."

*   *   *   *

Caeli counted the soldiers assembled in the courtyard below her preparing for battle. She'd witnessed the theatre many times. Who among them would return? What must it feel like to be so enraptured with impending death? She'd never understand men or their lust for power and control.

Caeli pushed on the side of her mirror, checking she had locked it in place, then wandered over to her bed and threw herself on the down bedcover. She pulled her father's letter out from under the pillow and read it again.

My Dearest Caeli,

Many seasons have passed and lives have changed since I last saw you. I sit here, hiding from creation and wonder what you must be like now. A grown woman with important responsibilities and duties. The mist rolls in from the sea almost daily and clouds gather. Though, they are never as dark as the thoughts that cloud my mind.

Sometimes your grandmother visits my dreams. She warns me of impending doom. I lament her eternal frailty. We share a wallow of endless torment as time refuses to yield for a mother and her son.

But time is not endless for the people of these lands. I write to you of a matter most urgent. One in which I need your help. I believe a young man, a traveller, has arrived in Enthilen. He's in grave danger. His fate is entwined with that of the kingdom and of us all. I know you see much from your tall spire. Set a vigil day and night. Should he arrive in Sardis, protect him, his life is precious. If you speak with him, send him to me with haste.

He has a birthmark on his right shoulder in the shape of a crescent moon. His name is Tom Anderson.

With deepest sincerity

Father

Caeli remembered the instructions from her small messenger. *Read it, then destroy it.* She'd already lingered too long. She held the letter above a candle and set the parchment on fire, watching the flames consume the words from her absent father.

A face peered through the peephole in her door. "Are you alright Princess? I smell smoke."

"Jürgen. Yes, I'm fine. I was trying to light a candle and had a small accident."

Caeli brushed ashes under her bed and rushed to the door. "Will you come in?"

Jürgen didn't hesitate this time.

"You look serious."

"My father leaves for the Riverlands War today. I'm concerned for his safety. Among other things."

"You can see him out of my window. He's preparing the troops for the king."

Jürgen glanced out the barred window of the Sunrise Keep, brushing his fingers across his neck, searching the empty space where his amulet used to hang.

"Your griffin," Caeli said.

"I gave it to my father. That he would return in victory, fate willing."

"You worry too much. He's a mighty and courageous warrior, like his son." Caeli stood right behind Jürgen so he could smell her perfume and feel her soft breath on the back of his neck. She raised herself up on tiptoes and whispered in his ear, "If the Dobunni rebels come for me, will you protect your defenceless princess?" Caeli stepped back and with a dramatic flourish placed the back of her hand on her forehead and pretended to faint, landing in the middle of her bed.

Jürgen turned away from the window. "I'll protect you with my life, Princess."

"Call me Caeli, silly. We are friends, aren't we? *Close* friends?"

"Of course, Caeli. Although, I don't think you're as defenceless as you pretend."

Caeli pouted.

Jürgen sat on the bed next to her. "You're safe here. Rebels could never make it into the inner circle. It's impossible to penetrate."

"There is one way. They bring prisoners in every day for executions. What if a prisoner loyal to the Dobunni rebels tried to attack the king?"

"The Shield would cut them down before they could draw a weapon."

"I guess you're right." Caeli sat up and placed her hand over the top of Jürgen's, staring into his honey-coloured eyes. She was much older than her young guard, though she felt the usual maturity of a woman her age had evaded her, a legacy of being imprisoned in the keep since childhood. Despite the immaturity, she'd developed the cunning of a survivor. However, there was no malice in her feelings for Jürgen. On the contrary, she was very fond of this fledgling soldier. But a higher duty called. One higher even than her duty to the kingdom. "Jürgen, can you travel outside the walls of Sardis?"

"Yes. Now I've completed my final training for the King's Shield, I'm able to travel freely among the circles."

"*Well*...remember when I said I would need your help one day? That day may come sooner than expected." Caeli paused. How much should she divulge to Jürgen? At the moment, she only needed to know if this Tom Anderson had stumbled into Sardis. Trying to protect the traveller could come later. She'd need Jürgen's help then too, but she didn't need to burden her chivalrous guard with that responsibility yet. Tom Anderson may never come anywhere near the royal city. "The son of a dear friend of mine may pass by Sardis soon and I need to know if he's here. I've promised to make sure that he's safe and well."

"I didn't realise you had any friends, Caeli."

Caeli's voice steeled. "I'm not as isolated here as you think. Visitors have come to my door over the yarles. You've been here only a short while."

"Sorry. That was callous of me. I don't doubt you have many friends. I can keep an eye out for him. It should be easy enough."

Caeli fluttered her eyelids. "Easy for such an honourable Shield."

"How will I know this person?"

"He's a young man. His name is Tom Anderson. I think he'll look lost."

"I'll do what I can..." Jürgen's voice trailed off. He stared at the back of Caeli's door, as if he was the one kept prisoner.

Caeli's eyes softened. "There's something else on your mind. You know you can trust me."

"You're Ewald's whore."

Caeli flinched at the word *whore.* It hurt so much more coming from

Jürgen's lips. But she knew he kept something from her. She pressed further. "The king might own my body, but he doesn't own me. I give to him only what I must to stay alive. I'm bound by my duty to the Erstürmen Kingdom, and I will honour that duty, but I have no fondness for Ewald. He's more a threat to the kingdom than the leader of the Dobunni rebels."

"What if I abandoned *my* duty? What would you think of me then?"

"I'd know that you had a very good reason for doing so."

Jürgen faced Caeli. "My father wants to leave Sardis. He wants all of us to leave. He believes the kingdom is about to fall. We're not safe here."

"How will you escape without being noticed?"

Jürgen shook his head. "I don't know. He and I can leave whenever we wish. But not my mother and sister."

Caeli saw an opportunity to forge an obligation. "I can get you out. All of you. No-one will notice until you're long gone."

"How?"

"I can't say, yet. But you have to trust me, as I'm trusting you with Tom Anderson."

"Who is this Tom Anderson?"

Caeli ignored Jürgen's question, grabbed his arm and trapped him with innocent, pleading eyes. "Please keep this between us."

Jürgen sighed, got up from the bed and peered out the window towards the sky. "I need to return to my post, Caeli. The change of guard will happen soon." He flashed a brief smile and locked the door behind him.

Caeli walked over to the window to watch the ebb and flow of the royal city. What *would* she do if the traveller arrived in Sardis? How could she possibly protect him from the king or anyone else? Caeli peered into the mirror to check the wrinkles on her face. Did Jürgen notice her wrinkles?

*　*　*　*

142

Built on an island in the middle of the wide, fast-flowing Anchep River, Sardis and the markets of Slumstadt could only be reached by crossing the Anchep Bridge, a huge structure with thick piers fashioned from ancient panalope trees, carpentered into tall trestles that resembled a forest growing out of the swirling brown water. The heavily lacquered wooden deck was wide enough for two wagons to travel side by side, high timber parapets, decorated with intricate carvings of fish and eels, protecting travellers from toppling into the treacherous river far below. The crossing formed another layer in the city's defences. Should an invading army ever threaten Sardis, the Erstürmen could destroy the bridge to halt their advance.

Under the trestles of the Anchep Bridge was one of the few quiet places away from the hustle of Slumstadt's markets, and a perfect place for a private liaison. A sandbar on the eastern side of the bridge, near the shore, stemmed the flow of the churning water, creating a calm pool. Watching water beetles skim across the surface of the pool, Rosalie and Harris dug their heels into the soft vermillion sand of the riverbank and clasped each other's hand.

"How's your father?" asked Rosalie.

"Better, I think. He's yelling at me again. It's when he goes quiet that I begin to worry."

Rosalie giggled and kissed Harris on the cheek.

"We didn't come here to talk about my father."

"Or my father," added Rosalie.

"Did you make them?"

"Make what?"

"You know what."

"*Hmm.* Well, I tried hard. I made one that looked like a knife. Then I made one that looked like a fork. Then another that looked like a spoon. Clearly, the metal gods were telling me I should eat, so I gave up and had a big roast dinner." Rosalie couldn't keep a straight face.

"I should ban you from the store."

"Oh no. No more rusty gold. How will I ever survive?" Rosalie doubled over with laughter.

"This isn't funny. I've been given a very important task."

"By who?"

"The *key* gods."

"Are they as scary as Volerdie?"

"You shouldn't mock your own religion."

"Why not? It's a load of nonsense. My father's infatuated with it."

"We weren't talking about our fathers."

"Forgot. *Alright.*" Rosalie reached into her dress and pulled out a piece of cloth securely bound. She handed it to Harris.

"How many?"

"I could make only two. There wasn't enough time for more."

"It'll have to do."

"What are they for?"

"I told you not to ask."

Rosalie pouted, then beamed with excitement. "Let's go for a swim."

"What? The water will be freezing."

"Scared? Can't swim?"

"I can swim, but..."

"Then let's go." Rosalie pulled off her dress, exposing thin, cream undergarments.

Harris remained fixed to the sand. "I'll watch."

"I bet you will. But if you want the full song, you're going to have to join the choir." Rosalie stood with her hands on her hips, watching Harris' eyes dancing across her body. "Well?"

"I can't..."

Rosalie jumped on top of her reluctant sweetheart and wrestled with his clothes. Seasons in the smithy had honed her muscles and although

Harris appeared to make an honest attempt to keep her at bay, his resistance proved futile. Rosalie got her hands under his tunic and pulled it up over his head. She stopped dead, mouth agape.

Harris pulled the tunic back over his chest and scanned the riverbank, as if a battalion of soldiers might march out of the water.

"What are those?" asked Rosalie.

"What are what?"

"We're not playing this game again. What are those scars on your chest?"

Harris exhaled and stared past Rosalie to the river behind her. "I knew this day would come. They're pledge scars."

"The rust merchants of Slumstadt take their business seriously."

"It's not a pledge to ironmongers. I've pledged allegiance to the Dobunni rebels."

The smile on Rosalie's face disappeared and she fell silent. She pushed Harris away and grabbed her dress, pulling it over her head. She started to walk off.

Harris seized her arm. "Wait, Rosalie."

"When were you going to tell me?"

"One day. Soon. I didn't want to put you in danger."

"Too late for that. If anyone else sees those scars you can bet they'll report you to Erstürmen soldiers. Are those keys going to the rebels? Have I aided and abetted a rebel plot?"

Harris didn't answer, but Rosalie only needed to look into his eyes.

"Didn't want to put me in danger? That's a cruel irony Harris Snape. I'm in more trouble than...than...Damn you! Damn you to the pits of Volerdie's dungeon." Rosalie stormed off, never looking back.

*　*　*　*

"Where's the king?" Hunfrid peered out of the door of the tiny, window-less room hidden in a secret corner of the inner circle of Sardis.

"He's surveying the troops. He won't notice our absence. For a while." Gerulf hunched together with Rostard, the King's Soothsayer, on a rotten bench seat, staring into the amber-hued glow of a lone candle. The wavering light fought against the damp air that cloaked the huddled conspirators like a shawl of treachery. A pressured claustrophobia hung heavy on Gerulf's thoughts. The walls appeared to pulse with the dance of the shadows from the flickering candle, as if he were trapped inside a cold, stone heart. Like Hunfrid and Rostard, he had his reasons for betraying the king. He knew they all wanted to secure more power.

Gerulf cleared his throat. "I have news from the Worshipful Master. The plan moves at pace. I must leave for Laodicea immediately."

"How do we know that you and the master are not conspiring behind our backs?"

"The Worshipful Master will reward those who progress his ambitions. If you're loyal, Rostard, he'll keep his word. Of this I'm sure."

"You're yet to reveal the identity of this Worshipful Master. I have trouble trusting in the unknown." Hunfrid shut the door and stepped into the candlelight to face his co-conspirators.

"He doesn't want to reveal himself, yet. In time, you will know every-thing, my dear Hunfrid, and you'll rejoice with all of Enthilen."

"How will he deal with the king?" Rostard waved his long, bony hand over the flame of the candle, as if to quell his shivers.

"Even I'm not privy to his entire plan. I assume this is the purpose of our meeting in Laodicea, to inform me of the next steps. The king must be killed, this much we know. However, the Worshipful Master wants Prince Adalwolf alive."

"When Ewald dies, Adalwolf will sit on the throne."

"It doesn't take a soothsayer to foresee this. Adalwolf may sit on the throne, but he'll not wield any power. His will is weak and easily bent. He won't be able to resist the demands of our master." Gerulf beckoned Hunfrid to sit and drew his accomplices close. "Don't you understand, my friends? We're on the cusp of a glorious new era that will usher closer the return of the greatest ruler of all."

"I don't claim to understand how all the pieces fit together."

"It is written in *Polus Sepcarture*, Rostard. Within the scripture verses, the future of Enthilen is laid out for all men to see."

"Only curates are permitted to read those words. The rest of us must blindly trust their interpretation."

The wooden seat creaked as Hunfrid shifted his stout frame. "What of these tainted grells?"

"They're the harbingers of change," said Gerulf. "They heed the Worshipful Master's bidding, clearing the path for his ascension. The white grell, Eroberung, stalks the lands south of here, though his charge is unknown to me. It's best not to meddle in the errands of corrupted grells. A particularly unpleasant death will befall any who make such a mistake. I know that Eroberung is the master's regent from Sardis to Süden Forst. You must follow his orders should he ever give you one. Be thankful if your path crosses only with him. The other three tainted grells are more ruthless."

~Chapter 13~

The morning sun decoupled from the horizon and Tom shivered, damp from last night's rain. Grin's snoring almost drowned out the dawn chorus of tiny birds bouncing between clumps of spiky grass. He smiled at his grell friend, content that Grin had time to rest and recover from his injuries, then watched the birds for a while, trying to find a species he recognised. One looked like a fairy-wren with a long, thin tail pointed towards the sky, but its feathers were bright red, not blue or dull brown like the wrens back home.

Tom rubbed his bare arms and turned to Thaly. "Can we make a fire?"

"Too risky. Will draw too much attention." Thaly dug under another boulder and pulled out a large, bound package, untying the string and beckoning Tom over. "We have spare clothes here, and weapons. I need to get out of these prison rags and you need to take off that animal fur...thing. Why are you wearing that anyway?"

"Grin made it for me. It was itchy at first. I've gotten used to it now."

"It makes you look like a grell child. Better to dress like a peasant or a goat boy if that's truly what you are."

Tom ignored the doubt in Thaly's voice. "Do you have any spare clothes for Grin?"

Thaly shook her head. "Nothing big enough for a grell."

Tom changed into a short tunic and long leather pants. The rebels didn't have any spare boots so he kept his moccasins. He took a sheathed long knife from the small pile of weapons, strapping it to his thigh. He used another leather strap to fashion a belt with a loop to hold the cutlass he'd stolen from the armoury in Süden Forst. "Can you teach me how to use these? I've never used a sword before."

Thaly's face hardened. "There won't be time for lessons. You'll be leaving soon."

The thought of leaving stoked Tom's anxiety. He knew little about the rebels, but they could fight. They could protect him if the need arose. Despite Grin's size, the grell wasn't a warrior. Tom needed warriors to defend him. From Eroberung. From the bad man.

"Where's Jacob?" asked Tom.

"He's scouting our surrounds. He didn't sleep last night."

"He kept watch all night?"

"He doesn't want to see any of us fall into enemy hands."

"Are all Dobunni so committed?"

"Jacob isn't Dobunni."

"He's not?"

"Not old Dobunni. His ancestors came from across the ocean and settled in Bethesda near the time of the Erstürmen invasion. He loves that city, though. He'd do anything to protect it."

"Do the Dobunni have their own language?"

"You don't know much, do you? Before King Faramund invaded Enthilen, the Dobunni spoke their own language. They were forced to relinquish it as part of the truce that saved Bethesda from being overrun. In exchange for keeping the Southern Vale. We still hold onto some of the old words, but nobody speaks Dobunni anymore. Not that I know."

Thaly pulled off her prisoner rags and began to change into fresh clothes. Tom blushed and averted his eyes, but still caught a glimpse of soft breasts dangling above a taut stomach. Something else captured his attention; two long, diagonal scars running parallel across Thaly's torso. Tom fixed his eyes on the ground while Thaly dressed.

"Haven't you seen a naked woman before?" said Thaly.

"Yeah, of course I have," lied Tom. "Just being polite."

Without warning, Jacob stepped into the campsite. "I leave camp for one moment and you two can't wait to get undressed." The older rebel laughed to himself as he searched the uncovered packages. "I don't think we're being followed. Hopefully, we've lost that white demon. We need more supplies though. But I have to rest first." Jacob sat in the wet ochre soil, bracing his back against a boulder, and sniffed the air freshened by the storm. "This is the first decent rain for many days."

Tom sat next to Jacob. "Did you see anything?"

"Wagons and traders moving along the road between Sardis and Süden Forst. Sometimes Erstürmen soldiers, escorting coffles of grell slaves to another punitive chore. You can rest easy; we're safe here. Our camp's surrounded by boulders and dense shrubs, and it's perched on the western side of a ridge away from the north road." Jacob raised his eyebrows. "I see you've got new clothes. Better than those furs. Don't want people thinking you're a wild grell. You might end up in slave chains."

"The tunic and pants *are* more comfortable, thanks." Tom paused for a moment before pressing further. "Jacob, can you tell me about Laodicea? I mean, Bethesda. I've never been."

Jacob nestled his buttocks into the damp soil, as if preparing for a long tale. "Three harvest seasons have passed since I last visited Bethesda. It's been my family's home for four generations. I was born in the Docklands. They look out across Traders Bay and the Veiled Occyan, a vast sea extending to the far horizon. The port bustles with merchants coming from faraway lands. Some buy fabrics and clothes from my mother and father who are renowned tailors. As a child, I'd sit at the window of their shop and stare out to sea, dreaming of riding a ship to exotic locations or back to the birthplace of my ancestors. The Dobunni built the city, but they didn't exclude others from settling there. Bethesda is a city of many cultures. It's this diversity that protects it from complete Erstürmen dominance. The Docklands are a melting pot of different peoples from many lands. The Southern Vale is mostly Dobunni and has held steadfast against the scowl of Erstürmen scum since the invasion. The King's Quarter is Erstürmen and the Terraces, the Terraces are where the rich traitors live."

"What do you mean?" asked Tom.

"The wealthy Dobunni and others. Those who raised themselves above the rabble through hard work or good fortune. Carved into the limestone cliffs that tower over the north of Bethesda are terraced dwellings with connecting passages. From balconies of stone, the rich look down upon the city. They have occupied the Terraces for generations. When the Erstürmen came, the terrace-dwellers placated the invaders with riches and loyalty in exchange for survival. They say this treachery bought them freedom. But they are trapped in their holes and rarely venture into the city or beyond. I don't call that freedom."

Jacob took his sword and scratched a rough map in the dirt showing Bethesda, a mountain range to its north and a narrow pass through the mountains. "We always thought Bethesda was vulnerable to an attack from across the ocean. We never expected a threat from the north. There's only one way to cross the Desolate Mountains — the pass of the damned — Detranté. It's narrow and treacherous. No army can march through in great numbers at once, they must travel single file along a rocky track at the bottom of a deep chasm with sheer sides towering above. Detranté is easily defended. The Dobunni had sentries among the cliffs ready to rain down arrows and rocks on any invader that tried to march through. The pass could be blocked completely at certain points to isolate groups of soldiers from one another. The sentries watched the pass day and night."

"Yet from the north the Erstürmen came." Grin had woken, and yawned loudly.

Jacob nodded. "The people of Bethesda didn't see them or know of their arrival until it was too late. The sentries that survived swore they saw nothing. The army didn't come through Detranté, but from the north there's no other way. How can you hide an army?"

"Could they have marched over the mountains?" asked Tom.

"Impossible."

Tom grabbed his old animal-skin tunic and searched inside its pocket. He pulled out his hand and offered an open palm to Jacob, the silver coin sitting in the middle. Grin's eyes grew wide. Tom noticed the concern too late.

Jacob plucked the coin from Tom's hand and twirled it between his thumb and forefinger. "Where did you get this?"

"It's from Lao...I mean Bethesda, isn't it?"

"*King's Quarter Treasury.* Only Erstürmen invaders use coins like these. But they wouldn't use this coin."

"Why not?" asked Tom.

"See the picture on the back? That's King Alaric, Ewald's grandfather. When a new king is crowned, all the old coins must be destroyed, replaced by those with an image of the new monarch. It's against the law to use this coin. You could be executed." Jacob handed the coin back to Tom. "This is a very old coin. How did it come into your possession?"

Tom stared in silence at the red sand.

Jacob persisted. "Let me guess, you found it in The Feign?"

Tom's heart pounded. *How long can I keep up this lie?* He looked to Grin for reassurance. The grell shrugged his shoulders. Tom faced Jacob. "Someone killed my grandmother. He dropped this coin. It's the only clue I have. I thought I might find him in Laodicea. Deliver him justice."

"Do you know what he looks like?"

"Yes. It was a long time ago, but yes."

"Why isn't your father seeking this justice? Or your mother?" asked Thaly.

"They never believed my story."

Jacob sighed. "You may find him, if he still lives. But Bethesda is a big city."

"And it's a long way from here," said Thaly. "You're on the wrong side of Enthilen."

Tom sensed doubt in Thaly's voice. He mumbled to himself, "I was tending goats in the plains..."

Thaly sprang to her feet. "Well, the water and food are nearly gone. You look after Grin until we return."

The rebels took a hunting bow, water skins and empty packs and left the campsite.

Tom waited until Jacob and Thaly were out of earshot. "I shouldn't have shown Jacob the coin, should I?"

Grin's face remained stern. "You have placed some of your trust in these rebels. I hope that is not a mistake. I caution you against revealing too much too soon. We cannot be sure what they will do with the information."

"Do you think we should just leave, before they come back?"

"I see no reason to fear the rebels, yet. They are leading us north. We could stay with them for a while longer, then head east to Laodicea. My wounds are not fully healed, and it is better we keep to the cover of the Scaur Hills for now, rather than risk travel on the open road or through the Dambay Plains. Soldiers from Süden Forst will be watching the roads. And the white grell."

The gaps between the boulders seemed to stretch open before Tom's eyes, as if a giant was yanking the stones apart. He searched the gaps with apprehension, expecting any moment that Eroberung would burst into the camp and wrap his thick, white hands around Tom's neck. He never meant to put Grin in such danger. Maybe he should continue on alone? "Frennan will be worried about you."

"He will, but I sense he knew this may happen. I refused to have you undertake this journey alone. We will travel together, at least until you reach Laodicea and begin your search for your grandmother's killer. Even goat herders can have grell slaves. I can pretend to be your slave."

"The King's Quarter is ruled by the Erstürmen. The blue book described them as heroes, but the more I hear about them, the less I like them. Even if we make it to Laodicea, I may never find my Nanna's killer, or the way home. We could risk everything and achieve nothing."

"Jacob appears wise. We should seek his further counsel before leaving the rebels. I will ask him if there is a way to get word to my father that we are both alive. Dobunni and grells have always been friends."

"I feel so guilty, dragging you into this mess."

"I am your friend, Tom. I am not going to abandon you at the time of your greatest need."

Tom and Grin rested in silence until mid-morning, dozing under speckled clouds. Tom had never experienced such a draining adventure. He jolted awake when an unexpected guest bounded into the circle of stones.

"A gundhirrwa!" said Grin.

Tom's mouth dropped open. "That's a wallaby. Bloody hell. There are wallabies here too."

"She is beautiful. Look at the markings on her coat, buff, black and tangerine. And she has a young one in her pocket."

Her pocket. Tom burst out laughing. A hearty guffaw fed by a mixture of exhaustion and disbelief, and thankfulness that the old Grin, the one in love with the beauty of this world, had re-emerged from the trauma of days past.

*   *   *   *

Thaly loosed an arrow and brought down a hare. "That will do nicely."

"Pity we can't have a fire." Jacob plucked berries from a thorny blemmel bush, a common plant on the eastern slopes of the Scaur Hills.

"We'll have to eat it raw." She grabbed the hare and stashed it into her pack, which she slung over her shoulder. "We have enough supplies now to move on. We don't need to go back to the camp."

"Are you suggesting we abandon Tom and Grin?"

"You were right, in Süden Forst, we had to be patient and wait for our opportunity to make an escape. And the opportunity came, just like you said it would, in the form of a skinny boy, barely a man. We took advantage of our opportunity and now we're free. We don't need Tom or Grin anymore. They're slowing us down."

Jacob rubbed his stubbled chin. "Something about Tom intrigues me. Did you see the scars on his palms? And that coin. That was a silver tausen. Not one to be lost so easily. On the black market it would be worth one thousand coins with the head of Ewald. My father told me that only a handful of such coins ever existed."

"Then we should take the coin. Imagine what we could buy."

"The black market is full of rogues, and you're not a thief, Thaly. I hope I trained you better than that."

Thaly flushed with embarrassment. She changed the subject. "The white grell pursues Tom. We're in danger if we keep the boy's company."

"Enthilen's a dangerous place for a rebel, no matter whose company we keep. The tainted grells are a new enemy we must face. I fear their master could be more heinous than any Erstürmen king. If the white grell seeks Tom, it may serve our purposes to make sure the boy is never captured."

Thaly rested her back against a boulder and shaded her eyes from the midday sun. She couldn't see an advantage in helping the injured grell or the boy any further, but she knew that Jacob would be weighing all the possible outcomes in his mind, well into the future. He rarely made rash decisions, unlike his pupil. Anger and frustration often overwhelmed Thaly. Although she'd grown up in the Scaur Hills, the labyrinth of rocks felt like a prison, not a home. Her home was somewhere else. In one of the villages that dotted the Dambay Plains, or maybe in Laodicea itself? With a warm fire and a mother and father that loved her.

Jacob strolled over with a sack full of blemmel berries. "We should head back."

"Emelin told me," said Thaly.

"Told you what?"

"Who my real mother and father are. Did you know?"

Jacob shook his head. "No. Emelin has kept her secret for many seasons. I know she considered never telling you. I guess the burden became too much to bear."

Thaly scuffed her boots in the sand.

Jacob rested his hand on her forearm. "Emelin adopted you as a baby. She loves you like her own daughter. Your real family is here. Among the rebels of Bagendon."

"Don't worry, I'm not interested in seeking the company of my parents. They disgust me." Thaly pulled away from Jacob, turned to face the north road at the foot of the Scaur Hills and froze. "Look!"

Jacob's eyes followed the point of Thaly's finger. At the edge of the road, a short hike away, crouched the white grell. Resting on one knee next to his giant horse, he hovered over a flat stone lying at the side the road.

"What's he doing, Jacob?"

"He's placed something on that rock. Something metal. I can see it glinting in the sun."

The rebels crouched, transfixed, as Eroberung studied the object he'd placed on the stone. Thaly thought she saw the object spin by itself. But that made no sense. His white horse whinnied, stamping the ground and tossing its head, as if spooked by an invisible threat. Thaly's heart jumped into her throat when Eroberung spun around and looked up into the hills to where she hid. She ducked behind a boulder with Jacob.

"Damn. Did he see us?"

"I'm too scared to look," said Thaly.

"We need to get out of here. He's hunting us."

~Chapter 14~

The central market of Laodicea, the meeting place of the four quarters of the city, thrived with activity. Traders sold the last of the fresh produce from the harvest season and residents of all locales mingled and bartered, stocking up on essentials and preserves to prepare for the rain and cold to come. While most came for food, visitors to the central market could purchase almost anything from the array of stalls, ranging from clothes, housewares, weapons and trinkets, through to various animals or even grell slaves.

Fires burned around the market to light the crowded paths, torch flames fluttering precariously close to the fabric walls of merchants' stalls. Two and three storey stone buildings ringed the entire square, the poorer residents of Laodicea from the Docklands and Southern Vale resting their backs against the cold stone walls, begging for coin. A few peasants drew market scenes and tried to sell the drawings to passersby. Others sang songs of ancient times. Most simply offered an empty hand. In the centre of the market, surrounded by Erstürmen soldiers on guard for any trouble, stood a statue of a woman looking into the distance. An open hand, faced down, rested against her forehead. The plaque at the bottom of the statue read: *The Seeker*. Most residents of Laodicea, however, had forgotten what she sought.

The more refined ladies and gentlemen visiting the market, mostly merchants or administrators, or high-ranking, off-duty soldiers, picked their way through the throng of beggars, navigating to the best stalls to secure wares for their houses. On this particular evening, the balmy air fuelled a jovial atmosphere. It would likely be one of the last warm nights before the storm season set in. The judgement of the pool of reflection approached, and gossip abounded on who may be favoured this season.

Felsie, the pool of reflection, lay at the foot of the limestone cliffs that towered over the north of Laodicea. Terrace houses with balconies overlooking the pool were prized by the wealthy because the owners could stare into the pool at their leisure. An ancient body of water, the sparkling, clear blue of Felsie was the reason that the Dobunni chose this place to build a settlement. In the early days, the pool provided fresh water, revered by the original settlers for its purported healing properties. In recent times, this legacy had been forgotten, Felsie now lauded for a different purpose; the judgement of the fairest of them all.

At the end of every harvest season, a competitor from each of Laodicea's four quarters would sit at the edge of the pool and stare at their own reflection until it was distorted by one of the ascending bubbles that occasionally broke the surface of the pond. Whomever was closest to the surfacing air pocket would be eliminated from the competition until one competitor remained. It could take days to determine a winner. If a contestant fell asleep or passed out, they were eliminated. The previous harvest season, Lady Queltra of the Southern Vale had lasted the longest, earning numerous gifts and favours, and special privileges for an entire cycle of the six seasons.

The light-heartedness of the market crowd leading up to the day of judgement belied the constant tension existing among the residents from the city's four quarters. While the original Dobunni families accepted different cultures and people into their city, the Erstürmen rulers didn't appreciate this type of cultural diversity. After their invasion of Laodicea, and the division of the city into four quarters, they had cleansed the King's Quarter of all but those of Erstürmen origin. Such exclusion didn't make the residents of the King's Quarter feel any safer.

*　*　*　*

On a cobbled street running along the north-western edge of the central market of Laodicea, strutted Widald, searching the stalls for a treat to take home for dinner. Satisfied that he'd completed a productive day of work at the Master's Hall, Widald held his head high, like a rooster on parade, his favourite bright yellow hat balanced on top of his proud bonce.

"Good eve, master."

Many residents greeted Widald as they walked past, dipping their hat or touching their forehead as a sign of respect. As Master of the King's Quarter, the king's regent in Laodicea, Widald held a position of particular importance. Each of the city's four quarters had a master. They met regularly to discuss the management of the city and attempt to maintain the fragile peace. Widald had to keep his wits about him during the meetings, lest a decision be made that angered his brother, King Ewald. All of the masters were cunning, in their own way, and promoted the needs of their quarter's residents whenever possible.

Widald stopped at one of his favourite food stalls. "How much for the honey devil-kuchen?" He patted his ample stomach, as if preparing it for the sweet, baked treat to come.

"Two coin mas'er."

"For one kuchen?"

"I cun give yer two fer t'ree coin."

Widald fished three coins from the pocket of his purple jacket and tossed them to the stall holder. The baker wrapped two cakes in paper and handed them to Widald who pressed his nose against the paper and sniffed. "Fresh?"

"Yar, just baked t'day mas'er"

"Lovely."

Widald strode on, dodging his way through the crowds, always ready to acknowledge the greetings from residents of his quarter. His thoughts turned to work and the poor circumstances that Laodicea found itself in. The coffers of the King's Quarter Treasury were almost bare and this harvest season had yielded a poor return. Tomorrow, he would chair another city council meeting with the other masters. More pointless discussions about problems that would never be solved. The city was running out of food. The Riverlands War, if ever won, would yield little benefit to the people of Laodicea. Only Sardis would enjoy those spoils.

Widald scolded himself for stressing over work as he opened the front gate to his yard, nodding to the guards as he passed through. The guards and the tall fence crowned with metal spikes that surrounded the grounds of Widald's house were new. As tensions in Laodicea rose, his wife, Adela, had demanded greater protection for their family.

Widald lived in the largest and finest house in the King's Quarter, befitting his position as master. Perched on the gabled roof, sculptures of gargoyles, winged beasts and fire-breathing serpents watched over him as he marched through the manicured garden that surrounded the entire residence. The statues gave him the shivers, but the previous master adored them. Widald nodded to the grell slaves that still tended the grounds despite the sun having set. Adela refused to allow the grells inside, forcing them to sleep in the stables with the horses and dogs. She preferred to employ peasants for minimum coin as maids and cooks.

Widald laboured up the stairs, between the stone columns of the portico, and opened the heavy, scarlet door to his house. In the entrance hall, he only had time to hang his hat and coat on hooks before his three youngest children came running along the hallway.

"Papa!" they cried in unison before giving his belly a collective hug.

"Oh, my goodness. Good eve children."

"Good eve, Papa. How was hall today?"

"Busy, busy, busy, Brunhilde. Very busy."

With small children hanging off his legs, Widald waddled into the dining room. Two more of his children sat at the table, teasing each other about their appearance. Widald's oldest daughter, Amelia, entered the other side of the room from the living quarters. He beamed at her and held his arms wide. "*Ahhhh*, here's my princess. You look beautiful this eve, my sweet."

"Thank you, Father"

"It's not long before the day of judgement. Are you ready, my sweet, to stare into the pool of reflection? Only by its divine provenance will we know who is the fairest and most beguiling of all the people in Laodicea."

"I'm ready, Father."

"Good, good, good. We can't have another Dobunni winning this season, can we? I've been telling all in the city council that my daughter, the beautiful Amelia, is sure to garner the pool's favour as this harvest season ends."

Widald's eldest son, Helmut, entered the dining room. "It's only a few days before the end of the harvest season."

"Yes, you're right, Helmut. The judgement of Felsie must be held soon. Before the onset of the storm season. We can't have all those raindrops disrupting the pool's surface now, can we? Chaos, that's what that would be, chaos. But now, let's eat! I have honey devil-kuchen."

The y oungest c hildren s quealed w ith d elight a nd g rabbed a t t he wrapped cakes, as Widald held them above his head. He laughed with loving heartiness. "Wait, wait, wait. Not for now. After our supper. Your mother will roast me over a fire otherwise."

*　*　*　*

Widald sat on a tall stool behind one of the four lecterns that faced each other in the timber panelled meeting room of the city council chambers. He read through his notes before the other masters arrived, his yellow hat resting on top of the lectern, the emerald-green feathers jutting from the jewelled headband glinting in the torchlight. The bustle of stall holders in the central market setting up for the day filtered in through open windows, making Widald drowsy. He jolted upright when Lady Lily LáDown, the Master of the Southern Vale, strode into the room.

"Good morn, Master Widald."

"Morn, Master Lily. It's a fine morn this day."

"Fine indeed."

Master Lily took her seat and traced her finger around the edge of the lectern, waiting for the meeting to begin.

Widald continued to read his notes, but kept an eye on the tall, stately woman sitting opposite him, her pale-olive skin framed by greying hair. Despite being fond of the Dobunni woman who he'd worked with for nearly twelve yarles, he didn't have the energy to engage in further small talk. The Erstürmen and Dobunni were sworn enemies. He always felt like a traitor whenever conversation between him and Lily became too friendly.

"Morn, masters."

"Morn, Master Sleame," said Widald and Lily in unison.

The Master of the Terraces, Lord Sleame Excelis, a haughty, discourteous man, considered the council meetings a complete waste of his time, whining about the imposition at almost every meeting. As he took his seat, Lord Sleame picked fluff from his velvet blue robes, as if each piece of lint had been contaminated with the wretchedness of the poor. Widald knew that Sleame had to walk through the western part of the Docklands, an area wracked with poverty, to reach the council chambers. It continually surprised him that Lord Sleame bothered to attend the meetings at all.

The three masters sat in silence, staring hypnotically at the top of their lectern. They waited for the last master to arrive; Dealhia Rossingbird, the Master of the Docklands. Always late, Dealhia gave the appearance of a bumbling, disorganised bureaucrat. But Widald knew this masked a cannier character that caught many off guard.

"*Sorrryyy.* Sorry I'm late." Dealhia tripped over her feet as she entered the meeting room, parchments flying from her arms and scattering across the floor. Master Sleame sneered as Dealhia kneeled to collect the papers. Master Lily left her stool to help.

"Sorry," said Dealhia. "Had to get the children off to the academy for lessons."

"I'm surprised you can afford lessons."

"They have scholarships, Lord Sleame. Scholarships for academic achievement."

"They must be very clever." Lily handed the papers to Dealhia and returned to her lectern.

"Thank you, Lily. They take after their father, I'm sure."

"I assumed it would be *fath-ers.*"

Dealhia appeared to ignore Sleame's jibe and took her seat at the last empty lectern.

"Enough of this chit chat," said Widald. "We've many important things to discuss. First on our agenda…"

"We've not decided on the agenda yet, have we Master Widald?" asked Lily.

"Well no, but I think we all know what the first item of business must be. The harvest season draws to a close and we haven't chosen the day of judgement."

"How surprising that you should consider *this* the most important item," said Sleame.

"Not because my daughter is the entrant for the King's Quarter. It's not just because of that. The city loves this event, and times are hard. We need something to distract the people, and soon, otherwise there'll be trouble."

"What happens when the event is over, master? The hunger will not recede," said Dealhia.

Master Sleame's face reddened. "Oh, for goodness sake. Seven moons from now. Do we agree?"

Widald considered if Amelia would be ready by then. Her mother had commissioned a beautiful dress, from the best tailors in Laodicea, which was sure to entrance the lake into granting her favour. But he didn't know if it was finished yet. "I have to confer with my wife."

"Nonsense. What say you, Master Lily?"

"I agree, Master Sleame."

"Good. All those in favour?" Three hands shot up. "Seven moons from now. All settled, Widald."

Widald's face flushed with annoyance at being overruled by the other masters.

Master Lily moved the meeting forward. "We have more pressing matters to discuss. The Southern Vale is running low on food and coin. What recompense does the kingdom offer its subjects?"

"Let the Dobunni starve."

"Your family are Dobunni, Master Sleame. Have you abandoned your heritage completely?"

"It's an awful matter. We're starving in the Docklands. Most of the merchant ships that arrive at the wharves are poorly stocked. Not that my residents could afford to buy anything," said Dealhia.

"We're in a terrible state in the King's Quarter…" Widald's stomach grumbled, as if to confirm his announcement, "…but what can we do about it? The king has sent troops to the Riverlands, yet the spoils of war will not reach Laodicea."

Lily looked squarely at each of the masters. "Events are conspiring against us, fellow masters. Merchant ships diminish in number. Our farms are failing as the wind carries the soil to the clouds. Sardis refuses to assist us. It's like we're being deliberately isolated. The weakest prey singled out by a pack of wild dogs before the fatal attack is launched."

"An attack!" blurted Dealhia. "I knew there was something important I needed to raise at this meeting."

"What are you talking about, woman?" Sleame turned in his seat to scowl at Dealhia.

"A ship's captain came to my hall two moons ago. On her journey here, she'd passed close to the Abrolous Isles. There she saw a fleet of ships anchored in the Bay of Fires. Barbarians."

"Most likely waiting to raid cargo vessels."

"No. This is different, Widald. There were many ships. She dared not get too close, but ventured close enough to spy heavily armed men and women stalking the decks. On the largest ship, standing on the bridge she saw a tainted grell, its whole body stained blood red."

The room went silent. Market smells and sounds continued to filter in through the open windows, as if nothing in Laodicea had changed, or ever would change. Freshly baked bread. Lambs bleating. Sweet incense barely masking butchered meat. Stall holders quarrelling over impingements on their space.

What will happen to the market when the barbarians come? thought Widald. Better to be home with his children sitting down to a nice meal than in this infernal meeting. He shook the thoughts from his mind. "Krieg."

"What?" asked Dealhia.

"His name is Krieg. The red grell. The grell of war."

"Are these ships preparing to raid Laodicea?"

"No, Lord Sleame. They're preparing to destroy Laodicea. While King Ewald hides in his circled prison, power is being methodically wrenched from his grasp."

Widald shook his head. "Now, now, Master Lily, those are treacherous words."

"Treacherous is he who seeks to usurp the king and enslave us all. I fear a malice greater than we've ever faced is preparing to show his hand. The red grell is not the first I've heard of. A grell with skin like the blackest burnt charcoal has terrorised our famers in the Dambay Plains. Wherever he emerges, crops fail and people starve. They call him Hunger. In Laodicea, Erstürmen soldiers are abandoning their king. They look to a new leader."

"I'm the leader of the Erstürmen in Laodicea."

"For how long, Widald?"

Master Sleame stood. "If war is coming, we must prepare. I will return to my people..."

Widald interrupted, "We should discuss the defence of our city. Only together can we defeat this threat."

"The residents of the Terraces do not trust the Erstürmen to protect them in times of war. We each must find our own path." Sleame strode from the room.

"And there is little hope for an Erstürmen–Dobunni alliance," said Lily.

"Then there's little hope for Laodicea," countered Dealhia. "The poverty-stricken people of the Docklands have but one choice. To run or to wait for war to come. I'm going to the port to warn them." Dealhia gathered her papers and left the room.

"I must leave also, Widald. If further news reaches your ears, I hope that you'll share."

"Yes, of course Lily. Of course." Widald slumped in his chair, alone, with his head in his hands. Thoughts raced through his mind. War? Would his family be safe in Sardis? Was there still time for the day of judgement? He should go home and pack.

Widald barely noticed a young child enter the meeting room. She pulled a rolled parchment from her tattered dress and reached up and placed it on the lectern. He raised his head. "Oh. Hello there. Aren't you a sweet little thing?" The girl pushed the parchment towards him. "What have we here? A letter?"

Widald opened the unsealed parchment as the girl ran from the room and disappeared into the central market.

> *Esteemed Master of the King's Quarter*
> *With great concern, I have uncovered critical information about*
> *a plot to kill our beloved king. This must be thwarted immedi-*
> *ately. I only trust to convey this information to you in person.*
> *We must meet, in your hall, on the night before Bargan next rises*
> *full. Under the cover of darkness.*

Widald rolled his eyes. "This, I *do not need*."

~Chapter 15~

Tom scrambled among the boulders of the Scaur Hills after the Dobunni rebels. He stopped regularly to let Grin catch up, the grell struggling to keep pace, his legs still suffering from being trampled by the undred. Tom knew Grin's anguish stretched deeper than the physical pain. His friend felt guilty at failing to save the female grell. Bruised bones and tissue scars would heal. Tom worried that the torment of failure would punish Grin until the end.

The wind picked up, careering through the gaps in the boulders and buffeting the four companions. The weather turned, making a difficult task even harder. Dark clouds raced across the sky, occasionally giving way to a patch of blue or glint of sunlight. Tom's ears ached in the howling gale and he struggled to keep his feet on the rocky ground. He glanced behind to see Grin falling further back.

"Wait!" Tom yelled to Jacob and Thaly up ahead. "We have to go slower."

Jacob looked over his shoulder; his reply almost swept away by the wind. "Eroberung is on our tail. We can't linger here. Need to get to the other side. Find somewhere to hide."

Tom waited for Grin, then helped the giant grell as best he could. Together, they pushed through the clumps of spiky grass and over loose, uneven terrain. Tom's feet burned inside his moccasins. "What I wouldn't give for a good pair of hiking boots," he mumbled to himself.

"I need to rest, Tom." Grin collapsed onto the ground, only the rags tied around his waist offering him any protection from the elements.

Tom yelled again and Jacob and Thaly slowed to a walk. He scanned the ridges that surrounded them, a strong gust of wind sending dust flying into his eyes and nearly knocking him off his feet. Tom sheltered next to a rockface and pulled his eyelid over his bottom eyelash, trying to clear the annoyance from his right sclera. As he blinked hard, he glanced up to the ridge on his east. Something...someone was there, silhouetted against the furious sky. *Eroberung.*

"I can see him!" Tom screamed.

Jacob spun around, raced back and pulled Tom and Grin in close. "Stop yelling. The wind will carry our voices. We need to find cover. Maybe we'll lose him."

The companions battled against the wind until stumbling upon the entrance to a cave partially hidden behind dense bushes. They squeezed inside, Jacob and Thaly crouched at the entrance, swords drawn. Everyone sat still and silent. Tom pinched at his tunic and counted in his head. It didn't calm his racing heart or still trembling hands. He sucked in air, as if struggling with an ascent up a tall peak.

The wind dropped. Grin pointed to a shadow passing over the surface of a large boulder near the cave entrance and raised his crutch like a spear.

Tom fumbled for his cutlass. *Eroberung's here.*

Thaly dropped her sword and nocked an arrow. They waited, their breaths rebounding off the sandstone walls. Something disturbed the bushes near the cave entrance. Thaly drew her bow. It walked into a clearing.

Grin's eyes widened and he grabbed Tom's arm. "Look. I have never seen one of those. What is it?"

"It's a boulder lion," said Jacob. "We're probably in her den."

Tom settled his nerves and peered over Jacob's shoulder. A large cat ambled past the cave. She resembled a cougar or mountain lion with sleek, rufous fur and a black tip to her long tail.

"They usually shy away from people," said Thaly. "She's no threat to us. She'll just have to wait until we're gone."

Jacob turned to Tom. "Are you sure you saw Eroberung?"

"I saw something. On the ridgeline."

Thaly lowered her bow. "We have enough to worry about without jumping at shadows."

It was more than a shadow, thought Tom.

"We'll wait here until we're sure it's safe," said Jacob. "Thaly and I will keep watch."

Tom retreated to the rear of the den and slumped against a rock wall, letting the cutlass fall from his hand onto the cave floor. What good was it anyway? He couldn't fight. He didn't know the first thing about using a sword. *I need to learn how to defend myself. If I'm going to confront Nanna's killer, I need to be the one delivering the justice.*

Tom spoke his thought aloud, into the empty half-light of the cave, "I want to learn how to sword fight."

Jacob kept his back to Tom, still watching for any threat. "Did they teach you nothing in The Feign?"

"The staff is a herder's weapon," Grin said, "not a sword. I do not know how to use one either."

Tom stared at the back of Thaly's head and could almost see her rolling her eyes. He decided to confront the rebels. "Why are you here? I mean, Grin's injured, I'm practically helpless. We need you, but you certainly don't need us. And Eroberung's after me, not you."

Jacob faced Tom. "How did you get those scars? On your hands."

Tom thrust his hands in his pockets as a knot set in his chest. "I picked up a rock, from the fire. It burned my skin."

"That was stupid," said Thaly.

"I don't believe you," Jacob said to Tom.

Tom looked at Grin who shook his head once. Tom understood; don't reveal too much.

Jacob continued, "We've thought about leaving you behind, but there's more going on here than I understand. You guard the truth closely, Tom Anderson. We share a common enemy, yet you can't tell us why the white grell pursues you."

"I don't know why," said Tom. "I'd never seen the white grell before Süden Forst. Never even heard of him. But..."

"But what?" asked Jacob.

"I think it has something to do with the murder of my grandmother, eleven yarles ago. I feel like her killer has lured me from my home by deception. I pursue him; maybe he pursues me?"

"If Eroberung captures Tom, I fear it will end many innocent lives," said Grin.

Jacob shook his head, then heaved a deep sigh. "My heart trusts your motives. I hope the trust isn't misplaced. You're right, Tom, you need to learn how to use a sword. Maybe we'll make you into a fearsome Dobunni rebel? Then you'll have a companionship at your back to help you deliver justice to your grandmother's killer. Thaly can train you."

Thaly spun around, eyes burning. "What?"

"It will do both of you good," said Jacob, turning back to guard the cave entrance. Eroberung didn't appear. As the moons rose, the companions vacated the lion's den to make camp nearby and let the feline return to her shelter.

*　*　*　*

Two days had passed since the encounter with the boulder lion. Jacob led the group to the western edge of the Scaur Hills, as far from the threat of Eroberung as possible. Here, the land changed to a flat, open expanse of sandstone sitting atop the steep-sided Riverlands Escarpment. Underfoot was solid rock, which meant they left few tracks and could travel swiftly, but the landscape offered little cover other than the occasional boulder or outcrop of shrubs. Jacob told Tom and Grin that the escarpment overlooked the fertile soils of the Riverlands Delta, pockmarked with wetlands and waterways as far as the eye could see. The Anchep River dominated the delta, nearing the end of its long journey from the Desolate Mountains, around Sardis, over the escarpment at Rārian Falls, through the Riverlands, and emptying into the southern ocean of Gadhang.

Despite her initial protest, Thaly had agreed to teach Tom how to fight. The responsibility seemed to elicit a distinct change in her demeanour towards him. Piercing glares almost disappeared. Her chestnut-brown eyes softened; sometimes even smiled. Tom began to notice the sheen of the thin layer of sweat that clung to her taut muscles during their sparring. Or the sway of her long black hair as she dodged the flailing stick he used as a sparring sword. His blossoming infatuation started to become a distraction.

Near the edge of the Riverlands Escarpment, with the sun overhead, Tom and Thaly began another training session.

"Watch your stance," said Thaly. "Which is your lead foot?"

"My left foot."

"Which one is that?"

Tom placed his left foot forward, bent his knee and thrust his left arm towards Thaly.

"Good. Turn your rear foot sideways. Remember, don't stand with your feet together. It's too easy to knock you off balance. A good fighter can lead with either foot and wield a sword in either hand. We'll need to work on that."

Tom furrowed his brow as he concentrated on Thaly's instructions, believing that the better fighter he became the more he proved his worth in her eyes.

"Let's practice sparring with real weapons." Thaly handed Tom his cutlass and drew her sword. "Get your stance right and thrust your sword towards me."

"What if I cut you?"

"You can't hurt me. Get in position, pick your mark and then strike."

Tom readied himself as Grin watched. The grell had almost recovered from his ordeal at Süden Forst and had abandoned the crutch. Jacob stood nearby, on lookout as usual, observing the track that ran along the foot of the escarpment.

Tom tentatively struck at Thaly and she parried his thrust, knocking the cutlass from his hand.

"You can't hesitate, Tom. Strike with more purpose."

She gave the cutlass back to him and took up a defensive position. Tom thrust again, and again she parried. This time he managed to hold onto his sword.

"That's an improvement at least. Try again."

Tom thrust again, Thaly parried. He tried again and again. Each time, Thaly dealt easily with his attacks. Tom advanced, pushing Thaly back towards a lip of rock. He saw an opportunity to knock her off balance and lunged forward. But he tripped on a loose stone and stumbled towards the ground, landing in Thaly's arms. She held him tight and he looked up into her eyes, smitten by their velvet gaze.

"You need to learn to stand on your own two feet." Thaly smiled and pushed Tom away.

His skin tingled as he lingered over the curves of her body, pressing against her tunic.

She glowered at him. "What are you looking at?"

"N-n-nothing."

"Don't be distracted during a fight. You'll get your throat cut."

Jacob interrupted the training session. "Follow me." He led the group to a boulder perched on the lip of the escarpment. Tom imagined one push and it would tumble over the edge. From behind this cover, the companions had a perfect view of the narrow dirt track below, linking Sardis with the farming communities of the Riverlands. Open woodlands with carpets of closely browsed grass stretching towards the Anchep River spread out before them. Further to the south, in the far distance, a patchwork quilt of fields stitched together by timber picket fences and hedges bounded each Riverland farm. Nearby, a waterfall crashed over the escarpment.

Jacob pointed towards the track. The head of a column of soldiers, their flags fluttering in the breeze, emerged from the cover of the tree canopy.

Tom crouched next to Jacob. "Who are they?"

"Erstürmen soldiers marching to war against the farmers of the Riverlands. Food is scarce, disease spreads, war soon follows. The soils of the Dambay Plains no longer produce the bounty they once did. The Riverlands are fertile, but the farming communities have resisted trading with the Erstürmen. King Ewald finally lost his patience. Now he's taking what he wants."

"Such an army should easily realise victory," said Grin.

"You would think, but the peasants have held fast for many moons. It seems they have powerful allies. Our scouts have spotted mercenaries among their ranks, directing their attacks."

Tom squinted into the sun at the throng of soldiers snaking along the road. The breeze caught the leading banner, revealing the outline of a creature in yellow fabric stitched atop a rectangle of crimson. "Is that a griffin?"

Thaly spat on the ground. "Now we know who leads the Erstürmen army. That traitor, Jurelle. I'd like to smite him with a single blow." She stood tall and drew her sword, thrusting it towards the marching column.

Jacob lunged at her and pulled her behind the boulder. "Stop waving that sword around. You'll draw their eyes."

"Let them come. I'll slay the Traitor General myself."

"Fools and death march lockstep," whispered Tom.

"What did you say?" Thaly turned a burning gaze on him.

"Just something my grandmother would say."

Jacob calmed his fellow rebel. "Sheath your sword, Athalee. The day you face the General may come sooner than you wish."

"I'll be ready."

*　*　*　*

The battalion from Sardis marched two abreast along the potholed track that led to the Riverlands farms. Jurelle rode out front on his trusted grey courser, Sphinux, sitting tall and relaxed in the saddle. Like the rest of his mounted soldiers, he wore a light armour of thick leather, the preferred attire for long marches. Jurelle expected little trouble until they reached the battlefields of Flüsse, the most densely populated region of the Riverlands. Yet, he remained watchful, especially of the escarpment to his left which offered a commanding view of the approaching army.

His bannerman rode next to him, holding aloft the only griffin to fly over these skies in generations. An emblem forever associated with the Stansfield family. Also of Dobunni ancestry, the bannerman had now pledged loyalty to the Erstürmen.

Behind Jurelle rode four dozen men on horses, a skilled and well-armed cavalry that would challenge any enemy. Six undred riders lumbered after the regular cavalry. While few in number, an undred unit could be devastating on the battlefield.

Six hundred men-at-arms marching on foot made up the remainder of the battalion; the grunts of the Erstürmen army from the outer circles of Sardis. They wore light tunics of blue and black, the traditional colours of the Heine Empire, with the characteristic Erstürmen spangenhelm protecting their head. Each soldier carried a halberd resting on their shoulder and a shield strapped to their backs. A third of the force had crossbows hanging from their belts. They marched under the ancient red and black banner of the curled, two-headed serpent; a sigil that dated back long before the beginning of Heine family rule. Jurelle had asked many in the inner circle if they knew what the sigil represented, but no-one had provided a convincing answer so far.

Following the marchers, ox-drawn wagons carried food, supplies and the heavy armour that would adorn the fighters during battle. The wagons also towed powerful ballistae capable of shooting heavy metal arrows into enemy ranks.

At the rear of the column trudged grells slaves, bare calves likely stinging from the slap of overseers' whips. Jurelle detested slavery, but he knew the giants were vital to transporting the resources of war, the crates strapped to their backs overflowing with food, bedding and weapons. The grells would also serve the soldiers in camp and clear the dead and injured from the battlefield.

Jurelle squinted as Sphinux walked out of a shady grove and into bright sunlight. As his eyes adjusted to the light, he caught a glint of something at the top of the escarpment. He waved his hand, calling up Segie, his sergeant-at-arms.

Segie moved his horse in next to Jurelle.

"Have you been watching the escarpment, sergeant?"

"From time to time, General."

"I'm sure I saw something near that large boulder..." Jurelle pointed to the top of the escarpment, "...like sun reflecting off metal. I think we're being watched. Pick your two best climbers and have them scout the top of the escarpment. If they find anyone there, kill them. We don't want our enemy being forewarned of our arrival."

"Yes, General."

*　*　*　*

In an abandoned farmhouse near the village of Breadelbane, in the shadow of the eastern edge of the Scaur Hills, Malphas waited in silence for his servant to arrive. He stood in the dusty shadows of a kitchen, furniture and cutlery left in place, as if the previous occupants had abandoned the house in a panic. Malphas dragged his bony finger along a dirt-laden shelf and held it to his nose, breathing in the days of desperation that had piled into the room before the farmers' final moments. He wondered if a family of corpses lay somewhere nearby.

Night closed in. Malphas' companion, Ende, the pale-skinned grell, raised her head as the front door creaked on its hinges and heavy boots clicked across the rotting timber floor. A plains rat scuttled into a hole in the wall. Outside, a screech owl hooted at the stars.

Eroberung entered the kitchen and bowed his head, holding out his fist towards Malphas. "I have a gift for you, Worshipful Master." He opened his hand to reveal the eyes of lost souls perched together in the middle of his giant palm.

Malphas let a faint smile escape, as he tottered over to the white grell. "Ah, the dark eyes. I'm reunited with them once again." He snatched the eyes from Eroberung and then looked up at the compliant white face before him. "What of the boy?"

"He escaped, master. The blood on the compass is old. It no longer guides me to his location."

"Then you have a problem."

"I will capture the boy, master. He is with two rebels and a wild grell. I believe the rebels will take him to their camp in the Scaur Hills. We have an ally in the camp."

"I'll give you one more chance. But you must carry a reminder of your failure. Kneel before me. Lay your hands out in front. On the floor."

Eroberung kneeled and crouched forward until his forehead rested on the floorboards, and stretched his arms in front of his head, palms facing up.

Malphas turned to the pale grell. "Ende."

Emotionless, Ende moved next to the white grell and with deft speed, swung a razor-sharp sparth at the floor, slicing Eroberung's left hand clean off at the wrist. The white grell jerked his forehead up, his face wracked with pain, but he made no sound. Thick blood, as black as pitch, oozed across the floor, consuming the dust.

Malphas pulled a vial from his pocket and placed it on the ground next to Eroberung's severed hand. "I have a few drops of Prince Adalwolf's blood left. If you fail again to bring me the boy, the remainder of your days will be in the service of the draughouls in the dungeon of desolation."

~Chapter 16~

Ewald knelt on a mauve cushion with white tassels, resting his clasped hands on the back of the ebony timber pew in front of him, and gazed down at the pentagonal tiles on the floor. His laboured breaths resounded through the empty kirika, his body detoxifying from the previous evening's binge on meduz, and horse meat fried slowly in rendered fat.

He imagined sinking through the floor of the kirika to the dungeon below. The Erstürmen always built a dungeon under their chapels, to remind parishioners that punishment was close at hand should they find disfavour with the curate or the Creator's faithful. The inner circle's dungeon had not held a prisoner for many seasons. Ewald executed those who displeased him, without hesitation. Yet, the executions did nothing to quell his paranoia.

How many people would he have to kill before he felt safe?

He toiled up off his knees and collapsed his bottom on the pew behind. Seven candles burned on the altar, dripping wax onto the polished obsidian. Adjacent to the flames, the pulpit lorded over the congregation projecting authority and piety, and damnation for the unbelievers. Anselm, the royal curate, was renowned for delivering powerful and frightful sermons, though Ewald had never heard any of them. He refused to attend community chapel; a perfect place for an assassination. He kept his devotion private.

"Good morn, Majesty." Anselm's shining white shoes smacked the pentagonal tiles with religious zeal as he strode down the aisle between the pews. He carried with him a book with a black leather cover. Ewald knew it was *Polus Sepcarture*, the scripture verses, believed to contain the will of the Divine Creator himself. He'd never read a single word from the book, trusting the interpretation of the verses to those with greater theological expertise.

Anselm stopped at the end of the pew. Ewald didn't bother turning his head, continuing to stare at the altar in front of him.

"Have you come to seek guidance from the Divine Creator?"

"What guidance might he offer?"

"That depends on your needs. He may guide you in the labours of rule or affairs more mundane. And the Creator is always ready to judge our worthiness to enter paradise."

Ewald picked a crumb from his beard and dropped it on the floor. "I imagine I'll be found wanting in that regard."

"If you've strayed from the path, Majesty, it's never too late to return. Renewed devotion will bring redemption. Volerdie can forgive true believers that stumble."

"I feel as if I've been stumbling for half a generation, Anselm. I've made my home a prison with no escape."

"You are the king. You do what you must to dodge the assassin's blade."

Ewald's eyes ached with the need for deliverance, as he turned them towards the curate. "Maybe that's their plan all along? Those who seek to hasten my end. Have me hide away behind these walls while my kingdom crumbles. My subjects have no respect for their king, only fear. The usurpers have defeated me without spilling a single drop of blood."

Anselm grasped the edge of the pew to steady the sway of his body, wavering on bowed legs. "In two harvest seasons, you'll reach the age of succession. Then Adalwolf will have to shoulder the burden of rule."

Ewald scowled. "He's weak. The boy will be consumed by the same maddening thoughts that torture my mind. Others will exploit his weakness to meet their own ends."

"You can remain in the inner circle if Adalwolf ordains it. Your son may welcome your guidance."

Ewald forced a smile. "He'd sooner see my severed head hanging from the wall outside the needle."

"My confrère, Lothar, sent word that Prince Hadufuns visited Süden Forst. The Wandering Prince may seek reunion with his brothers. If you bring all your family into the inner circle, they can shield you and Adalwolf from the machinations of usurpers."

Ewald turned away and sank back into the pew, staring into thin air, remembering times long past. "Hadufuns was always the wanderer. Even when we were children, he'd disappear for days on end. Walk off into the Scaur Hills or down the escarpment. No-one would know where he was or when he was coming back. Not that my father cared. Gerulf always managed to convince the old king that somehow Widald was responsible for Hadufuns' absence. Widald became father's whipping boy. Gerulf took an unsavoury pleasure in that fact." Ewald faced Anselm again. "Where *is* Gerulf?"

"He left for Laodicea three moons ago, Sire."

"What's he doing there? He's supposed to be training Adalwolf. Preparing him for rule."

"I'm not privy to his reasons."

"Not for the torment of his older brother, I hope. Widald is kind hearted and a fool. He'd welcome an assassin with open arms and thank him for the knife in his back. I shouldn't have made him Master of the King's Quarter. I should demand he return to the inner circle, like you suggest. Send Hunfrid to Laodicea. My heart cannot trust the Master of Executions, despite what Gerulf says. Though, I'm not sure Widald would embrace being an executioner."

"If I may suggest, Majesty, you could appoint Widald Umbo of the King's Shield and Gerulf Master of Executions."

A scoff escaped Ewald's pursed lips. "Gerulf would squeal at the demotion. It's best I leave well enough alone. Adalwolf will have other plans, no doubt. It's a pity he has no siblings to offer support."

"Romilda is now barren, Sire. The Divine Creator deemed it so after my penetrating... catechism."

"I should be thankful that I have an heir. Instead, I get more bitter with every moon rise. It was loneliness that drove poor Hadufuns to despair. That drove him away from the kingdom. He never recovered from the death of his wife, Godeliva. You know he killed her. Not deliberately. We were on a hunt, all of Oldaric's sons together in the woods at the foot of the Desolate Mountains. We came upon a deer. Hadufuns stalked the prey, arrow nocked. The rest of us followed. Gerulf accosted Widald for another supposed misstep. They wrestled. The deer bolted. Hadufuns loosed the arrow at the same time Gerulf flung Widald into his shoulder. The arrow missed its mark, but we heard a cry from the bushes. Godeliva was collecting berries to bake a pie to surprise her new husband. We found her with an arrow in her chest, still breathing. Still...awake. Hadufuns cradled her dying body until the sun set."

Ewald stood, brushing the creases from his royal blue robes. "How will history remember my reign, Anselm? What stories will the poets tell? The hunger and disease that consumes Enthilen won't stop at the needle. It will breach our defences soon enough. All of us will succumb to the infection. I can't stop it."

"Darkness will descend before Sardis falls, majesty. When we enter paradise, famine, disease and war will fade away, banished by a wave of the Creator's hand. We'll never want or fear for anything."

"I hope you're right, Anselm."

~Chapter 17~

Hadufuns rode into Laodicea as the sun set and the three-quarter crescents of Seena and Bargan floated in the night sky. The journey between Süden Forst and Laodicea normally took five days of solid riding, across the Dambay Plains and along the central and north roads. But Hadufuns had taken more than twice that long, stopping along the way at the Erstürmen outpost in the old grell city of Malang Gunya, and camping on the fringes of Laodicea for three days before finally entering the city. He remained uneasy about the letter and the meeting with his father, but he knew his guidance may help save the kingdom from collapse.

Hadufuns navigated his chestnut pony through the busy streets of the Southern Vale, making his way to the King's Quarter in the northeast of the city. An unadorned rider dressed in frayed cloth attracted little attention from passers-by, the dirty grey hood of his cloak masking the weathered face of the king's brother.

On reaching the King's Quarter, he slowed his filly to a walk as he neared the Master's Hall. The horse's hooves echoed on the cobblestones of streets strangely empty for so early in the evening. Two Erstürmen soldiers stood outside the stables next to the hall, confronting peasants cowering on the ground. Hadufuns dismounted and kept to the shadows of a portico, observing the exchange from a safe distance.

"Ya can't sleep here ya filthy scum. Get up!" A young Erstürmen soldier flung his boot into the ribs of an old man bedded down on a pile of hay. An elderly woman sat next to the man, clutching a tattered bag.

"Sorry, young master. We was just goin'." The old man tried to stand, doubling over from another swift kick to his stomach.

"Y'need to be quicker dan dat. Here, what's da old crone got in her bag?" The young soldier snatched the sack from the woman's grasp and emptied the contents onto the stones, a meagre haul of bread, potatoes and rags spilling out into the half-light.

An older soldier watched the encounter, leaning against a timber post and smoking. Hadufuns assumed it was bunbili weed rolled in fine paper, the favoured leaf of Erstürmen soldiers. The contents of the bag didn't appear to pique the old soldier's interest. "Looks like dese two been beggin'. Y'know beggin' on da streets of his majesty's quarter is punishable by death."

The woman clasped her hands together. "We ain't been beggin' sir. These are the last of our things. We're just…"

"Shut it." The young soldier thrust the blunt end of his halberd into the woman's face.

Hadufuns flinched at the sound of breaking teeth. He had seen enough. He walked out from the shadows and led his horse across to the stables.

The young soldier spun around and pointed the blade of his halberd at Hadufuns' chest. "'Who are you? Another filthy beggar?"

The old soldier stiffened, placing his hand on the grip of his sword. "He ain't no beggar. Not with dat fine horse."

Hadufuns raised an open hand. "Lower your weapon, soldier. I'm a loyal servant of King Ewald."

The young soldier scowled. "Says who? The king ain't got no *loyal* servants no more, just servants. And he won't have dem much longer neither, from what I hear."

As Hadufuns pulled the cowl from his head, the smirk on the old soldier's face disappeared. "Whoa, whoa, hang on." He placed his hand on the shaft of his companion's halberd, pushing it towards the ground as he leaned in towards Hadufuns. "Who *are* you?"

"I am Prince Hadufuns Heine, eldest brother of King Ewald, King of Enthilen and all her peoples."

"How'd we know dat?" The young soldier raised his weapon again.

"Put dat down y'fool," admonished his companion, before turning back to Hadufuns. "I knew ya looked familiar. I served in da King's Shield a while back. When King Ewald still visited Laodicea. I seen you and da king riding together."

"That was a long time ago. You have a good memory."

"My apologies, yur highness, for me simple-minded friend. He ain't even seen da king, let alone his brother."

"Apology accepted. Now, I need to stable my horse. These trespassers..." Hadufuns waved his hand at the peasants lying on the ground, "...seem to have made an honest mistake. I say let them gather their things and be on their way."

The soldiers moved to the side as the elderly couple collected their possessions. They paused as they passed Hadufuns. "Hail the king," said the old man, placing a trembling fist to his chest, before taking the woman's arm and limping away.

Hadufuns handed the reins of his horse to the old soldier. "See that she's fed and watered before you resume your duties. Hail King Ewald."

"Hail King Ewald!" The soldiers barked as Hadufuns strode from the stables.

It had been many yarles since Hadufuns had been inside the Master's Hall of the King's Quarter. Built from timber perched on stone foundations, the hall dominated the skyline of this part of Laodicea. The Erstürmen had expanded the footprint of the original Dobunni building by adding a second floor and extending the ground floor rooms. Outside, white-washed clay render covered the timber cladding, framed by exposed structural beams of dark brown. A roofed deck adorned the front of the building. Hadufuns smiled to himself as he pictured Widald standing on the deck, delivering speeches to adoring crowds assembled in the courtyard. Colourful decorations dissected the leadlight bay windows of the building, depicting thrones and sealed parchments, horses and riders, locusts, scorpions and jacinth, and a red dragon with seven crowned heads and ten horns.

Hadufuns tiptoed up the stairs of the hall and crossed the deck. He waited for a moment outside the main door, left ajar, pondering for a final time the wisdom of his actions. Behind him, the two soldiers from the stables skulked across the empty courtyard and down the street. Darkness cloaked the entrance hallway inside the building. Hadufuns searched the dark for signs of a trap. The Master's Hall could be accessed via multiple doors through which an assailant may have entered from the outside and prepared for an ambush. Though Hadufuns' instincts told him to be wary, the desire to serve the kingdom once again outweighed his caution. He stepped over the threshold.

The Erstürmen had divided the ground floor of the hall into twelve rooms used to receive guests, hold meetings of the quarter council or conduct the daily business of managing the King's Quarter. When the king or his immediate family visited Laodicea, they would be accommodated on the second floor which had been divided into six rooms and decorated with fine silks, masterful tapestries, rare timbers and porcelain vases. Once, Hadufuns had caught Widald napping in the king's chambers, his brother drowning in the duck down quilt and dwarfed by the four-poster bed that filled the room.

Hadufuns' eyes adjusted to the darkness of the entrance hall. At the end of the hallway, a sliver of light snuck out from under another door.

He rested his hand on the pommel of his sword and edged towards the glow, passing closed doors to his left and right. The dark wood panelling of the hallway swallowed the brightness and leeched Hadufuns' confidence as he reached the end door. His neck tingled as he eased the door open. It protested at the disruption, creaking like the ancient bones of a lost draughoul soul.

The flame from a white candle, melted to a porcelain saucer in the middle of a table, flickered from the draft that followed Hadufuns through the doorway. The amber hue of the candlelight illuminated a throng of parchments strewn across the table. Around the room, half-open cabinet drawers clung to their runners. A wooden box sat at one end of the table, papers and various trinkets stuffed inside. Otherwise, the room appeared empty.

Hadufuns scouted the perimeter of the room, in the dullness beyond the candlelight, searching for another exit. He found a door at the back of the room, between two cabinets, but it was locked. A loud scuffling coming from the entrance hall disrupted his contemplation. He retreated to a dark corner and drew his sword.

"My goodness. *Mmmm.* Delicious. This kuchen is delicious." Into the room tottered Widald, surrounded by the aroma of freshly baked buns. Hadufuns relaxed, but stayed hidden.

Widald plonked the buns onto the table, wiped crumbs from his mouth and began to pack more items into the box, muttering to himself the entire time. "No coin. No coin. The coffers are empty, your majesty." Widald chuckled before his demeanour turned serious. "Just pack the essentials, Widald. Stop fooling around. Anything of value, and important papers. Yes, important papers. Don't want them falling into enemy hands. War is coming. Pack it all and then get out of here."

Widald sifted through the parchments scattered across the table.

Hadufuns shifted his weight and one of the floorboards under his boots creaked.

Widald spun around. "Who's there?" He picked up the candle and swept the darkness. "Show yourself."

"It is I, brother. No need to set a fire here."

"H-H-Hadufuns? Hadufuns is that you?"

Hadufuns sheathed his sword and stepped into the light as his younger brother beamed. "It is you!" Widald put the candle back down and hugged Hadufuns. "How long? How long has it been?"

"Too long, Widdy."

"And *where* have you been? We thought you were lost forever."

"I *was* lost. Ambling through the kingdom and beyond like a lamb bleating for its mother. I've wrestled with the demons in my mind and they're at bay for now. It's time for me to return to the kingdom."

"What brings you to the fair Laodicea?"

"I hoped maybe you could enlighten me there, Widald."

"Your presence is a complete surprise to me. Though, maybe you've heard..." Widald pulled Hadufuns close and lowered his voice, "...war is upon us. Krieg has been seen in the Bay of Fires, standing tall on the bridge of a barbarian ship. A whole fleet litters the bay. Scores of ships people say, scores. They ready themselves to attack Laodicea. I'm sure of it."

"The barbarians have become bold indeed if they're considering an attack on Laodicea. Why is a tainted grell leading them?"

"The red grell is a portent of war. Nothing can be surer. Someone wants to see the city burn. I have to protect my family."

"So, you're fleeing, Widdy?"

"What else is there to do?" Widald glared at Hadufuns. "You fled the kingdom many yarles ago. Why shouldn't I?" Widald returned to sorting through the papers for a moment then jerked upright. He patted his purple coat and pulled out a parchment from the inside breast pocket. "I almost forgot. As if war isn't enough for me to deal with, this letter came six moons ago."

Hadufuns read the letter. "It's unsigned."

"Yes, yes, unsigned and unsealed. I don't know who it's from. Something about a plot to assassinate the king, as if that's news. I think there's been a plot to kill Ewald since the day he was born."

"I also received a letter about such a plot. It asked me to come here, on this night, just like yours. It was signed by our father and secured with the royal seal."

"Oldaric? He's still alive? I thought him long dead. *Long* dead. Why would he want to meet you here? Do you think my letter's also from him?"

"It's the same hand-writing. Something feels strange about all this, Widald. I can't accept that father is truly concerned about the welfare of Ewald or the fate of our kingdom, but his motives remain shrouded. He would be a frail old man by now. I doubt he'd consider another attempt to usurp the king."

"Maybe his intentions are true? Maybe a remorseful old age has cleared his mind and steeled his purpose as a..."

Hadufuns clutched Widald's arm, stopping his brother mid-sentence. Footsteps echoed along the hallway. He pulled Widald back into the shadows as the door to the meeting room swung open.

Framed by the jamb, a diminutive figure planted its feet in a confident stance. "Widald?"

Hadufuns sensed the tension in Widald's body as Gerulf entered the room and began perusing the parchments on the table.

"I know you're here, Widdy. You'd never leave behind a half-eaten kuchen."

Widald broke free of Hadufuns' grasp and stepped into the light. "I'm here."

Gerulf didn't look up from the parchments. "Good, good."

"I am here also."

Gerulf's head jerked up. "Hadufuns? Why are you…well, isn't this a pleasant surprise? Here we are, reunited at long last."

"Why are *you* here, brother?" Widald glowered, not bothering to mask the disdain he had for his younger brother.

"I'm here to see you, Widald. I bring a message from the king."

"What message?"

"Patience, Widdy. That can wait. It's been a long time since three sons of Oldaric were together. Let's sit and drink to our family's health. Do you have any meduz?" Gerulf pulled out a chair and took off his coat, exposing the hilt of his sword. He sat and beckoned his brothers to join him. "Sit, sit my brothers. Let's reminisce about old times."

Hadufuns hovered near the table. "I prefer to stand."

"Always wary, Hadufuns. We could use your vigilance in the king's court. Why don't you end your pointless wandering and return to Sardis where your talents can be put to good use?"

"There's nothing for me in Sardis. I choose to serve the kingdom in other ways."

"Serve? I haven't witnessed any of your valuable service. You hide it well." Gerulf fetched the kuchen from the table and took a bite.

Widald broke the tension. "Now brothers, please. There's no need for any hostility. I have some meduz in the cupboard here, let's drink." Widald sat and poured three cups of the milky liquid. He leaned across to Gerulf and whispered, "Hadufuns has a letter from our father. Asking to meet him here. This eve."

"Our father? He's dead, surely." Gerulf acted surprised, but Hadufuns wasn't convinced.

"Did you receive a letter, Gerulf?" asked Widald.

"No. My visit serves another purpose."

Hadufuns moved closer to the table. "What purpose might that be? It seems a strange happenstance that you should turn up on this night."

"You see conspiracy and sedition everywhere, Hadufuns. You should give your untamed thoughts a rest. You know how they torture you so."

Hadufuns thumped the table and towered over his younger brother. "What do you know of my thoughts?"

"Control your Shield, Widald. His breath is souring my meduz." Gerulf took a lingering swill of the drink as Hadufuns fumed. Widald placed a comforting hand on Hadufuns' forearm, stilling his anger.

Gerulf smacked the bottom of his empty cup on the table and belched. "I came to speak with the Master of the King's Quarter. I'm sure you know by now, Master Widald, that war is on your doorstep."

"How do you know this? Are you in leagues with the barbarians?"

"You're a witless fool, Widdy. The machinations of Enthilen swirl about you like a flock of buzzards, but you see naught past your fat stomach. You're not fit to be the Master of the King's Quarter. The fall of Laodicea will be on your head."

A draft of warm, stale air floated under Hadufuns nose. He spun around towards the back door. A giant shadow hidden in the darkness blocked his path. With lightning reflexes, Hadufuns drew his sword, but a monstrous black hand reached out from the dark, grabbed his forearm and snapped the bones in two. The creature lifted Hadufuns off the ground and flashed a forbidding smile etched on a stained, black face.

"What?" Widald jumped from his chair. "The black grell." He confronted Gerulf. "Traitor!"

Gerulf smirked and took another bite of kuchen. "That's a strong word, my brother. You shouldn't bandy it around so lightly." Gerulf waved his hand and the tainted grell released Hadufuns who collapsed to the ground.

"You bring Hunger into the Master's Hall. You threaten the king's

regent in Laodicea *and* his eldest brother. What purpose does this treason serve?"

"You were always a simple child, Widdy. How do you think I was able
to convince Father that you were responsible for all the missteps of his
children? And you could do nothing about it. Poor — gullible — Widald.
Even Hadufuns, the Wandering Prince, is more aware of the tides of
our kingdom. You're too consumed by your vanity, your cakes and your
pitiful city."

Hadufuns ached with Widald's fear. The panicked eyes of his younger brother darted around the room. But Hunger, the black grell, blocked
the only escape. Hadufuns' frustration boiled as Gerulf toyed with
Widald like a lion with a fawn.

"Let me talk slowly so even you can understand, Widdy. King Ewald
is failing. Our kingdom rots under his feet and he does nothing. Who
can arrest this situation? A new ruler must emerge to lead the Erstürmen
into paradise."

"Do you think that's you, Gerulf?" asked Widald.

"Not at all. I live to serve my king."

"You're not serving him now."

"That's where you're wrong. Ewald is no king, but there is another.
Ready to take back the throne that he should never have been forced to
relinquish."

Behind Gerulf, a hunched old man shuffled into the room through
the main door. His calloused skin glowed dull-orange in the candlelight,
pinprick holes pockmarking a bulbous nose. Hadufuns' eyes narrowed,
imagining ageless secrets hiding at the bottom of the deep, wrinkled
caverns furrowing the old man's brow and cheeks. Behind dull, grey
eyes resided a soulless pit masked by drooping eyelids.

A female grell shadowed the old man, her skin tainted a sickly
pale colour, as if inflicted with jaundice. Strands of long, white hair,

caressed the handle of the sparth she carried in her right hand like a walking stick.

Widald stammered, "F-f-father?"

Hadufuns pulled his aching body from the floor, nursing his broken arm, and staggered over to Widald's side. "Yes, it's him. It's all clear to me now. Our father has returned to take the throne he's always coveted. To do that, he needs to quash all other legitimate claims. He needs to kill us."

Warped ears twitched between strands of wiry hair. The old man's forceful voice belied his decrepit appearance. "Very clever, Hadufuns. Very clever. But the vessel that was your father is no more. While the body of Oldaric stands before you, the weakness inside him has been replaced by a force greater than any can imagine. It is Malphas that you face now. And it is I that will seal your fate and the fate of all Enthilen."

"You'll never take back the throne. Adalwolf is the rightful heir. You failed once; you'll fail again."

"That was a different time, Widald. A very different time. I have travelled to faraway lands and to me has been bestowed the ultimate blessing. Soon, darkness will descend on Enthilen. It is my singular right to hasten its arrival and prepare for the return of the Divine Creator."

"It's you directing these tainted grells, spreading fear and chaos throughout Enthilen," said Hadufuns.

Malphas caressed the skin of the pale grell with a crippled finger. "What a joy it was to corrupt a soul so pure and innocent. All of my servants were wild grells once. Peaceful, content. Until I completed their...rehabilitation. Bent their wills to my purpose. It is one of my greatest achievements."

"Father...you bring war to Laodicea," Widald cried.

"Laodicea is already at war, fool. War with itself. I plan to cleanse it. March with the faithful to Volerdie's ancient seat of power. Rid this cursed land of all unbelievers to prepare for the greatest ruling dynasty ever known. When the tumult reaches its peak, when day turns to night, the road to paradise will be revealed."

Hadufuns lunged at his father. The pale grell stepped from behind the old man and slashed her sparth across Hadufuns' face and chest. He collapsed at her feet, clinging to a dimming vestige of life. But he fought to keep his senses alert; to bear witness to the treachery unfolding before him.

Widald bolted for the door. Gerulf sprang from his chair, drew a sword and smote his brother in the back, cracking his spine. The air exploded from Hadufuns' chest as Widald's heavy, limp body toppled onto him.

Gerulf's heaving breaths filled the room with mist as night closed in. He presented himself to the man Hadufuns once knew as Oldaric; the now self-proclaimed Malphas. The youngest son knelt at Malphas' feet, head bowed, with his sword lying flat across the palms of his hands, as if the old man had already taken back the throne. "I pledge my allegiance to you, Worshipful Master. My loyalty and devotion will not be bounded."

"You've been a faithful servant, Gerulf. I could not have asked for a better regent in Sardis." Malphas tousled his son's fair hair. "You were always my favourite. I know you used this to your advantage. Misdirected my anger towards your brothers when it was you who should have been punished. I admire your cunning. Laodicea is about to fall. Sardis will soon follow. What role might you play in this new order?"

"Whatever is your will, Worshipful Master."

"Of course. Rise my son. I know I can always trust your loyalty."

Gerulf stood. "Our plan moves inevitably to completion."

"Inevitably it does. But there is one more piece to complete this night."

The light faded in Hadufuns' eyes, but he caught the last moments of another life. The black grell grabbed Gerulf's forehead and slit his throat. The traitor to King Ewald fell to his knees, his emerald gaze fading in the candlelight, blood pouring from his wound. Malphas rested his wizened hand on Gerulf's head and pushed his son's body to the floor. It slumped on top of his siblings.

~Chapter 18~

The storm closed in. Driving rain lashed the Scaur Hills and black clouds full of thunder and lightning careered over the jagged ridge-line. Heavy raindrops stung Thaly's skin and the wind screamed in her ears, as if the weather had decided to punish her foolishness. She crashed through dense vegetation, admonishing her actions with every scratch. Stupid, stupid, stupid! Why did she always let her emotions get the better of her? That stunt at the escarpment put the whole group in danger. Erstürmen scouts had climbed the rock face and were in pursuit. She'd drawn their attention, waving her sword around like a petulant child.

Jacob had placed her in charge of leading the group away from danger. Training under pressure, he called it. His voice inside her head helped to calm her thoughts. *We learn the most from our mistakes.* She wondered how many more mistakes she needed to learn from.

Thaly steeled her resolve and led the group back into the middle of the Scaur Hills, away from the escarpment. Below the ridgelines offered more hiding places and they needed to find somewhere safe and dry. Navigating through the hills in the dark was nigh impossible, even for someone who had spent her entire life here, and Thaly's instincts warned her that Eroberung would be waiting in the dark, ready to spring his trap.

Jacob yelled over the din, "We need to find shelter, now!"

"There!" Thaly pointed to a gap in the rocks in the far distance where an overhang with a recess underneath provided protection from the rain and wind. She quickened her pace, marching towards the shelter. As lightening illuminated the sky, she turned to see Tom and Grin struggling up the slope towards the shelter. Thaly raced back to help, offering another shoulder for Grin to rest his hand and steady still healing legs.

Together, the group crammed into the back corner of the overhang, as far away from the entrance as possible, welcoming the respite from the storm.

"At least it's dry here. This cavern is larger than I thought." Jacob dropped the satchel from his shoulder.

"It's good to get out of the storm, but this shelter feels like a trap. We can't linger here long."

"Nightfall is coming, Thaly. The scouts won't travel during the night. It's too easy to get lost. We should be safe here until dawn."

Tom shivered with cold or fear, his satin-grey eyes glistening with bewilderment like they often did. "What about Eroberung?"

"There's been no sign of him for five days," said Thaly. "I hope he's given up the pursuit."

"We should be wary nonetheless," said Jacob. "You did well to find this shelter, Thaly. I couldn't see anything in that storm."

"Neither could I," said Grin. "Despite the legendary keenness of grell eyes."

Thaly smiled, before the musty smell of charred wood wafted into her nostrils. "There's a fire pit here, surrounded by stones."

Grin sat on the red sand floor of the shelter and ran his hand over the surface of the rock. "Scrape marks on the rockface suggest this shelter has been hollowed out. Purposely enlarged."

Thaly crawled to the other side of the shelter, discovering etchings scratched onto the rockface. Drawn in white and red, simple representations of animals and people decorated the walls.

Grin joined her. "These drawings tell stories. Of hunts and ceremonies." A few of the human-like figures towered over the others, who fled in the wake of the giant hunters. Grin beamed with excitement. "This is a meeting place."

"For who?" asked Thaly.

Grin scratched his head. "My father told me tales of places such as these. I think this is a meeting place for mouldewerps."

"I doubt it's been used in generations. There are no mouldewerps anymore. The grells saw to that."

Grin flinched at Jacob's comment, as if struck by a stone.

"Are they dangerous?" asked Tom.

"They're tiny, like children," said Jacob. "They couldn't hurt anyone. Anyway, there's no need to be fearful. Mouldewerps disappeared from Enthilen a long time ago."

Grin's mood turned sombre. "When I was very young, my mother would recite a verse about mouldewerps:

> *Mouldewerps delve deep down*
> *In dwells deep underground*
> *Digging deep without a sound*
> *Mouldewerps delve deep down."*

"...and grells hunt them all around and grind their bones into the ground." Jacob smiled, apparently admiring his cleverness.

Thaly shot a piercing glare at her trainer, then turned to Grin. "Ignore him."

"What does he mean?" asked Tom.

Grin's face turned pale. "It is true. Some grells hunted mouldewerps. A long time ago. Sometimes for food. Sometimes for the thrill of the hunt. I am not proud that my ancestors did this. When grells spread throughout the Dambay Plains, they forced the werps into the surrounding hills. They have been lost from the plains ever since, but their dwells can still be found, though they have been vacant for generations. I have never seen a mouldewerp. My father has. He thinks they still exist somewhere, hiding from the world."

"The werps were here before the grells, isn't that so?" asked Thaly.

"Yes, that is true." Grin bowed his head and the group went silent.

Thaly sensed their exhaustion. "We need to rest. I'll take first watch." She sat at the front of the overhang as more lightning pierced the surrounding darkness. Thaly pulled her arms in tight to ward off the cold wind and waited for the thunder to arrive. She wished they'd packed coats among the supplies that had been hidden in their temporary camp. Behind her, Tom, Grin and Jacob dropped off to sleep. She smiled to herself as all three of them began a chorus of snoring that reverberated around the shelter. "Anybody hunting us is going to hear that all the way from Sardis."

The storm passed over and the night went quiet and still, nothing to disrupt Thaly's thoughts. She yawned and rested her back against the stump of a dead tree, stretching her legs out front. How long would Tom and Grin stay? she wondered. They didn't seem in a hurry to leave. And now Jacob had assigned her as Tom's trainer. What purpose did that serve? She wasn't ready to train anyone, especially given her proneness to foolish acts that put her and others in danger. That wasn't exactly leading by example. But Jacob must have his reasons. He must see something in her and Tom that she missed. With enemies closing in, keeping the group together appeared to be the right call for now. Even better if all of them could fight.

Thaly slumped against the tree, fighting hard to stay awake. But tired eyes won this battle.

*　*　*　*

Tom had a restless sleep on hard ground. He woke often, shivering from the cold. The season had changed dramatically with the storm. Grin had told him that this season was called guma; the Erstürmen called it the storm season. It would be followed by ngurung-ginya, the long dark, which Tom assumed was winter. After the dark came mumbal, the season of blossoms, dhawura, a short season of strong winds, then the growing season of yirra followed by the harvest season of gawimarra.

In between sleep, Tom thought about home. In his mind, he watched kangaroos grazing in the paddocks next to the rocky scrub. Threw a tennis ball against the chimney of a brick barbeque and hit the rebound with his cricket bat, all the time keeping score. Laughed at his mum dancing in the loungeroom to some silly song about cops and robbers, and cringed over a phone call made to his latest crush. The fun, the awkwardness, the confused insecurity of teenage years. Tom longed for those times. In this complicated and dangerous new world, he felt like a character in a play, as if none of it could possibly be real.

What if he found Nanna's murderer? Could he really kill someone if he had to? What does that feel like? The thought terrified him even more than being chased by a tainted grell. Grin and the rebels offered protection, but few answers. Tom desperately needed to make sense of the events swirling around him.

He reached into his pocket and pulled out his white hanky, embroidered by his Nanna and pressed into his hand by his loving mother when he left home. He wrapped and unwrapped the hanky around his thumb, pulling it tight in case this really was all a dream.

Would his mum wake him up in the morning?

Half-asleep, he rolled onto his side. Something sharp dug into his back. He reached around to move it out of the way, but it stuck fast in his skin. *Must be jammed in the ground.* Tom opened bleary eyes and sat up to see if he could deal with the source of his discomfort. Through the dull predawn light, a tiny shape emerged at the entrance to the shelter. Tom rubbed the sleep from his eyes, then jumped out of his skin.

"Shit. Wake up! Wake up! There's someone here!" Tom yelled in English, forgetting where he was.

Grin and the rebels stirred. More shapes, covered in short, dark fur, arrived to block the entrance. All of them carried spears in clawed hands.

"Wake up! There's more of them," said Tom, reverting back to Erstürmen.

"What?" Jacob yawned.

Thaly grabbed her sword. The shapes squealed. One of them thrust a spear at her hand, knocking the sword to the ground.

Jacob raised his arms in surrender. "We don't want any trouble. We're just seeking shelter from the rain. We'll be going now." More stone-tipped spears invaded the shelter, pinning the four companions against the back wall. The small creatures yabbered among themselves in a language foreign to Tom.

"What do you want?" asked Thaly.

A dozen spears surrounded Grin, trapping him in a pointed prison. The grell held his arms high. "I think...I think they are mouldewerps".

The creatures responded to Grin's voice with a cacophony of squeals and sharp jabs towards the grell's body.

Dawn broke and more mouldewerps came running up the slope and into the shelter. One of them, the tallest of the bunch, yelled in Erstürmen, "I smell a grell! I smell a grell in our dwell!"

The tall werp, standing as high as Tom's waist, rushed into the middle of the shelter. "I knew it. I knew it. A grell. I smell a grell. My nose is never wrong."

A handful of werps bounced around outside the shelter, hollering to their companions in a riotous commotion. Others kept their rudimentary, but effective weapons trained on Grin.

"Who owns this grell?" asked the tall werp.

Tom spoke up, "No-one *owns* him."

"A wild grell. Much more dangerous. Much more dangerous. *Hungrier.*"

"I am no danger to you," said Grin.

"Can't be trusted. We don't trust grells!"

"You should trust, Grin. He's my friend," said Tom.

"Grells hunt and eat werps. Always have. Always will."

"Not Grin."

"Grell expert, are you? Tell us why we shouldn't stick you here?"

"Grin is our ally. He's joined us to defeat the Erstürmen and take back these lands for grells and werps alike." Jacob lowered his hands. He raised them again when the stone tip of a wooden spear jabbed into his stomach.

"Ha. Take back what is not yours. Mouldewerps here long before grells *and* rebels."

"Listen, we're all in this together," said Thaly. "We should join forces to defeat the invaders."

"Erstürmen leave werps alone. Grells eat werps. Hunted us from our dwells. Now we hide in the hills for fear of being grell dinner."

"Sometimes it's important to forgive past trespasses. Look to the future." Jacob's argument didn't appear to have the desired effect.

"Only future for you will be decided by the elders." The tall werp, the only one to speak Erstürmen it seemed, signalled to his companions and they tied Grin's hands behind his back.

The tiny creatures collected all the weapons and supplies and herded Tom, Grin and the rebels out of the shelter and down the hill face.

"Where are you taking us?" asked Thaly.

"We need to confine this grell. Then the elders will decide what to do with all of you. Trespassing on mouldewerp land, using a sacred shelter. These are serious offences." The tall werp stopped in front of Thaly and gave her a long sniff. "You are in much trouble, rebel Dobunni woman. Much trouble."

Jacob interjected, "We're being tracked by Erstürmen scouts."

"Yes, yes, yes. We've dealt with them. They won't be bothering anyone. You're being followed by something much more dangerous than Erstürmen. Another grell. Yes, another *horrible* grell. The white one. Him we can't deal with. But he won't find our dwell. It's hidden well — from sight and smell!" The tall mouldewerp barked out orders in the strange language and the werps marched Tom and the others down the slope.

*   *   *   *

Tom's feet ached from walking all day. He was sure the mouldewerps were marching their captives around in circles to disorient them. More than once, they'd passed familiar scars in the rock faces, and places where the shrubs thinned for easier passage. On either side of Tom trotted one of the short, rotund creatures, spears always ready to prod him in the right direction, the tops of their heads bobbing next to his knee. Small, dark eyes sat either side of an elongated nose, shiny and black, that the werps used constantly to test the air around them. Tom thought the mouldewerps looked like a cross between a wombat and an echidna walking on two legs.

In the late afternoon, the werps marched their prisoners into a depression surrounded by dense vegetation. They descended a steep ridge before the vegetation cleared, revealing large holes dug under shrubs and rocks, and sometimes in dirt embankments. It reminded Tom of rabbit warrens, except the holes were much bigger, large enough for him to crawl into if he kept low. Out from the holes peered curious faces of salmon pink, and probing proboscises bending in all directions and sniffing; forever sniffing.

The armed werps halted and encircled their captives. They tied Grin to the trunk of a dead tree and forced Jacob and Thaly to crawl on their stomachs into a shallow hole in one of the embankments. Guards stood to attention outside the hole.

The tall werp turned to Tom. "Your fellow invaders will stay here. You come with me."

"I'm not an invader." Tom chased after the werp as he marched away. "Wait up! What's your name?"

"My proper name would be too hard for your rudimentary mind to process. Instead, you can call me Dwarrow."

"Are you the only one who speaks Erstürmen?"

"I'm one of the few who need to. I have dealings. Many important dealings. Because I'm small, you think I'm of no consequence."

"No, I don't think that."

"I speak many different tongues. Easier to hear your enemies' plans. One day the Erstürmen will come for us. I need to know when." Dwarrow scurried onwards until he came to a hole in an embankment between two rocks. "*Ahhh*, here we are. My dwell. Follow my nose!" Dwarrow ducked into the burrow.

Tom baulked at the tight fit. The claustrophobic tunnel looked uninviting, but he didn't have much choice. He got on his hands and knees and crawled into the pitch-black hole, his back pressing against its roof. Dwarrow had disappeared into the darkness, though Tom could still hear the werp snuffling up ahead.

"How do you see where you're going?"

"We use our nose. I can find my way easily enough following the smells. Soil smells, roots smell, bushes smell, rocks smell."

"Rocks smell?"

"Yes, yes, yes, rocks smell. And grells. Grells smell the worst."

"Grin won't hurt you."

"The assembly of elders will decide. We have other things to discuss. Do you have a name?"

"My name's Tom. I'm the son of a goat herder from...."

Tom stopped short as he crashed into something in the dark.

"Ow!" said Dwarrow. "You've squashed my foot."

"You didn't tell me you were stopping."

Silence filled the cramped tunnel, the darkness pressing in around Tom. And then the sniffing started. Tom thought he felt Dwarrow's wet nose trace across every part of his face.

"No," said Dwarrow. "No herder are you. No Dobunni either. No Erstürmen. You have a strange smell. I noticed it when we first met. A *very* strange smell."

Tom's heart skipped as he persisted with the lie. "I'm a herder's son from The Feign."

"My nose never falters. All is revealed in the darkness. Your smell is not from these lands. Not at all."

Tom panicked. Dwarrow didn't believe his story, but he didn't have another one, other than the truth. Could he trust this creature?

"I smell fear," said Dwarrow. "Are you afraid?"

"Yes."

"Don't be. Yet. You're safe for now. Eroberung has lost your scent."

Dwarrow shuffled ahead and Tom crawled after him. "How do you know about the tainted grell?"

"I'm a simple werp living in a humble dwell. But I have dealings.

Important dealings." Dwarrow lowered his voice, "I even deal with grells, but don't tell my neighbours."

"Then you could help Grin."

"The elders will decide. Not me."

"Where are we going?"

"Somewhere away from prying noses."

The heavy smother of the narrow, musty tunnel gave way to fresher air. Tom reached up but couldn't feel anything. He tried to stand, cracking his head on the roof. Nursing a bruised crown, Tom squatted in the pitch-black listening to Dwarrow shuffling about nearby.

"Is this a room?"

"Yes, yes. There, you're learning to use your nose."

All of a sudden, a bright light illuminated the darkness. Tom shielded his eyes from the glare.

Dwarrow held a small stone in the blush-coloured palm of his clawed hands. His wet nose glistened under the light and shadows hovered over his face as the werp brought the stone up to his tiny black eyes. "*Look at this.* I'm the only mouldewerp who has one of these."

Tom's eyes adjusted to the new light. "What is it?"

"A grell gave it to me. They call it a giba. A magic stone. Sacred."

"I've seen one. In Grin's milbi."

"*Hmph.* Well, mine's especially special. Sacred magic. That's what I was told."

The light of the giba revealed the inside of Dwarrow's dwell. Dirt shelves built into the soil walls housed clay pots and dried plants. In the corner was a depression in the floor lined with feathers and grass where Tom assumed the mouldewerp slept. Connecting passages led off in various directions, from which came wafts of fresh air that caressed Tom's sore head.

"The passages lead to my neighbours. We're all connected underground you know. Are you hungry?" Dwarrow sat on a stool in the middle of the tiny room.

"Yes."

"Do you have something to trade?"

"Trade?"

"Yes, yes, yes. Something to trade for delicious food. Takes time to prepare you know."

Tom patted his clothes. He had nothing in particular he could do without. He placed his hand on his hanky and rubbed the thin white cotton between his fingers. *My last vestige of home. Am I that hungry?*

"How about a sharp knife, will that do?" Tom pulled the knife that Thaly had given him out of the scabbard strapped to his thigh.

Dwarrow snatched the knife and brought it to his nose. "*Hmm.* The guards should have confiscated this already. With the other weapons. It smells like rebels. It will have to do. I'll keep it. You have a trade." Dwarrow stashed the knife near his bed and fossicked around one of the shelves, passing Tom a wooden bowl.

Tom didn't recognise the watery contents of the bowl, but starvation overrode his caution. He brought the bowl to his lips and tipped the liquid into his mouth. An acrid sting burned his nostrils and made his eyes water. He spat the food back into the bowl. "*Errrk.* What am I eating?"

"Fat, jimin grubs sautéed in their own juice, and boiled scallob leaves. Very tasty. Very tasty."

"It tastes and smells horrible."

"*Hmph.* You don't know good food. You need to train your nose better." Dwarrow squinted at Tom. "Do you trust your friends?"

"O-o-of course. Grin saved my life. Jacob and Thaly helped us escape from Süden Forst. I-I think I trust them."

"What were you doing in Süden Forst?"

Tom berated himself for letting the information slip. The more he talked to Dwarrow the harder it was to keep the pretence up. The shadows in the room started to dance around his eyes. Nausea threatened.

Dwarrow didn't bother waiting for Tom's response to his question. "Dobunni rebels only care about one thing. Kill Erstürmen and take back Enthilen."

"Why do they call this land Enthilen?"

"Erstürmen named it. It has to do with the history of this place, from long ago. The grells call it something else."

"Nguram-bang."

"You speak Grellian. I should have guessed. You've spent too much time with the giants." Dwarrow sniffed along one of his shelves. "Ah, here it is." He grabbed Tom's hand and pressed a large metal key into his palm.

Tom flinched as the key dug into his scar. "What do I do with this?"

"Keep it safe. Very safe. One day you'll need it."

In the sombre light of the small room, Tom became overwhelmed. He started to count the clay pots on Dwarrow's shelves.

"Thirteen pots, seven pouches, four cups — for when I have guests, five bowls...why are you counting?" asked Dwarrow.

"It's something I do when I can't cope. Try to stop myself being afraid."

"Then you have lots of counting ahead of you."

"I don't understand what's going on, Dwarrow. Can you help me?" Tom started to tell the mouldewerp the truth.

Dwarrow cut him off. "Don't reveal your truth so easily. Does the grell know?"

"Yes, Grin and his father, Frennan. They call me the birraman."

"The birraman. The traveller. If you were only that, your troubles would be much less. What about the rebels?"

"They don't know."

"Good. They shouldn't know. Too easily corrupted. The man already suspects something. I can smell his uncertainty. The girl, she wants to appear strong, but she wears a mask. When the mask comes off, she'll be broken and someone will need to fix her. They mustn't find out about you yet. They'll use you in their rebellion."

"Please help me, Dwarrow."

"I'm a simple werp living in a dark…"

"But you have dealings. You know things. You see…smell things. Why does a tainted grell hunt me?"

"Stay away from the tainted grells. They are slaves to a brutal master."

"I saw horrible things in Süden Forst. A priest prayed for the return of the Divine Creator. They sacrificed children in his name."

Dwarrow sighed. "I can't tell you all I know about these things. It would cripple your mind."

"At least tell me something. Have I been brought to Enthilen for a reason?"

"Almost certainly yes, although I can't be sure what that reason is, or who benefits from your presence here."

"And do you know who killed my grandmother or how I can get home?"

"No. That is beyond me. I know nothing of where you've come from, so have no hope of returning you."

"Can you tell me more about this world I'm in? I think the Erstürmen call it Ostamp?"

"Yes, yes, yes. That's right. The Erstürmen call all the known lands and seas Ostamp. That is where you are now, although, like all worlds, it will be what you make of it. At the dawn of time, when the eternal battle between good and evil began, many worlds were created. Some by those with good intentions and some by those with wicked intentions. In the end, it didn't matter. All worlds have good and evil, even the world that exists inside your mind. The Erstürmen believe that Ostamp was created by Volerdie, the Divine Creator, but not through his divinity alone. In the time before creation, so the Erstürmen legend goes, Volerdie shadowed another creator. In the darkness, he watched this creator fashion a world of mountains, valleys and oceans, and all the creatures that lived there. Volerdie became jealous. He wanted such a world to rule over, so he copied what he saw. However, there was one creature that Volerdie struggled to replicate; those that the other creator made in his own image."

"Do you mean humans? Dobunni, Erstürmen."

"Humans? Is that what you call them? Volerdie repeatedly tried and failed, resulting in abominations that he despised, especially the grells."

"The grells are Volerdie's attempt to make humans?"

"Grells and mouldewerps too. Maybe there are others. The Erstürmen say we are Volerdie's failures. That's why they hate the grells so much, and why one day, I fear, they'll turn their attention towards us." Dwarrow paused and sipped from his bowl.

"Volerdie didn't give up after his so-called failures. Eventually, what you call humans came into this world. The Erstürmen believe that they're the pinnacle of Volerdie's creation. For a time, Volerdie ruled over these lands, sitting on the throne of the dead in a city now lost. But he was never satisfied with his creation. He still coveted the world made by the other creator. The Erstürmen say that he abandoned Ostamp so he could fight for control over this other world. They want him to return, though. They desperately want him to return. When Volerdie returns, daylight will turn to dark and in the darkness the faithful will find paradise. That is what they believe."

"I read about Volerdie in a book. Where I come from, we also have stories that talk of gods and creators. A lot of people believe these stories, but I don't."

"You don't need to believe, Tom. But you must understand that there's a purpose to these stories, beyond what you see at the surface. How they're interpreted can decide the fate of this world and yours. Some use the stories to secure power and harm the ones they call unbelievers. If you understand the meaning of the stories, and how they might be interpreted differently, only then can you fight against those who would use the stories to oppress others."

The hole closed in on Tom. Sweat dripped into his eyes, as a heavy burden of responsibility threatened to crush him.

Dwarrow sighed. "I've said enough. Speaking of such things makes me weary." The werp leaned forward and placed a clawed hand on Tom's arm. "The eyes, Tom. Where are the dark eyes?"

"I think Eroberung has them."

"Oh. That is not good. That is not good at all."

~Chapter 19~

Straddling his heavily armoured destrier, Badulf surveyed the muddy battlefield from behind the safety of a makeshift palisade. Catching his reflection in the polished umbo of a metal shield, he barely recognised himself. Skin once taut with subcutaneous fat now drooped from his bones as the demands of war took their toll, every defeat seemingly etched in deep recesses criss-crossing his face. He almost fell from his horse, daydreaming about a victory that was always out of reach.

Laid out before him, the Riverlands battlefield of Flüsse had been churned over from the panicked hooves of war beasts and the leather boots of weary fighters. Puddles littered the field like pit traps waiting for an unsuspecting footfall. An occasional blade of grass fluttered in the stiff breeze; a lonely survivor waving the white flag of surrender. The woodland surrounding the field burned and tendrils of silver-grey smoke wrapped themselves around the bodies of dead Erstürmen soldiers like smouldering funeral shrouds. Badulf grimaced as the screams of the injured pierced the smoky haze, disrupting a moment of calm before the next onslaught ensued.

Like giant ghosts silhouetted against the haze, grell slaves lumbered through the carnage. They cleared the battlefield of the dead and piled the bodies in grotesque heaps, setting fire to the inert flesh with flaming torches. Enemy casualties trapped on the field were dispatched with a halberd to the throat by the slaves' overseers.

Mounted next to Badulf was Willem, one of his lieutenants. Both had been fighting the Riverlands War since the beginning, seven seasons past. They'd hoped for a quick and easy victory. At first, it appeared their prayers would be answered as the Riverlands farmers were taken by surprise at the size and ferocity of the Erstürmen attack. But the tide of battle soon turned when the farmers gained an unexpected ally; skilled fighters from an unknown land. Now, the Erstürmen soldiers played a waiting game, holding their ground until the long-promised reinforcements arrived from Sardis.

At one end of the battlefield, twenty Erstürmen archers with crossbows took cover in a shoulder-high trench dug into the black soil. Each archer had two bows and a 'loader'; another soldier whose job was to load the crossbow after each shot. This avoided the long delays between firing that were characteristic of this weapon and made archers vulnerable to counter attack.

The trench sergeant shouted and the archers positioned their crossbows over the lip of the channel, aiming them at the field. In the distance, barely visible over the crest of a rise, Badulf saw the heads of peasant farmers marching to battle bobbing determinedly towards their enemy. The archers held steady, waiting for the farmers to come into range, and the signal to fire. The grell slaves and their masters scattered as the farmers approached.

"Fire!" yelled the trench sergeant.

Badulf jolted upright as the archers loosed their arrows at the marching farmers. Most of the projectiles fell short of their targets. The farmers halted their advance and stood defiant with the blunt end of their spears, sickles and pitchforks planted firmly in the soft mud.

Badulf swung his arm forward; the signal to attack. From behind the palisade, charged thirty-six horsemen with swords drawn. Polished chanfrons adorned the foreheads of the swift, strong horses, the crinets covering their necks glistening in the sun. The battle cries of the riders seemed to fuel the adrenalin of their mounts, which galloped towards the enemy with madness in their eyes. The farmers scattered into the burning woodland. Behind them, from below the crest of the hill, emerged a wave of soldiers clad in light, flowing garments and riding strange beasts.

Badulf groaned at the sight of this new enemy. Another battle almost certainly lost, he thought.

Nevertheless, the Erstürmen cavalry continued its charge. The lightly-clad fighters turned their odd beasts away from the assault, drawing the Erstürmen into the middle of the battlefield. Thick mud sucked on the hooves of the horses, as the mounts struggled to gain traction. From behind the blackened trees of the woodland immediately north and south of the field, came scores of enemy riders. They surrounded the Erstürmen and announced the trap with blood-curdling screams.

Badulf remained indifferent despite the inevitable slaughter. "What *are* those banshees riding, lieutenant?"

"I think they're called kamels, Field Commander."

"Brutish, lumbering beasts. I've never seen fighters like these. We need to capture one of them for interrogation."

"It's rare for them to engage us during the day, commander. They're getting bolder as the war goes in their favour."

Badulf frowned. "Where are our reinforcements?"

"Our scouts say they'll be here before sunset."

"Signal the archers to advance. See if we can't save at least some of our cavalry."

Detached from the carnage, Badulf followed the battle for a moment longer then turned his war horse towards the main Erstürmen encampment.

* * * *

"Have the scouts returned from the escarpment, Segie?" asked Jurelle.

"No, General."

"Then we can assume the worst. Our enemy may well have been watching our progress."

"I doubt it was Riverlands farmers, General. They would have ambushed us by now."

"You're right. Maybe it was the Dobunni."

The Erstürmen reinforcements led by Jurelle veered west of the Riverlands escarpment and marched into the delta towards the front-line battlefields of Flüsse. They had already passed through a number of small villages currently under Erstürmen control. On either side of the track, thinning woodland gave way to green fields and sparkling waterways.

Jurelle began to understand why the Riverlands farmers would protect such a place. He turned in his saddle to face his trusted sergeant riding beside him. "What circle were you born in, Segie?"

"The fifth circle, General. My father was a carpenter. He was so proud when I joined the King's Shield. Got to see his son move up to the second circle. Make a good home for my family."

"How are your family?"

"As well as can be expected. We ask the Divine Creator for his blessing every day and my wife and children attend kirika when they can."

"Do you think that will help?"

"It's blasphemy to think otherwise, General." Segie glanced behind him. Jurelle did the same. The soldiers following were out of earshot.

Segie faced forward, his body slumping in the saddle. "Food's still scarce, despite our prayers. My wife works as a seamstress for extra coin. My sons wish to join the King's Shield like their father. My daughters are well schooled. I should be thankful for that. I hope one day they become wives in the inner circle. Then they'll want for nothing."

"Nothing but freedom," Jurelle mumbled under his breath, before approaching a more delicate subject. "What's the feeling among the men about the fate of the kingdom?"

"It's unwise to discuss such things, General."

"Your thoughts are safe with me." As Jurelle waited for an answer, he could almost hear the cogs turning inside Segie's mind.

The sergeant looked over his shoulder again. "There's a rift in the men. A few say Ewald shouldn't wait for the age of succession to abdicate. He should do it before the next two harvest seasons have passed and hand the throne to Prince Adalwolf. Men are losing faith in the strength of King Ewald."

"Do they think Adalwolf will be a better leader?"

"He couldn't be a worse leader, could he?"

Jurelle locked eyes with his sergeant. "There's more on your mind, sergeant. I can sense it."

Segie's chest rose and fell with a deep breath. He leaned closer to Jurelle. "There's a few men who talk in whispers and keep secrets. They think I don't notice, but the whispers are getting louder."

"What do they say?"

"Usurpers stalk the halls of the inner circle and in Laodicea. Power and allegiances are shifting. Men don't want to get caught on the wrong side."

A scout interrupted the General and his sergeant. "The main camp is coming up, General Jurelle."

"Inform the men, Segie. We need to find somewhere to pitch our tents."

*　*　*　*

Badulf lounged in an ornate chair of carved timber covered in the hide of a griffin. He carried the chair with him to every battle. It'd been in his family for generations. He sneered at General Jurelle Stansfield standing in front of him next to the battle table, the irony of the moment not lost. Badulf's family had skinned a griffin, even if he could not.

Badulf had been a lieutenant in the inner circle when King Ewald brought the leader of the Dobunni rebels into the fold. He signed a parchment with a handful of other commanders protesting against the move. The king ignored their pleas. Jurelle remained in the inner circle and Ewald made the ex-rebel leader a General, one rank above Badulf.

Both Badulf and Jurelle had seen fifty-one harvest seasons, though the passing of time had been a lot kinder to the Traitor General. He still walked tall and straight, and clean, tan skin clung tight to the muscles of his face, accentuated by piercing brown eyes.

Lots of easy yarles in the inner circle, thought Badulf. Not enough on the battlefield.

Badulf leaned forward as Jurelle shuffled a handful of miniature wooden soldiers around the battle table, planning the next offensive in the failing Riverlands War.

Jurelle looked up from the table. "How many men do you have left, commander?"

"Less than two hundred."

"How many did you start with?"

"What are you implying, General? I know the war's going poorly. It took a season for the king to send reinforcements. We've battled bravely with little support."

"Well, support is here now. What is the strength of your enemy?"

"It's hard to tell. They attack mostly at night in small groups, raiding our outer defences. We've even had attacks here at the encampment."

"The farmers are led by banshees, General, banshees riding kamels." Willem studied the battle table with apparent interest, at least more than he showed when Badulf planned the attacks.

"I don't believe in banshees, lieutenant." Jurelle scratched his head. "If they're riding kamels, these fighters must have come across the desert wasteland of Grōz Wüste. I've heard tales of a shining city where Grōz Wüste meets the sea."

"Germalians?" asked Badulf. "Is that who you think we're fighting? Germalia is many days ride west from here. Why come and fight in the Riverlands for these peasants?"

"I'm sure they have their reasons, commander. It matters little now. They're our enemy, and they're defeating us. What do we know about their defences?"

"We've sent scouts. None have returned. It seems their camp is well defended."

"They're outwitting you at every turn. A new battle plan is required."

Badulf bristled and slumped back in his chair.

Jurelle placed more miniatures on the battle table, then turned to his sergeant. "Segie, find out what you can about our enemy. Send men to scout their base camp and defences, and make sure they return. We prepare for an assault in two moons."

* * * *

The Erstürmen commanders perched on a ridge overlooking the main camp of the Riverlands farmers and their allies. The reinforcements had easily carved their way through the enemy outposts. Jurelle shifted in Sphinux's saddle, uncomfortable about the ease with which his army progressed so close to the farmers' stronghold. Nevertheless, he needed to take the battle to the enemy to secure victory. In front of the commanders, across an open field, stood a makeshift fort with timber and cobb walls as high as two men. At the top of the front wall, a rudimentary rampart supported archers and lookouts, and along the length of the wall's base, a palisade deterred charging soldiers. The farmers and their allies had retreated into the fort.

A disquieting tension descended over the Erstürmen ranks as Jurelle pondered his next move. His first concern was the field in front of the fort. "There'll be pitfall traps in the field that will swallow unsuspecting riders and foot soldiers. We need to lure them out from behind their defences so we can locate the position of the traps."

"Our scouts say the defences are weaker from the west," said Segie.

"Send a troop of riders there, Segie. Have them wait until the sun is directly overhead, then launch an attack on the western defences."

Jurelle turned to Badulf. "Send your archers to the edge of the field and have them set a fire in the front wall."

"Is that wise?" asked Badulf. "There's no cover in the field."

"I'm hoping it will force our enemy to show their hand. We need to know what surprises they have in store for us."

Badulf ordered the remainder of his longbow archers into the field. They sent flaming arrows towards the fort. A few hit their mark and small fires took hold in the timber wall. A volley of arrows flew from the ramparts, felling a third of the Erstürmen archers, but enough remained to loose further barrages of flaming projectiles. As fires spread up the walls of the fort, a wave of farmers rushed from the main gate and charged towards the Erstürmen archers. Jurelle's plan had the desired result.

"Watch them carefully, Segie. Draw a map of their movements in your mind." Jurelle ordered the archers to retreat and sent in a troop of foot soldiers to engage the farmers. As he expected, from the cover of dense vegetation to the south of the field, kamel riders charged into the fray. "Watch their course, Segie."

"We need to send in cavalry, General."

"Wait, commander. We've lured them out of the fort and they've shown us key defences." Jurelle glanced at the sky. "The attack on the western wall will begin soon."

"We can't wait much longer. Our men are being slaughtered."

"It's a cost we must bear. Ultimately, we'll win this battle."

Jurelle watched the kamel riders cut down the foot soldiers, piercing the gaps between the Erstürmen breastplates and plackarts with deft skill. As the battle ended, the mournful wail of a hurna filtered over the field and the kamel riders urged their mounts towards the west wall. The farmers retreated behind the palisade.

"Send down more archers."

"This is madness, General. You're repeating the same mistake."

"Send the archers, commander."

The Erstürmen longbows took up their position. The farmers charged again from behind the palisade, followed by more kamel riders from inside the fort.

"Watch how they move through the field," said Jurelle. "There are trap lines running east-west along the north and south boundaries of the field. The south line is breached there near that fallen tree. Segie, do you see that?"

"Yes, General. There's also a trap line running north-south in the centre of the field. It's breached in line with the main gate of the fort."

"Let's draw them closer. Have the archers retreat and order a small troop of foot soldiers to stand between us and them."

Jurelle's plan worked. The farmers and kamel riders engaged with the Erstürmen in hand-to-hand combat.

"Send more men into battle. Push the enemy towards the south."

The Erstürmen forced their enemy back and to the south of the battlefield.

"Send the undreds in, Segie. Have them attack from the south forest at the breach."

Undred riders charged from behind the commanders and galloped into the woodland south of the battlefield, the body of their mounts protected from sharp blades by thick leather tooled with intricate patterns of mythical creatures from ancient times. They turned their beasts directly north and rushed at the enemy, splitting the breach in the trap line almost perfectly. One rider misjudged the line and an undred disappeared into the ground, swallowed up by a pit trap camouflaged with branches and forest litter.

Perched on his horse next to Jurelle, Willem flinched as the trapped undred squealed. "Those pits have timber spikes at the bottom. Not a pleasant way to meet your end."

The undred's scream pierced the battlefield, and the farmers and their allies spun around to meet the new onslaught, but couldn't form ranks in time. In a long-practiced assault, the line of undred horns sliced through the enemy and impaled men and kamels with equal devastation.

"The battle is going well. We know where their strongest defences…" Jurelle stopped short as something flew past his face. It struck Badulf in the neck, his limp body tumbling from his horse. Willem and Segie also fell, throwing knives embedded in their chest.

"We're under attack," Jurelle yelled to the soldiers assembled at the base of the ridge. He turned to lead the counter-attack, but something smashed against his spangenhelm and his world went black before he hit the ground.

~Chapter 20~

Grin pressed his shoulder blades into the trunk of the dead tree to feel the ancient creature's strength, even though its life force had now faded. The final chorus of birdsong seduced his ears as the feathered creatures prepared to roost for the night. In the twilight, bats careered over his head in chaotic swoops searching silently for a winged meal. He immersed himself in the sights and sounds of this new environment, doing his best to connect with the nature of the landscape.

But thoughts of his forest home lingered at the back of his mind. The yurali bushes should have finished flowering by now. The leaves of the panalope tree would be dark red, falling to the ground with the slightest of breezes and covering the moss and lichen in a blanket of deep mahogany. Forest animals would be storing food or body fat in preparation for the long dark. And his father. His father would be alone in the milbi not knowing the fate of his son or the birraman that Grin had refused to abandon. The birraman who had disappeared with the tall werp. Another mystery to ponder in an ever more intricate web.

Grin tugged against the rope that bound his torso to the tree trunk. It didn't loosen. He smiled at his werp captors, trying to raise his spirits and reassure them he wasn't a threat. They replied with stern looks and whispers, and a lot of sniffing.

Cressets burning a smokeless resin encircled the dead tree and cast a dull light across the secluded vale that the mouldewerps called home. As evening fell, faint drumbeats drifted over the dwells. Mouldewerps shuffled out from their burrows, congregating around Grin. Between their tiny bodies he spotted Jacob and Thaly still kept prisoner in the cramped confines of the rock shelter. But Tom had not reappeared. Maybe the birraman had abandoned his grell friend?

The drumbeats stopped. Murmurs among the gathering faded. A lone voice wailed in the distance and a sharp and regular click echoed around the dwells. The crowd parted for a werp whose body had been smothered in red clay now dried and bound to her fur. The werp chanted and knocked together two polished sticks of resonant wood. Guided by the regular beats of the performer, ten mouldewerps with greying fur marched into the centre of the gathering and encircled Grin. They have arrived, he thought. The gathering of elders that would decide his fate.

Each elder carried a driftwood staff with the head carved into the shape of an animal. Grin recognised a few of the shapes; an owl, a lizard, a spider. The wailing and beating stopped. The ten elders simultaneously thrust their staffs into the ground, forming a circle of judgement. The crowd stood silent.

The eyes of the elders burrowed into Grin's mind. This new land had become something to dread.

A spine-chilling scream breached the stillness of the night and into the circle of elders leapt a werp. She thrust her spear menacingly towards Grin, dancing around him with manic fury. Each feint and taunt were accompanied by a yell of defiance rattling behind a wooden mask painted in ochre and carved with a predatory gape, pearl-white canines filed to flesh-piercing sharpness. A grass skirt swirled around her waist as she pirouetted in place, twirling the spear above her head. The stone tip drew blood as it grazed Grin's bare torso. The dancer spun madly, her frenzied pace building to a final crescendo before she collapsed with exhaustion at Grin's feet. One of the elders raised his hand and two werps came into the circle and carried her off.

Grin's heart almost burst from his chest, as if trying to escape the inevitable punishment. The still night offered no comfort. No hope for mercy. He gazed at the stars with distant eyes that saw no solace in the future. He needed to be saved, again. And there, on the fringe of the crowd, stood his only hope. Tom Anderson. The birraman.

*　*　*　*

Covered in dirt, Tom waved awkwardly at Grin. The expected smile of acknowledgement didn't come. He leaned down towards Dwarrow. "What's happening?"

"It's the assembly of elders. They will decide what to do with the grell and the rebels."

"What about me?"

"I've already spoken to them about you. You're free to go whenever you choose."

"I won't leave without my friends."

"You may have to."

An elder raised her hands to the sky and chanted in a strange language. "I don't understand what she's saying," said Tom.

"Our language is foreign to all but the mouldewerps of the Scaur Hills. The elder has announced that they will first decide what to do with the rebels. To identify a suitable punishment for their crimes."

"Jacob and Thaly aren't criminals."

"Ja-cob. A strange name. I smelled salt on his skin. He's from the Docklands in Laodicea."

"That's right. He's a good man, Dwarrow. Can't you tell the elders?

We made an honest mistake using your shelter, stumbling into your lands."

"I mustn't interfere with the judgement."

Tom peered over the tops of the werps' heads and fixed his gaze on Thaly. He whispered into Dwarrow's ear, as if the answer to his question might reveal a closely guarded secret. "What can you tell me about Thaly?"

"Her smell is ancient Dobunni mixed with an ancestry from a different culture. There's nobility in her blood, but it's tainted with anger and confusion, and the consuming desire for vengeance. If she cannot learn to control her fire, it will devour her."

*   *   *   *

Lying flat on her back, Thaly stretched her stiff body, fighting against the suffocation of the dirt hole, and berated her carelessness. She shouldn't have fallen asleep in the shelter. She should have been on watch. Seen the werps coming.

"Don't blame yourself. All of us were exhausted." Squeezed in tight next to her, Jacob rested on his stomach, seemingly engrossed in the werp ceremony.

Thaly raised her eyebrows.

Jacob smiled. "I know what you're thinking. We've been together long enough."

"Too long if you can read my mind." Thaly turned onto her stomach. "The crowd of werps keeps growing. How did so many remain hidden from us? Dobunni scouts have walked these hills for many seasons."

"I assumed the werps had vanished long ago. Out of mind, out of sight I guess."

Thaly pushed her feet against the back wall of the prison hole. "You're right, Jacob. There's something strange about Tom. How come he gets to stand there like one of them and we're forced to lie in the dirt?"

"It seems he's friends with grells *and* werps, though he claimed to have never seen these creatures before."

"Is he an Erstürmen spy?"

"I don't know, but I do know he's lying to us." Jacob raised himself onto his elbows and moaned. "My back's aching. Even if they let us go, I'm not sure I can walk anymore."

*　*　*　*

The night grew darker and Tom's eyes became heavy. "How long will the elders take to decide?"

"Oh, it could go on until sunrise, even longer," said Dwarrow.

"Can I talk to my friends?"

"You consider them your friends?"

Tom hadn't thought too much about this. Grin was his friend; he had no doubts about that, although he would always wonder why the grell befriended him, but Jacob and Thaly? At the moment, it seemed a friendship of convenience, more so for Tom and Grin rather than the rebels.

Dwarrow interrupted Tom's thoughts. "Regardless of the answer, you can't talk to anyone. You must not disrupt the dealings of the elders."

Tom slumped to the ground and closed his eyes. The rhythmic deliberations of the elders drifted into his unconscious and he fell into a half sleep, floating in a vast ocean like a piece of flotsam moving at the whim of unseen currents. Water soaked his body, weighing it down, pulling him towards the dark, cold depths. A hunched figure in the distance beckoned to him. His body went limp as he sank into the darkness. Suddenly, someone grabbed his arm and he gasped for air.

"Wait. Yes, I think they've made a decision," said Dwarrow.

"About Grin?"

"No, no, no. About the rebels." Dwarrow paused as the elders raised their staffs to the stars. "Good news. They're free to leave, but only under close guard until well out of scent of the dwells. And all their weapons and supplies must be forfeited. Oh, and if they ever return, they'll be executed. That's a better outcome than I expected. You should be thankful."

Tom smiled and waved a thumbs-up at Jacob and Thaly. His gesture didn't seem to please them.

Dwarrow tugged Tom's pant leg. "Now they're discussing the grell. This could take a while. You may wish to sleep again."

Tom fought to stay alert, for Grin's sake. Through the remainder of the night, the elders appeared to argue over what to do with their grell captive. In turn, each elder walked up to Grin and gave him a protracted and detailed sniff, their long noses bending in all directions to reach every crevice of his body. Grin always smiled when an elder approached.

A new morning dawned. The bats returned to their roosts and the birds stirred, ready for another day.

Dwarrow shook Tom's weary shoulder. "A decision has been made already."

"What have they decided?" Tom yawned.

"They have decided to cook him."

"What? No! You have to do something, Dwarrow."

"I can't do anything. I'm not ready to be a member of the assembly."

"They can't cook him."

Tom jumped to his feet and pushed his way through the crowd. He rushed over to Grin, latching onto the grell's arm. The elders clutched their staffs, as a disquiet rippled through the gathering.

"Have they made a decision, Tom? Is it good news?"

"No, it's stupid news. These werps don't know anything. I'll get you out of here, somehow."

Dwarrow pulled on Tom's tunic. "Tom, you must come away. The judgment has been made."

Tom spun around. "You talked to the elders about me, why can't you do the same for Grin? Why can't you tell them that he won't hurt anyone? You can't hold him responsible for the actions of his ancestors. That was a long time ago."

"It's not that simple."

"Dwarrow, can you ask the elders if I may speak on my own behalf?" Grin said.

Dwarrow scratched the pale skin showing through his furred stomach. "An intervention at this stage would be most inappropriate. I've already gained a reputation as a werp who engages in an array of inappropriate activities. One more might see me banished from the dwell."

Tom dropped to his knees and clutched Dwarrow's shoulders. "Please, Dwarrow. I can't complete this journey without Grin."

"*All right*, all right. But just this once. I don't want to be known as someone who harasses the elders or cavorts with grells." Dwarrow stomped off and began an animated conversation with the elders.

Tom sat in the dirt next to his friend. *This'll work out,* he thought. *It has to.*

After a short while, Dwarrow returned. "They will let Grin speak. I'll act as the translator. Don't say anything foolish, or threatening."

The elders crowded in around Grin. He spoke slowly so that Dwarrow could translate every word, "Dear wise and compassionate elders, I am Grinnian stone-grell. First born of Frennan and Mirrian, protector of Babir Birramal. Please accept my humblest and deepest apologies for trespassing on your land and using your shelter without permission. I am a young grell, naïve to the laws of mouldewerps. My father taught me to respect all living creatures that inhabit this world, and to love those who offer no threat to life. I apologise for the actions of all grells, including my ancestors, which have caused you so much grief and loss. I acknowledge that we blundered into the Dambay Plains with little concern for those who already called the plains home. We built our stone city and farmed the land, destroying the dwells of mouldewerps without regard for your future. We hunted mouldewerps for food. Sometimes for no reason at all. For all of these trespasses. For all of these inexcusable deeds, I am utterly ashamed and deeply sorry. If there is a way for me to right these wrongs, please charge me with this task. If the only way to alleviate your pain is through my death, then I will accept this judgement."

"No!" Tom cried, his outburst admonished by stern looks from the elders and Dwarrow.

Grin continued, "But if the wisdom of the elders sees another path for me, I will graciously accept it. We live in a different place to that of our ancestors. New invaders have stolen our lands. Mouldewerps hide in fear. Grells are massacred or enslaved. If I can arrest the wrongs of the past and protect mouldewerps in the future, then I offer my service to you until my life ends and my body rests in Bindari."

The crowd responded to Grin's words with silence. The elders talked among themselves for a short while and then spoke to Dwarrow.

"What did they say, Dwarrow?" Tom asked.

"They've decided to rest. The assembly will recommence when the sun is overhead."

Tom slumped to the ground, exhausted. The congregation disbanded.

Thaly called out from the prison burrow, "What's going on? Can we get out of this damn prison? Tom! Come and move these spear-wielding minikins."

*   *   *   *

The midday sun shone through tall cumulonimbus clouds that towered over the Scaur Hills like white and grey pyramids reaching towards another world somewhere beyond sight and memory. Tom sat next to Grin, resting his back against the dead tree, and counted the clouds as they drifted past.

"You are worried, Tom. You always count when you are worried."

"I don't know how to get you out of this, Grin."

"You have already saved my live once. It is too much to ask that you save it again. Maybe this is my recompense for the trespasses of my ancestors. Each new generation pays some of the debt incurred by their forebears."

"It's not fair. You haven't done anything wrong."

"The mouldewerps do not see it that way. I fear that I may not be able to join you on the rest of your journey."

Tom grasped Grin's forearm and whispered, "Dwarrow knows about me. He knows I'm different."

"I expected as much. My father always said that mouldewerps should never be underestimated. They can uncover secrets in the most unlikely of places."

"Dwarrow's coming."

The stout little werp strode towards Tom and Grin with his chin tilted to the clouds and his swollen chest hovering above his clawed feet. "I'm glad you haven't tried to escape. My assessment of you both wasn't misplaced. I have just returned from a private audience with the elders. We spoke about many things."

"What did they say about Grin?"

"Well, I've managed to avoid all your misadventures turning into a complete disaster, though some of the elders were not pleased about the final outcome."

"Get to the point, Dwarrow," said Tom.

Dwarrow cleared his throat and raised himself up on tiptoes. "My masterful negotiation skills have yielded a fruitful resolution for our, *errm*, I mean *your* grell friend. Grin has been placed at my service. He must report to me when summoned and fulfil any request I should give him. If he agrees to this, he'll be freed into my care, and I will be responsible for his actions." Dwarrow leaned in towards Grin and whispered, "This is the best outcome I could negotiate."

Grin beamed. "Master Dwarrow, I offer you my service without reservation."

"*Hmm.* I prefer *Lord* Dwarrow."

Down on his knees, Tom wrapped the tiny werp in a relieved hug and nearly knocked him over.

"*Hellloooooo.* We're still stuck in this damn hole. Ow." Thaly cried as the point of a mouldewerp spear dug into her side.

The mouldewerps freed their captives. Tom, Grin and the rebels spent a restful day and evening, feasting on whatever food they could stomach after learning quickly that the werp diet is an acquired taste. Dwarrow sat with his new acquaintances and appeared to revel in their stories of adventure. Most of the other werps kept their distance, but those that passed by always sniffed the air around the guests, as if searching for the scent of trouble.

The next morning, the four companions were brought before the elders for a final farewell. This time, Dwarrow translated mouldewerp into Erstürmen. "We accept your apology for your trespass, past and present. We will allow you to continue your journey. Speak not of your time here or try to find us again. There are others with less noble intentions who may seek us out. You will be guided from our dwell by one of our most knowledgeable residents."

"Who are they referring to?" asked Jacob

"They are referring to me," replied Dwarrow. "I will accompany you for a time. I have to keep my nose on my new grell assistant, after all."

Two werps joined Dwarrow to help lead Tom, Grin and the rebels away from the dwell. They stumbled along a torturous, winding path, the werps poking their guests with spears if they strayed too far in the wrong direction.

"Do you know where you're going?" asked Thaly.

"We're following my nose," said Dwarrow. "It's never led me astray yet." He grasped the smooth shaft of his walking stick and marched ahead.

"This is the blind leading the blind." Jacob staggered forward.

Dwarrow called over his shoulder, "Shall I return you to your prison, rebel soldier?"

"No thank you. We appreciate any help."

The group trudged after Dwarrow until midday. Then the two werp guards disappeared into the shrubs.

Jacob turned full circle. "This area is not familiar to me. Which way to our camp?"

"I'll lead you there. Easy to find. Smelly place. Very smelly. I can smell all that Dobunni stink from here!" Dwarrow pranced onwards, but his foot tripped on a rock. He fell forward, skidding along the ground on his portly stomach, his walking stick clattering across the stony path. "*Arrh!* I have dirt up my nose. My nose is blocked. I'm all, all... discombobulated!"

Jacob, Thaly, Grin and Tom burst out laughing.

~Chapter 21~

"Rostard. *Rostarrrrd!* Where *is* that warlock?" Ewald stumbled around the throne room in a drunken stupor, a half-empty barrel of meduz rocking on the floor as he staggered past. The news of his brothers' deaths had crumbled the last defence against a swelling paranoia. "They'll come for me next. Me next! I know it. Where's the damn soothsayer? How do I escape death?"

Hunfrid thrust his arm out to stop his king from toppling over. "He's on his way, Majesty."

Ewald spun around, knocking over a vase containing the ashes of his great grandfather, King Faramund, the Erstürmen king who had led his subjects from Nordland and first settled Enthilen. The porcelain vessel smashed into pieces and a cloud of ash settled on the tiled floor. Ewald didn't flinch. He had abandoned all pretence of caring for the history of Erstürmen culture. A long breath whistled through his lips as he hissed, "Dobunni assassins. Everywhere. They murdered my brothers. My beloved brothers. All three gone in one...foul...swipe." Ewald bent over and vomited next to the throne.

Rostard hurried into the room. "I'm here, my liege."

Ewald grabbed the soothsayer's shirt in a clenched fist and wrenched him towards his face. "Finally...finally...you show yourself. Where've you been hiding?"

"I've been consulting the giests for guidance, Majesty."

"Volerdie has abandoned me, Rostard. The Divine Creator has abandoned the king."

Anselm lifted his head. "Volerdie does not abandon those who offer appropriate worship, Sire."

"Are you saying I'm a heathen? How dare you!" Ewald swung at the pontifical curate, striking nothing but air as Anselm swayed out of the path of the flailing arm.

Ewald tumbled to the floor. He crawled over the painted tiles on hands and knees, head hanging between his shoulders, spittle and vomit dripping from his beard and bile burning the back of his throat. "What do you know about the death of my brothers? What do any of you know? All of you are assassins...waiting to thrust your blade into my spine... planning my downfall. My carcass...picked clean by bloodied vultures... *belch*." Ewald slumped to the floor, legs splayed out in front, leaning back on his hands, royal robes flung over the tiles like a discarded rag. He cast pleading eyes towards the soothsayer. "Speak to me, Rostard. How do I escape the clutches of my pursuers? What do the giests say?"

Rostard placed his long, spidery arms behind his back, as if to conceal the hands of treachery.

Ewald's blurred mind latched onto the thought. "What are you hiding, Rostard? What are you keeping from me?"

Rostard shuffled from one foot to the other and glanced at Hunfrid. Ewald caught the acknowledgement. He moved his inquisition to the Master of Executions. "I knew I couldn't trust you, Hunfrid. I knew it. You're all...*belch*...all conspiring against me. Hatching your little plans."

Hunfrid puffed out his chest. "I've always been loyal to you, Sire, and I always will."

Rostard crouched next to the throne.

He's got a knife! thought Ewald. This spider has a sting. "Get away from me." He scuttled his bottom along the tiles as Rostard tried to place a hand on his shoulder.

"I'm your soothsayer, Majesty. Not an assassin. I've consulted the giests, but their guidance is shrouded in uncertainties."

Ewald relaxed. "Their guidance is always shrouded. An imbecile could have made that judgement."

"The desires of those who directly serve the Creator are a mystery to mortal men. Their true intentions often hidden." Anselm flinched, as if Ewald would spring to his feet and attempt another strike.

But Ewald's mind had other concerns. "Rostard cavorts with spirits all the time, don't you, Rostard? You speak with them as if you're a demon yourself."

"I have visions, Majesty. The giests guide me through these visions."

"Dammit! What do they show you? Who seeks to hasten my end?"

"I saw giants with tainted skin heralding war, famine and death. A city wreathed in fire and weeping royal blood. And the coming of a horde."

"Death stalks me. Nothing's more certain. Sardis will fall. It's not safe here...but...I've nowhere else to go. Laodicea..."

"War is upon Laodicea, Majesty."

Hunfrid's announcement interrupted Ewald's train of thought. For a moment, he considered the protection of his subjects. "War?"

"Barbarians, in leagues with Dobunni rebels no doubt. They'll seek to destroy the King's Quarter. It's not safe for you there."

Ewald stared at a painted tile on the floor, depicting the coronation of his father, King Oldaric. "Not safe...not safe anywhere."

Rostard stood and rested his hand on the top of the pedestal where the vase of King Faramund's ashes had sat. "The giests also showed me a towering spire surrounded by water."

Ewald's mind grasped for a straw that might lead to his salvation. "Hurst? Is that what they mean?"

"I cannot guess, Majesty."

Ewald clutched the straw. "*Yeesss.* Hurst. The impenetrable finger of rock in the Nordargen Sea. My grandmother told me...that...that griffins nested on its peak. She said there were rooms built into the rock. *Secret rooms. I'd be safe there.*" Ewald slapped his forehead. He'd announced a potential hiding place to everyone in the room. He attempted a drunken misdirection. "Hurst...it's too far away. A long and dangerous journey. Better I stay in the inner circle."

"I agree, Majesty. Leaving the safety of Sardis would be unwise," said Anselm.

Hunfrid cleared his throat. "Rostard's visions show a clear path, sire. You and your family must abandon Sardis or face death."

"That's exactly what you want me to do, isn't it Hunfrid? Then you can proclaim yourself as steward of the royal city in my absence."

The Master of Executions raised himself onto his toes. "Nothing is further from my mind."

"I can't trust any of you!" Ewald retched, chunks of vomit cascading down his robes. "I can't...I can't...get out. All of you. Get out!"

*   *   *   *

"Nettie!"

Rosalie sat at the dinner table in the koken of her family's apartment as her sister burst through the front door and ran towards their bedroom. Their mother soon followed; her face flushed. Rosalie emptied her bowl of vegetable mash, then turned to her mother. "What's wrong?"

Heady stopped and slumped into a chair. "She's upset about chapel." She turned to her husband Yonna who came through the door with Petas and Allum trailing behind him. "Why have they started to sacrifice animals?"

"The curate believes it will appease the Creator," said Yonna. "Show that we're prepared to spill blood in his name. Our ancestors did it, long ago. We should never have abandoned the ritual."

Rosalie placed her fork on the table and pushed her chair back. "It seems we're getting more desperate for Volerdie's return. Where's it going to end?"

Yonna seemed to ignore the question. "You were missed at chapel again, Rosalie. The curate sought me out, especially. Told me that you would be forever lost to us if you refused to hear the Creator's word from the scripture verses."

"Can we eat now? I'm hungry," said Allum, who sat at the table next to Petas.

Rosalie smiled. "I've cleaned up all the mash. You'll have to eat stale bread." Allum poked his tongue out at her.

"We'll find something," said Heady as she stood and fussed around the shelves.

"The sermons seem to be getting longer," said Petas. "And the nave is more crowded than ever."

"True believers flock to the kirika to find their path to salvation," said Yonna.

"It must be well hidden," said Rosalie.

Yonna raised the corner of his upper lip. It looked like a snarl. "The path is found through personal sacrifice to placate and honour the Divine Creator; the sooner he returns to Enthilen the sooner all our troubles will end."

Heady began stirring a blackened copper pot that sat above a smouldering fire. She threw in a handful of herbs and the last vegetables in the house. "The Felshams have a sick child. Fever, chills, swelling under the arms. That's the third one I've heard about with those symptoms." She rested the stirrer on the inside edge of the pot and gathered five bowls, placing them on the table.

Rosalie noticed the beads of sweat pooling on her mother's gaunt face, her tall, thin body stooped under the burden of providing for her family. The last of the food simmered in the pot and the family had little coin to buy more. The smithy business had slowed. Her father hadn't sold anything in days.

Yonna tousled Allum's hair. "You worry too much, Heady. People get sick all the time, especially children. It's part of growing up."

"I'll leave you to your meal," said Rosalie. She stood and walked out of the koken, heading for the smithy. She passed Nettie, her head buried in a straw pillow, the cotton cover soaked in tears. Rosalie kept walking; she didn't have the energy to console her little sister.

* * * *

Shirt soaked in sweat and covered in ash and dirt, Rosalie pounded the fired metal between hammer and anvil, as if crushing the skull of a would-be assassin. She dipped the axe-head in water, steam wafting up into her face, and inspected her work.

Still too blunt, she thought.

Rosalie turned to place the axe-head back into the furnace, when a vision of Harris' face appeared on the surface of the water in the cooling tub. The apparition smiled at her, but Rosalie's thoughts remained stern. She hadn't returned to the Slumstadt markets since handing Harris the keys and discovering his secret. She couldn't return. Falling further in love with a Dobunni rebel had no future. If Harris stayed in Slumstadt, he would be exposed, eventually. And if the King's Shield discovered that Rosalie had kept the secret, she'd be executed beside her lover. Better that Harris leave Sardis and Rosalie forget that he ever existed.

"Where's your apron?"

Rosalie jumped as her father marched into the smithy. She thrust the axe-head back into the furnace.

"At least put your apron on," he said.

"I don't need it."

"I can't allow you to miss chapel again."

"Chapel's a waste of time."

Yonna grabbed Rosalie's arm and wrenched her away from the roaring fire, the axe-head dropping into the dust on the floor of the smithy. Rosalie clutched at the handle of the hammer, as her father's wiry grip tightened around her arm, not an ounce of fat blurring the lines of his taut muscles. She averted her gaze and tried to escape into the flames. But she couldn't avoid Yonna's scowl, the hue from the fire reflecting off the sheen of his bald head.

"Never say that, Rosalie. Ever. There are people in Sardis who would see you executed for such blasphemy. It's our duty to worship the Creator. The curate keeps a record of those who are absent. One day, he'll pass the names onto Ewald's Shield. Then they'll come knocking at our door. You'll attend the next sermon and every sermon after that."

Rosalie faced her father. "Why do you go, Papa? Do you believe it will change anything? People grow hungry and weak. Illness spreads. The Felshams never miss chapel and now their boy is sick. Why doesn't the Creator help those who worship him?"

Yonna softened his scowl. "I don't claim to understand Volerdie's motivations. Those who do are fools. Maybe he's punishing all of us for the failures of the unbelievers? When darkness descends..."

Rosalie snapped, "Where is this darkness? It always seems to be coming, yet never arrives. Maybe it's already here? Maybe hunger and death is all that we'll find in the darkness and paradise is a myth preached by the curates to keep us complicit."

"Stop it! Heretic!" Yonna threw Rosalie to the ground, knocking the hammer from her grasp. It landed on the point of her shoulder and she screamed, muffled by the dirt of the smithy floor. Rosalie pulled her knees to her chest with a trembling ache and curled up in the dust, terrified to move.

Yonna crouched over her. "Rosalie. I'm sorry. I didn't mean…my little girl. I'm just trying to protect you." He dropped to his knees, grasped Rosalie's hand and whispered a prayer to Volerdie for forgiveness.

*   *   *   *

"King Giltbert stood on the pebbled beach and thrust his sword towards the barbarian ships as they entered the Bay of Deception. Only the mighty king and his loyal Shield could protect the Erstürmen people from the blood-thirsty horde. The ships raced towards the surf, pulled by giant, harnessed whales that breached the water with each thrust. Archers behind the king notched their arrows, preparing to release the first volley. *Aim for the whales!* came the yell from the Field Commander. It had little effect. The arrows bounced from the beasts' thick hides like droplets of rain off a rock. The ships rode the waves into shore and barbarians spilled into the wake, lunging towards their quarry. A squire led a white undred to the king, the only white beast ever known to exist. Giltbert straddled the mount and clutched its reins. He waited for the horde to reach the shore. He was ready." Caeli leaned her shoulder against the prison door and balanced the open book in her left hand.

Jürgen stood on the other side of the small, barred hole in the centre of the door. "Giltbert, he's the great, great, grandfather of King Ewald?"

"That's right. And the first ever king of the Heine Empire."

"One day, I'm going to be a renowned warrior like Giltbert, able to slay a thousand barbarians with my unyielding sword. What happens next, Caeli?"

"The barbarians scurried over the pebble beach, emerging out of the Nordargen Sea like furious ants swarming from a nest. The King's Shield fought bravely, but they were overwhelmed. King Giltbert raced his undred up and down the beach, impaling barbarians with each pass. Enemies' swords lashed across the beast's chest. Finally, the animal fell. But the king stood tall, surrounded by the horde, flailing his battle axe at any who dared confront him. Yet, their numbers were too great. King Giltbert began to drown in the sea of barbarians. At the very moment when all hope seemed lost, a griffin swooped from the sky and plucked Giltbert from the flood, grasping the king in its talons and spiriting him away."

"Did he die?"

"King Giltbert was never seen again. Our ancestors believed that it was a sign that they must abandon the Nordlands and seek a new home. One to which they had a more ancient connection."

"So, they marched to Enthilen?"

"Yes. King Faramund led them. He was Giltbert's oldest son and the first Erstürmen king to rule from Sardis."

"What connection did they have to this land?"

"A few believe that the Erstürmen are descended from a people who lived in the Dambay Plains and built a city there a long, long time ago. Then, when the city crumbled and the land became tainted, they fled to Nordland. But Enthilen was always the first home of the Erstürmen." Caeli closed the book and sighed. "I'm tired of reading. Do you want to sit with me a while?"

"I can't." Jürgen placed his mouth to the bars and whispered, "I've lost my key."

Caeli threw the book on her bed and clutched a handful of hair, rolling split ends between her thumb and forefinger. "Oh. That's a shame. I'm sure you'll find it again."

"I hope so. If my sergeant finds out, I'll be removed from the King's Shield."

"We can't have that happen. Any news from your father?"

"There hasn't been a message from the Riverlands since he left. My mother's worried. She won't admit it, but she paces around our apartment day and night. I've never seen her in such a state."

"Are *you* worried?"

"I have to stay strong for my mother and sister."

Caeli released her hair and stretched her hand through the barred hole. Jürgen leaned his halberd against the wall, took off his gauntlet and rested his hand on top of hers.

"You *are* worried," she said. "Your hands are cold."

Jürgen snatched his hand away. "I should get back to my duty."

"I'm sorry. I didn't mean to offend. Please don't be upset. Both of us need friends now more than ever. Tides of change ebb and flow through the inner circle. The king hasn't visited me for twenty-four moons. And there have been no executions for three days. No royal parade. No pomp."

Jürgen put his gauntlet back on and retrieved his halberd. "You sound almost like you miss the executions. I don't."

Caeli pulled her hand back inside the door. "I've never watched one. Not a single one. But I can't block out the screams. They'll haunt me until I die."

Jürgen stepped away from the door and resumed his guard position, staring intently down the spiral staircase that led to the top of the Sunrise Keep.

Caeli frowned through the bars. Would her brave soldier abandon her?

*　*　*　*

Deep in the night, three armoured wagons, each escorted by a dozen riders from the King's Shield, passed through the main gate of Sardis and crossed the bridge over the Anchep River. When they reached the outer limits of Slumstadt, they went separate ways, each heading to a different location.

~Chapter 22~

Tom, Dwarrow and Grin strolled ahead of Jacob and Thaly, who had dropped behind to gather wild berries and yams, confident they'd foiled Eroberung's pursuit. The clouds above the Scaur Hills parted and the warm sun calmed Tom's nerves. Underfoot was flat and open, as if someone had cleared a path to make walking easier. Tom enjoyed the hike, thinking back to the bush tracks he used to explore near his home. Dwarrow and Grin had been telling each other stories the entire trip; Tom decided to join in the storytelling.

"Back home, I had a favourite tree. The only tree in our front yard. It was probably hundreds of *years*...I mean yarles old, and huge. There was a hollow...a hole at the base of its trunk, so big I could crawl into it. I used to hide all sorts of treasure down there. When I got older, I learned to climb the tree. Halfway up the trunk was a deep bowl surrounded by limbs where I could escape from the world. I felt calm there, watching things going on around me, not having to be part of it. No responsibility. No need to worry about how to act or what to say. Then one day my arse...my father set fire to the tree..." Tom stopped in mid-sentence as the tip of a sword pressed into his throat. He sensed his accoster smiling behind the black cloth that masked the lower half of her face.

"Well, isn't this an unusual group?" she said. "A grell, a mouldewerp, and a boy. What're you doing wandering the Scaur Hills?"

Two more masked figures, swords drawn, surrounded Tom, Grin and Dwarrow.

Dwarrow sniffed the air. "Rebels. I smelled you a while back. I thought we might pass by unnoticed. I guess that was wishful thinking since we're so close to your home."

"What do you know of our home?" asked the rebel with her sword still threatening Tom's throat. He started to count the long, scattered brown hairs that clung to the front of her shoulders.

Before Dwarrow could answer, Jacob rushed up to the group. "Emelin?"

The brown-haired rebel turned from Tom. "Jacob? Jacob and Athalee? We thought you were dead."

"You can sheath your swords; these strangers are with us."

Emelin returned her sword to its scabbard and removed her mask. Her companions, two younger females, did the same.

Emelin gave Jacob and Thaly a hug. "What tales have you to tell?"

"We have many tales," said Thaly. "They can wait until we reach Bagendon."

Emelin looked down at Dwarrow. "It's been many an age since anyone has seen a mouldewerp. I wasn't sure what it was at first."

"We've come from a…ow." Jacob flinched as Dwarrow thrust his walking stick into the rebel's thigh.

The werp sniffed Emelin's pant leg. "There are a few of us left. We stay hidden from Dobunni rebels and other…troublemakers."

"It seems this werp was leading *you*, Athalee. Have you forgotten how to find your home?" The young rebel with blonde hair and dimples smirked as she wrapped her mask around her neck like a scarf.

Thaly's posture stiffened. Tom noticed her clenching and unclenching her fists.

"We've had a long journey, Dayna. Taken prisoner at Süden Forst, tracked by the white grell and Erstürmen scouts. We need rest and food," said Thaly.

"Well, well, you *have* been busy. Of course, clever scouts would never be taken prisoner in the first place." Dayna stared at Tom, as if she was sizing him up.

"You better introduce us to your friends, Jacob," said Emelin.

"This is Dwarrow. He's been our guide through the less travelled parts of the Scaur Hills. Grin is a wild stone-grell from Babir Birramal, and his friend here is Tom Anderson. Tom helped us escape from Süden Forst."

"Such a weak and sickly-looking boy. How did he ever help you escape?" asked Dayna.

"He's stronger than he looks, and he knows when to keep his mouth shut," said Thaly.

Emelin rolled her eyes. "Well, at least you two are happy to see each other. I suggest we head to Bagendon before moonrise. You're just in time for the Pledge Feste tomorrow eve."

*　*　*　*

Tom's eyes widened as he rounded a steep cliff face. The rebel camp of Bagendon loomed ahead, nestled between huge sandstone boulders and rock faces, and surrounded by stone and timber walls topped with ramparts and lookout towers.

Emelin led the group towards the heavily fortified south gate. As they passed through, Tom's head bowed under the weight of the steely glare from guards decked in chainmail coifs and hauberks. One of the guards stamped the blunt end of a glaive on a rock, as if to accentuate his intent should any trouble come from the new arrivals.

Inside the walls of Bagendon, well-crafted stone houses stood side-by-side with basic shelters of fabric and wood tied down with rope, laid out in a grid pattern, criss-crossed with rudimentary dirt streets full of thousands of people.

This is more of a town than a camp, thought Tom.

Standing inside the south gate, Grin pushed to the front of the group. Another grell emerged from the crowd, smaller than Grin with fair skin, long, reddish-blonde hair, and one eye of lilac and one of turquoise. The grells greeted each other in the formal way before engaging in a short conversation in Grellian. Tom caught only a few of the words.

After the grells parted company, Grin turned to the group. "That was Austran. Her mother is a stone-grell and her father a weald-grell. She was born in Giigal and given the crest of marrumin. She is a long way from home."

"What's she doing here? Is she a slave?" asked Tom.

"The Dobunni do not have slaves. She is a rebel soldier."

Emelin led the group along the main street of Bagendon. Lined with houses and shops, the street bustled with people on foot or horseback, or pulling wagons carrying supplies. A young boy chased a drift of piglets through the crowd, dogs barking as he passed.

A few of the residents glared at Dwarrow and whispered to each other behind their hands. He mumbled to Tom, "Why is a werp such a novelty? These people need to clear their nose, and get out more."

Tom shirked from the crush of people, the most he had seen since arriving in Enthilen. Filthy faces frowned at him as he passed, their astringent body odours stinging his nostrils, escaping from the holes in ragged clothes. Tom expected people to start begging him for coin at any moment. He relaxed when the group arrived at a modest timber dwelling that might offer him respite from the crowd.

On the front step, Emelin turned to Jacob. "I imagine you'll want to go home to Payton. He's missed you. I can entertain our guests until tomorrow. Then, I think all of you should speak with Ryder."

Jacob bid his farewells. Rohesia, the rebel scout that had accompanied Emelin and Dayna on patrol, also said goodbye.

Emelin held the door open. "Well, friends. Please accept our hospitality for this eve. Come inside."

"Don't you want to see your family too, Thaly?" asked Tom.

Thaly pressed her fingers into her left temple. "Unfortunately, this *is* my family."

"Athalee has been adopted into our house and we are more than grateful to have her," said Emelin.

"This means Athalee and I are like sisters. Aren't we, Sis?" Dayna beamed and wrapped her arm around Thaly's shoulder as they walked through the door.

Tom could feel Thaly cringing. He smirked and felt guilty immediately. But he'd learned something about the guarded young warrior. She had a family of sorts. A family that could peel back her armour and expose her humanity.

Inside the house, a fire smouldered in the corner, smoke escaping up a stone chimney. Tom's mouth watered at the scent of cooked food, wafting from a blackened cauldron that hung near the coals.

"Please, sit." Emelin waved her hand at a long table surrounded by wooden stools.

Dwarrow trotted past three beds, oxen hides stretched over wooden frames, and plonked himself on a stool.

Grin ducked under the timber beams that supported the vaulted, thatched ceiling, knocking his forehead on a clatter of utensils that hung from hooks driven into the wood. He crouched low onto a stool; his legs splayed out on either side.

Tom smiled as a picture flashed into his mind: a giraffe, legs akimbo, trying to drink from a waterhole.

"What smells so awful in here?"

"Dwarrow, don't be so rude," said Tom.

Emelin laughed. "It's probably our breakfast, Dwarrow. Don't you like porridge?"

At the mention of porridge, Tom forgot his manners. "I love porridge. It's my favourite breakfast. In fact, it's my favourite meal full stop. If you don't mind…I mean, I haven't eaten porridge in ages."

Emelin glanced into the cauldron. "There's a serving in here from this morning, but it's very dry. You'll need to add milk and heat it again."

"Not a problem." Tom picked out a metal spoon from the cooking implements arranged along the mantelpiece above the fireplace. "Where's the milk?"

"In that pot," said Emelin, pointing to an earthen jug sitting in a recess in the wall.

Tom poured milk into the cauldron then caught himself. For the first time since arriving in Enthilen, he felt almost at home in the somewhat familiar surrounds of the Dobunni cottage.

Thaly and Dayna squeezed next to Grin and Dwarrow. Tom stirred his porridge and watched Emelin empty the shelves of foodstuffs; root vegetables, slabs of blue and yellow that looked like cheese with mould growing on it, and small loaves of baked dough that seemed heavy in her hand. She placed the food on the table.

Dwarrow sniffed the baked dough. "Do you have any slitherweed? Or jimin grubs? Or toad jus?"

"No, sorry. You'll have to eat proper food here," said Emelin.

"*Hmph.* Proper food."

During the meal, the group exchanged stories, although Tom remained quiet and Grin and Dwarrow didn't expose his secrets. Thaly did most of the talking, regaling her adopted family with tales of their adventures. A warmth flowed through Tom as he listened to Thaly's stories. He'd never seen her so animated, and her voice soothed his thoughts even further.

Dayna had ignored Tom most of the evening, but all of a sudden, she moved her seat next to his and grabbed his forearm. "So, where are you from again, Tom?"

"The Feign. In the foothills of the Desolate Mountains. My father's a goat herder..."

"How fascinating. Tell me about your escape from Süden Forst. However did you free those hapless Dobunni scouts?"

"I feel like Jacob and Thaly rescued me. I was being chased...."

"By who?"

"Eroberung was in Süden Forst. I already told you that, Dayna," muttered Thaly.

"And you ran away from the white beast rather than fight?"

"We had no choice."

Dayna rubbed Tom's bicep through his tunic. "You must be amazingly strong to be a goat herder. How do you control those beasts? I'm terrified of goats."

Thaly groaned. "For goodness sake. Is it time for bed yet?"

*　*　*　*

Tom, Grin and Dwarrow slept on the floor of Emelin's house. Emelin had managed to find clothes that fit Grin; long pants and a tunic borrowed from another grell who had joined the rebel cause. Grin refused the offer of boots.

In the morning, Jacob arrived to take the new visitors to meet Ryder, the leader of the rebels. He led them to the meeting hall in the centre square of Bagendon, telling Tom that the Dobunni called the large, elongated stone building the longhouse.

Inside the longhouse, a fire pit radiated warmth from the middle of the main room, smoke escaping past exposed timber trusses and through a hole in the thatched roof. Trestle-tables and benches along each wall flanked the fire. A few people sat on the benches conversing or eating while guards hovered near the doorways, watchful of Tom and his unusual companions as they stood inside the main entrance of the hall with Jacob.

At the far end of the room, surrounded by a handful of rebels, stood a tall, muscular man with long grey hair and a thick grey beard.

Jacob whispered into Tom's ear, "That's Ryder."

A younger woman with high cheekbones and pale blonde, almost white hair, rested a hand on Ryder's shoulder. As Tom approached, she trapped him with ice-blue eyes that set a lump in his throat. He bowed his head, trying not to stare.

Ryder greeted Jacob with a smile and a bear hug. "Jacob Seamaster. You've finally returned. I was almost worried."

"We were delayed somewhat. My friends here led us to safety. Let me introduce Tom Anderson, Grinnian stone-grell, and Dwarrow...mould-ewerp. This is Ryder, the leader of our group, and his lufu, Brynlee."

"Welcome. Friends of Jacob are friends of mine and Dobunni rebels everywhere." Ryder engaged Grin in a formal grell greeting. "It's always good to have another strong grell in our camp. And a werp. The little ones haven't been seen in these parts for a generation. What news from the south, Jacob?"

"Süden Forst is in disarray. People pass through the gates unchallenged. Theodoar tries to maintain a pretence of control, but his men don't respect his leadership. The fort is ripe for overthrow, should we consider it a useful base."

Ryder stroked his beard. "How were you delayed?"

"To my embarrassment, we were captured by a patrol from Süden Forst."

"Despite the lack of leadership," said Brynlee.

"We were imprisoned in the dungeon. Luckily, the gaoler was too lazy or drunk to put much effort into the torture. He lost interest in us when they caught Grin. Then Tom came to rescue his friend and freed us all."

Ryder turned to Tom, eyes sparkling. "It seems we owe you a debt of gratitude. I often find that the biggest surprises come in the smallest packages."

"That's what I always say," said Dwarrow.

"Where are you from, Tom?" asked Ryder.

"The Feign," he replied. "In the Desolate Mountains."

Ryder beamed. "I know it well. My grandparents had a farm there. Mountain sheep. Anderson did you say? That name isn't familiar to me."

Tom kept his nerve. "We're very isolated. Hardly see a soul regardless of the season."

"We also saw a battalion of Erstürmen soldiers marching to the Riverlands, led by Jurelle," said Jacob, as if changing the subject to save Tom from further interrogation.

Ryder spat on the dirt floor of the longhouse. "The weasel comes out of his hole to bite another hand that once fed it. The Erstürmen are losing the battle for the Riverlands. They have underestimated their enemy, like they underestimate us. Jurelle will fall. We needn't concern ourselves with him." Ryder patted Dwarrow on the head. "Where did you pick up this werp?"

"We keep our noses to the ground." Dwarrow pushed Ryder's hand away with his walking stick.

"We were being tracked by Erstürmen scouts and got lost in the Scaur Hills. Dwarrow and a few of his companions saved us and led us to safety."

"Well, Jacob, that is quite an adventure. You're all welcome here. Rest and recover. Stay as long as you wish. The Pledge Feste will be held this eve. It's the biggest celebration of all the six seasons." Ryder leaned into Jacob's ear, though Tom overheard the whisper. "After that, the leaders will meet to discuss our next move. I'm sure you'll want to attend this meeting."

*   *   *   *

Around midday, Tom, Grin and Dwarrow wandered the streets of Bagendon looking for something to eat. Jacob and Thaly had other things to attend to, leaving the trio to their own devices. They attracted looks of curiosity from the Dobunni rebels. Jacob had told Dwarrow to expect attention. Most Dobunni had never seen a mouldewerp, let alone one in the company of a grell.

All three were famished. Grin had proposed they try hunting in the hills nearby, but Dwarrow would have none of it, preferring to search the food stalls along the dirt streets hoping to find a tasty morsel.

"We have no coin, Dwarrow," said Grin.

"Don't worry, my dear grell. I've enough coin for all of us."

Wherever he went, Dwarrow carried a leather satchel slung over his shoulder, and many pouches dangled from the twine tied around his waist, which also held up his tiny britches. He didn't wear a tunic or coat, his furry hide seemingly enough to keep the cold at bay. Tom thought the werp likely hoarded a huge pile of coins in a dark, secret corner of his dwell. There could be riches beyond measure hidden in that hole.

"Why do you wear pants, Dwarrow?" asked Tom. "You're hairy enough not to need them."

"You see those looks I'm getting already. Imagine what a kerfuffle there would be if I was naked." Dwarrow grabbed Tom's arm and pulled him in close. "Plus, I have a few secret pockets where I keep my most precious possessions."

I knew it, thought Tom. *I bet he has gold and diamonds stitched into his pants.*

Dwarrow's long nose bent in the middle, almost turning back on itself as he sniffed the air. He spun around and marched towards a stall with wood-fired, clay ovens roasting a variety of foodstuffs. He grabbed an empty crate and clambered on top, his head peering over the tables at the front of the stall. "Excuse me, kind sir."

The cook turned from his oven, his eyes almost bursting from their sockets. "Well I never. Not in a generation would I 'ave expected to see this. A talkin' pig!"

"I'm no pig, sir. No pig at all. Haven't you read your history books? Surely they'd include an account of the original inhabitants of these lands."

"I cain't read nor write. Don't need to. I know how to work the ovens." The stall holder leaned over the table, his nose almost pressing against Dwarrow's. "Ya ain't 'ere to 'ave a go at me about the roast pork are ya? If they're one of yer cousins, I knew nothin' about it."

"I'm a mouldewerp, sir, not a pig."

"Mouldewerp, hey? Yer a good size for me ovens. Whaddya taste like?"

Grin stepped forward. "Mouldewerps are not for eating."

The cook backed away. "Right, right, just askin'. He looks too tough to skin either ways." He wiped his hands on his apron. "What can I get for yers?"

"Do you have any roast pusclegrubs?" asked Dwarrow.

"Nup."

"What about slitherweed or fesctree roots?"

The stall holder shook his head.

"Mole intestines? Dried giggerboogers? Wormsley droppings?"

"None of those. We got roast pork, roast hare, roast deer, pickled lizard..."

"Pickled lizard!? Why didn't you say? I'll have a large jar please." Dwarrow turned to his companions. "Does anything take your fancy? There isn't much choice it seems."

"Roast hare will do me, thanks Dwarrow," replied Tom.

"I will have the roast deer with forest greens and yams," said Grin.

"How much for all that?" Dwarrow asked the stall-holder.

"Fifteen coin."

"Fif...Fifteen coin!? That's preposterous. How can you get away with charging such exorbitant prices?"

"Times are 'ard and food is scarce. I got to pay me suppliers. If ya don't like it then head off into the hills and go forage for yerselves."

"I say, this world has gone downhill since us mouldewerps stopped running the show."

Dwarrow paid for the food and the three companions walked to the centre square of Bagendon where the rebels prepared for the Pledge Feste. Residents collected wood for a huge bonfire and set up seats and tables for the feast. Tom soaked up the atmosphere, scanning the buildings and stalls that flanked Bagendon's square, advertising on painted wooden signs weapons, fabrics, food, meduz, cooking utensils and so on. "What's meduz?" he asked.

"Horrible stuff," said Dwarrow. "I had a sip once. Made my head spin."

The new arrivals sat in silence on a bench seat, the bustling crowd of Dobunni rebels working around them. Tom's mind wandered. He thought about home, picturing his mum standing in the kitchen, a flowery apron tied tight around her small waist, smile beaming under curly brown hair as she made him dinner. Then he heard his grandmother's voice, reading from Dr Seuss. He saw her broken body lying on his bedroom floor, and next to the big gum tree at the bottom of the driveway, a ghostly apparition appeared to remind him of his cowardice.

Tom gasped for air.

"Indigestion?" said Dwarrow. "You should have had the pickled lizard. It's very tasty."

Tom put his wooden plate on the seat. "No, it's not the food. Dwarrow, have you ever been to Laodicea?"

"Now and then. I try to avoid it. Too many unsavoury types walking the streets."

"I think I need to go there."

"Whatever for?"

Tom glanced at Grin for reassurance. The grell nodded his head and stood. "I will let you two talk. I have spotted more grells on the other side of the square. I should go and introduce myself."

Grin left, and Tom tried to steady his nerves. "I know you said you don't want to hear all of my story, but I need help."

"Whatever you choose to tell me, I'll keep it safe."

Tom recounted more of his tale to Dwarrow, including the murder of his grandmother, and the discovery of the blue book and the silver coin. He didn't say anything about the dark eyes bringing him to Enthilen, but he got the impression that Dwarrow knew some of that already since the werp had asked about the eyes during their conversation in his dwell. "Grin and I are going to the King's Quarter in Laodicea to find my Nanna's killer."

"*Hmm.* It would be easier to find a three-legged worm under the Dambay Plains. It sounds like the errand of a fool and his foolish companion."

"I have to try. You understand, don't you? My mind won't rest until I've sought justice. It's the only sense I can make out of all this. The last time I saw Nanna's ghost, I thought she was reaching out for me, but maybe she was pushing? Pushing me to find redemption."

Dwarrow scratched his stomach and drank the last of the pickled lizard brine straight from the jar. "There's no doubting your intentions are honourable, but you shouldn't be in such a hurry to travel to Laodicea. There's another path you might take. One that is more likely to lead to the answers you seek."

"What are you talking about?"

"There's someone you should meet. She can make better sense of all this. You and I could travel to…"

"What the? Hey, Dalton. Did ya shee thish? Thish boy's talkin' to a dog."

Two men stumbled up to Tom and Dwarrow, their bodies lurching from side to side.

"Dat's no dog. It'sa bear cub."

"Can we roast it?"

Dwarrow stood and clutched his walking stick. "On your way, please. No-one is roasting anything."

"Creakin' crickets. Did ya hear dat, Rolph? Itsh talkin' t'me."

"Grab hold of it. I got me knife."

Dalton latched onto Dwarrow's tiny arm and flashed a peg-toothed smile.

Tom sprang to his feet. "Leave him alone."

Rolph pushed Tom in the chest. "Back off, boy. Best ya be mindin' ya own business." The rebel drew a long knife from his belt. "Let's find a pole t'hang it from. We need t'cut its throat then let it bleed out."

Tom stepped between Rolph and Dwarrow. "I said, leave him alone."

Rolph grabbed a handful of Tom's tunic and pushed the knife up under his throat. "You should learn to leave well enough alone, boy."

The foul reek of Rolph's breath seeped into Tom's airways and his lunch threatened to explode from his stomach. He counted the reddened capillaries in the bloodshot eyes of his tormentor, as the knife pressed into his skin. Somewhere among the cloud of fear, Thaly's calm voice drifted into his head.

Use the weight of your opponent to your advantage.

Tom took a step back and Rolph stumbled forward. Tom pounced, grabbing the rebel's shirt, dropping his shoulder and flinging the attacker behind him. The knife nicked Tom's throat as Rolph collapsed to the ground.

Tom grabbed the knife from his lunch plate and pointed it at Dalton. "Let him go."

Dalton sneered. He lifted Dwarrow off the ground and threw him into the bench seat, the werp's head cracking against the timber.

Tom flashed his blade and cut the rebel's arm. Rolph staggered to his feet still holding the long knife.

From the crowd, Jacob rushed to Tom's side. "What's happening here?"

"Thish boy needs a whippin'," said Rolph.

"They attacked us," said Tom. "Dwarrow's hurt."

The mouldewerp lay motionless in the dirt next to the seat.

Jacob glared at the rebels. "Be off, before I throw both of you in the gaol."

The drunk rebels pushed past another man standing behind Jacob. The man kneeled next to Dwarrow.

"Leave him," said Tom, brandishing his knife.

"It's alright, Tom," said Jacob. "This is my lufu, Payton. He's a healer."

Payton ran his hand over Dwarrow's body. "He's breathing. Nothing broken it seems. He'll have a lump on his head. I'm hopeful that's all. He should wake again soon enough. I'll take him to our quarters, Jacob. I can tend to him there." Payton cradled the mouldewerp in his arms. "They're heavier than they look."

"I'm going with you," said Tom.

Jacob rested his hand on Tom's forearm. "Payton is a skilled healer. Dwarrow is in good hands with him, and you'll just get in the way. We should clean that cut on your neck, then talk some more."

"Do I need to keep this knife with me?"

Jacob laughed. "The Dobunni rebels are a motley bunch. I can't vouch for all of them. Most are true of heart, but there are a few who'll stick you in your sleep for a bag of grain."

Tom's eyes flicked across the faces of passers-by, prepared for another assault.

"Lower your knife, Tom. The danger has passed. You fought well. Thaly will be impressed."

"Impressing Thaly may be the biggest battle of all."

Jacob beamed a broad smile. "You're a fast learner. If you're true to your word, Thaly will lower her defences eventually. She's still finding her place in this world. But I trust her with my life."

"It seems you're beginning to trust me, too. Asking Thaly to teach me how to fight. Bringing me here to your home."

"I know you're keeping things to yourself. I guess you have your reasons. But there's no malice in your actions. I can see that." Jacob placed his arm around Tom's shoulder. "Let me introduce you to some more pleasant rebels. You can assist us with the preparations for the Pledge Feste."

*   *   *   *

"Sit next to me, Tom." Dayna patted the space adjacent to her on the bench.

Tom sat in front of a huge bonfire that signalled the beginning of the Pledge Feste. It seemed that all of Bagendon had turned out for the event. Thousands of men, women and children milled around the fire and the communal spaces nearby. Many sat at long tables, drinking from large mugs and feasting on roasted meat and vegetables. Despite the professed scarcity, thought Tom, the rebels had still managed to gather enough food for a decent banquet.

Sitting on the opposite side of her adoptive sister, Thaly leaned across to Tom. "How's Dwarrow?"

"Oh, that's right," said Dayna. "I heard you fought off two horrid ruffians. You didn't tell me you're a warrior as well as a goat boy."

Tom ignored Dayna's painful ingratiation. "Dwarrow's recovering. He's drifting in and out of consciousness...waking. His mind is a bit muddled. Payton is confident he'll make a full recovery, but it will take longer than he first thought."

"More time for us to get to know each other." Dayna rubbed Tom's forearm.

"Jacob said you fought well," said Thaly.

Tom's body warmed at the recognition from his tutor. "Thanks to your training."

"Where's Grin?"

"He's with two other grells. They're conducting their own ceremony in the hills tonight. Secret business."

A stiff breeze swirled up, launching embers into the moonlit sky and fluttering the many banners staked around the fire.

"What do all these banners mean?" asked Tom.

"They're the sigils of the families that make up the Dobunni people," replied Dayna.

Tom leaned towards Thaly. "What's your family's sigil, Thaly?"

"They're just stupid pictures."

"Athalee has been adopted under our sigil. Two stalks of grain bordering a wooden bowl. Our family were farmers, and very good ones. Long ago we had a huge farm on the Dambay Plains, near the grell's stone city, before the Erstürmen came."

As they spoke, a man wandered past balancing a tray of mugs brimming with froth.

"Meduz!" said Dayna. "Let's drink together."

All three took a mug of the milky, grainy alcohol.

"I don't drink much," said Tom.

"Time to learn, goat boy." Thaly swigged from her tankard.

Tom sipped the meduz and spluttered as the alcohol burned his throat. "What's this made of?"

"Fermented grain," replied Dayna. "My father would make his own at home. He's dead now. Killed by the Traitor General."

Tom took another sip of meduz. Not as bad as the first. He could get used to it. After a few more tastes, he started to enjoy the drink, although the strong alcohol snuck up on him. "There won't be any...sacrifices tonight, will there?"

"What do you mean?" asked Dayna.

"People or animals. Killed for the sake of some...god."

"Don't be stupid. We're not savages."

"Do the Dobunni believe in the Divine Creator?"

"Of course not. You don't know much, do you?"

"The Feign is an isolated place."

Thaly stared into the fire as she spoke, "The original Dobunni settlers worshipped different gods, each responsible for a particular emotion; love, jealousy, anger, fear, among others. If you needed guidance dealing with an emotion, you prayed to the respective god. The Dobunni built statues of these gods throughout Bethesda and people would visit the statues to speak to the gods. I'm told it was a private thing. When the Erstürmen came, they tore down the statues. We haven't bothered to build anymore here in Bagendon. I guess most people believe this home is only temporary. Still cling to the thought that we'll return to Bethesda one day."

"What's going to happen at this Pledge Feste?" asked Tom.

Thaly turned in her seat to face Tom. "Those brave enough will pledge allegiance to the cause of the Dobunni rebels. They'll be accepted into the companionship determined to expel the Erstürmen from Enthilen. A lone fighter can do only so much, Tom, to bring forth the justice they seek. But together, victory is assured."

The crowd became more raucous as the night wore on. Men yelled and sang. Women shrieked and laughed. Fights broke out among the revellers. The noise throbbed in Tom's ears, probing his groggy mind. Defences weakened, he talked openly about his adventures in Enthilen. A few people gathered around him, attracted by the tales.

"...I followed Grin into the dungeon. Well, first it was a chapel or something. There was a big crowd...and...a sacrifice...and this white demon tried to grab me. I ran. Down the corridor. Into the dungeon, looking for Grin."

"How brave of you, Tom," said Dayna

"I couldn't find him. Well, actually, I found Jacob and Thaly first. They hid me under the straw. Eroberung came. He almost had us. A scream distracted him...a scream from Grin being tortured...*belch*..." Tom sucked in the smoky air, "...Jacob sent me back to get the keys off the guard. He was knocked out...the guard I mean...the other one was sleeping. Then the three of us saved Grin. Well, really, Jacob and Thaly saved Grin...killed two Erstürmen. We hid in a wagon to the hills, and then we saw a boulder lion and...and...white grell...and Erstürmen soldiers heading to the Riverlands War..." Tom accepted another cup of meduz and began drinking.

Dayna squeezed Tom's thigh. "Were you scared, Tom?"

"We were safe on the escarpment, though Thaly did..."

"Thaly did what?"

"Nothing...anyway...they must've spotted us because two scouts climbed the cliff...we stumbled onto the mouldewerps and they helped us..."

As Tom told his story, Brynlee moved into the growing circle of rebels that surrounded him. The bonfire hadn't melted the shine in her ice-blue eyes; her long, blonde hair tied back in a pony-tail, accentuating high cheekbones. He thought she looked like a queen and could see why Ryder had fallen for her. Dayna sat almost in Tom's lap, caressing his back. His spine tingled and he smiled at her. He'd almost forgotten about Thaly, until she jumped from her seat and made her way out of the circle of onlookers, disappearing from his view.

A man dressed in chainmail pushed his way through the crowd. "Who'll take the oath tonight?"

"I'll take it!" yelled a girl standing near Tom.

She looks younger than me. He turned to Dayna. "What's happening?"

"She's pledging her allegiance to the Dobunni resistance."

The man led the girl from the circle towards the bonfire.

"Will you take the pledge, Tom?"

Dayna's question swirled around Tom's frothy mind. Alone in a crowd of strangers, no trusted friends to guide him, rebel eyes burned through his skin. He reached for his hanky, clenching and unclenching his fist around the bulge in his pocket. *One, two, three, four, five...*

"Of course, if you're not willing to fight the Erstürmen, they'll continue to slaughter grells and Dobunni alike. I can see that you're scared. Only the bravest men and women take the pledge."

"I'm brave."

Dayna leaned across and brushed her lips over his ear. "Prove it."

The crowd around Tom closed in. Words from his past filtered into his mind. *Please, Tommy, get help...face your fears...it is a noble cause to seek justice...a lone fighter can do only so much...a companionship at your back.* Tom swayed uneasy. The flames from the bonfire melted together. Faces blurred. Dayna smelled sweet, like lavender. Her eyes lingered on him.

It's time, he thought. Tonight is when he would join a companionship for justice. Justice for Jean Anderson; his grandmother. Tom jumped from his seat. "I'll take the oath!"

The crowd around him cheered. A few of them slapped Tom on the back. Dayna beamed.

Ryder entered the circle. "I will accept you into the resistance, Tom Anderson."

Brynlee guided Tom to the bonfire. Ryder pulled a knife from the fire, its tip glowing white. "Tom Anderson. Will you answer the call of the resistance?"

Tom staggered forward, slurring his reply. "Yesh, I answer the call."

"Remove your shirt. You must be marked as a Dobunni rebel."

Tom took off his tunic and handed it to the blonde woman with the piercing eyes. She waved a torch over his body, inspecting his skin. "His skin is clean. He's ready to accept the allegiance scars."

Ryder hovered in front of Tom's chest with the hot knife in hand. "It's a gentle touch, but it will hurt and it will scar. You'll be marked forever as a Dobunni rebel. Do you understand?"

"Yesh."

"Tom Anderson of The Feign, I bring you into the resistance." Ryder traced the point of the blade diagonally across Tom's chest. Tom clenched his teeth, trying not to cry out, but a yelp escaped nonetheless. He collapsed into Brynlee's arms. She held him upright while Ryder traced another scar underneath the first. "I accept your pledge and hereby proclaim you as a Dobunni rebel, member of the companionship, protector of the Dobunni people and their lands for now and always."

Dayna squealed and clapped her hands.

Tom hung like a rag doll in Brynlee's grasp.

Grin pushed his way through the crowd. "What have you done, Tom?"

"I found help. To deliver justice to Nanna's killer." Tom stared past Grin, searching for Thaly. She'd be proud of him now, wouldn't she?

The crowd of revellers parted and there stood Thaly, locked in a passion-ate embrace with another woman. Tom's mouth dropped open and he thought his heart stopped beating for a moment.

Dayna kissed his cheek, grabbed his hand and wrenched him upright. "Dance with me, strong rebel warrior."

Music filtered over the crowd and the Dobunni started to sing.

"Long ago, the invaders came
Stole the daylight, stole our name
Burned our city, set to flame
But we will rise, rise again.

Rise again, warriors brave
Break the chains, free the slave
Strike the king, kill the knave
We will rise, rise again.

Rise again, warriors all
Break the shield, climb the wall
Shake the tower, watch it fall
We will rise, rise again.

Rise again, don't hide away
Soon will be, our victory day
In our homeland, we will stay
We will rise, rise again."

~Chapter 23~

Lady Lily LáDown dug her chewed fingernails into the top of the lectern in the meeting hall of the Laodicea City Council, watching the door with trepidation, still in shock over Widald's assassination. She'd heard the rumours that Dobunni assassins had killed the king's brothers, but she had information that painted a different picture. Acting on that would have to wait. After Dealhia delivered the news about an impending barbarian attack, Lily had hardly slept, spending most of her time in meetings, planning for a defence of the Southern Vale. Poorly armed, her fighters would be no match for the barbarians. She had dispatched a messenger to Bagendon to plead for reinforcements, but doubted the rebel army would reach Laodicea in time. Evacuation plans also consumed her mind. Lily had identified the Erstürmen outpost of Gestade as a place where refugees may find shelter. Even the Dobunni considered the outpost's Field Commander, Hartmut, a noble and fair leader.

Lord Sleame trudged into the room, his usually immaculate plumage now somewhat dishevelled.

"I thought you would have escaped long ago," said Lily.

"My family won't leave. Neither will most of the terrace dwellers. They've reinforced the barricades and plan to negotiate a truce with the victor. I'm hoping this meeting offers a chance to avert war."

"That's my hope, too. I'm not sure why."

"Widald is dead. Who are we supposed to be negotiating with? My notice for this meeting wasn't signed, but it said this was the only path to peace."

"You know as much as I, Lord Sleame. Maybe barbarian sympathisers have already infiltrated the city? I imagine they'll demand an unconditional surrender."

The clinking of a metal necklace announced the arrival of Dealhia as she rushed into the room. Auburn hair stuck out at all angles, as if she'd just woken, her puffy face etched with worry. "Am I late again?"

"You've outlasted Widald, Dealhia. There's something to say for that."

"You're melancholy today, Master Sleame."

"Death stares us all in the face, Master Dealhia. Pomposity offers me no protection."

"How are the Docklands preparing, Dealhia?" asked Lily.

"We've gathered as many weapons as we can find, and armed all the able-bodied men and women. But our arms are basic and our strength sapped by hunger. We can't defeat the barbarians."

"You may avoid the barbarians all together, should you choose." A hoarse, unforgiving voice floated into the meeting room from the doorway where a giant frame blocked the daylight, the growing blackness threatening to swallow the masters in a single pulse.

Lily recognised the enemy she now faced. Hunger; the black grell. He entered the room and towered over Widald's lectern; his shining black head pressed to the cedar ceiling.

"Quell your fear," snarled Hunger. "I am not here to end your lives. I called a meeting, and a meeting we shall have. And I, as the new Master of the King's Quarter, will take my rightful place in the ruling council."

Dealhia and Sleame dropped their heads, but Lily kept her eyes fixed on the black grell.

Sleame mumbled at the ground, "There'll be no city to rule when the barbarians are done."

"It is true, Lord Sleame, that Laodicea teeters on the edge of destruction. My brother, Krieg, has an unquenchable desire to inflict the ravages of war on your people. But he can be tamed. All that is required is for you, my fellow masters, to agree to terms."

The muscles around Lily's jaw tightened. "What may those be?"

"You must pledge allegiance to Prince Adalwolf."

"King Ewald isn't dead, is he?" asked Dealhia.

Hunger paused for a moment. "Ewald still lives, but the age of succession is upon him, and his days as king grow dim. We must prepare for a new kingdom, forge new alliances, bow before a new leader."

"Who do *you* serve, Hunger?"

"I serve the people of Enthilen, Master Lily."

"Who then, is Malphas?"

"Where did you hear that name?"

For the first time, Lily averted her gaze from Hunger's interrogation.

"Is this Malphas person someone we should be negotiating with?" asked Sleame.

"Malphas does not negotiate with contemptible worms." The black grell fell silent for a moment, as if collecting his thoughts. "Your choice is simple, pledge fealty to Adalwolf or suffer the annihilation of Laodicea. When Adalwolf ascends, we begin the resurrection of ancient Pergamos, and prepare for the return of the Divine Creator."

"Only the Erstürmen believe in Volerdie and Pergamos. This land was ours before the invaders came," said Dealhia.

An enraged Hunger smashed his fist through the lectern. "Liar! In the Dambay Plains is the lost city of Pergamos. Our Creator's seat of power. Those sacrilegious wild grells built their childish shrines right on top of it. They sensed the unbridled power of the life force that once resided there. And he will return. Of that, you can be sure. He will return to guide all believers into paradise and preside over an endless reign."

Lily lifted her head. "The Erstürmen consider only themselves as believers. Do you think your master will find a place for you in paradise, Hunger? A place for a tainted grell?"

Hunger snarled. "My master will honour my service. Of that, I have no doubt."

Sleame shook in his seat. "Pledging fealty to Adalwolf while King Ewald sits on the throne is most irregular. We must have time to consider your proposal."

Hunger calmed his heaving chest. "You have one day. I will be in the master's residence in the King's Quarter. Come to me there to pledge your allegiance, or face execution."

*   *   *   *

Two days after the meeting with Hunger, Lily sat with Dealhia in the Master's Hall of the Docklands. The black grell had wasted no time in setting up his headquarters in Widald's old home. Apparently, Widald's family had fled Laodicea, although nobody knew where they went. Hunger had formed a militia from Erstürmen soldiers already willing to denounce King Ewald and pledge fealty to Prince Adalwolf. Lily had heard stories of the militia ransacking the streets of the King's Quarter, demanding loyalty to Adalwolf and publicly executing those that refused.

In the poverty-stricken Docklands, all eyes watched the sea, waiting for the arrival of the barbarian ships. Residents built barricades along the jetties and docks that lined the port of Traders Bay. Men, women and children armed with rusted swords, farm tools and fishing hooks crouched behind the blockades waiting for the tsunami to arrive.

Dealhia drummed her fingers on the map table, interrupting Lily's thoughts. "You're not thinking of pledging allegiance to Adalwolf, are you Lily?"

"Of course not. And I know you won't either. Hunger's deadline has passed anyway."

"What about Lord Sleame?"

"He can't see much beyond saving his own skin. I imagine he's already bowed before a new master."

"It seems only the Southern Vale and the Docklands will stand together against the barbarians." Dealhia turned to her lieutenant, Cedrald. "How many men and women guard the docks?"

"No more than a few thousand, Master Dealhia. We have commandeered a handful of boats to intercept the barbarians. Most of the merchant ships have already fled the port."

"How go the plans for the evacuation?"

"Soldiers have searched every house in the Docklands. Those unable to fight have been given priority. We're amassing wagons and horses, as many as we can find, but it's pitifully short of our needs. Most will have to walk."

"Where are they walking to?"

Lily smiled at Dealhia's oldest son, Yannus, a sergeant in the Docklands Guard. He was the spitting image of his mother. "The ruling councils of the Docklands and Southern Vale have decided to send our refugees to Gestade," she said.

All eyes turned on Lily, as the room filled with murmurs of disapproval from the handful of Dockland's fighters present.

Lily straightened her back. "I know it's an Erstürmen outpost, but it's the best choice...the only choice we have. Field Commander Hartmut is still loyal to the king, as far as we know. It doesn't count for much, but the alternative seems infinitely less appealing."

"Will the Dobunni rebels stand with us?" asked Cedrald.

"I've requested aid from Bagendon. I hope it reaches us in time."

A young boy burst into the meeting room. "Masters! The barbarians are coming!"

*   *   *   *

In the deep cave that Malphas had called home for many seasons, under the Desolate Mountains north-west of Laodicea, a haunting of soulless draughouls milled around a throne fashioned from petrified bodies and adorned by the head of a beast: the throne of the dead. They watched it day and night for a sign. Any sign.

Malphas paced around the cave, hands clasped behind his back. "Soon, Ende. Soon all the pieces will be in place."

"Yes, Worshipful Master."

"Eroberung is close to finding the boy. Prince Adalwolf will soon be king. Many yarles have I waited for this day. Many long and arduous journeys have I taken. The throne of the dead. The eyes of lost souls. Pergamos. I found them all. There is no doubt that Volerdie has chosen me to prepare Enthilen for his return. When Tom Anderson and Prince Adalwolf are in our grasp, all will be in readiness to begin the eternal reign. Then we can leave this infernal cave and sit in the grand hall of Pergamos, as is our right."

Another draughoul entered the cave. "Master. Wagons leave Sardis. Three wagons."

"Our quarry has been flushed. Send for Hunger. We travel now."

~Chapter 24~

In the crisp dew of predawn, among a grove of trees a half-day's ride from Bagendon, Eroberung stood, towering over a cloaked figure who shivered before him.

"V-V-Vater Eroberung."

"You have news for me?"

"You asked me to watch for a young man with a naevus in the shape of a crescent moon. Tom Anderson."

"Where is the mark?"

"On his left shoulder."

"Excellent. Where is the boy now?"

"Safe."

"He must come to me unharmed. Bring me the boy and the severed head of the rebel leader."

"I can deliver them to you, but I want something in return."

"Such as?"

"A safe haven, and a place in the new order, serving your master."

Once the boy is delivered, the master will not need your service, thought Eroberung. But a pretence should be maintained until that moment. "How would we enact this trade?"

"When my treachery is exposed, I'll need protection from the rebels.

The inner circle of Sardis is still the safest place in Enthilen. Once there, I will hand over the boy and Ryder."

"The inner circle is impenetrable."

"The rebel leaders meet today. They grow restless for an attack on Sardis, to end the reign of King Ewald and his heir. One of the rebels will propose a plan. He discussed it with me during an...intimate moment. I will support his proposal at the meeting. He'll argue that the best chance for assassins to reach the king is as prisoners chosen for execution. He has a key that will unlock the shackles of the condemned."

Eroberung breathed deeply, tasting the dampness of the air, then scowled at the trees around him; useless creatures of little worth. He despised the nature of the lands above ground, preferring the dark stillness and emptiness of the underworld.

The boy is in the rebel stronghold, thought Eroberung. The blood compass confirms it. He could torture this arriviste right now. Attempt to bleed compliance from her black soul. But it is unlikely she will give up the boy without securing something for herself. Her selfishness appears to override any fear or loyalty. Subtle deception is needed to lure Tom Anderson away from the clutches of the Dobunni rebels.

Eroberung rubbed the bandaged stump of his left wrist, a constant reminder of his past failure. The proposal by the traitor had merit. A plan that he could use to his advantage. Have the Dobunni deliver the boy right into the heart of Erstürmen strength. Ewald has abandoned Sardis. The master's spies confirm it. It is likely the rebels will not know this, yet. They must be convinced that the king still hides in the inner circle until their plan is enacted.

"Your plan has little chance of success," said Eroberung. "But I could improve the odds by easing your passage into the inner circle. Those loyal to the Worshipful Master grow in number each day. Enough occupy the royal city to ensure your safety until we meet again in the king's courtyard. Ryder and the boy must be with you. If the rebels assassinate the king, so be it. You and the boy will be safe, I guarantee it."

Shoulders slumped under the cloak. "Ryder may consider this a suicide mission."

Eroberung's frustration brewed. "You must convince him that this plan is his only hope of reaching the king." He turned his back and marched towards his white stallion, then spun abruptly to face the traitor. "Wait...wait. Tell him that there is a secret passage that leads out of the inner circle. He will agree to the plan if he thinks there is a chance to escape."

"Such a passage is a myth. A fanciful tale born long ago."

"It matters not. Your job is to make him believe." Eroberung straddled his horse. "The boy must be kept alive. Should he die before his time, both of us will endure pain beyond imagine."

*   *   *   *

"Dayna's not interested in you. It's all an act to annoy me." Thaly lashed her blunted halberd at Tom's chest. He blocked it with a wooden shield, the blow shuddering through his arm. But he kept his body balanced for a counter attack.

"It seems no-one's interested in me." Tom swung at Thaly with a sparring sword, almost knocking the halberd from her hands.

"What are you talking about?"

"Who was that girl you were with? At the Pledge Feste?"

"Ebba? Why should you care?"

Tom pirouetted and smacked his sword into Thaly's side. She winced and backed away. He closed in on her. "I pledged allegiance. I thought... maybe...maybe..."

Thaly dropped her arm and held a hand up in deference. "Thought what?"

"It would mean more...I would mean more to you."

Thaly's chest rose and fell with deep breaths. "Let's rest."

Tom relaxed his posture and the two companions sat in the shade of one of the few trees left in Bagendon. Although the air was cool, the sun still drew a sweat and Tom needed respite from its gaze.

"Why do you seek my approval?" asked Thaly.

While Tom had flirted with the idea of trying to be more than a friend to Thaly, he realised after the Pledge Feste that friendship was likely the best he could hope for. "I need friends, Thaly. Brothers and sisters to stand by my side."

Thaly took a gulp from a waterskin. "I hardly know you. The *real* you." She passed Tom the waterskin and trapped him with a steely glare. "You're not a goat herder's son, are you?"

Tom drank from the waterskin and wiped his mouth. He'd prepared for this moment, surprised it hadn't come sooner. He traced the dirt with the soles of his worn, filthy moccasins.

"Tom?"

"I can't...I can't tell you the whole story. I don't *know* the whole story. The more I learn, the more confused I get."

"A lot of things seem new to you, like you've never experienced them. Are you even from these lands?"

Thaly's guess came uncomfortably close to the mark. Tom knew that if he wanted her help, he needed to relent, at least a little. "No, I'm not from here. It's hard for me to describe my homeland or how I arrived in Enthilen."

"Did you come from across the oceans?"

"Yeah, that's probably the best explanation for now."

"Why have you been befriended by a grell and a werp?"

"In all honesty, I think Grin would have adopted me regardless of the circumstances. I almost drowned in a forest stream. Grin saved me, and showed me a generosity I've never experienced before. Dwarrow...he seems to know more about my situation than I do. How that's possible... or why...I don't know." Tom sought Thaly's soft brown eyes. "Thaly... I'm afraid I'm in danger. I don't really know what the danger is. I don't know where it comes from or who it comes from. I want to ask for your help. I *need* your help, but in asking I'm placing you in the same danger."

"Being pursued by one of the tainted grells isn't a good sign. Do you think this is about your grandmother's murder?"

Tom struggled to compose himself. "Yes, though I can't be sure."

Thaly went silent for a moment, then stared off into the distance. "I wanted Jacob to leave you behind, back in the Scaur Hills. I couldn't see any point in helping you. You could have been an Erstürmen spy for all we knew."

"I'm not a spy."

"No, you're not. I can see that now. If you were, you'd fit in much more easily. Your awkwardness stands out like...like the testicles of a tufted goliath."

"A what?"

Thaly smiled at Tom. "Doesn't matter. And you wouldn't have pledged allegiance to the rebels if you ever wanted to return to the Erstürmen. The scars on your chest mark you as Dobunni now. Your enemy is my enemy. We are the companionship. Together, we'll deliver justice."

Right there, under the shade of the lonely tree, Thaly seemed to grow in front of Tom's eyes into a brave, strong, unbreakable warrior. Something unfamiliar flowed through his body. A brimming confidence. "We'll deliver justice," he repeated. "What's it like? Taking someone else's life."

"I've only ever killed one person."

Tom's eyes widened. "Grin's torturer? In Süden Forst?"

"Yes. He was the first."

"How did you feel?"

"Like it wasn't me. Like somebody else held the sword and plunged it into his stomach while I watched. There was no joy or remorse. Only emptiness. It felt like a creature had taken over my body. A creature who could kill as easily as picking berries. It terrified me."

I can't be scared of that creature, thought Tom. *I need to embrace its malice when I confront Nanna's killer.*

* * * *

With the sun at its highest point in the sky, Jacob entered the Dobunni longhouse and took the last seat at the meeting table of the leadership council. He glanced at the faces gathered around the table. A few he knew well; others, less so. How much could he trust each of them? Were they all as devoted to the Dobunni cause as he was?

Sitting at the head of the table, Ryder nodded towards him and smiled. "Well, now we're all here we can begin. My friends, for a generation we've hid in these hills, launching attacks on Erstürmen soldiers. Yet, the invaders still rule and we're too few in number to defeat them in open conflict. Our only hope to bring down the kingdom is to cut off its head and watch the usurpers fight over the carcass. Then, when the warring parties are weakest, we'll strike. I know you've heard rumours that the king's reign is threatened. That predators stalk his every move. We can't wait for them to pounce. We must master our own destiny. Ewald will make way for Adalwolf and a divided Erstürmen will rally around their new king. I'm sure of this. I've seen blind faith in leadership many times."

"How do you propose we reach the king and the prince?" asked Jacob. "They hide in the inner circle behind the city's seven walls and never venture out."

Ryder nodded to a young man sitting to his left. Jacob had met him only a few times, but he remembered his name; Harris Snape, a scrap-metal merchant from Slumstadt who had pledged allegiance to the Dobunni rebels during the Pledge Feste six seasons ago.

Harris leaned forward in his seat. "There's a way into the inner circle, which we can exploit. My father's stall in Slumstadt's markets is right next to the deeping pits. The Erstürmen gaol. Whenever I work the stall, I see the King's Shield come to take prisoners from the pits and lead them into the city. Those prisoners never return. Ewald's passion for executions is well known. I believe the prisoners are selected to quench his thirst."

Jacob and Emelin locked eyes and raised their eyebrows almost as one. He respected her judgement more than any other rebel. Jacob knew that Ryder was grooming him to be the next Dobunni leader, but he thought Emelin would be a much better choice.

Emelin turned in her seat to face Harris. "What are you suggesting?"

"That some of us get taken prisoner."

"What?" Alfred, the oldest member of the leadership council, almost jumped from his seat. "That's preposterous. Such a plan is suicide."

Jacob frowned as Brynlee raised her hand. Ryder had insisted that she and Harris be permitted to attend this meeting, despite neither being members of the council. Jacob couldn't persuade the Dobunni leader otherwise.

"Let Harris speak," said Brynlee. "We should at least show the courtesy to hear his plan."

"I know it's fraught with danger," said Harris. "Rebels will die. But, if enough of us are taken prisoner, surely a few will survive to be selected for execution. That will get us into the inner circle to face the king."

Edith, a young woman with fair skin, rubbed the top of her bare arm, as if a chill had descended on the room. "Once inside the inner circle, then what?"

"The prisoners are shackled to a long chain. The guards carry the key. But, here's the thing…" Harris leaned in close and his hand disappeared under the table. It returned as a clenched fist, which he opened slowly. "I have a copy of that key. Two copies."

"How did you get those?" Alfred asked.

"One day, when I was watching the prisoners being taken out of the pits, a guard dropped a key on the ground without noticing. When the soldiers disappeared into the city, I searched among the dirt and found the key. I took an imprint in wet clay and returned the key to the ground. Soon after, a flustered guard raced back out of the city and collapsed to his knees, searching the ground for his lost treasure. You should have seen the look of relief on his face when he found the key."

Jacob jumped as Harris plunked the keys onto the table.

"The daughter of the finest metalsmith in all of Sardis made these keys," said Harris. "She doubts her skill, but I don't. I'm sure they'll unlock the shackles that bind the prisoners."

Ryder picked up a key and cradled it in his palm. "You trust this metalsmith?"

"Yes. I didn't tell her what the keys were for. She knows nothing of the plan. Except…" Harris paused, rubbing his hand across his chest.

He's keeping something from us, thought Jacob. "Except what?"

"Nothing. As prisoners, we could walk into Sardis with two keys, hidden somewhere in our clothes. At the right moment, we unlock the shackles."

"The needle," said Brynlee. "That's where we must strike."

"What?" asked Edith.

"The only way into the inner circle is through the needle, a narrow passage that pierces the final wall. We will pass a guardhouse…"

"How do you know this?" interrupted Alfred.

"I know because I was selected from the deeping pits and led into the inner circle to face execution before the king. And I escaped."

Emelin, Edith and Alfred gasped. Jacob noticed that Ryder and Harris remained unmoved.

The rebel leader leaned in towards his companions and placed the key back on the table. "It's true. At least I believe it to be so. Last harvest season, when we found Bryn, she was fleeing Erstürmen soldiers. Her wounds were deep and her wrists still shackled."

"That doesn't explain how you escaped the inner circle," pried Edith, keeping her eyes fixed on Brynlee.

"There's a secret passage. Within the needle guardhouse. It leads out of the city."

"How did you find this passage?" asked Alfred.

Brynlee stared at the table, as if struggling for a response. "When I was a child, wallowing in the mud of Slumstadt's streets, I befriended an old woman who claimed to be descended from the Dobunni of Iglund. She told me many stories, but the one she coveted the most was about an underground passage that led from the bottom of the Sunrise Keep all the way to the woods outside Sardis."

"The old Dobunni watchtower of Al Mōr Sŭrl," said Alfred. "The Erstürmen re-named it the Sunrise Keep."

"If there's a secret passage out of the inner circle, then we can use it to enter the circle," said Emelin.

"I don't remember where the passage opens to the outer world," said Brynlee.

"Surely, that is something you *would* remember," said Alfred

A red blush spread across Brynlee's cheeks. "I was fleeing my captors. I didn't have time to take notice of my surroundings. Anyway, the door to the passage can only be opened from inside Sardis. That's what the old woman told me. You can't use it to enter the inner circle."

"Where *exactly* is the door?" asked Jacob. He'd heard tales of secret passages buried deep beneath Sardis' walls, but he dismissed the idea as fanciful. If such passages exist, surely the Dobunni would have discovered them by now?

Brynlee shifted in her seat and adjusted her tunic, as the light of the longhouse fire turned her blonde-white hair tangerine. "In the needle guardhouse, there's an armoury. Along the back wall of the armoury is the entrance to the passage, hidden by stones. Push in the right place and part of the wall swings open."

"How has this passage remained hidden from us for so long?" asked Emelin.

Edith glared at Ryder. "Both Harris and Brynlee have been rebels for only one cycle of the six seasons. I have serious concerns about this entire proposal."

Alfred leaned back in his chair and winced, as if worn bones rubbed together. "None of you are as old as I am. And you have too easily forgotten the history of your people. Before she died, my grandmother told me the story of the last Dobunni survivors of Iglund, the village where Sardis now stands. The village that once surrounded Al Mōr Sŭrl. She said the villagers escaped the Erstürmen invaders through a tunnel under the Anchep River. When the Erstürmen found the tunnel, they blocked it completely so it could never be used again. However, the passage could have been re-opened."

"Or was never blocked in the first place," said Harris.

Jacob shook his head. "There's no guarantee that any of this is true. How can we trust our lives on hearsay?"

"Bryn is here," said Ryder. "Sitting right in front of us. She escaped Sardis."

"We need to consider this proposal carefully," said Emelin. "First, a group of us must be taken prisoner. This will require committing a crime that doesn't warrant immediate death, though I'm sure some of us will die. The rest will be taken to the deeping pits. Some will rot there until their last breath. Maybe, just maybe, a few of us will be chosen to stand before the king."

"We could rescue those that remained in the pits," said Harris, too eagerly for Jacob's liking.

Jacob pressed further. "What if those taken prisoner don't hold the keys? We only have two."

Harris rubbed the stubble on his face. Jacob waited for an answer.

"Well?" said Jacob.

"My father..." said Harris. "My father will bring the keys to the prisoners. He'll drop them through the grate. He passes the deeping pits every day on his way to and from work. His presence there won't cause any suspicion."

"Does your father know of this plan?" asked Ryder.

"He knows some of it. He can be trusted. He has no love for the Erstürmen."

"How will he know who to give the keys to?" asked Emelin.

"I'll show him. Those that go. I'll take all of us to our market stall so he can see everyone's face, right before we commit the crime. He has a very good memory for faces. And I want to be the first to volunteer for this mission. To show that I have confidence the plan can work."

"Those selected for execution will be shackled and led into the inner circle, or so we believe." Emelin glanced sideways at Harris and Brynlee. "At least two of us would need to be selected. It's impossible to unshackle your own hands even with a key. In the needle we have an opportunity to overpower the guards. Then what?"

"We enter the inner circle as free people and confront the king."

"We'll need weapons, Ryder," said Edith.

"Ranged weapons," clarified Brynlee. "The royal family sit on a balcony overlooking the executions. I saw them there before I escaped.

In the guardhouse armoury I found crossbows. If we can get these, we can strike."

Ryder stroked his beard. "My friends, let's adjourn to consider this proposal. It's a desperate one, I agree, but we are desperate people, and I'm prepared to do anything to turn our fortunes around. We should think on this overnight."

The rebels filed out of the longhouse. Jacob waited until the others left before grabbing Ryder's arm and pulling him to one side. "We need to talk. About Tom Anderson. Eroberung has been hunting him since Süden Forst."

"What could a tainted grell want with a goat herder from The Feign?"

"I don't think he's from The Feign. There's more to Tom's story than he's willing to divulge."

"Should we be worried? Is he a threat?"

"My instinct says no, but my head is fogged. He knows little about our ways or these lands. He's not Erstürmen. I doubt he would have pledged to the Dobunni cause if he was, even if he wanted to hide his true identity. The pledge scars last a lifetime and they're not welcome among our enemies."

"What about the wild grell? I've always found them to be honest souls, and they have no love for the Erstürmen."

"Grin is devoted to the boy."

"So, not a spy. Apparently, a friend to both grell and werp. Now pledged allegiance to our rebellion. Hunted by the white demon who has killed some of our own. Maybe it doesn't matter where Tom comes from? You're not Dobunni, Jacob, but I've not met a more loyal servant of our cause."

That's true, thought Jacob, his family wasn't Dobunni, but he didn't try to hide his origins. "I've never avoided questions about where I came from. Or tried to pretend I was someone else. It feels like Tom Anderson is doing this, but I don't know why."

"He's young. I'm sure there can't be much to it. Maybe he's trying to escape a shame from the past? All of us have done things we are not proud of. Maybe he's searching for a new beginning?"

Jacob sighed. "You're probably right. I'm worrying for nothing."

Ryder wrapped his arm around Jacob's shoulder. "Jacob Seamaster. Always on guard. Never tires of the watch. If Tom makes a mis-step I know you'll see it. And if need be, I'll sharpen the axe that removes his head."

*   *   *   *

Brynlee dragged the lash slowly across Ryder's naked back. The leather straps, studded at the end with metal spikes, traced over cuts already made into his skin. Her lover's shallow panting bounced from the walls of the bedroom. She could sense Ryder's nervous arousal, maybe even apprehension about what came next. It made her skin tingle.

She yanked on the ropes that tied him spread-eagled to the bedposts, smiling as the knots pinched his skin. He lifted his head from the pillow and winced.

"Shall I strike you again?" she asked.

"Yes," he whispered.

"Address me properly."

"Yes, Suzerain."

Brynlee raised her arm and struck her lover. Ryder cried out; his face etched with pain. Naked, she paced around the bed surveying her handywork as droplets of blood formed on his skin. "Ryder. The greatest rebel leader that ever lived. That is what they say, isn't it?" Brynlee knelt beside the bedhead and whispered in his ear, "What they don't know are your secret desires. Desires that only I can fulfil. Desires fuelled by the unending quest to bleed pleasure from pain. And the stakes are raised higher each time, are they not?"

"Yes, Suzerain."

Brynlee struck Ryder again. He buried his face into the soft furs covering the bed and moaned. She dropped the lash and cut his hands free of the ropes. Digging her nails into the reddened flesh around his wrists, she yanked him over onto his back, straddled his waist and guided him inside her.

The Suzerain controlled the thrusts, taunting her lover with near climaxes before slowing her pace again and again. The lustful tension built until the sweat on Ryder's face threatened to drown him. He grasped Brynlee's hips and she ground her pelvis into his. Groans exploded from the lovers' mouths, then their muscles relaxed. The Suzerain dismounted her serf.

Brynlee lay on her side and traced her finger over the pledge scars on Ryder's chest. Though not necessary, he'd taken the oath three times to demonstrate his commitment to the rebel cause and to his people. She knew he'd do anything to route the Erstürmen from Enthilen.

"Harris' plan. It's the best chance we have of ending the reign of Ewald and Adalwolf."

"It could be a trap."

"I've known Harris since he was a boy. Watched him grow up in the streets of Slumstadt. It was the Dobunni resistance that offered us both a way out of the poverty. He's loyal. You scarred him yourself."

"It's possible Harris is an unwitting pawn in a bigger plan."

"Would anyone in Sardis risk giving Dobunni rebels the keys to the inner circle?"

Ryder sat up, resting on his elbows. "A growing number of residents of the royal city would rejoice at the announcement of Ewald's death."

"And expediate the coronation of Adalwolf. Another Erstürmen king to continue the oppression of the Dobunni. Both heads of the two-headed snake must be removed. You said it yourself, our destiny is ours to master. Now's not the time for hesitation. Your people look to you for decisiveness. For leadership. Ewald and Adalwolf sit side-by-side on the balcony overlooking the executions. I've seen them. Perched on a ledge like sitting ducks."

Ryder clutched Brynlee's finger. "How did you escape execution? You never told me."

"Hunfrid, the Master of Executions spared my life. But he only wanted me for a pet. To keep me locked away, a shackled plaything. One day, a maid heard my sobbing. She unlocked the door and turned her back. Still shackled, I ran for the one place that offered a chance at freedom. And there it was, just like the old lady said."

Ryder collapsed onto his back. "If we can find this passage again..."

Brynlee lowered her cheek onto his scarred chest. "We'll find it. My memory of its location is clear. The assassins could escape to fight another day. To bask in the glory of their deed. But..."

Brynlee's cheek raised with Ryder's deep breath. "But what, Bryn?"

"I should be one of the chosen assassins. To show them that I believe in the chance to escape. To give them confidence...and hope."

"It's too dangerous, I can't..."

"But you must. You know in your heart, you must." Brynlee felt Ryder's heart beat a little faster.

"Harris has already volunteered," he said. "He must be sure his keys will release us."

Brynlee traced her finger in circles around the outside of Ryder's nipple. "And you will go. I know you have too much honour to let others go in your stead. But we must take more than three."

"Yes. At least eight."

"How will the others be selected?"

"The Testament of Fire. It's the only way. I won't accept further volunteers."

Brynlee hovered over her lover's chest and lowered her mouth onto his nipple, biting the raised, pink skin. He moaned softly and she smiled to herself. *The Testament of Fire.* She knew the ritual. That would be her chance to ensnare Tom Anderson in this plan. The boy with the mark on his shoulder; the naevus shaped like a crescent moon. She'd seen it during the pledge ceremony. The Erstürmen revere the marked, though she didn't know why. But it didn't matter. Tom Anderson was the treasure she would trade for a life far from the poverty-ridden streets of Slumstadt, and far from serving the warped desires of the rebel leader.

*   *   *   *

The following morning, Tom stood with Grin, Thaly and Dayna around the smouldering coals of the Pledge Feste bonfire. Ryder had called for a gathering of all Dobunni pledged to the rebel cause. Since the sparring session the previous day, when Tom had revealed some of his story to Thaly, she'd lowered her defences and he now felt more at ease in her company. Maybe, also, it had something to do with his pledge to the Dobunni rebels. He'd become one of them now. Welcomed into the companionship. Although, Dayna seemed to have lost interest in him. Not that he cared. He didn't have time for flirting. His thoughts had turned to convincing Thaly and Jacob to accompany him and Grin to Laodicea to find Nanna's killer.

Ryder stepped onto a raised platform overlooking the crowd of Dobunni rebels and raised his arms to the sky. "Rebels of Bagendon! The time for hiding is over. The time to strike is now!"

Rousing cheers echoed through the crowd.

"The Erstürmen army is strong. We cannot defeat them in battle. But we do not need to. The kingdom will fall when Ewald falls!"

"Death to the king!" shouted a few in the gathering.

"We have a plan that will strike at the heart of the Heine Empire. When we succeed, the Erstürmen Kingdom will collapse into chaos. The two-headed snake will devour itself. And when it does, our army will be ready to tear asunder whatever carcass remains."

Ryder waited for the cheers to die down. "I do not ask any of you to volunteer for this mission. I am almost surely leading some of you to your deaths. But lead you I must. I will not ask others to go where I fear to tread." Ryder turned to Brynlee, standing next to the platform. "Brynlee will accompany me. She's our best hope of escaping the clutches of the enemy."

Murmurs rippled through the crowd. A few of the rebels standing next to Tom whispered to each other behind raised hands.

Ryder continued, "And Harris Snape. The metal merchant from Slumstadt. He's the architect of the plan. He'll join us because he knows the plan will succeed. He wants to be the rebel that launches the arrow that slays Ewald!"

The cheering crowd around Tom grew louder.

Ryder raised his hand to still the excitement. "I cannot speak openly about the details of the plan, lest enemy spies reside in our midst. But we'll need more than three rebels. Therefore, I ask for five more of you, to be chosen using the ancient custom — the Testament of Fire. Stoke the fire, we shall begin." Ryder stepped down from the platform.

Jacob moved in between Tom and Thaly.

"What's this plan, Jacob?" asked Thaly.

"I can't say too much. A meeting of the leadership council early this morning agreed to it. Eight rebels will attempt to enter the inner circle of Sardis and assassinate Ewald and Adalwolf."

"How will they do that?"

Jacob shook his head. Tom sensed Thaly becoming tense.

"Sounds like a fool's errand," said Thaly. "Fools walking right into the gaping maw of death."

Jacob leaned across to Tom. "Your name will be offered to the fire."

A lump set in Tom's throat. "I don't...I don't understand what's happening."

"He's not one of us," said Thaly. "He shouldn't have to do this."

Tom understood Thaly was trying to protect him, but her statement still hurt. *He's not one of us.*

"He has scars on his chest," said Jacob. "All those pledged to the Dobunni must offer their names to the Testament of Fire. It's the custom and the fairest way. Let the flames decide."

People walked through the crowd with trays of wooden plates, no bigger than an adult's hand, soaked in water. Each rebel took a plate as the trays passed by.

"What should I do, Thaly?" asked Tom.

"Every Dobunni rebel must write their name on a wooden plate. All the plates will be thrown into the fire at once. Then we'll recite the chant of the chosen. The fire is doused and the selection of names made. The first five plates that are drawn from the fire unmarked will join Ryder, Bryn and Harris."

Tom took a wooden plate and turned it over in his hand.

"Use your knife to scratch your name onto the plate," said Thaly.

Tom reached for his leg. The knife was gone; he'd traded it with Dwarrow. The mouldewerp still rested under Payton's supervision. Tom glanced at Grin for guidance.

The grell rubbed Tom's shoulder. "I cannot interfere with a Dobunni custom. You have made the pledge and you must honour it. I will beseech the land for your safety."

With a trembling hand, Tom took Thaly's knife and scratched his name into the face of the wood. He counted the letters as he laid them on the plate.

The tray-bearers returned through the crowd to collect the plates and confirm that the name on the plate belonged to the person who handed it to them. Tom added his to the pile and received a dot of blue dye on his forehead to herald his loyalty. The fire billowed white smoke, as trays of plates were thrown into the flames. When the tray-bearers completed their duty, the chant began.

> *"Let the testament begin*
> *The fire, within*
> *Chose the name*
> *Unmarked by flame*
> *A knife on edge*
> *Honour the pledge*
> *With each breath*
> *Victory or death."*

The crowd repeated the chant until the tray-bearers doused the flames, plumes of white and grey smoke funnelling to the sky.

*　*　*　*

"I will select." Brynlee didn't wait for any protests. She walked straight into the hot coals, ignoring the searing pain on the soles of her feet, and plunged her hand into the ashes. She drew out the first plate, half blackened by the flames, frowned and threw it to the side. She drew another plate, unmarked by fire. The crowd stilled to silence. Brynlee yelled out the name scratched into the wood, "Alvena Myerscough!"

A woman stepped forward. "That is I."

Brynlee drew another name. "Randel Beckwith." Randel emerged from the crowd and stood next to Alvena.

Brynlee found two more plates that the fire had spared and read out the names of the chosen. This left one more name to call. A strong easterly breeze disturbed the still morning air, whipping up smoke and blanketing the crowd. A fiery-red ember spiralled into the sky and escaped the mounting tension among the gathering.

Brynlee reached into the ashes. As her hand disappeared from view, she moved her fingers under her pants and pulled out a wooden plate hidden there. She brought the plate from the ashes and cried out the name with particular authority, "Tom Anderson!"

*　*　*　*

The blood drained from Tom's face and the ground beneath him began to lurch and spin. *What the hell have I done?*

He barely noticed Grin crouching in front of him, speaking in that deep voice that he usually found so soothing. "Every decision we make has a consequence. I would ask to go in your stead, but I fear the rebels would not accept me. Ancient customs must be respected. You offer yourself to great danger. I will do whatever I can to keep you safe."

Brynlee stepped from the ashes and approached Tom. "Do not fear, grell. I'll protect the boy."

Ryder gathered all of the chosen next to the smouldering fire. Despite its warmth, Tom stood, shivering. He bit down on his tongue, as if that might quell the shakes.

"We hold the covenants of our ancient laws close to our hearts," said Ryder. "Your names were offered to the flames and you have been selected. It's an honour to be accepted as a Dobunni pledge and to serve in our name. Our task will challenge us all. For some, it will be the last challenge they ever face. But our names will be remembered forever, and songs will be sung about the glory of our deeds. We leave at sunset."

*　*　*　*

The sun set, and the rebels chosen by the Testament of Fire prepared to travel to the outskirts of Sardis. Tom stood next to a pony that Ryder had picked out for him. She was small and old, and dried mud clung to her grey coat, but Tom stroked her neck like she was the most prized horse in the Dobunni cavalry. Back home, his neighbours had horses and they had taught him how to ride, at least enough not to fall off or scare the horse into a mad panic.

Well-wishers gathered around the chosen, bidding final farewells. Grin lumbered through the crowd, head and shoulders above the rebels, his towering frame pushing its way towards Tom.

Tom looked up at his friend. "I don't know her name." He could tell Grin wanted to smile, but the grell's mouth remained flat and lifeless.

"I thought I was doing the right thing, Grin. Collecting allies. Fighters like Thaly and Jacob that could help us reach Laodicea and bring justice to Nanna's killer. But look at me now. I've been a fool all along."

Grin crouched in front of Tom. "When I was a young grell, not long after I received my facial crest, my father, older brother Merran, and I lived in our milbi. One day, the Erstürmen raided all the grell shelters along the edge of Babir Birramal. They killed our neighbours and were coming for us. Frennan refused to leave the milbi, his sense of place forged by many seasons in the forest. He pleaded for Merran and I to go. Save ourselves. As we ran into the forest, we heard the war cries of the Erstürmen. When I thought of my father standing alone against the enemy, I stopped running. Merran did the same. We decided to go back home. To face whatever destiny awaited us. Maybe it was a foolish choice, but our intentions were true. When we arrived at the milbi, a band of grells stood shoulder-to-shoulder with Frennan, defending our home. Help had arrived when it was least expected. We charged into the fray without thought or fear and the scales of battle tipped. The Erstürmen retreated. Our home was saved, though…" Grin took a deep breath, "…though my brother fell. As he lay dying in my father's arms, he looked into my eyes and spoke his last words. *We made our choice with sincere hearts, Grin. It was the right choice, no matter the outcome.*"

Grin cupped Tom's cheeks. "Deep inside you, Tom, is courage and loyalty that you fail to recognise. But I see it. Let it guide you. You will face danger, but it is better to live a brave and honest life, no matter how brief, than linger in infinite deceit."

Tom wrapped his arms around Grin's thick neck, then pulled away. "Did you speak with Dwarrow? Payton wouldn't let me see him."

"Yes. When I told Dwarrow of your plight, he was most upset. Most upset indeed. He said that this should not have happened. He called you a few names that I will not repeat here and muttered something about fixing the mess." Grin whispered in Tom's ear, "He told me to make sure you took your key and that, if the chance came, you should trust Princess Caeli."

"Princess Caeli? Who's that? I've never heard that name."

"I can offer you no more."

Jacob made his way through the crowd and smiled at Tom. "The unexpected has a habit of following you around. Not long ago, I wondered if I could trust you. Now, you prepare to risk your life to end the Erstürmen oppression. You are an enigma dressed as a conundrum, Tom Anderson."

"If I had a choice, I'm not sure I would willingly enter Sardis," said Tom.

"There are few who would. But you freely chose to pledge allegiance to our cause, and you haven't fled from that commitment. I admire your courage. I hope to admire it for many seasons to come. Stay near Ryder; he'll protect you if he can."

As if he'd heard his name being called, a clean-shaven Ryder walked over to Jacob and placed his hand on his friend's shoulder. "It's time for us to leave." The rebel leader turned his back on Tom and Grin, but Tom overheard the hoarse whisper Ryder delivered to Jacob's ear. "I fear I'll not return from this journey, my friend. If I fall, you must lead our people in my absence. When Ewald and Adalwolf are dead, prepare for an attack on Sardis. But wait until the predators have feasted and their bellies full. Gluttony makes for a listless mind."

Jacob nodded and disappeared into the crowd.

"Mount your horses!" Ryder yelled to the chosen.

Tom searched the crowd for a face he hoped to see one last time. She was there, standing next to Emelin, her arms crossed, her expression stern and unyielding. Thaly. When solemnity ruled Thaly's mind, Tom felt like a scolded child. But he adored her smile and, for whatever reason, the ache for her approval wouldn't subside.

Tom turned his back and took the reins of his horse. As he grasped the pommel of the saddle, a hand clutched his forearm.

"Do you at least remember your training?" asked Thaly.

"I remember," said Tom. "Though I'm not sure how much fighting I'll be doing. It seems we're going unarmed."

Thaly shook her head. "This is madness. How are you going to defeat the Erstürmen unarmed?"

Harris walked his horse over to Thaly. "Only the chosen eight will be told the details of the plan, when they arrive in Slumstadt."

Thaly hugged Tom, tight. "I can't save you from this. You understand, don't you?"

Tom nodded. "Maybe I'll learn how to save myself." He climbed into the saddle, turned his horse and followed the others towards Sardis.

* * * *

"Jacob! A messenger from the Southern Vale has arrived."

Jacob rushed past the guard and out of the longhouse, as a young woman dismounted her horse. He called out to her, "What news from Bethesda?"

"I've been sent by Lady Lily LáDown. The brothers of the king have been assassinated. All of them. Laodicea is on the brink of war. Barbarian ships gather in the Bay of Fires. The red grell stalks their decks. Master Lily calls for aid. We cannot defend the city alone."

* * * *

Grin packed food in a backpack and looped a longbow and quiver of arrows over his shoulder. He planned to follow the rebels to the outskirts of Sardis. At least he could make sure Tom reached the royal city unharmed. After that...

"Grinnian stone-grell." Dwarrow strode through the door of Emelin's house. "I call on your service per our arrangement and binding agreement."

"Dwarrow. You have recovered."

"Yes, and not a moment too soon it seems. Not a moment at all. Where is that fool of a boy?"

"He has left already."

"I feared as much. We have no time to lose. No time indeed."

"I am going to follow the rebels to Sardis."

"No. Change of plans. My business is much too important. I need haste and speed. Faster than my little legs can carry me. Grells run like a wild storm careering over the mountain tops. I've seen them. I'll ride on your shoulders. We leave immediately."

Torn between his duty to Dwarrow and his desire to look after Tom, Grin's shoulders slumped.

Dwarrow climbed onto the table next to him, looking almost directly into his eyes. "Trust me, Grin. There's only one way that Tom can escape this predicament and I know the way. If you want to help Tom, you must help me."

~Chapter 25~

Malphas sat astride a small, sickly pony, his juniper robes camouflaged among the shadows of predawn that filtered through a grove of trees on the western edge of the Lokan woods. In the valley below him, a closed and armoured wagon, drawn by six burly horses, hurtled along the road to Laodicea. Even from this distance, Malphas could hear the metal doors of the wagon groaning against the reinforced timber frame, as the carriage wheels jolted over ruts in the road. Small slits in the side of the door allowed air to flow in and passengers to peer out. The wagon-driver, perched on a box seat, did his best to control the frenzied beasts that pulled the carriage forward.

At a junction in the road, the wagon took a sharp turn left, heading north towards the Desolate Mountains and the pass of Detranté. A dozen heavily armed cavalry escorted the wagon. They flew no banner and wore no helmets, their armour covered by plain, grey cloaks, but Malphas knew they were from the King's Shield. Nothing differentiated this wagon from the other two that had also left Sardis on the same morning except for one thing: its cargo.

As the company laboured up a winding rise, Malphas waved his hand and Hunger walked his giant, black horse into the middle of the road at a point where the pass narrowed with a precipitous drop on either side. The rider leading the wagon escort must have seen the black grell. He shouted a command and everyone slowed. The wagon-driver yanked on the reins of his chargers and pointed a wavering finger at the horizon.

Hunger sat motionless on his horse. As dawn broke, the first rays of the rising sun outlined his silhouette, an armoured right arm brandishing a double-headed axe.

How magnificent, thought Malphas.

With the sun in their faces, the cavalry squinted towards their barrier. Malphas recognised the lead rider; General Veremund, a commander of the inner-circle guard during the time when Malphas called himself King Oldaric and ruled over Enthilen.

Veremund's old and weak, thought Malphas. Couldn't they have found a better commander for such an important mission?

Veremund wielded his horse around and scouted the edges of the road.

Pointless, thought Malphas. The sides are too steep to traverse and littered with rocks and channels that would break a horse's leg in an instant. And the road is too narrow to turn the wagon around. You're trapped, Veremund.

Hunger waited on his master as the horses of the King's Shield tossed their heads, eyes wide with terror and desperation. Malphas raised his hand to hold the grell in place.

Veremund turned his horse towards Hunger and yelled into the rising sun, "Riders of the King's Shield, form your lines! We'll charge this black demon and trample him to the ground."

The riders formed four lines, three abreast, and drew their swords. Veremund barked the order and they galloped towards Hunger. He remained unmoved; eyes fixed on Malphas. The soldiers were almost upon the black grell when another grell on a pale horse sprung from the roadside and in a series of precise, maniacal sweeps, slashed a keen sparth across the throats of the first line of riders. A row of headless bodies fell from the soldiers' panicked beasts.

Ende, thought Malphas. *She's always so...clinical.* He dropped his hand and Hunger urged his black stallion forward, thrashing his battle axe, as if it were fuelled by the scent of terror. He careered into the second line and the King's Shield descended into chaos. Terrified horses bucked their riders. Soldiers fell in quick succession, failing to mount any resistance against the onslaught. The encounter ended in a blink, littering the road with dead bodies.

Hunger and Ende steadied their horses in front of the wagon. Malphas urged his pony out from the shadows and trotted her down to the wagon-driver who sat frozen on his box seat. The pony tensed under Malphas' body as they passed the slaughtered horses. He leaned forward and stroked her on the neck, pulling up next to the front of the wagon.

Malphas addressed the wagon-driver, "My pony's unnerved by all this. Pity there has to be so much bloodshed. But we do what we must to secure the future."

Buckles on the reins jangled with the wagon-driver's shaking hands.

Malphas nodded towards the reins. "You can probably let those go now. Under the circumstances."

"Ye-ye-yes," said the driver, dropping the reins at his feet.

"Do you wish to live this day?" asked Malphas.

The driver nodded. "P-p-please."

"Then get off your perch and run back to Sardis. Tell them that Dobunni rebels ambushed the wagon and assassinated the king. Tell anyone who'll listen."

"D-D-Dobunni rebels. I understand. Killed the king."

"If you fail in this task..." Malphas tilted his head towards the pale grell, "I'll send Ende over there for you and your family. Deep in the night. Their screams will bleed your ears until she grants you blessed release."

The wagon-driver jumped from the box seat and sprinted back down the road. Malphas walked his pony back to where Hunger and Ende waited at the head of the horse train.

"Hunger, open this metal box please."

The black grell dismounted and strolled around the wagon, dragging the point of his axe along the sides. The high-pitched screech spooked the bridled horses, but they stood in place, Ende blocking their path. Hunger stopped at one of the slits in the side of the wagon and pressed his nose against the metal, sniffing the air inside. He took a step back, grabbed the edge of the door with one hand and wrenched it from its hinges. He returned to stand at Malphas' side.

Malphas called out, "Ewald. I know you're in there." With no response from the wagon, he turned to Ende. "I can't hear anything over this damned snorting."

Ende dismounted, the billowing shirt covering her wiry frame flapping in the morning breeze. She ambled up to the train of horses harnessed to the wagon and executed each one without pause. Malphas placed his hand over his nose and mouth as the smell of fresh blood began to overwhelm him.

When Ende finished her chore, he composed himself again. "There's no use hiding, Ewald. You've been hiding your entire life. The time has come for you to face your destiny." Malphas waited for a reply, then sneered, "If you don't come out, I'll have to send in my grells to pull you out."

A dirty brown boot stepped onto the wagon's running board, and a plainly dressed, clean-shaven man, eased himself onto the road.

* * * *

Ewald squinted ahead. Framed by the rising sun, an old man slouched atop a small, bay horse. Standing next to him appeared to be two grells;

one huge and dark, the other shorter and stooped, clutching the handle of a sparth, as if she might topple over at any moment.

"Your feeble attempt at disguise doesn't fool me, Ewald," said the old man.

"Who are you?"

"You don't recognise your own father?"

"Oldaric?" Ewald's legs buckled. He grasped the side of the wagon to steady himself. "But you're dead."

"Not so much dead, as…transformed. My body hasn't changed. But my soul. My soul has gained an eternal power beyond anything you can imagine."

Ewald glanced into the wagon at the sword resting against his seat. He wasn't much of a swordsman and had no hope of defeating the grells. Romilda and Adalwolf cowered inside. He winced at the fear in their eyes, then turned to confront the fate that had finally captured him. "How did you know I'd be in this wagon? Who are the traitors that serve you?"

"The other wagons were empty, Ewald. It was simply a matter of elimination. Now, what of your family? I'd like to see them again also."

The springs on the wagon creaked and Romilda stepped onto the road.

"Ah, here she is. The beautiful Queen Romilda. I see Ewald has also dressed you in rags. How unbecoming for the Queen of Enthilen. But, I guess, you were always the faithful servant of your king. Well…*almost* ever faithful. And what about young Adalwolf. Where's the boy?"

A trembling prince slinked from the breached sanctuary. At that moment, Ewald wished he had four sons. Four strapping young men that could dispatch the usurper and his vile, tainted servants without raising a sweat.

"Don't be scared, Adalwolf," said the man Ewald knew only as Oldaric. "You've nothing to fear from me. Isn't that so, Romilda?"

Ewald turned to his wife. "What's going on?"

Oldaric chuckled. "So, you haven't told the prince. Well, why would you? We need to keep certain matters secret to avoid the wrath of the king."

Ewald's curiosity overrode his fear. "Told him what?" Romilda's silence made him more desperate. "Told him what!?"

Oldaric's smile faded. "Told Adalwolf that King Ewald is not his father."

Ewald clutched the side of the wagon tighter. The road under his feet appeared to buckle and tilt. He imagined the lifeless heads of his decapitated Shield rolling towards him in a grotesque wave. The smell of blood and rent flesh swamped his nostrils. Already, flies swarmed around the open wounds of the still warm corpses, feasting on the carnage. Ewald dropped his head towards the ground and vomited.

"It seems this has come as a surprise," said Oldaric. "I find that puzzling. You're not a man, Ewald, let alone a king. You can't even get that whore pregnant. The one you locked in the keep. You're a pathetic creature with no quality to lead and no-one to continue your line. The end of your reign cannot come soon enough."

"Father?"

Ewald lifted his head at the sound of Adalwolf's voice. For the first time in many yarles, he searched his son's eyes for a confirmation of love, but saw only confusion. His son's eyes. *His* son. His? Ewald turned to Oldaric. "Who *is* the boy's father?"

The smile returned to Oldaric's face. "Seriously, Ewald, you haven't worked it out yet? Romilda and I consummated our relationship in secret. She screamed with delight to have a real man inside her. Risked everything to sneak from the inner circle right under your nose. Time and time again, such was her lust for me."

A knot set in Ewald's chest at the revelation of intimate treachery.

The one thing he could be proud of, siring an heir, may be a lie. He confronted Romilda. "Is this true?"

Romilda turned away from him and spoke to her son, "It's true, Adalwolf. I should have told you."

Oldaric shifted in his saddle. "My old bones are aching. It's time we ended this family reunion, there's so much to be done. Do you wish for a swift passing, Ewald, or are we going to have to hunt you down? Mind you, the latter will not be pleasant."

The black grell stepped to one side, as the pale grell moved towards Ewald, her sparth raised above her head and glinting in the sun.

"Ah yes, it's fitting that Ende should be the one to smite you down. I think a beheading is in order."

Ewald's eyes narrowed as Ende approached. He reached around the back of his tunic and drew a dagger from his belt. Wrapping a crushing arm around Adalwolf's chest, Ewald pulled the prince in close and pressed the tip of the blade against the young man's throat. "If he is your son, then you should care about his future."

Oldaric raised a hand in deference. "Think about what you're doing, Ewald. Your brothers are dead. Soon, you will join them. Who do you want to see crowned in your absence? All of Enthilen believes that Adalwolf is your son. There's no need for them to think different. When Prince Adalwolf becomes king, history will record that it was the heir of the brave King Ewald that took the throne. The brave King Ewald who singlehandedly saved his family from Dobunni assassins."

Ewald grasped the handle of the dagger tighter. "Lies. Vile, twisted lies. Adalwolf believes none of it. I'm the rightful king. Adalwolf will be crowned when I reach the age of succession, as is the custom of our people. A custom you scorned long ago. Call off your tainted monsters and turn away. Otherwise, your son...*ugh.*" Pain shot across Ewald's back. He dropped the dagger and collapsed to his knees. Romilda stood over him, holding the sword from the wagon. He looked into her marble-grey eyes and saw a reflection of his own madness burning her irises.

Adalwolf stepped behind his mother.

Oldaric clapped a hand on his thigh. "Bravo, Queen Romilda. Finally, you've broken your tormenter's spell."

Romilda dropped the sword. Still kneeling in front of her, Ewald lifted his head, grasped her hand and sought salvation. "Why? We were in love, once. Did that mean nothing? I still love you."

"How melancholy one gets when faced with imminent demise," said Oldaric. "The drunken, raucous, foul-mouthed Ewald disappears, replaced by a more sensitive and loving king. The chilling wind of death clears the clouds from a sullen mind and urges the heart towards reconciliation."

Ewald released Romilda's hand. "The people will never accept you, Oldaric. Even if you hide behind Adalwolf's crown."

The black grell helped the old man climb off his horse. The moment Oldaric's feet hit the ground, Ewald's lips parted in shock. The bent, crippled old man he thought was his father grew before his eyes, standing straight and tall. A clear, cruel voice shattered the dawn. "Malphas. Your life ends by the will of Malphas."

*   *   *   *

Adalwolf clutched his mother like a toddler learning to walk. His sobbing father knelt before him, head hanging towards the ground. The old man who called himself Malphas waved his hand and the pale grell tottered over to the king. She didn't say anything, or pause to offer at least a moment's reflection on Ewald's legacy. Instead, she flashed her glinting blade and Ewald's head thudded onto the dirt road.

Romilda gasped and Adalwolf buried his face in her tattered dress. The man he thought was his father was dead. That meant...that meant he was king, didn't it?

Malphas cleared his throat. "Adalwolf. Come closer. Let me see you. My son."

The pale grell tugged at Adalwolf's arm. He relinquished the safety of his mother's embrace and stepped towards Malphas who grabbed him on both shoulders. "Look how you've grown. What a fine king you'll make. I'm sure Gerulf began to prepare you for this moment before his unfortunate demise. But don't worry, I'll be at your side the entire time, and look..." Malphas reached into a pocket of his tunic, "I have a gift for you."

Malphas placed two polished glass eyes in Adalwolf's cradling hands. Adalwolf swayed, silently, mesmerised by the flaming pupils flickering in a well of obsidian.

"Do you know what they are?" asked Malphas.

"The eyes of lost souls," Adalwolf whispered.

"Do you know what they offer?"

"Eternal life."

"Eternal life, my son. Your chance for immortality is close. Very close."

Hunfrid sat on his horse outside the main gate of Sardis waiting for an important guest. His co-conspirator, Rostard, sat next to him, the nervous energy that characterised the soothsayer directed towards fidgeting with his robes or twisting the reins of his horse. Around them, Slumstadt still bustled with activity despite the markets looking more bereft each day as food and resources dwindled. Soldiers in the King's Shield mingled with civilians and turned a blind eye to minor infractions.

That will soon change, thought Hunfrid. Those that remain loyal to Ewald will be routed out, replaced by men who pledge fealty to the new order. Men that will answer to him; Hunfrid, Steward of Sardis.

Hunfrid was one of the few who knew that Ewald and his family had abandoned Sardis. Indeed, it's what he'd hoped for. What he and Rostard had been ordered to achieve in a letter sent by the Worshipful Master. While Hunfrid had questions about the Worshipful Master's motivations, the death of Gerulf had rattled his nerves. No-one was safe in this emerging new world. He needed to be on the right side of history.

To avoid exposing his hand too soon, Hunfrid continued the ruse that Ewald was gravely ill and confined to his quarters with his family at his side. He'd managed to convince most in the inner circle that Ewald had proclaimed him Steward of Sardis until the king recovered from his illness. But the ruse could last only so long. Although a growing number of soldiers had been coerced into the usurpers circle of trust, others remained stubbornly loyal to the king. The arrival of Hunfrid's guest would change all that.

Hunfrid covered his nose as the stench of the deeping pits nearby wafted on an easterly breeze. Adjacent to the outer wall of the royal city, the notorious Erstürmen gaol more commonly known as the deeping pits were little more than holes dug into the ground with rusty steel grates placed over the top. Though the pits were often crowded with prisoners, on this night, only a handful of inmates occupied the cells. Arrests had been sporadic as the chain of command broke down, and disease had infected the cells, killing many prisoners already weak from hunger. Hunfrid hadn't overseen any executions in days because this would draw attention to the absence of the king and could expose the mutiny before he was ready.

Rostard stopped fidgeting and sat bolt upright in his saddle. Hunfrid removed the hand from his face and searched the dim light of early evening. A huge white stallion trotted up the main cobbled road towards the royal city, carrying a rider dressed in a long, brown cloak with a scarf wrapped around his head and face. His right hand held the reins while his bandaged left wrist hung loosely at his side.

As the rider got closer, a gap in the scarf exposed white skin surrounding eyes that must have been lilac once; now befouled black.

Hunfrid followed Rostard's lead and straightened his back. "Vater Eroberung. Welcome to Sardis."

"You must be Hunfrid. It would be wise, Hunfrid, to keep your voice down. My presence here must remain secret for now. Who is this with you?"

"I am Rostard, Vater Eroberung. A soothsayer."

"Visions of things yet to come pollute your mind. I never had much time for failed prophecies. Did your visions announce my arrival?"

"N-n-no," said Rostard. "It was a draughoul."

"Of course. My master's messengers seem to populate the entire landscape."

Eroberung glanced over his shoulder at the crowded Slumstadt markets. Despite the mask, Hunfrid couldn't mistake the white grell's scowl.

"Time for us to leave this cesspool of penury behind," said Eroberung. "Take me into the inner circle."

Hunfrid looked at Rostard, but the soothsayer bowed his head. The responsibility for leading the white grell into Sardis would fall to the new steward.

The trio entered the main gate unchallenged and easily passed through the checkpoints at remaining circles where Hunfrid had managed to roster on guards sympathetic to the usurpers. However, he hadn't been able to arrange for ease of passage through the gate to the second circle, the one immediately outside of the inner circle.

As the three riders approached the entrance to the second circle, a young guard stepped into their path. "Hail King Ewald!" The guard thumped the breastplate on his chest with his right fist.

"Hail," muttered Hunfrid.

"State your business."

Hunfrid was about to speak when Rostard interrupted. "Is this your first time guarding the circle gates?"

"It's not my usual charge. I've been called to this duty to protect an ailing king."

"Do you know to whom you speak?"

The guard squinted and shook his head.

"I'm the King's Soothsayer and this is his Master of Executions, Hunfrid, who has now been proclaimed Steward of Sardis by the king himself. It would be wise not to delay us further."

The guard glanced across to his colleagues sitting in the guardhouse, apparently engrossed in a game of alquerques.

Hunfrid pulled open his cloak to expose the armour of the King's Shield, embossed with the sigil of the two-headed snake curled in an incomplete circle.

The young guard's eyes widened, then drifted across to the masked Eroberung sitting atop his white horse.

"Who's this?" asked the guard.

"He's a guest of King Ewald," replied Hunfrid. "If you don't let us pass, it's likely that you and I will meet again, at your execution."

The guard approached the white grell. "Why do you cover your face?"

Eroberung leaned forward in his saddle. That was enough to send the guard stumbling backwards, clutching his chest. As the guard's halberd clattered onto the cobblestones, Hunfrid spun in the saddle, towards the guardhouse, but the boardgame still held the other soldiers' attention. The young man slunk away into the shadows and the three riders urged their horses forward.

Hunfrid and Rostard led Eroberung to the king's private quarters, avoiding confrontation and having their passage eased by the strategic placement of soldiers keen to see the end of Ewald's reign. A few residents crossed paths with the three companions, but at the sight of the masked giant, they scurried away like rats from a fire.

Inside the king's quarters, Eroberung removed his mask. Hunfrid stifled a gasp. He'd never seen a tainted grell up close before, and wasn't prepared for the disfigurement that had resulted from the removal of the grell's facial tattoo. Raised and reddened scars littered the lower half of Eroberung's face; a network of pain entwined like the tangled web of a huge spider.

The white grell settled into the king's chair, as if reacquainting himself with an old friend. "Ewald is dead. The Worshipful Master will see to that. We must keep this a secret for now. Rebels are coming to assassinate the king. They will abandon their plan if they learn of his demise."

"Why should we assist a rebel plot?" asked Hunfrid, realising too late the stupidity of questioning a tainted grell.

Eroberung sneered, "Because they bring with them a naevus. A boy who the Worshipful Master needs for the resurrection. The rebels want to breach the inner circle. They plan to be taken prisoner and selected for execution."

"There have been no executions for six moons."

"That must change. Gather all the men loyal to our cause. Place them at the circle gates and in the markets. Tell them to look for a woman with white hair and blue eyes. She will be with a young man, no more than a boy, and a tall man with grey hair — the leader of the rebel scum. All of them must come to me unharmed. Let them be taken prisoner, then lead them here to face execution. If we facilitate their plan, they will simply walk right into the inner circle where we will be waiting." Eroberung leaned back in the king's chair and stretched out his legs, thighs as thick as tree trunks. The chair creaked under his weight. "Do not fail me, Hunfrid. It is your responsibility to deliver the boy into my arms."

Hunfrid steeled himself. The new order had arrived, and he must find a place somewhere at its head.

*　*　*　*

A knock came from behind Princess Caeli's mirror. She put down her book, jumped up from her bed and raced over to the door, peering out of the peephole to an empty landing. That *is* strange, she thought. She unhooked the latches on the mirror and pushed it across the wall, exposing the secret passage behind.

Inside, a tiny figure inhaled. "Princess Caeli. How lovely it is to smell you again."

"Oh, Dwarrow. How wonderful it is to *see* you again. I wasn't expecting a visit from you." Caeli dropped to her knees and reached out to hug her friend.

"No, no, no. Well, it's an unexpected visit to be sure and an unusual journey for me, but a speedy one." Dwarrow lowered his voice, "I had help from a grell. They're faster than a pebble hare fleeing a boulder lion. I felt quite ill perched high on his shoulders watching the ground below me flash past. I thought I'd fall at any moment. Had to hang on for dear life. Wrapped my arms around his head."

"Where's your grell friend now?"

"He's much too big to navigate the secret passage. I made him wait for me at the other end." Dwarrow snuffled towards the door to Caeli's prison. "Is it safe to speak freely?"

"Yes. There's no guard. That's never happened before."

"*Hmm*, well, things are changing very quickly, very quickly indeed. Nothing surprises me anymore."

"What news do you have for me, Dwarrow?"

"Especially important news, Princess. *Particularly* important. The boy with the mark…"

"Dwarrow. Did you read the letter from my father?"

Dwarrow dropped his head and shuffled his tiny clawed feet.

Caeli's heart melted. "Oh, I can't stay angry with you. You know that. I should've guessed that my father's letter would've been too much for your curiosity to resist. So, what news do you have of this Tom Anderson?"

Dwarrow puffed out his chest. "I've met him."

Caeli sat back on her haunches, mouth agape. "Dwarrow…you are amazing. You must bring him to me." She leaned forward and scratched

Dwarrow's stomach. The werp responded with something that resembled a smile.

But his face turned serious. "I'm afraid that's not possible, Princess. He's gotten himself into quite a quandary."

Caeli sat on her bed as Dwarrow paced around the room telling her about the rebels' plans. At least, as much as he claimed to know after overhearing one of the rebel leaders talking to his lover who happened to be Dwarrow's healer. Caeli had no reason to doubt Dwarrow's story, but she knew the werp always kept a few secrets hidden away behind his disarmingly cute face. Nevertheless, it seemed her mission to speak with Tom Anderson had become more than a little complicated. Indeed, it appeared she may have to save his life. She'd need help with that.

Dwarrow stopped pacing. Caeli sighed. "My goodness. He seems to have gotten himself into an awful mess. How did that happen?"

"According to my grell friend, it was the result of a dangerous concoction of meduz, bravado and the need for affirmation."

Caeli slumped into her quilt and stared at the shelves of books lining the prison walls. "What can you tell me about this Tom Anderson, Dwarrow? I mean, I know you won't tell me everything, despite our friendship. And I already know a few things, like he's travelled here from a faraway land."

"I'm not sure I know much more than you, Princess. Tom must have carried the eyes of lost souls, but he's lost them. Or they were stolen by the white grell who now pursues him. Why? I don't know. But Tom's presence here is no accident. He claims to seek justice for the murder of his grandmother and I don't doubt his motives. Yet, something tells me that Tom has been brought to Enthilen for another purpose. One completely beyond his control. The whole thing doesn't smell right to me. Not right at all, Princess."

Caeli shut her eyes and thought back to the letter from her father. *I write to you of a matter most urgent...a young man, a traveller, has arrived in Enthilen. His fate is entwined with that of the kingdom and of us all... protect him, his life is precious. If you speak with him, send him to me with haste.*

Caeli opened her eyes and sat up. "The rebel plan won't work. I haven't seen the king in days and there have been no executions."

"No executions? That would be most inconvenient."

Caeli's mind raced. "I need to find out what's going on. I have a friend who could help us. If he ever returns to guard duty. Or maybe I could send a message with one of the maids? We can't let Tom fall into the hands of the Erstürmen..." Wait. She was Erstürmen. Were her own people to be so feared? Who, exactly, was the enemy?

Caeli turned to Dwarrow for comfort, but the tiny werp had already disappeared back down the secret passage.

~Chapter 27~

Jurelle lay conscious on a stretcher, keeping his eyes shut, furtively assessing his new surroundings. The flap of a tent smacked nearby, rattled by a stiff breeze that stroked his face and carried familiar sounds and smells. People chattering, the clang of metal on metal, groaning beasts, their unmistakable stench occasionally overridden by a sweet, smoky aroma that reminded him of cured meat. Jurelle opened his mouth, stretching the stiff muscles near his temples. The lump on his head throbbed. How long had he been knocked out? He felt around his neck. The griffin amulet, Jürgen's amulet, was still there. At least they didn't steal that.

Jurelle sensed somebody standing right next to him. He opened his eyes and tried to sit up.

A tall woman with brown skin and black hair pushed him back down, grabbed his arm, and started to bathe him. *"Enturé en lut nie alowe yien?"*

Jurelle shivered as the woman rubbed a cloth drenched in cold water over his naked body. She leaned over his chest and pulled his other arm towards her.

"Where am I?" Jurelle muttered.

"Et dolla kielas Erstürmen."

"I don't understand what you're saying."

The woman smiled and kept washing. Jurelle lay recumbent in the middle of an open, circular tent. Four guards dressed in thin, tan-coloured cloth covering their entire body except their hands and bare feet stood at opposing points around the inside perimeter of the tent. Each guard had a long, polished cutlass tucked under a black belt of plaited hide that cinched the tan cloth at their waist. Cream-coloured veils covered the guards' faces, but Jurelle could tell from their posture that they were female.

The washer woman finished her chore and gestured for him to stand. She dressed him in a simple white robe and the four guards escorted him from the tent.

Outside, the size and noise of the settlement swamped Jurelle's senses. Still feeling the effects of the concussion, he staggered between rows of tents and racks of weapons, the guards guiding him through crowds of dark-skinned people, mostly women, and past a large canvas pavilion with seating for many hundreds and cooking fires ablaze. In the distance, kamels corralled in temporary wooden pens moaned laments at their confinement.

A guard grabbed Jurelle's upper arm and dragged him towards a tent decorated with scenes of sparkling blue oceans and white pillars of stone entwined with flowering creepers. Inside, covering the floor of the tent, rugs woven from threads of many colours intertwined into pictures of landscapes Jurelle had never visited. Guards encircled the entire inside perimeter, their light cloth illuminated by flames encased in ornate metal lanterns hanging from the ceiling.

A raised platform draped in fabric of dark blue with white gold trim filled the centre of the tent. There, on small canvas chairs, sat three women all with brown skin and raven hair. The guard shoved Jurelle in front of the women and placed herself between his back and the tent entrance.

"General Jurelle Stansfield of Sardis. Born Dobunni under the sigil of the griffin, and once the leader of the Dobunni rebellion. Now a commander in the Erstürmen King's Shield. Welcome, General. My name is Zenais, and these are my colleagues, Pelagia and Eutropia."

Jurelle swayed unsteady, scanning the inside of the tent.

"I imagine you're wondering where you are," said Zenais.

"I assume I'm meeting the allies of the Riverlands farmers," mumbled Jurelle.

"You're in the command headquarters of the 2nd/43rd battlement of the Germalian Exercitus," replied Pelagia.

"Germalians. I guessed as much. No room for men in your army?"

"Men play a...supporting role in our culture, General," said Zenais. "Given their propensity for erratic temperament, we prefer to keep them away from the weapons."

"You're ignoring half of your military capacity. The stronger half."

Eutropia smiled. Her face was softer and kinder than Zenais', but it made her observation sting even more. "And yet, we are still defeating the Erstürmen Shield and their much lauded General."

Jurelle bristled at the insult, then checked his anger. "More reinforcements will arrive soon. The tide will turn in our favour."

"No more men are coming to help you, General," said Zenais.

"Am I a prisoner here?"

"You'll be free to leave in due course, but we have much to discuss and it would be wise for you to listen."

Pelagia stood and paced across the platform, head down, like a wading bird stalking prey. "The Erstürmen are losing the Riverlands War. They have underestimated the strength and determination of their opponent. If they continue to misjudge us, death will be the reward. But for you, General, and for you alone, we offer a choice other than death. A different route, should you desire to take it."

"You're a descendant of the original Dobunni settlers. Once a respected warrior and leader among your people. Forced by the Erstürmen invaders to choose between servitude or secret rebellion. You chose servitude rather than hide like a mouse in a hole, and for the love of a woman; King Ewald's sister no less. Some call you the Traitor General. The rebels in those hills…" Eutropia waved her hand towards the Riverlands Escarpment, "that watch this conflict from afar, spit out your name in disgust. What redemption might there be for a traitor? Are your descendants destined to always serve the Erstürmen kings? Your son is already a King's Shield, is he not?"

Jurelle's head spun, more from the revelation that these Germalians knew so much about him than from his injury. He checked the tent again. No hope of an escape. Maybe it wasn't necessary? His captors seemed more interested in his family history than learning about the forces that challenged them in the Riverlands War.

"How do you know…" started Jurelle.

Zenais interrupted, "The depth of our knowledge is matched only by the shallowness of yours, it seems."

"I've heard stories about your land, far across the western wastelands. Men are treated like slaves. I didn't need to know anymore."

Pelagia lifted her head and fixed her eyes on Jurelle. "A closed mind withers on the vine. An open mind bears fruit sublime." Her lilt hung in the still air of the command tent.

Jurelle became impatient. "I've never had much time for riddles."

Eutropia raised her voice, "Ewald's rule is coming to an end. The young Prince Adalwolf inherits a fading kingdom ripe for conquest. The people of Enthilen stand at a crossroad. What path will you take, General Jurelle? Who will you serve when Ewald falls? In the shadows lurks a usurper, desperate for an eternal reign. Should he succeed, Enthilen will be entombed in a torturous depravity without end. And the disease will spread, even across Magna Avium, the land the Erstürmen call Grōz

Wüste. It will lap at the walls of our capital like a seeping bile of death. The harbingers of the reckoning already poison the land; tainted grells stained with the colours of conquest, famine, war and death."

"Who is this usurper you speak of?"

Zenais continued, "He's already removed his veil. In Laodicea he struck and all the king's brothers fell in a single night. The Germalian Empire is not blind, General. The failure of men to recognise what is unfolding before them will be their downfall."

Jurelle's mouth sat open as his mind tried to process the Germalians' warning.

"Who might gain from the death of all those with a claim to the throne?" asked Pelagia.

Jurelle blinked slowly, as if it might clear his blurred thoughts to reveal the answer Pelagia sought. "Adalwolf? Is Adalwolf behind all this?"

"Adalwolf does not orchestrate this madness," said Zenais.

"Then who does? Stop playing games with me."

*   *   *   *

Jurelle picked his way through the Erstürmen infirmary, the muddy field sucking at his bare ankles as he absorbed every moan and scream from the wounded soldiers that lay around him. Dark puddles full of bloody sediment pooled on the ground, the storm season bringing forth sheets of mist that draped over the dying in cold comfort. He had learned that the battle at the peasant fort had turned against the Erstürmen soon after the attack on the commanders. A final defeat waited on the horizon, preparing to crush the failing strength of the king's army. Even General Jurelle Stansfield couldn't turn the tide of this war.

Jurelle stepped over a corpse laying in the mud and recognised the face; Balack, the young soldier that he'd spoken to in the inner courtyard of Sardis. It appeared Balack hadn't learned to use fear to his advantage.

"General?"

Jurelle turned at the sound of a familiar voice. Behind him lay Segie, on a bed of horse hide stretched across thin branches lashed together with animal gut and twine. His trusted sergeant rested his hands on a bandaged torso while a healer moved about him treating the wound with potions and soothing incantations.

"General? Is that you?" Segie waved the healer away and rolled onto his side, flinching from the effort.

Jurelle stood next to the stretcher and rested his hand on the sergeant's shoulder. "You're alive, my friend."

"This hole in my chest will take some healing, but I'll see a few more moonrises yet. I barely recognised you without your armour. What happened? You've been missing for days. I thought you must be dead."

"I was knocked out. Woke up in our enemies' camp. Germalians. From across the desert. They kept my armour and weapons and dressed me in these...robes." Jurelle ran his fingers across the thin, cream fabric draped over his body.

"I've heard sea-farers talk about them. Must admit, I didn't take much notice of their stories. The Germalians let you go?"

"Strangely, yes. I had an audience with their commanders."

"Did they demand a surrender, General?"

"No, they wished to speak of other things." Jurelle frowned at Segie's blood-soaked bandages. "The throwing knife pierced your armour?"

"It was made of some kind of metal no-one's ever seen before. I'm going to keep it for a souvenir."

"Has there been any news about the king's brothers?"

"All dead. Murdered by Dobunni assassins. A messenger came last eve."

The Germalian commanders didn't mention Dobunni assassins, thought Jurelle. Someone is twisting the truth.

Segie clutched Jurelle's hand. "That's not the only news. It seems the king has taken ill and is confined to his quarters. Hunfrid is now Steward of Sardis. Men loyal to the king are abandoning their posts. They say Ewald's dying and the prince is not fit to rule. The royal city is in turmoil. Many in the camp blame the Dobunni for all this trouble. You're no longer safe here, General. Some won't rest until your blood is spilled."

Jurelle looked over his shoulder almost expecting an assassin to be already standing there, knife raised. Naught threatened but a field full of the dead and dying, and those providing comfort. He pushed the tips of his fingers into his temples, processing Segie's news. There seemed little point in trying to win the Riverlands War. Likely he had lost the support of his men, and soon, obstinance would become outright hostility. He needed to return to Sardis. With the tumult caused by Ewald's failing, and the scrabble for power that was bound to follow, the inner circle would be no place for a Dobunni or those descended from one. His family was in grave danger. He had to save them.

Jurelle stared along the muddy track that led back to the royal city. "There are moves afoot that were unforeseen. A storm gathers to break upon the innocents. I must return to Sardis."

Segie sat up from his hospital bed. "What about the war, General?"

"Did Badulf or Willem survive the attack?"

"Willem died on the hill right before we were overrun by banshees…I mean, Germalians. The men told me that the enemy drove our entire army back all the way to camp. I blacked out for most of it, but I remember being carried by a grell slave. She saved my life. No-one knows what happened to Field Commander Badulf. His body was never found."

"Then the war's over, Segie. The only thing left that is worth fighting for is the love of family. When you're able, gather the men and announce that they're free to choose their own destiny."

323

~Chapter 28~

Tom and the other seven rebels chosen to assassinate Ewald and Adalwolf, set their horses free before they were in sight of Sardis. They'd been riding for two days, the short, stout horses, adept at navigating the narrow, twisting paths through the Scaur Hills. Despite limited riding experience, even Tom found the going easy, his mount landing her footfalls with aplomb while he concentrated on staying in the saddle. As reward for the hard labour, Ryder granted the equines freedom, though he told Tom they would most likely return to Bagendon.

The rebels changed their clothes, presenting as a group of destitute peasants looking to beg for food in the Slumstadt markets. Harris kept the two keys and would hand them to his father when the group arrived in the markets.

Tom also had a key, wrapped up inside his white hanky and shoved into a pocket next to the coin from Laodicea. He kept the coin because it reminded him of his true purpose. His reason for being here in Enthilen. Find Nanna's killer. If he was going to achieve this goal, he needed to get out of Sardis alive.

Leaving the rocky slopes of the Scaur Hills behind, the group trudged through dense thickets of thorny shrubs that eventually ceded to reed beds and muddy bogs as they entered a floodplain. Raised above the bogs, the main road to Sardis from the west ran right through the middle of the floodplain. When the group reached the road, they joined with other travellers moving to and from the royal city, blending into the desperate throng.

Around mid-morning, the rebels crested a rise that gave a commanding view of the road ahead. The seven concentric rings of the royal city spread out before them, surrounded by the sprawling shanty town of Slumstadt. To reach Sardis, the rebels had to cross a towering bridge.

Tom pushed to the front of the group, his mind struck with awe and terror. He counted the trestles under the bridge.

Ryder moved in next to Tom and told him a story as they walked together. "Sardis is built on an island in the middle of the Anchep River. Before the Erstürmen came, the only thing on the island was the fishing village of Iglund. There was no bridge back then, only a ferry pulled by ropes. By all accounts, it was a hair-raising passage fighting the treacherous Anchep currents. This discouraged most from crossing. So, Iglund was known as a quiet village. In the town square, the Dobunni built a watchtower, Al Mōr Sŭrl, to look out to the east. When the invaders came, they destroyed the village and murdered most of the people. They kept the tower and now call it the Sunrise Keep, building their walled city around it, protected on all sides by the Anchep. As the river rushes west, it eventually meets the Riverlands Escarpment. There, at Rārian Falls, it plummets to the floodplains below. An attack on Sardis from the west is virtually impossible. Only a narrow trail zigzags up from the base of the falls to the top of the escarpment. An attacking army would have to crawl, in single file, and the track is easy to defend from above. King Faramund, Ewald's great grandfather, was the first king in Sardis..." Ryder trailed off as the rebels approached the bridge.

A bustling crowd of peasants jostled Tom, funnelling his path towards the start of the bridge. The ramshackle hovels and lean-tos of

Slumstadt lined the road. Row after row of sheltered poverty, as far as Tom could see. Dogs barked, children squealed, hawkers spruiked their wares, all at bargain prices. Smoke slunk through the crowd, carrying smells of ash or charred meat. The smoky aroma mixed with the rancid assault of open sewers, rivulets of human waste trickling along every muddy street. Ryder had told Tom what to expect when they reached Slumstadt, but the reek of failed humanity still overwhelmed him.

The rebels had no choice but to move with the human tide. Their boots clicked on the lacquered wooden deck of the bridge over the Anchep. Black banners with red, two-headed serpents, fluttered from the parapets where fish and eels sprang from the carved timber.

Tom sucked in each breath, wringing the claustrophobia for energy. Thoughts hurtled around his head. What had he gotten himself into? And how was he ever going to get out of it? He peered over the railings along the side of the bridge, hypnotised by the swirling brown water below. *Jump? I'd never be able to fight the current.*

Tom started as Ryder shouted above the crowd, "Stick close together! Once we're over the bridge, the market isn't far. We'll talk further then."

Tom trailed the rebel group like a faithful dog, hoping the opportunity for salvation would present itself before he passed the point of no return. Brynlee kept close behind him. In fact, he couldn't remember a point in the whole journey when she wasn't right on his tail, as if she expected him to make a break for it at any moment. As if she had declared herself his keeper.

When the rebels reached the markets of Slumstadt, Ryder gathered everyone close. "Harris will take all of us to his father's stall, so the scrap-metal merchant can see our faces. Then Harris will give him the keys and he will return them to whomever is in the pits."

"What if this man's courage fails?" asked Alvena. "What if he betrays us to the Erstürmen?"

"He won't," snapped Harris. "My father is sympathetic to our cause, despite not taking the pledge."

"We have to trust each other," said Ryder. "What else do we have? After reaching the stall, we'll split up into groups of two or three. Tom and Bryn will come with me. Remember, don't force a soldier's hand. Steal a small amount of food, feint an escape and surrender as soon as you feel threatened."

Harris led the group to a stall selling rusty scrap metal. Behind the tables, an old man with deep-set eyes and a weathered face decorated with wrinkles that never ended looked up and nodded.

Harris' father, thought Tom. He lined up with the rest of the group, lingering at the table, as if interested in making a purchase, remembering to look up occasionally so the old man could see his face. Commit his face to memory. The whole process seemed awkward and obvious, and Tom expected to be sprung by Erstürmen soldiers at any moment.

As the final member of the group passed the stall, Tom saw Harris slip his closed hand into a beaten-up old metal box, then snatch it back. Harris' father removed the box from the table and placed it at the rear of the stall.

Keys delivered, thought Tom.

Ryder grabbed Tom's arm and led him and Brynlee into the centre of the market. There, soldiers dressed in the armour of the King's Shield milled around market stalls. Tom recognised the attire from Süden Forst and the army marching to the Riverlands War. Above the din of the crowd, his heart thumped in his ears.

One of the King's Shield, perched high on a stage, pronounced to the assembled traders, "Our glorious king bids you all good tidings and blessings from the Divine Creator. Today, the inner circle is eager for fresh fruit from the woods of Lokan and salted meats from the high plains of the Desolate Mountains. Traders should approach the bidding corrals now for the best prices. The slow will receive less as the hunger of the inner circle is satiated."

Traders pushed forward into corrals, shoving and yelling to attract the attention of the King's Shield.

Ryder guided Tom and Brynlee close to one of the corrals. "I'll steal something from here. When I do, run with me." He pointed to a canvas tent not far from the corrals. "We stop running when we get to that tent. Hopefully, the soldiers' reflexes will be slow and they'll be satisfied with a capture."

Ryder pushed into the corral.

Tom froze, mesmerised by the two-headed snake embossed on the silver breastplate of the King's Shield; the curled animal, face-to-face, ready to devour itself.

Brynlee comforted him with gentle susurrations. "We'll be fine. The plan will work, I can feel it. Stay with me. I'll lead you to safety after we've dealt with the king."

There was a commotion among the traders. Ryder burst from the crowd carrying something under his arm. He ran straight for the tent. Brynlee grabbed Tom's hand and dragged him with her as she chased after Ryder.

"Hoi! Dey stole me food. Stop 'em! Guards!"

"Halt! Halt in the name of the king!"

The rebels made it safely to the tent and stopped. Four soldiers pounced on them, pinning the thieves' arms behind their back.

"Ran out of puff, heh?" said one of the captors. "We'll keep da meat. Yur goin' to da deepin' pits."

* * * *

"Jürgen?" Caeli peered out between the bars of her prison door, hoping that the young guard would be on duty.

"I'm here, Caeli."

"What's going on? I've not had a guard for two moons. My only visitors have been the maids bringing me a few scraps of food and water. Unless there's a guard here to let them in, they can't change my chamber pot. Or bring me water for bathing."

"The inner circle is in turmoil. Soldiers are abandoning their posts."

"Where is the king?"

"He's not been seen for days. A few of the soldiers say he warms his death bed. Others claim he's already dead. Murdered by Dobunni assassins. Hunfrid has been appointed Steward of Sardis, but order is breaking down."

"Oh Jürgen, this is an awful calamity. I don't want to add to your worry..."

"I'm here for you, Princess."

"I need your help. That young man I spoke of, Tom Anderson, I fear he may be taken prisoner and thrown into the deeping pits." Caeli locked eyes with Jürgen through the hole in the thick wooden door that separated them. But she couldn't hold the gaze lest it reveal her exploitation. Her use of Jürgen to serve another purpose.

"There's more to this story than just looking out for a friend, isn't there?" said Jürgen, as if he had finally understood her motives.

Caeli returned her gaze. "I don't want to draw you in any further... yes, there's more to the story. I know only a small portion of it; a chapter in a long book. I do know that I need to keep Tom safe. The sooner he leaves Sardis the better."

"Are you asking me to risk my life?"

Caeli's heart broke. How could she do this to a friend? Someone who'd shown her nothing but kindness. Someone who she might even love, if she ever really understood what that was. But her broken heart turned cold, encased in a layer of ice to protect it from further harm. She could do it, because she knew she had to.

Caeli squeezed her hand through the bars and Jürgen took hold of it. "This is much bigger than us and the kingdom," said Caeli. "The fate of all Enthilen may be at stake. Should Tom fall into the wrong hands... well...well I don't know what will happen. Something brutal and horrible from which there's no escape for any of us. I know I'm asking for a lot, Jürgen, but you're the only one I can trust."

Jürgen's kind young face turned grim, as if a heavy responsibility had aged him on the spot. "If Tom Anderson's in the deeping pits, we need to act quickly. Hunfrid has called for a resumption of the executions beginning at sunrise tomorrow. Your friend may well be chosen for this fate."

"There's still a chance we can save him."

"What do you need me to do, Caeli?"

* * * *

Tom watched a half moon and a three-quarter moon floating side by side in the night sky. He closed one eye and imagined he could track their trajectory across the rusted metal grid that covered the top of his cell in the deeping pits. Standing on tip toes, he reached for the grid; still another arms-length above him. He thrust his hand in his pocket, wrapping it around his hanky. The key poked out through the worn cotton and dug into his welt, and the silver coin jammed into the webbing between his fingers.

Next to Tom, Ryder, Brynlee, Harris and Alvena sat with their backs against the red clay wall of the cell. Their outstretched legs filled most of the remaining space. Behind them, a few of the previous prisoners had scratched their names into the clay: William, Rena, Darius.

Tom reached across and traced his fingers over the names. *What happened to them? Where are the other three rebels? Already dead?* There was no sound from the neighbouring cells. The only view out, directly above.

Harris' father had already delivered the keys. Dropped them through the grate as he scuttled past in the early evening. Tom tried not to smile at the old man as he passed, in case it caused him to stumble. But he couldn't help feeling relieved. Harris took one key and Brynlee the other, placing them inside a small, secret pocket stitched into the waistband of their pants.

Why don't I have one of those pockets? thought Tom.

"You might as well sit and rest, Tom. We need to be prepared for anything," said Ryder.

Tom's moccasins disappeared into the sticky mud floor that reeked of urine and faeces. "I'm fine standing."

"Can you use a crossbow?"

Tom thought about lying, then caught himself. "I've trained only with a long bow and a sword."

"Let's hope we're not relying on you to fire the fatal shot," said Alvena.

"We should have thought of that," said Harris. "Brought our best archers instead of leaving fate to the Testament of Fire."

"All of us can fire a bow," said Ryder. "The Testament was the fairest way. We have already forsaken too many of our ancient customs. I refuse to relinquish that one as well."

"The first part of our plan has gone well," said Brynlee. "We must be hopeful now that some of us are taken into the inner circle."

"What if they leave us here to rot?" asked Alvena.

"They won't," said Brynlee.

Tom thought Brynlee's statement exuded a confidence the rest of the group didn't seem to share. He blurted out the next thought that popped into his head without considering the consequences. "I shouldn't be here."

"Do you think you're more important than the rest of us?" asked Alvena.

"No. It's just...well, Grin and I were travelling to Laodicea before we met Jacob and Thaly. Before all this happened."

"Before Jacob and Thaly kept you safe from the clutches of Eroberung."

Harris and Alvena raised their eyebrows at Ryder's revelation.

In Tom's mind, the red clay of the prison walls started to melt, like scarlet wax held too close to a roaring fire. Soon, the hot wax would ooze across the ground, burning his ankles the moment before it set hard and trapped him in place with only the truth able to set him free.

Ryder's voice regained its prominence among Tom's thoughts. "We've all made sacrifices to be here, Tom. When you pledge allegiance to the Dobunni rebels, the needs of the many take precedent over the needs of the few. Each of us have agreed to sacrifice our own desires for the betterment of the companionship. You should feel honoured to be given this opportunity."

Honoured for the opportunity. Above Tom, the stars sparkled through clouds drifting over the deeping pits. *I wonder if one of those stars is Earth?* He jumped when a guard stood over the grate, blocking the view.

"Looks like yur da lucky ones. Quick execution for ya next morn. Don't 'ave to waste away in da pits like other poor bastards."

Ryder smiled at Tom; a smile he tried to accept as reassuring. But in the shadows, anxiety pressed. He returned to his stargazing, and started to count the stars before admonishing himself. *Don't be an idiot, Tom. Accept your fate and do something you can be proud of. Even if it lasts only a moment.*

The night wore on and one by one the rebels fell asleep. Tom fought to stay awake, but his eyelids grew heavy. He had almost nodded off, leaning against the prison wall, when a shadow passed over the rusted grid and whispered his name.

"Tom Anderson."

Tom jerked his head up. A tall young man wearing the armour of the King's Shield crouched on the edge of the pit, moonlight catching the polished silver through his parted cloak. The soldier nodded at Tom and smiled, then disappeared into the night.

~Chapter 29~

Jacob sat with his thoughts in the longhouse waiting for the remaining rebel leaders to arrive. Unexpectedly, he'd been dropped into a well of responsibility that weighed heavy on his mind. The future of the Erstürmen Kingdom was uncertain and, it appeared, the end may be near. How might the rebels gain advantage from this? Or avoid complete destruction? The king's brothers were dead. Possibly the king himself. The plan to breach Sardis with assassins could be all for naught. Maybe he should send people now to rescue anyone in the deeping pits? War threatens Bethesda. Did he have the fortitude to lead the rebels to face such challenges? Emelin would do a better job.

Jacob buried his head in calloused hands as Emelin, Alfred and Edith, their faces strained and sleep-deprived, entered the longhouse and sat next to him. All four wallowed in silence, as Jacob tried to muster the energy to begin the discussion. "We must march for Bethesda," he announced.

"You're not the leader of this council," said Alfred. "The decision is not yours to make."

"Ryder asked me to lead the people in his absence."

"We have no confirmation of this. And it's not how the Dobunni choose their leader. We must have a vote."

"We don't have time for that," said Emelin.

"What about the poor souls that have been sent to Sardis?" asked Edith. "We can't just leave them."

Jacob sighed and propped his elbows on the table. "Get taken prisoner, selected for execution, assassinate the king and prince, then escape. It was madness all along. I should never have gone along with it. But you're right, Edith, we have to send someone to the deeping pits to rescue any survivors."

"I'll lead that group," said Emelin.

"Laodicea is your home, Jacob, and your family's still there. Does this cloud your judgement?" asked Alfred.

"*Bethesda* is the spiritual home of all Dobunni. I'd protect it with my life, family or no family."

"Lady Lily wouldn't call for aid unless the situation was dire. Her plea cannot go unanswered," said Edith.

"We need to act decisively and quickly," said Jacob. "Events are transpiring much faster than anticipated."

"Do we leave Bagendon unguarded?"

"No, Alfred. I want you to lead a caretaker force to protect our settlement. Edith and I will march with the remainder of our army, to war."

Alfred shook his head. "What if this is all a ruse to empty Bagendon of its army? The Erstürmen could be waiting in the hills to attack at any moment. You may march to Bethesda, but you might return to ashes."

"We'll have to take that chance," said Emelin.

"Wasn't Ryder's plan to attack Sardis when Ewald falls?" asked Edith.

"The time for that may yet come," said Jacob. "But our immediate threat is to the east."

*　　*　　*　　*

Thaly walked, head bowed, along the main street of Bagendon, kicking stones into pools of dirt. Everywhere around her people prepared for war. Shouldn't she be pleased at the thought of battle? She's a warrior after all. Tom and the other rebels were probably dead already, sacrificing their lives for the Dobunni cause. Grin and Dwarrow had disappeared, and Jacob and Emelin were busy preparing the army. Alone, doubt had crept under her guard. The feeling was totally foreign and she fought hard to stay afloat amid a storm of second thoughts.

Thaly kicked a rock. "Ow. Damn that hurt." She sat on a tree stump, took off her boot and rubbed her toes.

Dayna pushed her way through the crowd. Thaly rolled her eyes as her adoptive sister approached.

"Greetings, Sis. I've volunteered to go with Emelin and save any rebel prisoners. Do you want to come with me?"

Why the hell is she so cheery? thought Thaly. "What's the point? They're all dead anyway."

"They might not be. We can't leave them to rot in the cells. What about that boy you like?"

"Tom. And I don't *like* him. I just feel..."

"Protective of him."

Thaly raised an eyebrow.

Dayna smiled. "I know you better than you think. You always want to protect those unable to protect themselves. Remember that baby goat we found in the hills? You rushed a boulder lion to save it." Dayna sat next to Thaly. "I know we're not real sisters, and we see the world differently..."

"And you spend too much time trying to get under my skin."

"Yes, I'll admit it. I'm a brat of a little sister. But despite all that, you're the person I most want to be like. You're strong and decisive. You know where you're going and you care."

"I don't feel strong. I feel lost."

"Is it because you're questioning your purpose?"

Thaly turned to Dayna. At some point, her little sister had started to grow up and she'd missed it completely.

"Jacob made you Tom's trainer to teach him how to fight. But you know that's only part of a trainer's role. You're also expected to be a counsellor and guide. And now Tom's gone, no wonder you feel lost."

"I wasn't ready to be a trainer," said Thaly.

"I'd be happy if you were my trainer. I got stuck with Alfred."

Thaly smiled at Dayna. A smile that said thank you.

Dayna stood. "I'm going with Emelin to save Dobunni rebels from the deeping pits."

Should I go too? thought Thaly. Would Tom be there? She shook the thoughts from her head. "I promised Jacob I'd help him defend Laodicea from the barbarians. We've been through a lot together. I can't let him down."

"The time may come when Tom Anderson needs you again. If we rescue him from the pits, I'll protect him with my life. And I'll make sure he understands how fortunate he is to have you looking out for him."

Thaly stood and held her sister tight.

~Chapter 30~

Dawn broke, and a sliver of dull light crept across the wretched walls of the deeping pits. Mist descended on the royal city, droplets lining up along the bars of the grid fixed over the rebels' cell. A single drop of fresh, clear water detached from the metal and landed in Tom's eye. He let it dribble down his cheek, embracing the tiny essence of life.

Through the mist, six guards appeared, hovering over the pit like vipers poised to strike. The hinges of a small trapdoor squealed and a rope ladder dropped into the cell. The guards thrust halberds towards the prisoners, grazing their weary heads.

"One at a time!" yelled a guard. "Men first, den da women, den da boy."

Ryder ascended the ladder. As soon as he reached the top rung, two guards grabbed his arms and clamped shackles around his wrists, padlocking the manacles to a long chain.

Tom couldn't help but notice. The guard used two different keys; one for the shackles and one for the padlock. *Two — different — keys. Shit. Shit. Shit!*

Harris followed Ryder up the ladder, then Brynlee, Alvena and finally, stumbling behind, Tom.

*   *   *   *

Jürgen stood in the guardhouse of the needle, craning his neck out the door, waiting for the prisoners to approach from the second circle. He'd managed to convince one of the rostered-on guards to change duties for the day, and through the confusion and indifference of the current environment, nobody had questioned the change. He shared guard duties with an old soldier who looked like he'd seen many harvest seasons.

The doddery elder chose today to conduct an inventory of the armoury weapons. "Most of these swords need to be sharpened. Bows re-strung. I can see to it after the executions."

"Yes," mumbled Jürgen.

"Where's Randall? I ain't see you here before."

"He was rostered to other duties. The circle commander sent me instead."

"I'm Crick."

"Jürgen."

"You look young. How long you been a King's Shield?"

"Less than six seasons."

"Well, you chose to serve the king in interesting times. I doubt I'll be here much longer. Getting too old for all this politics."

Jürgen glanced out the door again.

"The prisoners won't be coming yet," said Crick. "Takes a while to get them from the pits to here, all chained and such. Wonder if we'll see the king today? My wife says he's already dead."

*   *   *   *

Caeli stared out her window to the courtyard below. She hadn't slept all night. Normally, royal executions would be preceded by the gathering of crowds, the unfurling of banners, and the pomposity of the royal family's arrival. However, the courtyard below her remained empty and quiet.

She rubbed sweaty palms over her dress, picking up a thin book and fanning her face. Her prison felt like an oven as the morning sun burst in through her window.

It might not happen today, she thought. What if there's a delay? They could take the prisoners elsewhere. The king could be dead. Tom Anderson could be dead.

As Caeli fretted, Hunfrid and Rostard strode into the middle of the courtyard and stood there, eyes fixed on the point of the needle.

*   *   *   *

Unmasked and naked from the waist up, Eroberung marched with authority along the hallways of the inner circle, flanked by a band of heavily-armed militia who'd pledged fealty to Prince Adalwolf and agreed to follow the orders of Hunfrid, Steward of Sardis.

Civilians shrank against the walls as Eroberung passed. A woman with three children in tow, screamed and yanked her family out of his path. Two of Ewald's Shield challenged Eroberung and were struck down with brutal efficiency. The militia targeted decorations celebrating Ewald's reign, ripping tapestries and paintings from the walls, and crushing pottery and vases underfoot.

Hysteria among the residents of the inner circle spread as Eroberung made his way to the royal balcony over-looking the courtyard. He sat on the throne Ewald used to oversee the executions, resting a sword against his knees. The militia stood guard behind him, dispatching in bloody carnage any who dared challenge the new order.

*   *   *   *

Jurelle had been riding all night. Although his courser, Sphinux, was

340

drenched in sweat and near exhaustion, he urged the stallion up the steep switchbacks that traversed the face of the escarpment adjacent to the Rārian Falls. As he reached the top, he shielded his eyes from the rising sun and tried to channel what energy he had left into his horse for one last sprint towards Sardis.

* * * *

Tom focussed on Alvena's back as he trudged along cobbled streets at the end of a corroded chain. The shackles on his wrists pinched his skin, pulled tight by the padlock connecting the shackles to the chain. He twisted his arms, trying to relieve the pain. Brynlee walked ahead of Alvena, then Harris and Ryder. Two guards led the procession, another guard trailing Tom.

Tom went over the plan in his head. *In the needle, we'll bunch together. Harris and Ryder will unlock each other's shackles, Brynlee and Alvena will do the same then free me...but...we only have one type of key. What if it unlocks the padlock and not the shackles? We're going to have to deal with these bloody shackles. What if it doesn't unlock anything? Shit, fuck! Calm down. Calm down. Dwarrow's key. Maybe that'll unlock something. Who was that soldier last night? Calm down, Tom. Breathe. When we're free, we run for the armoury. Ryder said we could leave if we wanted. Find the secret passage and escape. He'd face the king alone if he had to. Why'd he say that? The others said they'd fight with him, to the death. What am I going to do?*

* * * *

Through the open door of the smithy, Rosalie heard the rhythmic clink of the metal links knocking together before she saw the two guards leading a tall, grey-haired prisoner, shackled and padlocked to a long chain. As the next prisoner in the line trudged past the door, head lolling between drooping shoulders, she gasped and stepped back into the shadows.

He was there; Harris Snape, on his way to be punished for his secret. The wicked charm had crumbled. The handsome face apparently burdened with the uncovering of the deception. Rosalie wasn't surprised. She knew it would come to something like this. There's no hiding from the authority of the Erstürmen Kingdom. But it hurt to feel this way. To accept that any disloyalty should always end in death. To so easily dismiss what was once a burgeoning love because of your own selfish fear. Her heart broke a second time.

As the last prisoner ambled past, a crimson tweak alighted on the window sill outside the smithy, puffed up its bright red chest feathers and serenaded Rosalie with a melodic trill that reminded her that beauty still existed in this world. She smiled at the bird and returned her attention to the shackled young man passing her window. He's not much more than a boy, she thought. And he looks terrified. She wondered about his crime. Part of her felt like taking a fired axe, rushing from the smithy and smashing the axe down onto the chain. To set them all free. To show the Erstürmen rulers that defiance could never be extinguished. Her heroic thoughts vanished when Yonna walked into the smithy and stood beside her.

"Hasn't been an execution for a while," he said. "They're going to get what they deserve. Filthy scum. Don't waste your pity on them, Rosalie."

*　*　*　*

Jürgen peered out of the guardhouse doorway for the tenth time.

"You nervous, son?"

"No, I'm fine. Just making sure I know when they're coming." Jürgen needed to decide what to do with Crick. The old soldier seemed harmless enough, but he couldn't risk his interference.

A yell came from the entrance to the needle. The line of prisoners had entered the second circle.

*   *   *   *

Caeli paced next to her open window. She had piled books on the window ledge. Lots of books.

Why's the white grell here? she wondered. Look at him sitting there on the royal balcony surveying the inner circle like a bear on a clifftop. People are being slaughtered behind him. He doesn't even flinch. Hunfrid and Rostard have been waiting in the courtyard for ages. Staring at the needle. Are they waiting for the...?

A soldier in the inner circle announced the arrival of the prisoners, interrupting Caeli's thoughts. She braced herself against the window ledge and with a determination born from years of abuse, willed events to transpire as she planned.

*   *   *   *

The guards led the prisoners into a narrow corridor, the sides almost brushing Tom's shoulders. *This must be the needle,* he thought. *This is where it's going to happen. We need to slow down. Stop walking so fast!*

Up ahead, Tom could see Harris prise his fingers into the secret pocket and search for the key, but the young rebel struggled to get close enough to Ryder to unlock the shackles. Metal pinged on stone. *Shit, someone's dropped their key,* thought Tom. Brynlee's face went as white as her hair. Tom passed the guardhouse. He glanced inside and locked eyes with the soldier who'd whispered his name in the deeping pits.

Suddenly, everyone stopped dead. Shouts came from the guards leading the prisoners. Tom peered over Alvena's shoulder. Books rained down into the courtyard beyond. Scores and scores of books.

The soldier in the guardhouse leapt from the doorway and ran a knife across the throat of the guard behind Tom. The soldier raised his sword, as if to smash through the chain, but Tom thrust his hands into the soldier's face, Dwarrow's key pressed firmly between his fingers. His apparent rescuer took the key and unlocked Tom's shackles. Before Tom could protest, the soldier dragged him into the guardhouse, past a bound and gagged old man, and through a back door that led to a staircase.

*   *   *   *

Dammit! thought Harris. It's the padlock key. Flustered, he managed to free a still shackled Ryder from the long chain. A guard turned to face the prisoners. Ryder spun his body around and threw his arms over the guard's head, garrotting him with the chain that joined his shackles together. Harris took a key ring from the guard's belt before the guard's limp body collapsed to the stones. He freed Ryder from the shackles. Another guard confronted them. Ryder drew a sword from the first guard and thrust it into the stomach of their attacker. The rebel leader freed Harris.

*   *   *   *

Distracted by the tumult at the point of the needle, Brynlee momentarily forgot about Tom. She turned back towards Alvena who stood paralysed. On the ground behind her lay empty shackles and a dead guard.

A lump set in Brynlee's throat. One half of her promise to Eroberung had disappeared. "Where's Tom?"

Alvena didn't reply, as if terror had struck her mute.

"Where's Tom!?"

Alvena stammered, "I-I-I don't know."

"Idiot. Release me, so I can get to the armoury. I dropped the key. It's behind you."

Alvena knelt, grasped the key and held it out towards Brynlee.

"Unlock me!"

Alvena released Brynlee from the chain. Still shackled, she raced into the armoury and tripped over an old man propped up against the wall. She yanked off his gag. "A boy. Did you see a boy?"

"Through the door." The old man tilted his head towards the back of the room.

Brynlee tried the door. It wouldn't budge. "Damn it." She grabbed a knife from the armoury and returned to the needle.

Alvena held her hands out. "Unlock my padlock. Please."

Brynlee's jaw clenched with malice a moment before she plunged the knife into the rebel's chest and twisted the blade.

*　*　*　*

"Damn that whore!" Hunfrid screamed as books rained down from the top of the Sunrise Keep. He rushed over to the point of the needle. Two guards lay dead. Two rebel prisoners stepped into the sunlight; swords drawn.

"Where's Brynlee?" asked Hunfrid.

"What?" The tall rebel with the grey hair blinked, as if confused by the bright sunlight breaching the wall of the inner circle.

From the shadows of the needle, a soldier from the second circle emerged with a rebel held captive in his grasp.

"Bryn," whispered Hunfrid.

She turned her pale-blue eyes towards him. "Can you tell this imbecile to release me?"

Before Hunfrid could respond, a chilling scream from the balcony pierced the tension.

"Where is the boy?!" Eroberung leaned over the balustrade, clutching the railing with his right hand, blood dripping from his fingers. "WHERE IS THE BOY?!"

Hunfrid glared at the soldier from the second circle.

"Only found dis one alive. Dere's another dead woman, back in da needle."

"Find him now!" ordered Eroberung. "He has a naevus on his back, shaped like a crescent moon. Strip every young man bare until you find the marked one."

*   *   *   *

Tom bent over, breathless. "Wait. What about the others?"

"I'm here only for you."

Tom bounded after the soldier up a steep, spiral staircase. He sucked in each breath, unable to ask where they were going. They stopped at a thick wooden door with a barred hole in the centre.

The young soldier leant down and called through the bars, "Caeli."

A soft, freckled face peered out from the door. "Jürgen, you're amazing. I want to give you a big hug."

"We need to hurry, Princess. They'll come after us soon enough. I never found my key."

"Not to worry. Tom, do you still have the key Dwarrow gave you?"

For a rare moment, Tom's mind stopped racing and he stared, dumbfounded, at the princess. *How does she know...*

"Quickly now, we've not much time," said Caeli.

Tom had held the key tight in his fist all the way up the stairs. "Does it open *this* door?" he asked.

"It opens many doors."

*   *   *   *

Eroberung stormed across the courtyard, his leather boots slapping against the stones. He pushed pass Hunfrid and Rostard and confronted Brynlee, smacking her across the face with his bloodied right hand. "We had a deal. Where is the boy?"

The traitor reeled back. She gathered her composure and spoke through blood-stained teeth, "He was with us. Something happened in the needle. Someone took him through the guardhouse. There's a back door."

"Where does that door lead?"

"To the Sunrise Keep, Vater," replied Rostard.

"Search every stone in that keep until you find him. Kill anyone who stands in your way."

Rostard gathered the militia and headed to the keep.

Hunfrid forced the prisoners to kneel on the hard, cobbled stones, hands clasped behind their heads, surrounded by halberd blades.

The younger rebel looked up at Eroberung. "Where's Ewald?"

Eroberung glowered. "The king is dead, fool. Your plan is for naught. But…I will spare your life if you bring me the boy."

"I'll find him," Brynlee sobbed. "I'll honour our deal. I want to serve the Worshipful Master."

"You had your chance and you failed." Eroberung raised his sword.

"No," said Hunfrid.

Without pause, Eroberung lashed his blade through the air and decapitated the woman with the cold eyes and white hair.

Hunfrid doubled-over, as if Eroberung had struck him instead.

The white grell hovered over the rebel with the grey hair. This must be Ryder, he thought, their pitiful leader. His eyes glisten with bewilderment. "Did you think she loved you?" asked Eroberung. "It seems poor Hunfrid thought the same. But there was no love in her, only a lust for self-preservation." Eroberung crouched and studied Ryder's shattered face, relishing the moment of exposed weakness. "The fearless rebel leader, played for a fool by a peasant girl. Is this pain enough for you to draw pleasure from, or shall I lash your flesh until it hangs from your bones?"

*　*　*　*

"Princess Caeli?"

"Call me Caeli. I'm a friend who can help you, Tom Anderson."

Tom wasn't surprised that Caeli knew his name. Nothing surprised him anymore. Standing inside her room, his eyes flicked between the door and the child-like princess. Jürgen had locked them in the room and returned Tom's key through the barred hole.

"Don't worry," said Caeli. "Jürgen will protect us. At least for a while."

How long's a while? Tom started to count the rows and rows of books stacked high on shelves up to the ceiling.

Caeli rushed over to one of the shelves and grabbed a book that she thrust into Tom's hand. "This is one of my favourites. Have you read it?"

Through the Looking-Glass, and What Alice Found There.

Tom's hands trembled and he dropped the book on the floor. "Where... how...how did you get this?"

"It was a present. It's a wonderful book. Alice meets Tweedledum and Tweedledee and the Red Queen and sees all sorts of amazing things, and has wonderous adventures and..."

"Can you read it?"

"Of course."

"Who taught you Eng…"

"Sorry, we don't have much time for small talk. I have important things to tell you." The princess glanced out her window. "The white grell is here. They'll never stop hunting you, Tom. I know somewhere safe and someone who can answer all your questions."

Tom floated with Caeli's musical lilt, enticed by the sparkle of her hazel eyes. "I'm here to bring justice to the man that murdered my grandmother. After that, I want to go home."

Caeli stepped from the window and spoke in English, *"Don't be afraid, Tom. You'll find the answers you seek in the graveyard of the grells. They call it Bindari. Find the gorge running east towards the sea. At the bottom of a steep and slippery stair, there is a light that never goes out. Walk towards the light…you'll find a door. To open the door, you must solve a puzzle. Only you will know the answer. Tell no-one why you seek this place. No-one."*

There was a commotion outside Caeli's door. Jürgen, the brave young soldier who had saved Tom, confronted intruders.

"They're here," said Caeli in Erstürmen. "You must go."

"Go where?"

"Why, through the looking glass of course." Caeli fidgeted with the edge of a full-length mirror and then slid it across the floor, exposing a dark hole in the wall.

The clang of swords from the other side of the door made Tom jump. "B-b-but…"

"Follow the passage. It goes only one way. Keep going and don't turn back."

Tom hesitated. He plunged his hand into his pocket and pulled out the silver coin, handing it to Caeli. "Take this. As a thank you."

Caeli held the coin to her face, studying both sides. "I haven't seen one of these since…since I was a child." She wrapped her fist around the coin and pushed Tom towards the wall. "You must go."

He squirmed into the hole. "Why don't you come with me?"

"They'll know there is another exit if I do. I'll stay here and befuddle them with my innocence. It's my duty."

A cry of pain and a thud filtered into Caeli's room. "Quickly." She pushed Tom into the passage and slid the mirror back in place.

*　*　*　*

Somebody thumped on the keep door. "Open this door you little bitch. We know the boy's in there." Caeli recognised the voice; Rostard, the King's Soothsayer. He'd come to visit her from time to time. To taunt her.

She ambled up to the barred hole. "What boy? I'm the only one who's occupied this room for nearly eighteen yarles."

Rostard's face went bright crimson. "Open the damn door!"

"It would hardly be a prison if I could open my own door." Caeli raised herself on tiptoes. On the floor outside her room lay Jürgen, motionless in a spreading pool of blood. Hardened by seasons of abuse at Ewald's hand, her heart still harboured a coracle of softness for the young soldier. She refused to let it sink amid the battering storm lashing her tiny world. "You didn't need to kill him. He was one of the few good men left."

*　*　*　*

Jurelle leapt from Sphinux and raced through the needle into the inner circle. He baulked at the sight of a huge white grell pacing around two peasants kneeling on the ground, surrounded by soldiers. Hunfrid sat on his haunches next to the peasants, sobbing.

350

"Ah, the rebel traitor approaches," said the white grell.

Jurelle searched his memory for a name. Stories of a white grell terrorising western Enthilen. The grell called himself Eroberung.

Three soldiers confronted Jurelle.

Eroberung interjected. "Wait. Give him a chance to pledge allegiance to a new master. He is quite accomplished at that. What news from the war, General?"

"I'm not your General. What transpires here?"

"Well, we have before us the leader of the rebel scum and one of his rats. You were a leader of the Dobunni once, were you not? Now, they despise you more than they despised poor Ewald. There is no respect for a traitor, their fate sealed with the first treacherous thought." Eroberung pointed his sword at the decapitated head of a woman, her long white hair tangled over the cobblestones of the inner circle like tree roots searching for nourishment.

"Where's the king?" asked Jurelle.

"I am tiring of that question," said Eroberung. "Enthilen has a new master now. Pledge fealty to King Adalwolf and I may spare your life."

"Never."

"Oh well. Hunfrid, wrench yourself from your misery and prepare for the executions. We have three offerings now. Maybe Ryder would like to kill the Traitor General? What a delicious irony that would be. One he could savour a moment before his own death. See, I am a compassionate soul after all."

A yell came from the top of the Sunrise Keep.

Eroberung glanced up at Princess Caeli's window. "I hope they have found the..."

Jurelle took advantage of the distraction. He drew his sword and thrust it towards the grell. A soldier sprang in front of the point, the blade plunging into his side. The man Eroberung had called Ryder grabbed the soldier's halberd and challenged the other guards. The younger rebel sprang to his feet, disarming another soldier. The rebels gained the upper hand. Hunfrid lifted himself from the cobblestones and scurried away into the shadows.

Eroberung's scarred face swelled with anger. He flailed his sword in a frenzy, slicing open the young rebel's chest.

"No!" Ryder lunged at Eroberung. The grell parried, running his sword through the rebel's stomach.

As Jurelle dispatched the last of the soldiers, Eroberung towered over the rebel leader poised to strike again. Jurelle dropped his sword and seized a halberd, hurling it at the white demon. It lodged in Eroberung's thigh, but that only seemed to fuel his anger. "You should have pledged allegiance to Adalwolf while you had the chance." The white grell swung his sword at Jurelle, but his injured leg threw him off balance. Jurelle dodged the blade and grabbed another halberd, thrusting it into the grell's side. Eroberung screamed. He lashed out again, staggering across the stones of the inner circle like a drunken king infected by the madness of his thoughts. Jurelle gathered his sword and plunged it into the grell's chest. Eroberung's knees buckled. Jurelle hovered over the white grell preparing to deal the final blow.

Eroberung's right hand clutched the shaft of the halberd lodged in his side, his wheezing breaths bouncing from the walls of Sardis' inner sanctum. He wailed, pulling the bloodied halberd from his flesh. "End it. Is there not a drop of rectitude in your well of treachery?"

Jurelle lashed his sword across the white grell's throat. He crouched next to Ryder who writhed on the ground. The rebel leader calmed his breaths and steadied his body. "I...I...remember you. I was only a boy...you...you were my hero. Revered by your people. They...they call me the greatest Dobunni leader who ever lived. I know that isn't true. That mantle is yours. We need you now...now more than ever."

Jurelle took Ryder's hand. "The Dobunni will never accept me. I have no place among the rebels."

"There's no place for you here, either. Monsters rule Enthilen now."

"The tide will turn. One day. However, I won't have a hand in it."

Ryder spit blood into the heart of the Erstürmen Kingdom. "A traitor drew me here, and a traitor tried to save my life. What am I to make of this world?"

"Love can lead you to treachery or death. But, in the end, only love matters." Jurelle mopped the blood from the rebel leader's chin, providing a final comfort.

With his last breath, Ryder whispered, "Your daughter needs you."

As Ryder closed his eyes, Jurelle noticed Jürgen's griffin amulet lying on the cobblestones next to the dying rebel. It must have been torn off in the fight, he thought. He wrapped his hand around it as the pounding boots of more soldiers resounded across the balconies of the inner circle.

Jurelle sprang to his feet and sprinted to find his family.

~Chapter 31~

Grin sat cross-legged outside the cave that Dwarrow had disappeared into, its entrance much too small for him to squeeze through. The mouldewerp had been coy about where the cave led.

"All you need to know," Dwarrow had said, "is that I'm going to save Tom. Your job is to stay put."

The cave opened on a densely vegetated foothill at the far western edge of The Feign. Being so near to The Feign reminded Grin of the goat-herding story he had concocted for Tom. Given the events of past days, it now seemed a futile thing to have done. Convince Tom to pretend he was someone else.

Further west, on the horizon, Sardis was a speck in the distance, at least a day's walk for a grell. Grin had a commanding view of the main road between the royal city and Laodicea, as it brushed the northern edge of the Scaur Hills and meandered through the valley towards the ocean. Across from where he sat, on the other side of the road, the Dambay Plains began. If he walked due south across the plains, he would eventually arrive at Babir Birramal. Then it would be a short journey home.

Grin had been watching the cave entrance for four moons and three days. He had been unable to muster the energy to go hunting or gathering food, fearful that he may be needed at any moment. Worried about the fate of his friend. Dwarrow had returned and disappeared twice during Grin's watch; always flustered and fretting. Tom Anderson had still not appeared and Dwarrow was growing more concerned as each moment passed. The werp had brought Grin some food, a mash of moss and insects, and reinforced the point that he must keep guard at the cave entrance until told otherwise.

Grin tossed the last portion of mash into his mouth as the sun rose on the fourth day of his duty. A hunger ached in his stomach and his connection with the land began to waver, the trees and shrubs of the foothills unfamiliar to him. The resonate song of a shrike-thrush, also common along the edge of Babir Birramal, rang out from a shrub, bringing him a little comfort.

He rested his eyes and thought about his father, hoping that the old grell had gathered enough stores for ngurung-ginya, the long dark. Jacob had sent a message with a Dobunni scout: Grin and Tom are safe. Frennan would welcome the news, would he not?

In the early morning sun, a dot in the west moved towards Grin along the main road. It grew in size, revealing a long line of cavalry and foot soldiers marching in haste towards Laodicea. Banners and standards flapped against the easterly breeze. A banner with the sigil of a whale flew at the head of the column. Grin's keen eyes spotted Jacob Seamaster riding beneath the banner. He crouched at the entrance to the cave and yelled into the darkness. An echo responded. He needed to find out why the rebels marched east. Dwarrow would not mind if Grin abandoned his post for a moment, would he?

He jumped to his feet and sped down the hill.

*   *   *   *

Bouncing on a hard, leather saddle, Jacob focussed on the road ahead until his temples ached. Behind him, the rebel cavalry numbered a few hundred, bolstered by about five thousand foot-soldiers. At the rear of the column, a handful of grells towered above the Dobunni rebels, pledged to fight for the rebel cause.

Jacob knew his forces wouldn't be enough to ward off the barbarians. Rebel arms were basic with no heavy weapons that could inflict damage on ships. Many soldiers had no armour, and Jacob lacked experience in large-scale conflict. Yet, thousands of lives now relied on his acumen for war. He couldn't fail them with stupidity.

"Looks like a grell up ahead."

Jacob jumped as Thaly yelled into his ear. He peered into the distance. "Careful. It might be a tainted grell."

Thaly galloped ahead and yelled over her shoulder, "I think it's Grin!"

The grell stood in the middle of the road, waving at the oncoming army. Jacob urged his horse after Thaly. They arrived at Grin's side together.

"Where have you been?" asked Thaly. "We thought you and Dwarrow had abandoned us."

"I was requested to assist Dwarrow with an important dealing. He tells me he is going to save Tom."

"How?"

"I do not know. He has disappeared down a hole for now. I am supposed to wait for him."

Jacob waved his army forward while he stayed behind to speak with Grin.

"It looks like you are marching to war," said the grell.

"Barbarian ships threaten Bethesda. We go to protect our home. Will you come with us?"

"I am at Dwarrow's service. I have strict orders to wait for him. I should not have left my post, but I wanted to speak with you and let you know that Dwarrow seeks to rescue Tom."

"Well, that would be a mighty feat. A tiny werp breaching all of Sardis' defences. Why is he risking his life for Tom?"

Grin avoided Jacob's gaze and dropped his chin to the road.

"I know there's more to all this," said Jacob. "And I seem to be the one who knows the least of it." He turned to Thaly, thinking she may have found out more about Tom.

Thaly shrugged. "All I know is that he's travelled from far away and he wants to find the man that killed his grandmother."

"So, he's not from The Feign after all?" Jacob asked the question, but didn't expect an answer.

Grin surprised him by looking up. "No, he is not. He is what we call a birraman. A traveller. Someone who has come from a different place, far from here. A strange place like nothing we have ever seen."

"Yet, he carries with him a silver tausen from the King's Quarter. Where did he get that?"

"The murderer dropped it. Then disappeared."

Jacob's head began to ache. "I can't fathom all this."

Thaly steadied her horse. "We need to protect Tom, even if we can't be sure of the reason. Grin and Dwarrow understand this. The white grell wants him. Our enemy wants him. We can't let them have him. I want to go with Grin. To wait for Tom."

Jacob watched the tail end of the rebel army file past.

Thaly clutched the reins of Jacob's horse. "I'll ride like the wind to catch up with you, before you reach Bethesda."

Jacob nodded. "You've been loyal to the Dobunni for many seasons, Athalee. I trust your word and I know your feelings are torn. Go with Grin. I hope Dwarrow is as wise as he appears to be. I'd like to see young Tom again too."

~Chapter 32~

Tom pulled his knees to his chest, trying to ward off the pitch black that enveloped him like a sarcophagus. On the other side of the mirror, it sounded like a battering ram pounding into Caeli's door. Tom counted the thuds. In the silence between the hammering, Princess Caeli's soft voice attempted to soothe the soldiers trying to breach her sanctuary with a wistful calmness that bewildered Tom.

How is she so brave? His trembling body shook any bravery from his bones. Anxiety and fear now ruled his mind. He pinched his tunic... *seventeen, eighteen, nineteen.* Wound his hanky around his finger, then unwound it, wound it again, unwound.

Wish I was home. Get in the wardrobe. Slam the door shut. Crawl up into a ball. Stupid dark eyes, stupid rebels, stupid fucking plan. Idiot Tom. Idiot, idiot, idiot. Dwarrow, Caeli...how do they know about me? What do they know? Mum, God...help. Stupid to think I could find Nanna's killer. Stupid to think I could bring him to justice. Kill him. Stupid.

A crack shattered the darkness. Yells and screams and an awful din told Tom that the soldiers must have breached Caeli's door. He heard her wail, "Leave my books!", before something smashed the mirror, breaking the glass.

The shock cured Tom's paralysis. He scuttled further into the darkness like a mole burrowing through the soil, complete and utter black masking the path forward.

Tom bumped his head against the smooth walls of the narrow passage, its floor always descending. Down he crawled, down from the top of the Sunrise Keep, down into further darkness. Then the tunnel floor levelled out and he pushed forward, crawling as fast as his aching hands and knees would allow.

Water sloshed around his wrists and dripped onto his head. He held his breath to stop the sound bouncing from the walls and reached up towards the ceiling. Above him, the muted roar of rushing water magnified his terror.

The river. I'm underneath the river. I must be already outside of Sardis' walls. A damp claustrophobia threatened to smother his escape. He quickened his pace.

After crawling on hands and knees for what seemed like hours, the passage widened and Tom could stand and creep along, his hands out front, feeling his way in the blackness. He kept his ears pricked for any noise either up ahead or from behind, but he could hear only the soft footfalls from his moccasin-covered feet. Stooped over, he pushed forward, focussing on his breathing.

Walk and breathe. Walk and breathe. Wait. Wait. I hear something. Up ahead. Scuffling, coming towards me. Breathe. Quietly. Listen. Listen… It's nothing. Nobody there.

Tom stepped forward.

No. There it is again. Someone's coming. What should I do? Go back? Stand still in the dark and hope it passes by?

Tom thrust his arms out sideways. The back of his hands smacked the walls of the tunnel long before his arms reached full stretch. Whatever was up ahead would bump into him if it came this way. Tom searched his tunic. All he had for a weapon was a key. He grasped it in his fist with the bit sticking out between his fingers.

Feet shuffled along the stone floor.

It's getting louder. Shit. They're close.

Tom flattened himself against the passage wall. The key slipped about in the grasp of his sweaty hand. He gripped it tighter and practiced stabbing out into the black to fend off an attacker. Footfalls and laboured breaths terrified his ears, but the darkness had no shape. Tom braced himself.

The shuffling stopped. The sniffing began. "Ah, finally, finally. I've found you. I don't remember this tunnel being ever so long, even though I've traversed it many times."

"Dwarrow? Dwarrow is that you?"

"Well of course. Who else would it be?"

Tom slumped against the wall and wept.

"Goodness, no need for that, and no time. No time at all. We need to be going. Pull yourself together."

Tom wiped tears from his face. He listened to Dwarrow fossicking about next to him, then, suddenly, a blinding light illuminated the two companions. Dwarrow had brought his giba.

"It's magic..." Tom muttered.

"Magic is rare in this world, Tom Anderson. What little exists should be cherished or feared depending on who wields it."

Tom dropped to his knees, beamed into Dwarrow's small, salmon-coloured face with its long, probing nose, and wrapped him in a suffocating hug. "Thank you, Dwarrow. I'm so glad you're here. So glad you recovered."

"Can't...can't...breathe..."

Tom released the embrace and smiled.

"It is nice to be appreciated for a change," said Dwarrow, "and I think

I owe you a debt of gratitude. Jacob told me that you managed to fight off those ruffians in Bagendon. Saved me from further...harm. Anyway, we'll have time for hugs later, now we have to run. Follow my nose!" Dwarrow disappeared down the passage.

Tom jumped to his feet and sped after the light of the giba. "Are we safe now?"

"Not yet. If the mirror is broken, they'll find the passage and follow us. However, a few more challenges will cause them delay."

What challenges? thought Tom.

"How's the princess?"

"Caeli? I'm not sure. Soldiers broke her door down..."

"And the other rebels?"

"I didn't see. An Erstürmen soldier, Jürgen, unlocked my shackles and took me to Caeli's room. That key you gave me..."

"A very *special* key."

"Eroberung was in the inner circle."

"Oh. King Ewald no longer rules Enthilen. He's probably dead, not that mouldewerps will mourn his passing."

Dwarrow and Tom raced along the passage, past red brick walls and arched roofs that seemed so strong they'd last for generations. Their feet slapped on the smooth stone floor, masking any other sound. Tom glanced over his shoulder, expecting pursuers to be upon him at any moment. They never came.

Dwarrow stopped when he reached a heavy steel door, bolted and locked. He took a key from a pouch, opened the door and urged Tom through before locking it behind them.

"Your key will also unlock these doors. If the Erstürmen or these new demons find the passage they won't have a key. That should slow them down a bit. Then there's the Gaping Hollow, and the draughouls of course."

"The what?"

"You'll see. Let's rest here for a while. We're safe behind this door, it's as thick as a grell. If they come to it, it will take strength to breach."

Dwarrow and Tom rested their backs against the brick wall, illuminated by the giba. The mouldewerp pulled food from one of his pouches.

Tom screwed up his face, almost too scared to ask.

"I can sense what you're thinking, Tom. You never know where your next meal is coming from. We must eat when we can."

"What is it?"

"Slitherweed. I found it right outside the entrance to the cave. That bumbling beast of a grell walked all over it."

"Grin?"

"Yes, Grin. He's waiting at the other end."

Tom smiled at the thought of seeing his friend again. "Why didn't he come with you?"

"Too big. Couldn't fit into the hole. There are lots of advantages to being small, you know. Anyway, better he keeps watch at the entrance, just in case."

"What about Thaly...Jacob?"

"I didn't have time to organise a search party. I imagine they're safe and warm in their little town hidden in the hills."

"Princess Caeli told me I should go to Bindari."

"*Hmm*. Where the grells go to die. I wonder why she sent you there?"

"I promised her I wouldn't say."

"*Hmph*. Well. Keep your secrets then. All I know is that the princess is one of my most trusted friends. You should heed her advice."

"Where is Bindari? How do I get there?"

"You'll need to ask a grell. It's a sacred place. Only the initiated know where it is. I doubt they'll tell you. Initiation doesn't improve their manners one little bit. Anyway, enough questions. It's time for a rest."

Tom slouched next to Dwarrow and closed his eyes. He nodded in and out of sleep, too exhausted to stay awake, but too wary to give in to deep slumber. He woke fully at the sound of Dwarrow's barking snores and shook the mouldewerp's shoulder. "Dwarrow. Be quiet. You're snoring."

"What...what...oh, was I asleep?"

"Yes. You snore so loud; it could wake up the dead."

"You shouldn't have woken me. Werps are at their most dangerous when asleep. Our olfactory senses are heightened to unimaginable levels. One tiny scent of danger and I could have split you in two with a single blow. Never wake a sleeping werp."

Tom half-smiled, unsure if Dwarrow was being serious. They both staggered to their feet. Dwarrow gathered the giba and led Tom through two more locked doors. After the last door, the secret exit from Sardis changed from a brick-lined passage to a natural cave with jagged rock walls and growing deposits of calcium salts forming cathedrals of stalagmites and stalactites.

"Who made this passage, Dwarrow?"

"The Dobunni. A long time ago when they built Al Mōr Sŭrl. They wanted an escape from the watchtower should Iglund ever be attacked. The Erstürmen invasion erased the secret from the memory of most of the rebels. Legend has it that the last residents of Iglund bricked over the tunnel entrance in the Sunrise Keep when they escaped. They were never seen again. Erstürmen royalty were too obtuse to see what was right under their nose. However, the mouldewerp elders remembered."

"How much further before we reach the end?"

"Not far. First, we must cross this." Dwarrow shone the giba into the darkness ahead, illuminating the steep walls of a deep chasm.

Tom crept close to the edge and peered into the abyss. "How far down does it go?"

"Far enough. My magic stone cannot pierce its blackness. The elders say the chasm has no end. If you fall into it, you'll keep falling until the air is squeezed from your chest. They call it the Gaping Hollow."

"How do we get across?"

"Too far to jump, much too far. I have a way, though." Dwarrow searched among the rocks and pulled out a pile of rope and timber. He laid it flat on the ground — a ladder with smooth and straight tree branches for rungs, lashed between two long pieces of rope. The werp draped a loop in one end of the ladder around two metal spikes embedded in the ground right at the chasm edge. "Are you a good throw?"

"Why?"

"At the free end of the ladder is a rope that forms a snare. We need to throw it across the chasm and have it catch on the spikes on the other side, then pull it tight. I always take forever to get it right. It's quite frustrating."

"I see, it's like a lasso. The ladder would form a bridge that we can walk across."

"Ah...not exactly. We need to take the ladder with us. Stop others from following. Plus, I need the ladder to cross back over, should I want to visit the princess..." Dwarrow's shoulders slumped and he bowed his head.

"She's a survivor, Dwarrow. She'll find a way to stay alive."

"Of course, she will. I need to stay positive." Dwarrow stood up straight. "When the rope snares the spikes on the other side, we free this end and swing across. Then we climb up the ladder."

Tom processed Dwarrow's instructions. *Did the werp really mean to swing across on the ladder? How the hell are we going to do that? Focus on the now.* Tom took the end of the rope and swung it above his head until he thought he had enough momentum to bridge the divide of the Gaping Hollow. He let the snare go. It fell well short of its mark, disappearing into the dark below. He gathered the rope and tried again, and again he failed.

"Maybe I should try after all," muttered Dwarrow.

"Let me have one more go." Tom swung again, calling on all the reserves of energy and concentration left in him. The snare sailed over the gap and caught the metal spikes on the other side. "Hey, I got it."

"Excellent. Excellent. Excellent. Pull it tight. Secure the ladder. We don't want to tumble into the hollow and keep falling until our chests burst."

Tom pulled the ropes taut.

"I'll crawl out a bit and grab onto one of these rungs. You'll need to free the rope on this side, simultaneously seizing the last rung before the ladder falls into the chasm."

Dwarrow placed the giba in a pouch tied around his neck. Though dulled, the light from the stone still shone through the cloth, guiding the werp along the ladder and into the gap. He grabbed a rung with both clawed hands and held tight. "I'm ready now."

Tom baulked at the next step in the plan. "Are you sure this is the only way to get across, Dwarrow?"

"Yes, yes, yes. Don't think too much about it. Take the tension off the rope, release it from the spikes and hang on for dear life."

Focus on the now. Tom grasped the last rung of the ladder with a sweaty, scarred palm. With his free hand, he tugged at the rope, trying to wrench it off the spikes, but there was too much tension. Tom pulled harder, trying to account for Dwarrow's weight. The rope released from one of the spikes and the ladder jerked sideways. One of Dwarrow's hands slipped from the smooth branch while the other one dug into the bark with life-saving determination. "Careful now! You almost lost me there."

Tom mustered all his remaining strength and freed the rope from the second spike, at the same time grasping the final rung of the ladder as it swung across the Gaping Hollow. He cried aloud as the far, sheer wall careered towards him. He heaved his legs out in front and bent at the knee, bracing for the impact. However, the lower part of the wall was undercut, and the adventurers swung into emptiness before hitting solid rock with much less force. The rope held and Tom and Dwarrow climbed the ladder, safely making it to the other side.

"See. No trouble at all." The mouldewerp pulled up the ladder and unhooked the snare. He stashed the ropes and branches into a hole in the cave wall, retrieving his walking stick at the same time. "Let's see someone follow us now. Well, that's the easy bit over. Only one more challenge before we reach the end."

"Easy bit? *Another* challenge?"

"I hoped we'd pass without them noticing, but you made such a racket at the crossing."

"Who are you talking about?"

"Draughouls."

"Draughouls? Frennan told me about those."

"Horrid, soulless creatures. They give me the shivers. They move swiftly about the land using their knowledge of ancient routes and underground passages. The elders say draughouls can pass through solid rock or disappear and re-appear in distant locations in moments. They are easily corrupted and forever in servitude of the trappings of Volerdie, especially the throne of the dead and the eyes of lost souls."

"Are they dead?"

"Not dead, still dying. Their souls have been captured by the dark eyes. When someone's life is taken by the eyes there is no peace. Their soul is trapped for all eternity and their body lingers, roaming this world seeking deliverance. Rotting. Putrefying. Waiting for the final decay. The body withers, eventually..." Dwarrow paused and sniffed. "They're coming."

"What do we do?"

"There's nothing we can do. We can't hide. We must face them and hope they'll let us pass. They're hard to kill and stronger than an undred, despite their appearance. I've met them many times before. Their mood oscillates on a whim. Sometimes they pay me no attention. Other times they talk about ripping me apart and painting the walls with my blood. I'm not sure what they'll make of you. Let me do the talking."

Around a bend in the cave floated five creatures, pale and decaying, like frail, crooked monsters. Although bent over, one stood taller than the others; a grell draughoul with its right arm severed at the shoulder.

Run! Tom's mind screamed. Nowhere *to* run.

Dwarrow stood looking brave and firm.

The draughouls approached Tom, their alabaster bones pressed against loose, torn skin. His mind flashed back to the rocky scrub near his home. The old woman that forced the eyes of lost souls into his hands. She was a draughoul.

"You disturb our rest," hissed one of the creatures.

"It's just me, Dwarrow, passing through again. Lovely weather..."

"The werp."

"That's right. Would love to stay and chat but we have to be getting along."

A draughoul wearing Erstürmen armour pressed his face up to Tom's. "Who this?"

A lump set in Tom's throat.

"A friend of mine," said Dwarrow. "Helping me out. My nose isn't like it used to be. I get lost more easily now. He won't be back. This is his only trip."

"Where you from?" the Erstürmen draughoul asked Tom.

"He's heading home now, actually. Back to the Desolate Mountains..."

"Let him *speeeeak.*"

Tom's dry mouth craved for the right response. "As Dwarrow said, I'm on my way…"

"You invaded our home. Why?"

"Dwarrow needed a guide…"

"Liar. The werp smells everything. You escape Sardis. Who hunts you?"

"Now, now," said Dwarrow. "You're drawing a long bow there. No-one's hunting us. We were visiting a friend."

A draughoul latched onto Dwarrow's stubby arm, its bony fingers clamped like a shackle. "Keep you here. Wait and see if anyone comes to find you."

"That's completely unnecessary," said Dwarrow. "I'm the only one who's used this cave for a generation or more. Well, beside your good selves."

The draughouls encircled Tom and Dwarrow. "Will let you go," said the grell draughoul. "Must answer one question first."

"What is it?" asked Dwarrow.

"Where are the eyes?"

"I have no idea what you're talking about."

"The eyes that have our souls. Where are they?"

"N-n-never heard of them."

As one, the five draughouls flashed piercing stares at Tom. Beads of sweat seeped from his forehead, as if the draughouls were squeezing the aqueous truth from his mind.

They know, thought Tom. *Who I am, where I've been, where I'm going.* He couldn't hold back the truth. "The white grell has them."

"He knows," the draughouls hissed. "He *knowssss*. Take us to them. Take — us — now!"

The grell draughoul grabbed at Tom with his giant left hand.

Dwarrow raised his walking stick. "I hoped it wouldn't come to this."

He lashed out, knocking one of the creatures to the ground and creating a gap in the circle. "Run!"

Tom and the mouldewerp bolted past their wretched assailants and sprinted towards the entrance to the cave.

~Chapter 33~

Lily stood on the Docklands wharf as the barbarian fleet filled Traders Bay. The ships had been anchored outside the heads that guarded the bay for days, as if waiting for a signal to begin the attack. She counted forty-eight barbarian ships cutting through the chop, the twin hulls of each vessel connected by a flat, square deck that supported dormitories housing hundreds of warriors. Made from the light, pliable timber of the meladoor tree, the hulls curved upwards at the front, each bow painted with a pair of eyes; ivory sclera and seaweed green pupils.

Having grown up in the Abrolous Isles, east of Enthilen, Lily was more familiar with barbarian ships than most in Laodicea. The isles were a favourite raiding spot for the barbarians, and her village had been raided three times before she'd seen six harvest seasons. After the third time, her family moved to the mainland and settled in Laodicea. Soon after arriving, Lily discovered previously unknown Dobunni relatives and began to learn more about her ancestry and place in the wider world.

Lily squinted into the morning sun rising above the ocean. Regular spouts of mist shot up from the surface of the water, catching the light and drifting off among the waves, seemingly offering no harm to anyone. Lily thought the dancing spouts would look beautiful if they weren't so terrifying. Like most ships that visited Laodicea, barbarian vessels didn't have sails or masts. Whales pulled the ships; teams of giants harnessed to the front of the vessel, spouting air and water as they came up to breathe. Many sea-farers had learned to communicate with and train whales using a complex series of whistles broadcast underwater via specially designed tubes. After calling up a pod of whales, sailors would attach harnesses to the sea creatures. Then, with enormous strength at their command, the whales pulled the boats through the water, guided by a whale-master on the bow of the vessel and a small crew responsible for tensioning each harness. This method freed sea-farers from the whims of ocean breezes. Each ship had its own pod of whales who would respond only to the whistles emanating from that vessel.

Lily had heard many tall, sea-faring tales from whale crews who visited the taverns in the Southern Vale. As a young woman, she had dreamed about driving her own pod of whales and sailing off into seas that had never been explored, at least not by anyone she knew. But duty called, and her fate as a Lady and Master of the Dobunni quashed her dreams of escape.

The shouts of the barbarian whale crews surfed across the tops of the waves splashing against the piles of the Docklands wharf. As the barbarians neared Laodicea, Lily followed them scampering about the decks of the boats, releasing their whales from the harnesses and preparing their rowers by threading oars through the oar-holes that ran the length of the starboard and port sides of the ships. Lily's heart quickened when the red grell, Krieg, appeared on the foredeck of the largest ship.

His powers of influence must be compelling, she thought. She'd never heard of anyone being able to unite the disparate barbarian tribes scattered across faraway lands into such a coherent and deadly force. Krieg must have promised them all of Laodicea's riches.

She glanced over her left shoulder towards the Terraces where most of Laodicea's wealth resided. Terrace-dwellers scurried about the balconies built into the cliff face, erecting timber barricades and arming anyone with idle hands. She thought of Lord Sleame strutting through the halls giving orders.

All of it was pointless. Laodiceans could never defend themselves against the barbarian horde. To make things worse, Hunger threatened to attack from the King's Quarter, a militia at his beck and call. The Docklands, Southern Vale and Terraces faced certain annihilation.

To what end? thought Lily. Hunger had demanded that all citizens pledge fealty to Prince Adalwolf or die. What had happened to King Ewald? Was he dead? Lily had never met the prince, but she'd heard stories of a nervous, shy young man. Did the temptation of power turn the meek prince into a voracious monster? And what of this mysterious Malphas? He who seems to have remained hidden for so long, but now emerges from the darkness to spread a different kind of terror.

Dealhia marched along the wharf and interrupted Lily's thoughts. "We're as ready as we can be. Boats have been anchored in the harbour and packed with heavy cargo. They'll disrupt the passage of the barbarians somewhat. Might even damage their ships should they collide."

Lily sighed. "It won't have much effect."

"Archers hide on the boats. Barricades and palisades have been erected along the entire length of the docks. Our armouries are empty. We can do no more."

"Our forces stand with you, Dealhia. When…if the barbarians get the upper hand, we must retreat to the Southern Vale. We'll make our final stand there. I've ordered our larger buildings to be reinforced. Turned into makeshift fortresses. Our best chance is fighting the barbarians at close quarters in the winding streets of the vale. Out in the open, their advantage is too great."

"Have you heard from Bagendon?"

"The rebel army marches as we speak, yet they're still at least three, maybe four moons away. I fear they'll arrive too late. We can hold off the barbarians for only so long."

A messenger bolted along the wharf towards the masters. She doubled over, panting, before eventually composing herself. "Master Lily, Master Dealhia. Barbarians have landed at Sand Bēċe. Over one hundred ships."

Dealhia's usual ruby face turned white. "What? That's only a day's march from here."

"They'll attack the south wall," said Lily.

"We're surrounded on all sides."

"They want to eliminate us, Dealhia. Squeeze the life out of every last citizen of Laodicea not beholden to the madness of Erstürmen rule. Even if we'd pledged fealty to Adalwolf, I doubt they would have called off the attack."

Dealhia pointed into Traders Bay. "The barbarians have dropped their oars. Krieg is coming."

~Chapter 34~

Gasping for breath, Tom stopped and strained his ears for a warning that the draughouls were upon them. The darkness of the cave kept its silence.

Dwarrow grabbed his hand and dragged him along. "No time for sightseeing. They'll be coming, but they won't leave the safety of the cave. Not without good reason. We need to reach the outside first."

Tom ran after Dwarrow, following the welcome light of the giba. *When's this cave going to end?* As the thought left his mind, a circle of daylight appeared up ahead. Dwarrow crawled through the hole on his hands and knees. Tom squeezed through, flat on his stomach. He lay there on his back, panting and squinting hard into the bright sunlight directly above. As Tom's eyes adjusted to the light, a colossal shadow blocked out the sun, hoisted him into the air, and smothered him with a rapturous bear-hug.

"You are safe. I cannot believe it!"

"*Hmmmph....*" muffled Tom. "I thought I was safe. Now I'm being crushed by a giant grell."

Grin held Tom aloft, at arms-length, and beamed. "I prepared myself not to see you again. I have never felt so foolish."

Tom couldn't help but smile along with Grin. He'd missed the glistening lilac eyes that sat above muwin, Grin's facial crest. He never thought he'd be so happy to see a huge, black spider.

Grin placed Tom back on solid ground. Standing behind Dwarrow, Thaly thrust her hands onto her hips. "You're the luckiest lubberwort I've ever met, Tom Anderson." She walked over to Tom and pecked him on the cheek. "I'm glad you're alive."

He grinned like a fool who'd discovered a chest of gold.

"It seems we will be forever in your debt, Master Dwarrow."

"Your debts are piling up, Grinnian stone-grell. I hope I don't send you broke."

Tom and Thaly laughed together; a brief, welcome respite.

"Where does this cave lead?" Thaly asked Dwarrow.

"It's a secret. But if the Dobunni didn't forget their history so easily then you'd know. A book in the library at Laodicea holds clues..."

"I can't read."

"I can teach you," said Tom.

Thaly pushed Tom away. "I don't need you to teach me."

"What of the others?" asked Grin. "Was the mission a success?"

Tom sat on the ground, exhausted from his journey through the cave. "I don't know. An Erstürmen soldier rescued me from the needle before I saw anything."

"You were in the needle?" said Thaly.

"That was the plan. We were taken prisoner and selected for execution. We were supposed to free each other in the needle before confronting the king."

"What a stupid plan. The inner circle would be crawling with King's Shield. No-one was ever going to get close enough to Ewald to kill him."

"Someone already has," said Dwarrow. "At least I'm fairly certain of it. Eroberung and his henchmen rule Sardis now. The kingdom of Ewald has fallen."

"Maybe that's got something to do with the threat of war in Laodicea," said Thaly. "Barbarians are preparing to ransack the city. The rebel army of Bagendon marches there now, led by Jacob."

"War? How unpleasant. No place for a werp. No place indeed. It's time I returned to the elders. They'll be longing for news, and I have much to share."

"I can carry you, Dwarrow, if you desire," said Grin.

"No, that's not necessary. I was unwell after our last trip. Couldn't stop my nose from spinning in all directions. I have other modes of transport I can call on. I release you from my service, for now. But don't go getting into too much trouble. I'll need you again one day."

"What should *I* do, Dwarrow?" asked Tom.

"*Hmm*. Well. I've just rescued you from one nasty predicament, only a buffoon would walk straight into another one. If there's war in Laodicea, I wouldn't be going anywhere near the place. Better to heed the advice of Princess Caeli."

"Princess who?" Thaly asked Tom.

"Caeli. She helped me escape the inner circle." He reached inside his pocket to the empty space where the silver coin used to sit. "I gave her my coin. As pay...to thank her for helping me. It was a stupid thing to do. But it's all I had. I think she paid for her kindness with her life."

Tom felt the burrowing of Thaly's searching brown eyes. "An Erstürmen princess helped you escape Sardis?" she asked.

"Dwarrow trusts her. I trust her...I think...although, we spent only a moment together."

"That coin was valuable. Beyond anything you can imagine." Thaly grabbed the reins of her horse. "I'm going to Laodicea, to fight beside Jacob and honour my pledge to the Dobunni. If that means nothing to you, Tom, maybe finding your grandmother's killer still does?"

Does it? thought Tom. *Caeli said to find Bindari.* He rubbed his chest, feeling the ridges of his pledge scars through his tunic. *I'm a rebel now, for what it's worth. One of the companionship. All of them are going to Laodicea. What better chance will I have to confront the murderer with an army at my side? But Grin? Grin could go home. He doesn't need to risk his life further.*

Grin spoke, as if he'd read Tom's thoughts, "We set out from Babir Birramal to reach Laodicea, so you could do the one thing that gave your presence here purpose. If that is still your destination, I will not abandon you. I will follow you to the end. But Laodicea is not the same as it was when we left the milbi. It has become much more dangerous. I would not think any less of you, Tom, should you seek another path. War changes everything. You should not consider yourself under any obligation."

Tom retreated into his thoughts. He glanced at Thaly, seeing a flash of anger pass across her face. Or maybe he imagined it? He'd set out to do one thing. One important thing. But was there any hope in finding Nanna's killer with a war raging?

Thaly mounted her horse. "I can't dally here any longer. My place is with the rebels."

I'm a fighter, thought Tom. *I have a purpose and an enemy, and brothers and sisters to stand beside me. I'm not going to crawl under the bed and hide anymore. Bindari can wait.*

"I'll go with you," he said. "If I'm not in the way."

Thaly smiled. "Actually, I'm beginning to like you. Just a little bit. You can ride pillion. My horse is strong and my saddle will accommodate two."

"I can run beside you," said Grin.

Tom turned to his grell friend. "You don't have to."

"I am not going to leave you, Tom."

"It's all settled," said Thaly. "We ride for Laodicea. My heart already breaks at what we'll find there."

Dwarrow smacked his forehead. "It's worse than I thought. You're all fools. How can I possibly argue against such witlessness? At the very least, stay away from any tainted grells. And especially stay away from their master."

"Who *is* their master?" asked Tom. "I know you're keeping things from me."

Dwarrow inhaled deeply and clutched his walking stick. "I've heard a name, but no more than that. The tainted grells serve a crooked old man called Malphas."

It seemed Tom's torment had a name. *Malphas.*

Dwarrow turned and walked away, calling back over his shoulder, "That's all I know. That's all I want to know." He disappeared into the shrubs.

Without another word, Tom mounted Thaly's horse and the three companions began their journey to Laodicea.

~Chapter 35~

Adalwolf wandered through the empty streets of the King's Quarter in Laodicea. He hardly remembered the place, having visited only one previous time as a child, before his fath…King Ewald became too paranoid to leave the inner circle of Sardis. He wondered where all the people were. Hiding in their homes, most likely. Hoping the barbarians don't come to batter their doors down.

Adalwolf fixed his eyes on the back of Malphas, the old man that limped ahead of him, still dressed in the juniper robes he'd been wearing when his tainted grells ambushed the armoured wagon from Sardis. Adalwolf tried hard, but couldn't see a single drop of blood on the robes, despite the carnage at the ambush. Not a single drop. The old man had managed to remain unspoiled. This old man who claimed to be Adalwolf's father, who *wanted* Adalwolf to be king, unlike Ewald, who always threatened to keep the throne from his son. A corner of the king's scarred mind might have known that he could never sire an heir. That Adalwolf could never be his son. Maybe that's why he was so reluctant to abdicate?

Next to Malphas walked Ende, the pale grell. Adalwolf's heart beat faster whenever she looked at him, as if she were casting a silent spell that would ultimately see his demise. The blunt end of her sparth clacked against the cobblestones as she pushed herself forward, the light of the moons bouncing from the shining tip.

Malphas led Ende and Adalwolf around a corner and Adalwolf gasped at the sight of hundreds of soldiers standing to attention in the square outside the Master's Hall. Malphas pushed him to the front and, as one, the soldiers dropped to their knees, both arms hanging limp by their side. Some wore the silver armour of the King's Shield. Others wore armour that Adalwolf didn't recognise; dull and blacker than the night around him.

Adalwolf stood there, dumbstruck, the joints in his body locked together, as if his bones and flesh had frozen solid.

Malphas whispered in his ear, "Tell them to rise."

"R-r-rise," Adalwolf stammered.

"Louder," said Malphas.

"Rise."

The nearest soldiers stood and the others followed. Out of the corner of his eye, Adalwolf caught Malphas nod to the front row of soldiers. In unison they thumped their breastplates with their right fist and yelled, "Hail King Adalwolf! Hail the king!"

The remainder of the soldiers followed in kind.

The gathering parted in formation, leaving a clear path to the main door of the Master's Hall. Malphas and Ende tottered towards it, and Adalwolf followed, fearing to make eye contact with a single soldier. As they entered the meeting room of the hall, the black grell with skin darker than charcoal sprang to his feet. He strode around the map table and dropped to both knees, bowing his head and holding out his hand towards Malphas. "Greetings, Worshipful Master. Laodicea is ready to fall."

Malphas clasped the black grell's left hand. "Excellent. You've served me well, Hunger. Our new king would welcome a pledge of loyalty."

Still on his knees, Hunger turned and bowed before Adalwolf, holding out his hand.

As Adalwolf stared into the black skin, an unexpected nightmare enveloped his mind. A crown he never coveted would soon adorn his head, placed there by a man who was no more than a stranger with ambitions beyond Adalwolf's comprehension. Queen Romilda still whispered to her son, but her desperate susurrations offered little comfort or guidance, only warnings of the perils to come. Malphas had become the dominant voice in Adalwolf's ear. Yet, Adalwolf couldn't decipher the true meaning of the words Malphas infused into his thoughts. However, one thing was clear, there was no room in Adalwolf's future for weakness or indecision.

"Take his hand and accept his fealty," said Malphas.

With trepidation, Adalwolf rested his hand above Hunger's. It resembled the tiny hand of a pale doll drowning in a black lake. The tainted grell bowed low and brushed his forehead across Adalwolf's knuckles, a sign of submission and loyalty.

"Rise, Hunger," ordered Malphas. "I have news from Sardis. It is not welcome news. That blunderer, Eroberung, has failed us again. I should never have given him another chance. His arrogance was his downfall. Eroberung's death should be a lesson to all of you. Humility is a valuable mis-direction that distracts the attention of your enemies from your true purpose. We'll find another white grell, when the time is right."

"What of the boy, Worshipful Master?" asked Hunger.

"The rebels from Bagendon march to defend Laodicea, as we expected. My spies have seen a rebel girl trailing them. She rides with a boy and a wild grell running beside. I'm certain it's our quarry. The grell is never far from the boy's side. Set a watch on the edge of the city. When they come, you must be ready, Hunger. I want him unharmed."

Malphas turned to Adalwolf and ran his crooked fingers through Adalwolf's curls like his mother sometimes did. "We must prepare, my son. Soon your destiny will be upon you."

~Chapter 36~

Perched on his horse, Jacob overlooked his home town of Bethesda, renamed Laodicea by the Erstürmen invaders. Scores of barbarian ships crowded into Traders Bay, firing burning lances into timber buildings. Vast plumes of black smoke drifted on the breeze, tall, thin clouds rising up like a wistful forest and blocking out the morning sun. Jacob's chest burned, as if the flames licking the jetties and wharfs of the Docklands had set his heart ablaze.

A barbarian army encamped south of the Southern Vale, cutting off any escape along the coast and blocking the rebels' path into the city. The low, stone wall protecting the inland boundary of Bethesda had already been breached, attackers swarming through like a cloud of wasps. From the parapets atop the wall, Dobunni soldiers from the Southern Vale rained arrows down at the sieging army. The barbarians countered with boulders covered in burning tar flung from enormous catapults. The projectiles exploded among houses huddled together, eave-to-eave, behind the wall, setting whole neighbourhoods alight.

The screams of injured and dying Dobunni soldiers tortured Jacob's mind.

"What are your orders, Field Commander?" Maxton Nash, Jacob's lieutenant, shifted in his saddle.

"The barbarians have attacked on two fronts. It seems they have no intention of occupying Bethesda. They aim only to destroy it. Yet, the King's Quarter remains unscathed. My guess is that the Erstürmen or whoever's in charge down there are in leagues with the raiders. Our best option is to march for the Southern Vale from the south."

"That's a dangerous route, taking us along the flank of the sieging army. I doubt we can fight our way through to the south gate."

"Do you have a better option, lieutenant?"

"If the barbarians aren't attacking the King's Quarter, we could try to clear a path through there. March our army to the Southern Vale through the centre of the city."

Jacob called on his memories of Bethesda, picturing the narrow streets of the King's Quarter and the closed enclave of the Bethesda market, surrounded by two and three storey stone buildings. "There are too many places for an ambush. We don't know what lurks in the King's Quarter."

"If we send in archers first, we could position them in the Terraces overlooking the city. They'd provide cover for the remainder of the army."

"I doubt the terrace-dwellers would welcome us with open arms."

"I was raised in the Terraces, Field Commander. My family still lives there. I can convince them to help us."

Jacob shook his head and continued to reel at the carnage playing out before him.

Maxton persisted with his plan. "There are ways to escape the Terraces if the need is dire. Through caves that burrow deep into the cliffs and lead out to hidden valleys in the Desolate Mountains."

Jacob chewed the inside of his cheek. The gates to the King's Quarter sat wide open and undefended. It appeared the enemy didn't expect a rebel attack through there. It could be his only chance to surprise them. He turned to Maxton. "Prepare a scouting party, lieutenant.

One hundred riders. Mainly archers. I'll lead them through the King's Quarter and to the Terraces."

"I should go with you."

"No. You're second in command. I need you here. Give me the names of your family and I'll ask for their help if need be. If our mission fails, you'll have no choice but to march for the south gate. Focus all your efforts on reaching the gate and getting as many soldiers through to the Southern Vale as possible. We can't defeat the barbarians in open combat."

*　*　*　*

After nearly three days of hard riding, Thaly approached the trailing end of the rebel army as it closed in on Laodicea. She galloped through the battalion, searching for Jacob. Apparently, he'd gone on ahead to survey the battlefield. Grin sprinted beside her, and Tom clutched her waist like he would never let go.

At that moment, her responsibility to Tom hit her hard. As his trainer, she was leading him to war knowing that he could hardly fight. Would Jacob have done the same thing? When did responsibility for a single life outweigh the needs of many lives? Never?

War meant sacrifice. Tom or Grin could leave if they wanted. She wouldn't try to stop them. But she'd follow Jacob and the rebels to whatever awaited beyond the walls of Laodicea.

Jacob split from a group of archers at the head of the army as Thaly arrived. She dismounted, revealing Tom sitting in the saddle behind her. "He who was lost is found again."

"Tom!" Jacob pulled the young man from the horse and wrapped him in a hug. "I feared no-one would return from Sardis."

"I may be the only one," said Tom.

"Emelin is leading a group to rescue any prisoners still alive. There is hope."

"Five of us were taken to the inner circle. I was rescued in the needle. I don't know about the others."

"Who rescued you?"

"An Erstürmen soldier called Jürgen."

Jacob's smile faded, replaced by a look of confusion. "Why single you out? How did you escape from the inner circle?"

"Jürgen took me to Dwarrow who guided me through a secret passage that led out of the city."

Thaly frowned. Tom had omitted his meeting with Princess Caeli from the story. Again, he hid things from those who were trying to help him. She needed to press him harder for the truth. About everything.

"So, there *is* a secret passage," said Jacob. "I dare not believe it."

"Dwarrow said the Dobunni built it when they raised the watchtower," said Tom.

"I'd heard the stories. Often vague or embellished. I erred by not believing them. The Erstürmen destroyed a lot of our recorded history when they invaded, so the stories were hard to confirm."

A soldier approached Jacob. "Field Commander. The scouting party is ready."

Field Commander, thought Thaly. She'd never heard anyone call him that before. She realised then how lucky she'd been when Ryder assigned Jacob as her trainer.

Jacob pulled Thaly, Tom and Grin in close and explained his plan.

"I'm coming too." Thaly glared, daring Jacob to deny her.

"We're going with Thaly." Tom nodded at Grin who smiled.

Jacob frowned. "Well, you'd better arm yourselves." He took the reins of his horse and gathered the raiding party.

Thaly turned to Tom. "I can't help you find your grandmother's killer.

Not now. My bond with the companionship is too important. We go to Bethesda to fight the barbarians."

"I understand," said Tom. "My commitment to the living outweighs the one I have to the dead. There'll be another time for that. I want to fight by your side. For all our sakes."

Thaly rested her hand on Tom's shoulder and tried to smile.

*　*　*　*

Tom sat in the saddle clutching Thaly's waist as she galloped her horse towards the main gate into the King's Quarter, ahead of the other members of the scouting party. Laodicea loomed up ahead of them. Tom had finally made it. The one place in Enthilen he wanted to see. The place where he hoped justice could be served. Eventually.

He turned to Grin, running beside them with bow and quiver bouncing on his back, but the grell kept his eyes fixed ahead, as if dispelling all other thoughts besides moving forward as fast as he could. *Focus on the now.*

"Do you remember how to fight?" Thaly yelled over her shoulder.

"I remember. You made me practice enough." Tom clutched the grip of a small falchion that hung at his side. He could wield the sword easily with one hand. It would have to do.

Thaly's horse moved up next to Jacob's the same moment he raised his hand and yanked on the reins, slowing his horse to a canter, then a walk. "We need to be cautious. Nothing to be gained by rushing through the gate."

"I can't see any guards on the wall," said Thaly. "I'll wager the Erstürmen are in leagues with the barbarians. Probably attacking the Southern Vale as we speak."

"It's possible. I'll ride on ahead and check the gate. You keep everyone

386

else here. When I give the signal, charge forward. We'll sprint to the Terraces as fast as possible."

Tom clutched Thaly's waist tighter.

*   *   *   *

Jacob approached the main gate of the King's Quarter, keeping his eyes fixed on the guardhouses sitting either side and on the top of the wall. Even if the Erstürmen *were* attacking the Dobunni in the Southern Vale, they'd still want to keep watch on the quarter gate, wouldn't they? He stopped his horse in the shadow of the portcullis, winched up and hanging above his head like the blade of a guillotine. Nothing moved through the stone archway of the gate. The streets on the other side appeared empty, as did the circular guardhouses to his left and right.

Jacob glanced over his shoulder to the scouting party waiting beyond the reach of an archer's arrow. He dug his heels into his horse's flank and walked her through the gate.

*   *   *   *

Tom gasped. "What's he doing?"

Around him and Thaly, a few in the scouting party became agitated.

"Wait for a moment longer," said Thaly, calm and confident. "Wait for the signal."

Horses tossed their heads and stamped, as if reacting to the tension coursing through the muscles of their riders.

Jacob reappeared, raised his arm in the air, then dropped it to his side. Tom almost fell from the saddle as Thaly and the scouting party charged forward.

Four hundred horses' hooves resounded along the cobbled streets of the King's Quarter announcing the arrival of the Dobunni rebels. The wind rushed through Tom's hair. He wanted to scream a blood-curdling war cry that would chill the bones of any arsehole that had murdered an old woman. *I'm here, you fucker! I'm here for revenge!*

Tom wielded the madness in his eyes like a battle axe. The few civilians still brave enough to walk the streets of the quarter seemed to shrink in his wake. It fuelled his bravado. He dismissed the Erstürmen soldiers that leant on their halberds and watched the rebels speed past. *Too frightened to do anything, bastards? You should be.*

Jacob led the group towards the Terraces. They raced through the streets, everything proceeding as planned. Tom assumed the Erstürmen had been caught napping or were paralysed with fear.

"You may not have to fight," Thaly said to Tom.

Tom's adrenalized smile disappeared when a loud crack echoed through the streets. His horse wailed and collapsed to the ground, sending him and Thaly crashing to the cobblestones. Tom rolled into the gutter, dodging a hail of riders and horses falling around him, a calamity of frenzied hooves almost trampling his body. An arms-length above him, a metal cable had been stretched taut across the narrow laneway. Tom counted more than twenty horses that had fallen to the ground in a single swathe, their legs sliced open by the sharp cord, plunging the rebels into chaos.

Soldiers dressed in black armour poured out of the buildings along the laneway and attacked the rebels from all sides. Tom crawled towards Thaly who lay, eyes closed, next to a wall. He reached for her recumbent body, then blacked out as a cloth smothered his mouth and nose.

* * * *

Thaly opened her eyes, her throbbing head assaulted by the clang of clashing swords and the wail of terrified horses. With all her strength, she propped herself up against a building, trying to avoid the frightful chaos. Her eyes drifted in and out of focus. Above her towered the Terraces of Laodicea built deep into the white cliffs of Hansen's Bluff. At the side of the bluff, cut into the bedrock, a long and steep stair led to the top.

Thaly blinked hard. Bounding up the stairs, the shadow of a grell carried a motionless body over its shoulder. The grell disappeared around a corner.

She sought Jacob, and found him standing back-to-back with Grin, fighting for their lives. Erstürmen soldiers pressed in around them. Erstürmen? Their armour looked different to the regular attire.

Jacob forced a gap in the ambushers and led Grin to Thaly.

"We need to get out of here." Jacob knelt and grabbed Thaly's arm.

"Where's Tom?" asked Grin.

Thaly shook her head to clear her thoughts. Tom wasn't on the street. She took a guess. "I think...I think a grell shadow has him. He...he...he was climbing the stair." She pointed towards the Terraces.

"A black grell," said Grin. "I can see a black grell carrying a body. He's heading for the top of the bluff."

An enemy soldier raised his sword, poised to strike Jacob's head, but collapsed when Grin fired an arrow through his throat. His quiver empty, Grin seized the soldier's weapon and swung it with a fury that Thaly had never seen from a grell. He managed to hold back the throng of soldiers bearing down on her and Jacob.

Jacob yelled above the advancing chaos. "Retreat! Retreat to the main army!"

The Dobunni rebels still mounted, turned their horses and headed back towards the gate, collecting injured companions where possible. Others ignored Jacob's order and fought on, but were soon swamped.

Thaly could see the pain in Jacob's eyes. She needed to release him. "We can't do any more for them. We need to save ourselves."

Jacob helped Thaly to her feet. "Grin, this way!" He dragged her through an open door and into a house. Grin fought off their pursuers and the three companions barred the door behind them.

"It won't hold for long." Jacob pressed his back against the door.

Thaly pictured enemy soldiers outside splintering the timber. "Tom needs us," she said.

"What do you know about him?" asked Jacob. "First Eroberung, now the black grell. Why do tainted grells hunt him?"

"He didn't tell me. But we can't just leave him."

Grin slumped to the floor. "When Tom arrived in Enthilen he carried with him the eyes of lost souls. Then Eroberung stole them. He wanted to take Tom as well. I do not know why."

"What are these eyes?" asked Thaly.

"Evil trinkets," replied Grin.

Jacob's face set hard. "I've heard of them. People can use them to steal souls. Turn others into draughouls. Some say they can make you immortal."

"There's one more thing," said Thaly. "Dwarrow told us that the master of the tainted grells is called Malphas." She jumped as something pounded into the door, cracking the timber. "Tainted grells wreak havoc on our homeland. If this Malphas seeks to use Tom to fuel our destruction, then we have no choice but to stop him."

Jacob nodded. "We'd better search for another exit."

lurred shapes drifted in front of Tom's eyes, their faint, distant voices dissolving in the mist. His groggy head lolled towards the ground. *I'm upright, but not standing. Where are my feet?* Tom tried to move his legs, but they were lashed to a pole driven into the ground. He wriggled his fingers, frozen dark-blue like the cover of the blue book. His shoulders ached from arms spread-eagled and bound to a timber cross.

I'm hanging on a crucifix.

A strand of drool detached from Tom's lip. He felt it slide down his chin as his swollen tongue pined for moisture. A salty wind blew across his face, carrying thunder clouds in off the ocean.

Someone's here. Right in front of me.

A hand reached up and grabbed Tom's jaw, turning his face towards vacant eyes.

Little Tommy's memory whimpered. *I know that face. I know who you are. Leave my Nanna alone. Get off her. Stop hurting her. Leave us alone!*

A brittle, dispassionate voice invaded Tom's memory. *"The eternal reign begins with you. When darkness descends, the faithful will enter paradise."*

English. This old man's speaking English. Tom tilted his head down, his eyes searching the man's hands. And there he saw them; two round scars, one in each palm. *He's used the dark eyes. This fucker's travelled.*

He's been inside my bedroom. Tom yanked his wrists against the ropes binding him to the crucifix. The twine burned his skin.

"*Do you admire the symbolism, Tom? A sacrifice on a crucifix will finally herald the return of Volerdie to Enthilen. A resurrection, so to speak. The irony is delightful. Although, it's lost on everyone here except you and I. Don't bother resisting, Tom, your fate is sealed. When the crescent moons shine bright, your time has come to serve the Divine Creator.*"

*   *   *   *

Grin hid with Jacob and Thaly behind dense bushes at the top of Hansen's Bluff, crouching low to keep his huge frame out of sight. After escaping from the house in the King's Quarter, they had ascended the stairway unnoticed. Mouth agape, he was mesmerised by the spectacle playing out before him; Tom Anderson suspended above the ground, bound to a wooden cross, and confronted by an old man in white robes. Behind the old man stood three tainted grells, black, red and...and.... *she's here,* he thought. The pale-skinned grell from the dream he had the moment before Tom Anderson arrived in Enthilen. The grell who offered him a hand as he floundered in the darkness.

He grasped the handle of a knife and tensed.

Jacob must have noticed the movement. "Not yet."

Next to the three tainted grells, stood a young man clutching his hands out front and rubbing them together, as if the wind chilled his bones.

"Is that the prince?" asked Thaly.

"Yes," said Jacob. "Adalwolf. The man in white robes...I'll take a stab and guess that he's Malphas. I don't like our odds against three tainted grells, but there's no time to go for help. If we're going to rescue Tom, we have to do it now."

"We have to rescue him," said Grin. "We have to."

"When the moment is right, I'll rush the grells. Thaly, you take the prince and hold him hostage while Grin cuts Tom free. We keep Adalwolf with us until we reach safety. Hopefully they value his life as much as we value Tom's." Jacob placed his hands on Thaly and Grin's shoulders. "Prepare yourselves for a folly that may end all our lives."

*　*　*　*

Malphas waited for the crescent moons of Bargan and Seena to poke through the gloomy, dark clouds. He reached up and traced his finger across Tom's bare chest. *"Why have you despoiled your body with these awful scars? A misstep I'll dismiss. I'm proud of you nonetheless, Tom. Nanna would be proud too. You learned our language and read the stories. And you've managed to navigate your way through Enthilen, as I'd hoped. Now you can fulfil your destiny as a true Erstürmen hero making the ultimate sacrifice."*

Malphas noticed Tom's pupils dilate as the boy's head lolled towards the tainted grells.

"I see you're admiring Hunger, Krieg and Ende. Your time with the wild grell has likely addled your mind. You probably see grells as pure, even angelic? Souls that can never be tainted. I thought the same, once, then found I could bend them to my will...after thoughtful coercion. I relished in the challenge of taking such a simple, naïve creature and turning it into a dispassionate executioner. A servant that inflicts pain when I command. Volerdie would now be proud of his creation, rather than ashamed, don't you think?"

Malphas flinched as anger exploded from Tom's mouth. *"Fuck you. Murderer!"*

He quickly regained his composure. *"Am I? Who exactly have I killed?"*

"I saw you...in my room. You killed my Nanna...you killed her...."

"Are you sure it was me?"

"I saw your face…lying on the floor…you wrote the blue book."

"Oh yes, I wrote the book. That's hardly a crime. Be careful, Tom. A judgement made in haste, finds truth the only waste."

Malphas turned from his quarry and announced in Erstürmen, "Enough of this prattle. Adalwolf. Come closer. It's time for you to understand your prey."

Prince Adalwolf dragged his feet towards Tom, rigid arms hanging from his side, fists clenched in tight balls failing to quell his shudders.

"Stop quivering, pitiful child," said Malphas. "We're on the cusp of the greatest ruling dynasty since the Divine Creator resided in Pergamos, and you tremble like a little girl surrounded by wolves. It has taken me over thirteen yarles to bring to fruition this day, and what timing. On the night of the crescent moons no less. Volerdie is pleased. I'll not have your weakness destroy everything." Malphas grabbed Adalwolf's arm and hauled him over to face Tom. "Here you both are, together at last. I've waited so long for this moment. Born at the same time in different worlds, both with the same mark. The sign that you could live a life eternal, but only if one soul dies by the other's hand. Show him, Adalwolf."

Adalwolf opened his fist. The eyes of lost souls sat together in the middle of his palm.

"Look into the dark eyes, Tom. In their blackness is where your soul will be trapped for all eternity, while your body roams Enthilen searching for release."

The clouds over Hansen's Bluff parted and two shining crescent moons illuminated the coming sacrifice.

"It is time." Malphas grasped Adalwolf's forearm. "Remember, my son, hold the eyes tight, like I showed you, both in your right hand. Then thrust your fist into his chest with all of your might, and hold it there. But brace yourself. There'll be quite a jolt when you steal his soul."

Malphas turned to his tainted grells. "Stand back! No-one can interfere with the transfer lest the entrapment fails and this wretched boy is lost to us forever."

*   *   *   *

Adalwolf stood alone in front of Tom, his right hand clenched in a tight fist, arm outstretched, all the colour drained from his face.

This is the prince, thought Tom. *The one we were supposed to kill in Sardis. And the old man. He must be Malphas.* Malphas. *The arsehole who killed my grandmother.*

Adalwolf looked as frightened as Tom felt. It appeared the young prince couldn't control his shaking. He kept his eyes fixed on his hand, as if avoiding Tom's gaze. Tom drew forth what little courage remained in his aching body. "You don't need to do this, Adalwolf. We're the same age. Born on the same day. That has to count for something, doesn't it?"

The prince faced the ground and announced, serf-like, "I'm the vessel for the return of the Divine Creator. Through me, his kingdom will rise again and I will enter paradise."

"It's a lie," said Tom. "Volerdie doesn't exist. Paradise is what we make, here and now."

"Silence!" Malphas' scream appeared to shake Adalwolf from his trance. The prince glanced over his shoulder. Malphas' voice calmed. "Paradise awaits, King Adalwolf. When you take his soul, you'll rule forever. The crown that lasts an eternity."

Adalwolf raised his fist towards Tom's chest, clutching his forearm with his left hand. He locked eyes with Tom, drew his right arm back and thrust it forward, punching Tom hard in the ribs.

It felt like someone had rammed their fist down Tom's throat and tried to wrench his stomach back out through his mouth. Foam bubbled around his tongue and his arms and legs yanked against the ropes holding him to the cross.

"*Aaahhhh!*" Adalwolf screamed, his arm recoiling like he'd punched a stone wall. He fell backwards onto the grass.

"Get up. Get up and finish him!" yelled Malphas.

"It hurts," said Adalwolf.

"Embrace the pain like a man. Like the king you were born to be."

Amid the convulsions, the last thing Tom saw was Adalwolf pulling himself from the ground and taking a step towards him.

* * * *

Thaly sprang from cover, knocking Adalwolf off balance before the prince could reach Tom again. She grabbed Adalwolf's hair and dragged him along the ground, positioning herself between the crucifix and the enemy. Grin began to cut Tom free while Jacob raced towards Malphas and the tainted grells.

The black grell stepped forward to protect his master and the red grell blocked the escape back down the stairs. Jacob ducked under the black grell's swinging axe, doing his best to keep the monster at bay. He thrust his sword towards the grell's stomach, but the grell deflected the blow, knocking the sword from Jacob's grasp.

Thaly pulled Adalwolf to his feet, holding a sword to his throat. "I'll kill him!"

The red grell, a huge, hulking beast, loosed an arrow that pierced Thaly's forearm. She dropped the sword and Adalwolf broke free. Thaly jumped on him again, wrestling the prince to the ground.

Grin freed Tom and cradled him in his arms. The red grell fired more arrows.

"Krieg! Wait!" Malphas yelled. "You might hit the boy. We need him alive until Adalwolf has trapped his soul."

Injured, Thaly couldn't keep hold of Adalwolf. He fought her off and raced back to Malphas, the master of the tainted grells.

"Stand behind me," Grin said to Thaly.

She froze, waiting for a command from Jacob who stood, unarmed and vulnerable, in front of the black grell. She thought she saw a tear dribble along the scar across his cheek before he yelled at her, "Run! Get out of here!"

No! her mind wailed. No.

"Thaly," said Grin. "We can't defeat them. We have to save Tom."

Without taking her eyes from Jacob, Thaly stepped backwards towards the edge of the bluff. The black grell slashed his battle axe across the back of Jacob's legs and her trainer...her friend collapsed to his knees.

Malphas stepped between the black grell and Jacob. "Wait. Let Ende come forth."

The pale grell shuffled over and raised her sparth above Jacob.

Malphas grabbed Jacob's head and twisted his face towards Thaly and Grin. "I'll spare his life. And yours. All you need to do is return the boy. He'll be mine eventually."

"He's lying," said Jacob. "He'll kill all of us."

Like a demonic colossus, the red grell, Krieg, planted his feet across the top of the stairs that led back down to Laodicea.

Thaly and Grin stepped closer to the edge of Hansen's Bluff.

What do we do? she thought.

Malphas grinned, as if he'd read Thaly's mind. "Your choices are few. There's only one choice that will save your lives. Return Tom, unharmed. Let him fulfil his destiny."

Holding Tom tight in his arms, Thaly could sense Grin teetering on the brink. "Don't listen to him," she whispered.

The grell's foot slipped on the edge of the cliff, sending rocks tumbling into a lake far below.

The pool of reflection, thought Thaly. How deep is that?

The smile disappeared from Malphas' craggy face. "Careful now... careful. Grin...is that right? Grinnian stone-grell? I met your grandfather once. In Malang Gunya on the day we liberated it. I know you don't want to hurt Tom. Move away from the edge and bring him to me."

Grin brushed his thick fingers across Tom's pale, lifeless face. He hugged his friend's body then confronted Malphas. "You are the spawn of a demon. Enemy of nature. I have no fear in my heart for you."

"We could jump." Thaly's heart sank at the idea of fleeing. Jacob needed her. She could rush the pale grell. Knock the sparth from Ende's hands. Shield Jacob's hunched and broken frame with her bravery.

Malphas continued tormenting Grin, "You are an honest soul, Grinnian. Such purity is rare among wild grells. I admire this. But do not wrong me. I would love nothing more than to crush your failing dreams and taint your skin like the servants that stand beside me."

Grin peered over his shoulder, down at the lake. "Even if we survive the fall, I cannot swim."

Tears welled in Thaly's eyes. "It's our only choice."

Grin nodded. "Then we jump."

The same moment Thaly, Grin and Tom stepped off the edge of Hansen's Bluff, a shining sparth flashed through the night air towards Jacob's neck.

To be continued in

Book II:
At the End of Everything

and

Book III:
She Will Rise

Free extras for readers

To receive free, colour images (digital files) of the maps of Ostamp and Enthilen, and a free short story, contact the author at the following website: **https://relevationtrilogy.com**

Appendix (Book I)
A Guide to Ostamp

Abrolous Isles — a group of sparsely populated islands off the east coast of Enthilen.

Al Mōr Sŭrl — watchtower built by the Dobunni in the old settlement of Iglund (an island in the middle of the Anchep River). The watchtower was renamed the Sunrise Keep by the Erstürmen and incorporated into the inner circle of Sardis.

Anchep River — major river running through the north-west of Enthilen and surrounding Sardis.

Babir Birramal — large forest covering the southern region of Enthilen, occupied by stone-and weald-grells.

Bagendon — a town built in the Scaur Hills by Dobunni rebels pledged to overthrow the Erstürmen Kingdom.

Bargan — the name of one of the two moons in the sky above Ostamp.

Bay of Deception — a bay in Nordland where King Giltbert made his last stand against barbarians.

Bay of Fires — a deep, protected bay surrounded by the Abrolhos Isles and often used by barbarian ships from Oder and Sexton for anchorage.

Bethesda — the Dobunni name for Laodicea.

Bilawi tree — a tree with needle-like foliage found in Enthilen.

Bindari — secret location of the graveyard for stone- and weald-grells.

Birraman — stone-grell name for travellers from far-away lands.

Birth twins — two individuals born at exactly the same time; one of them on Earth and the other in Ostamp. Birth twins usually don't look alike and can be different genders. However, they will always have the same birthmark, which persists until death.

Blood compass — gold pentagram that spins of its own accord after a single point of the star is dipped in the blood of a birth twin when their twin occupies the same world. There were once five compasses; only one remains.

Blue book — a book left for Tom Anderson that translates the Erstürmen language to English, and tells stories of Erstürmen culture.

Breadelbane — abandoned village on the western edge of the Dambay Plains near the Scaur Hills.

Calendar of life — the most sacred place in Malang Gunya. An open, circular temple surrounded by marble pillars with paintings decorating the tiled floor depicting important aspects of grell culture.

Crest — facial tattoo worn by all free grells. Each crest is unique, representing a plant or animal that the grell is responsible for protecting.

Curate — a holy man in the Erstürmen culture.

Dambay Plains — huge grassland region in the centre of Enthilen once occupied by mouldewerps and stone-grells.

Da Und Sepcarture — Ancient name for the First Scripture.

Deeping pits — gaol adjacent to the outer wall of Sardis.

Desolate Mountains — a large mountain range in the north of Enthilen, marking the border between Enthilen and Nordland.

Detranté — narrow pass through the Desolate Mountains connecting Nordland with Enthilen.

Divine Creator — another name for Volerdie.

Dobunni — settled Enthilen after the stone-grells and built Bethesda,

Iglund (a village on an island in the middle of the Anchep River, now the location of Sardis) and the watchtower of Al Mōr Sŭrl. Came as peaceful settlers rather than invaders. Ousted from much of Enthilen by the Erstürmen and now mostly confined to Bagendon and the Southern Vale in Laodicea.

Dobunni rebels — those Dobunni pledged to overthrow the Erstürmen Kingdom. Most live in Bagendon, but some still live in secret in the Southern Vale.

Docklands — one of the four quarters in Laodicea. Wharf area next to Traders Bay.

Draughouls — creatures that have had their soul captured by the eyes of lost souls. Only humans, grells or mouldewerps can become draughouls. They exist in a state of almost suspended animation, but they aren't 'undead' as such. They can be killed or, over time, their body will wither away to nothing. However, a natural demise takes a very, very long time.

Dwell — name for both a specific hole in the ground where a mouldewerp lives, and the collection of holes in a given location. Akin to 'home'.

Enthilen — Land in the eastern half of Ostamp occupied by Erstürmen, Dobunni, stone- and weald-grells, mouldewerps and others.

Erstürmen — settled Enthilen after being ousted from what is now called Nordland by barbarians (the ancestors of Nordmen). Came as invaders and conquerors, claiming Enthilen for themselves regardless of other inhabitants.

Eyes of lost souls — two obsidian glass eyes with flaming pupils. One of the seven treasures from the throne of the dead.

Felsie — also called the pool of reflection. A lake in Laodicea located at the bottom of Hansen's Bluff.

Field Commander — rank in the Erstürmen army usually bestowed on those commanding one of the Erstürmen outposts. This rank is immediately above that of lieutenant and below that of General, although many in the military view General and Field Commander as equivalent ranks.

First Scripture — also known as *Da Und Sepcarture* in the old language of Pergamos. Ancient parchment believed to be written by Volerdie in his own blood documenting his lore and secrets.

Flüsse — the central, most fertile and densely populated region of the Riverlands.

Gadhang — large ocean to the south of Enthilen. Crossed by the first stone-grell settlers.

Gaping hollow — deep chasm that breaches the floor of the cave leading to the secret passage into Sardis.

Garrabari — ancient stone- and weald-grell celebration involving dancing and singing, telling stories and sacred ceremony. It happens when both Seena and Bargan, the two moons, are full.

Germalia — region in the western half of Ostamp occupied by the Germalians. Main city, Portum.

Gestade — Erstürmen outpost on the central east coast of Enthilen.

Giba — a stone sacred to stone- and weald-grells that casts its own light.

Giigal — Weald-grell city on the south coast of Enthilen.

Grōz Forst — Erstürmen name for Babir Birramal.

Grōz Wüste — large desert in the western half of Ostamp claimed by Germalians (who call it Magna Avium), but includes disputed territory claimed by both Germalians and the Pordillo.

Hansen's Bluff — limestone cliff to the north of Laodicea and overlooking the city.

Heine Empire — name for the unbroken reign of kings from the Heine family, beginning with King Giltbert Heine.

Hurna — a horn used to rally troops in battle.

Hurst — tall pinnacle of rock in the Nordargen Sea where Erstürmen kings of old would hide treasures and jewels and where, legend has it, griffins used to nest.

Iglund — Dobunni village once located on an island in the Anchep River now home to Sardis.

King's Quarter — one of the four quarters of Laodicea occupied by the Erstürmen.

King's Shield — elite Erstürmen soldiers who have vowed to protect the king with their life.

Kirika — building in most Erstürmen settlements containing a chapel for worshipping Volerdie, and other rooms. Often built underground and above the dungeon.

Laodicea (Bethesda) — port city on the north-east coast of Enthilen at Traders Bay. Divided into four quarters (King's Quarter, Southern Vale, Docklands and The Terraces) and occupied by Erstürmen, Dobunni, and others. Dobunni settlers built the city and named it Bethesda.

Lieutenant — rank in the Erstürmen army immediately above that of sergeant-at-arms and below that of Field Commander.

Magna Avium — Germalian name for Grōz Wüste.

Malang Gunya — ruined stone-grell city in the middle of the Dambay Plains in Enthilen. The Erstürmen maintain an outpost in the ruins.

Master's Hall — largest building in each quarter of Laodicea used by the quarter's master to conduct various business.

Meduz — grainy, milky alcoholic beverage found throughout Ostamp.

Meladoor tree — barbarians use the timber from this tree to make their ships.

Mendeal herbs — herbs found throughout Enthilen and used for medicinal purposes.

Milbi — small stone shelter used by stone-grells.

Mouldewerps — long-time inhabitants of Enthilen. Previously lived in the Dambay Plains until ousted by stone-grell settlers who used to hunt mouldewerps for food and sport. Now live in small and secretive groups mostly in the Scaur Hills.

Needle — a narrow passage connecting the inner circle of Sardis with the second circle. The only [widely known] way to gain access to the inner courtyard.

Nordargen Sea — sea to the north of Nordland.

Nordland — land to the north of Enthilen occupied by Nordmen (descendants of barbarians).

Ostamp — land mass that includes Enthilen, Germalia, Nordland, Pordillo Territory, Grōz Wüste and Babir Birramal.

Overseer — leader of a group of twenty grell slaves.

Panalope tree — a favourite tree of stone- and weald-grells used for various purposes. The largest tree species in Babir Birramal.

Pergamos — a lost and ruined city lying underneath the foundations of Malang Gunya. Believed by some Erstürmen to once be occupied by their ancestors. Also believed to be Volerdie's seat of power when he ruled over Ostamp and other lands.

Pledge Feste — name of the ceremony in which the Dobunni ask for citizens to pledge allegiance to the Dobunni rebels and their cause.

Pordillo Territory — land in the south west of Ostamp occupied by Pordillo nomads.

Rārian Falls — where the Anchep River tumbles over the Riverlands Escarpment, west of Sardis. The Erstürmen maintain guardhouses at the top and bottom of the road that zig-zags down the face of the escarpment next to the falls.

Riverlands — fertile farmland wedged between the Scaur Hills and Groz Wüste. Occupied by unaligned farmers and villagers.

Riverlands Escarpment — steep, sheer cliff running along the western edge of the Scaur Hills.

River Milawa — river in the Dambay Plains and closest river to Malang Gunya.

Sardis — royal city of Enthilen occupied and built by the Erstürmen, comprised of seven concentric circles. Each circle of the city is occupied by Erstürmen of different status; the closer to the inner circle the higher the status. The inner circle is occupied by the royal family and trusted court.

Scaur Hills — a rocky range running along the western edge of Enthilen marking the border between Enthilen and the Riverlands and eventually Grōz Wüste.

Scripture verses — also called *Polus Sepcarture* in the old language of Pergamos. A black book believed to be an interpretation of the First Scripture. Only curates are normally permitted to read and interpret the scripture verses.

Seena — the name of one of the two moons in the sky above Ostamp.

Sergeant-at-arms — rank in the Erstürmen army immediately above that of soldier and below that of lieutenant.

Silver tausen — very rare and valuable coin.

Slumstadt — shanty town/ghetto on the fringes of Sardis.

Softstone — stone used for grell totems.

Southern Vale — one of the four quarters of Laodicea occupied mostly by Dobunni.

Stone-grells — [grells] early inhabitants of the land now known as Enthilen. Built Malang Gunya and occupied the city until being ousted by the Erstürmen. Currently live in isolated shelters known as 'milbis' along the northern edge of Babir Birramal (males only), or as guests of the weald-grells in Giigal (women and children only).

Süden Forst — Erstürmen outpost in the south of Enthilen on the edge of Babir Birramal.

Sunrise Keep — Erstürmen name for Al Mōr Sŭrl; one of the two keeps in the inner circle of Sardis.

Sunset Keep — one of the two keeps in the inner circle of Sardis.

Tainted grell — a stone-grell whose skin has been tainted by Malphas using arcane, evil arts. There are four tainted grells with four different skin colours: Eroberung (white), Krieg (red), Hunger (black), and Ende (pale).

Terraces — one of the four quarters of Laodicea occupied by wealthier residents.

Testament of Fire — a ceremony used by the Dobunni to select rebel soldiers for critically important missions.

The Feign — the southern foothills of the Desolate Mountains.

Throne of the dead — believed to be Volerdie's throne. Made from desiccated, ossified bodies.

Thyatira — ruined city in Nordland once occupied by the Erstürmen before they were expelled from the north of Ostamp by barbarians.

Totem — soapstone about the size of a taper candle. Grells etch the story of their life on its surface and totems are handed down to family members or buried with the grell.

Traders Bay — bay neighbouring Laodicea where the city port and docklands are located.

Umbo — title bestowed on the figurehead/commander of the King's Shield. Rarely participates in actual battle.

Undred — giant, horse-like creature with a single, curved horn protruding from its forehead.

Vater — a title given to the tainted grells, meaning 'Father.'

Veiled Occyan — ocean to the east of Enthilen.

Volerdie — A god worshipped by the Erstürmen. Also known as the Divine Creator.

Weald-grells — [grells] once identified as stone-grells until the tribal war that saw them abandon Malang Gunya and settle on the south coast of Babir Birramal at Giigal.

Worshipful Master — preferred title of Malphas [Oldaric].

Yarle — Erstürmen word for a time period covering six seasons/three hundred and sixty days.

Yirany — yellow tuber eaten by grells.

Yurali bush — common shrub in Babir Birramal.

Extras

The Relevation Trilogy Book II:
At the End of Everything

~Prologue~

Hál tilted her head back as the draughoul servant lifted a wooden cup to her lips and trickled cool, clear water into her mouth. The chain of the heavy jewel that hung around her neck pinched her skin, reminding her of the burden and the treasure she had borne for a generation. The jewel was a symbol of the infinite possibilities of future lives.

Through crumbling archways, sunlight poured into the ruined monastery, perched high on the northern face of the Desolate Mountains above the town of Revelé. The light refracted through the jewel's many gemstones, sending a rainbow of colours dancing across the monastery walls.

The draughoul removed the cup and stood beside Hál's stone pedestal. She smiled. "Thank you, Pida. The season of storms does not usually bring such warm days."

"The cycle of seasons forever changes."

"Yes, I guess you're right. Did I ever tell you the story of my ancestor, Lycious?"

"I cannot remember it."

"Then, it's a nice day for a story." Hál nestled the stump of her legless torso into the soft, white cushion sitting atop her pedestal and closed her eyes. She reached inside her mind, seeking memories of ancient times that came from someone else, but now belonged to her. "Long ago, before the stone-grells came, even before mouldewerps spread across the Dambay Plains, pilgrims and explorers from distant shores wandered the forests and mountains of the land the Erstürmen call Enthilen. Some sought treasure, others knowledge. The pilgrim Lycious desired both, her quest driven by whispers of the lost city of Pergamos where once dwelled he who created all.

"The journey began in her homeland, far from the shores of Enthilen, where Lycious spent her youth pursuing knowledge of the lost city until one story consumed her entire being; the fall of Pergamos and the flight of Volerdie from the world that he created. She learned that Volerdie's wrath destroyed Pergamos. A cataclysmic event that saw buildings tumble and paved streets buckle underfoot, wiping the city and many of its people from living memory. Those left alive claimed that Volerdie himself, the Divine Creator and ruler of Pergamos, ruined the city in a fit of jealousy. A bitter envy of another world whose beauty he coveted above all else. Volerdie disappeared, but Lycious suspected that the ruins of the lost city lay somewhere hidden under the soil, housing a wealth of treasures. No greater legacy, she believed, was the written word of the Divine Creator himself; *Da Und Sepcarture* — The First Scripture, for it contained Volerdie's Lore and many secrets, including the path to immortality.

"In the town of Maline in the land of Oder, Lycious stumbled across an ancient library in a dusty basement under the town's watchtower. On damp, decaying shelves, she discovered a text of fragile, yellowed pages bound together with frayed string. With obeisant fingers, Lycious turned to the first page; a map scratched onto the parchment in faded black ink. It showed a land across the ocean west of Oder. In the middle of vast plains, someone had marked a cross next to the words *Pergamos, Throne of the Creator.*

"Lycious stole the book, gathered her possessions and began a pilgrimage to find Pergamos. In a tiny canoe, she travelled alone for seven seasons, finally reaching the eastern shore of Enthilen. Dehydrated and famished, Lycious stumbled on an entrancing freshwater pool, luminously clear and nestled at the foot of limestone cliffs. Drinking from its store, the pool replenished her strength and will, encouraging her to continue the journey. With the moons and stars as guides, Lycious travelled south-west until reaching the place where the map showed Pergamos once stood. But there she found only dirt and rocks.

"Undeterred, Lycious dug. For many days, using her hands and sharp sticks, she burrowed deep into the loam soil of the plains until blood dripped from swollen fingers and dry, calloused palms screamed with every thrust. Exhausted and ready to abandon hope, Lycious' arms jolted when her digging stick hit a large, flat stone. She gouged at the soil around the stone until she'd uncovered all its edges. *This is it*, she told herself. *This is the way in.*

"Prising a long, thick branch under one edge of the stone, Lycious dislodged it from its resting place, exposing blackness and emptiness below. She pushed the stone aside and cast a flaming torch into the darkness. It landed on the floor of a chamber, right under Lycious' feet. Without hesitation, she jumped down into the void and collected the torch, shining its orange glow into dark corners that hadn't seen light for many generations. A labyrinth of snaking passages lined with statues and pillars, and forgotten rooms full of the trappings of a civilization long gone, basked in rare illumination. Pergamos unveiled by the flames.

"Lycious searched day and night, unable to tell one from the other in the underworld. She discarded many treasures, looking for the one thing that had plagued her thoughts for so long; The First Scripture. Eventually, her persistence reaped its reward. Behind thick oak doors encased in metal, which squealed as she squeezed her tiny frame between them, Lycious found the most elaborate of halls. At its centre, a throne of gruesome contortions haunted the darkness, desiccated bodies entwined to support the authority of the Divine Creator. She examined every surface of the throne, casting the light from the flaming torch into every shadow and prising her fingers into each crevice until something gave way. Lycious' heart skipped as she opened a secret compartment and withdrew a scroll, tied with cured human skin and sealed with seven wax seals.

"Holding the parchment to the torchlight revealed words scrawled on both sides, written in blood. Not a drop of saliva lined Lycious' dry throat. She gasped for air, forcing it into her lungs as disjointed thoughts raced through her mind. Was she worthy to break the seals? Would Volerdie strike her down?

"Lycious refused to abandon her journey at the moment of greatest discovery. She broke the seven seals and cut the cured skin, reverently unfurling the ancient document. With no doubt in her mind, she'd discovered The First Scripture; Volerdie's Lore. The language was a vestige of another age, but Lycious had studied antediluvian languages in her homeland for many seasons. Days and nights blended into one as she read the text, over and over, her attention always returning to one passage: *Let the marked take the dark eyes from the throned beast, and hold tightly. Unto them eternal life may be granted.* Lycious' mind danced. What a treasure immortality would be! She must be one of the marked. One of Volerdie's chosen, she thought, not understanding the true meaning of the words.

"Lycious again sort Volerdie's throne, but found the eye sockets of the beast's head that sat atop the backrest empty. She searched all the rooms and passages for days without success, before deciding that the dark eyes had been stolen and that somewhere in the lands surrounding Pergamos she'd find them.

"Taking the scripture, Lycious began a new pilgrimage to find the eyes. She maundered for the rest of her life until aged and nagging bones pleaded for an end. Eventually, a debilitating paranoia crippled her mind; a consuming terror that someone would steal The First Scripture and uncover all its secrets before she did. One day, hiding in a cave above the shore of a wild ocean, she heard a piercing shriek and rushed out to see a white griffin flying overhead. Without thinking, she ran onto the beach to revel in the wonder of the strange creature. The griffin swooped down, grabbing Lycious in its talons and carrying her to a nest on a pinnacle of rock surrounded by perilous seas."

"Hurst?"

"Yes, Pida. The griffin had carried her to Hurst, the lonely stone tower in the Nordargen Sea. Lycious was sure that the creature would tear her asunder, but something drew it away. Alone again, she refused to accept the griffin's nest as her grave and found the top of a stairway carved into the rock on which the nest lay. Cautiously, she descended the stair." Hál opened her eyes and faced her servant.

"Is that where the story ends?" asked Pida.

"Oh, no. That is only the beginning."

*   *   *   *

"I found it, brother," Oldaric crowed. "I found The First Scripture. I scoured these lands for yarles and now all has come to me."

"The Scripture! What does it reveal?" Widukind leaned forward, almost toppling from his stool into the campfire.

Oldaric smiled at the eagerness plastered all over his younger brother's face. "It has many secrets, dear brother. *Many* secrets." He drew a knife from his belt and held it above the fire, twisting the blade in his hand as firelight bounced off its keen surface and disappeared into the dark. Flashing a wicked grin, he plunged the knife into his chest.

Widukind gasped.

Oldaric cackled like a drunk witch, the bone handle of the knife protruding from his ribcage dancing along with the mirth.

"Take it," said Oldaric.

"What?"

"Pull the dagger from my flesh."

With a trembling hand, Widukind reached across and yanked the knife from Oldaric's chest. Eyes wide, he examined the clean, bloodless blade.

Oldaric knew that Widukind idolised him. He hoped this new magic would fuel the adoration. "Eternal life, Widu. I have become immortal."

"How is this possible?"

"Like most of our kin, you forget your lore and history. Long, long ago, our ancestors christened this land Enthilen and lived at peace under the watchful eye of Volerdie himself, in the royal city of Pergamos. But, when Pergamos fell, the scattering of ancestors that still lived abandoned Enthilen and nearly expunged the city from their memories. The machinations of Erstürmen kings then consumed our time and distracted our attention from the only ambition of any importance." Oldaric took a charred tree branch from the ground, swivelled on his seat and stoked the fire. The glowing amber hue silhouetted the transfixed expression on Widukind's face, as flames licked the dampness from the night.

Oldaric lingered a little longer amid the silent anticipation before continuing, "My banishment from Sardis by the myopic Ewald was a sign from the Divine Creator. Volerdie wanted to free my thoughts and time so I could complete his bidding. In the library in Laodicea, I found a text that told the story of Lycious, a fortuitous thief who, long, long ago, stumbled on a scroll of considerable importance. Presented as no more than an apologue, the story still had a truthfulness that I couldn't shake. From the description, I guessed what the scroll might be. The author of Lycious' tale claimed that she was last seen travelling through Detranté towards Nordland. I followed in Lycious' footsteps, walking until the north land met the sea. But I found nothing. No trace that she'd ever passed that way. No person that knew of her existence. I was about to turn back when I remembered Hurst, the tall, rocky outcrop in the Nordargen Sea where once griffins nested and the Erstürmen kings of old hid many treasures. Maybe Lycious also hid a treasure there? I had to find out, dear brother. I plundered a boat from a wild Nordman and travelled through the waves. Thirst and hunger almost defeated me until finally I saw a stone spire jutting from the horizon and the ocean swell crashing onto jagged rocks. I'd found Hurst."

Oldaric threw the branch into the fire and reached under his stool for a silver goblet half-full of meduz. He took a swig and wiped his mouth. Still examining the knife, as if at any moment blood would seep from its blade, Widukind's eyes yearned with devoted curiosity. Oldaric knew then that his younger brother was hooked.

"Over rocks and through decaying passages, I searched until finding a stone door hidden within a wall and sealed from the inside. With toil and torment, I broke the seal and discovered a room that looked like it hadn't been visited for many generations. A tombstone lay at rest in a corner, one word scratched onto its surface: *Lycious*. It appeared she'd prepared her own grave and buried herself alive. I opened the lid of the stone coffin and inside found a skeleton clutching a threadbare scroll. I prised the document from bony fingers and cast my eyes on the bloodied script. There was no doubt; I had found The First Scripture. That fool Giltbert died right on top of it! His skeleton and armour were scattered across the crest of the pinnacle, likely the remains of a griffin banquet. If he had more wits, he could have escaped the griffin's talons and found immortality instead of death."

"I still don't understand how you discovered eternal life, brother."

"You don't *discover* eternal life, Widu. You *earn* it. Remember how our father used to tell us that the eyes of lost souls were a window to eternity?"

"That's just a metaphor. The dark eyes don't exist."

Oldaric reached into his pocket and withdrew a clenched fist, holding it towards the firelight. He beamed and spread his fingers, revealing the dark eyes sitting in his palm.

"They're real!" Widukind's mouth hung open, the knife dropping from his hand into the grey dirt of The Feign.

"After studying The First Scripture, I began my search for Volerdie's throne — the throne of the dead — and for the eyes of lost souls. In one of Lycious' pockets, I had found a crude map. Before it disintegrated in my hands, I saw where she'd marked the location of Pergamos. The Erstürmen settlers led by King Faramund hadn't found it, hidden under the foul temples of those pagan grells. Even when our father, Alaric, routed the last stone-grell from Malang Gunya, he was unaware that the heathen city stood atop the one place he longed to find. It's a tragedy he died before he could begin the search. And he was so close, Widukind. So close."

Oldaric took another sip of meduz. "It fell on me to brave the atrocities of Malang Gunya and discover the entrance to Pergamos, deep under the soil of the Dambay Plains. Searching every corner of every underground room, I found a grand hall worthy of a throne, but it contained only the dais on which a throne might sit. As I stumbled in the dark, something glinted in my torchlight, under a pile of rubble. I swept away the dirt and there lay the eyes of lost souls. Volerdie's Lore explains their use. And the lore did not fail me, brother. I've used the eyes and to me has been bestowed the greatest gift of all."

Widukind sucked in deep breaths, as if gasping for every detail of the revelations laid out before him. "Can I read the scripture, Oldaric?"

"It's in a language you'll not understand. I spent many moons learning to interpret its meaning. There's no need for you to do the same. I can guide you." Oldaric placed the dark eyes back in his pocket. "Why do the Erstürmen revere the marked?"

"Because we believe that a mark at birth is a portent to a long life."

"Our mother was overjoyed when you were born and she saw the naevus on your leg. Now she had two sons with birthmarks. Maybe somewhere in her heart she understood the real potential of these blemishes. Volerdie has marked us, Widukind. Chosen *us* for a special purpose. The First Scripture explains the significance of these marks. When a marked child is born in this world, another child with the same mark is born in Volerdie's adopted world at exactly the same time. The world to which the creator fled when Pergamos fell. This child is your birth twin. They may not look like you, but you will both share the same mark until your end. It is the soul of your birth twin that you must capture with the dark eyes. It is their life that you must end if you wish to become immortal."

"How is it possible to find our twin if they exist in another world?"

"Hold the eyes, one in each hand, and you'll be transported to the world where Volerdie fled. I've been there. It's a vile and desperate place ruled by machines; you won't want to linger long. Through fortitude and cunning, you must find your birth twin. Then, with the dark eyes grasped tightly in your right hand, hold your fist against their heart. They'll twist and scream, but you must remain strong. Keep the eyes next to their chest. When their life is gone, trapped within the dark eyes, only then will you be able to return home, bringing with you the gift of immortality."

Widukind dropped his head into his hands. "Oldaric, you're making my head spin."

Oldaric dug his fingers into Widukind's shoulder. "Steel yourself, my little brother. There's more that you must know. About the young Prince Adalwolf and another child, and the blood connection that links us all."

Acknowledgements

T his story began in 1982 when I was 15 years old. My eldest sister, Frances, took me to a store in Adelaide, South Australia called Trims (still going strong!) to buy a second-hand typewriter. I chose a small, turquoise-blue, ribbon typewriter because it was the only one that I could afford. For those of you born after 1990, do a Google image search to see what a typewriter looks like.

And so, the journey began. Over the next 2 years, I punched out around 100 pages of text. I say punched, because I'm sure that at some points I actually did punch the typewriter. Learning to type was frustratingly slow, made even more so by having to correct the many mistakes using correction fluid (Google image search) and fussing around with worn typewriter ribbons. Nevertheless, the basic premise of the story you now hold in your hands or view on your screen was forged during this period.

During this early writing, my best friend at the time, Ritchie Collins (aka Jack Friend), was a great sounding board for my various ideas. He was a brilliant artist and did some sketches of a few characters from the book. Alas, I never kept them, along with many other things from my younger years which I now wish I had.

Time moseyed on and, as John Lennon aptly put it, life got in the way. I left school at 17 and spent 6 months on the dole, doing a short course in creative writing during this time. However, I needed a job and had to put the book on hold. I remember planning out the entire plot and typing out each chapter heading on its own piece of paper, before filing all this neatly away in a large, lever-arch binder (Google image search).

The 100 pages of text and the chapter headings disappeared sometime in the following years. I didn't return to writing until well into my 40s. However, this story never left me — percolating around in my head for decades (although the end result is very different to the story I started when I was 15). During my 40s, I would, on irregular occasions, take notes about the plot and characters. I ended up with about 70 pages of notes before I sat down and began to write the story out properly, around the time I turned 50. I guess you could call it a mid-life crisis since time was running out for me to actually finish this thing. The upside to all this was that the writing came very easily because the story had been with me for so long.

I'm glad I waited until now to write this book. I've loved and lost more than once, experienced grief and unbridled joy more than once, fought the demons of anxiety and depression, and seen this fight in others much too often. I understand a lot better than my 15-year-old self the challenges and rewards of life. Hopefully, this is reflected in the characters in this story.

Many people read draft chapters or complete drafts of *When Darkness Descends*. I thank all of them for their kind words and constructive criticism — Margrit Beemster, Ian Boyd, Raf Freire, Neil Padbury, Manu Saunders, Maggie Watson and Ashlea Zivanovic. I especially thank Tansy Roberts from TasWriters for opening my eyes to the importance of point of view, and helping me forge a much closer bond with my characters.

However, no-one has shared this journey with me more than my beautiful soulmate, Gayle. Over more than 20 years, Gayle tolerated all the long discussions about plot lines and character development, motivations and justifications. She had many good ideas and helped me weed out the really stupid ones. She read multiple drafts of this book and picked up lots of errors that I failed to see. This story would be much less without her.

About the author

G. W. Lücke shares a small part of Tasmania with his partner, a mischievous border collie and a menagerie of animals and plants. He has no spare time, but when not writing, fills the days with gardening, growing food, forest and beach walks, and being healed by the nature that surrounds him.

www.ingramcontent.com/pod-product-compliance
Lightning Source LLC
Chambersburg PA
CBHW020007120726
47903CB00004B/1174